She Did Not Want To Know . . .

An isolated mansion . . . a beautiful, bewitching and tormenting woman . . . a terrible drama of passion, violence and madness . . . a curse that would not cease until it claimed its victim. . . .

Like grotesquely shaped parts of a jigsaw puzzle, these bits and pieces of the truth emerged from the darkness of the past. But still Elizabeth hesitated to put them all together . . . to see at last the face of shame, guilt and horror that would be revealed. . . .

Would it be the face of her beloved . . . ?

THE
Breaking
Point

•

MARY ROBERTS
RINEHART

A DELL BOOK

Published by
DELL PUBLISHING CO., INC.
750 Third Avenue
New York, New York 10017

Reprinted by arrangement with
Holt, Rinehart, and Winston, Inc.
New York, New York

Printed in the U.S.A.

Previous Dell edition #0795
New Dell Edition
First printing—March 1970

Chapter One

"HEAVEN and earth," sang the tenor, Mr. Henry Wallace, owner of the Wallace garage. His larynx, which gave him somewhat the effect of having swallowed a crab-apple and got it only part way down, protruded above his low collar.

"Heaven and earth," sang the bass, Mr. Edwin Goodno, of the meat market and the Boy Scouts. "Heaven and earth, are full——" His chin, large and fleshy, buried itself deep; his eyes were glued on the music sheet in his hand.

"Are full, are full, are full," sang the soprano, Clare Rossiter, of the yellow colonial house on the Ridgely Road. She sang with her eyes turned up, and as she reached G flat she lifted herself on her toes. "Of the majesty, of Thy glory."

"Ready," barked the choir master. "Full now, and all together."

The choir room in the parish house resounded to the twenty voices of the choir. The choir master at the piano kept time with his head. Earnest and intent, they filled the building with the Festival Te Deum of Dudley Buck, Opus 63, No. I.

Elizabeth Wheeler liked choir practice. She liked the way in which, after the different parts had been run through, the voices finally blended into harmony and beauty. She liked the small sense of achievement it gave her, and of being a part, on Sundays, of the service. She liked the feeling, when she put on the black cassock and white surplice and the small round velvet cap, of having placed in her locker the things of this world, such as a rose-colored hat and a blue georgette frock, and of being stripped, as it were, for aspirations.

At such times she had vague dreams of renunciation. She saw herself cloistered in some quiet spot, withdrawn from the world; a place where there were long vistas of pillars and Gothic arches, after a photograph in the living room at home, and a great organ somewhere, playing.

She would go home from church, however, clad in the rose-colored hat and the blue georgette frock, and eat a healthy Sunday luncheon; and by two o'clock in the afternoon, when the family slept and Jim had gone to the country club, her dreams were quite likely to be entirely different. Generally speaking, they had to do with love. Romantic, unclouded young love, dramatic only because it was love, and very happy.

Sometime, perhaps, some one would come and say he loved her. That was all. That was at once the beginning and the end. Her dreams led up to that and stopped. Not by so much as a hand clasp did they pass that wall.

So she sat in the choir room and awaited her turn.

"Altos a little stronger, please."

"Of the majesty, of the majesty, of the majesty, of Thy gl-o-o-ry," sang Elizabeth. And was at once a nun and a principal in a sentimental dream of two.

What appeared to the eye was a small and rather ethereal figure with sleek brown hair and wistful eyes; nice eyes, of no particular color. Pretty with the beauty of youth, sensitive and thoughtful, infinitely loyal and capable of suffering and not otherwise extraordinary was Elizabeth Wheeler in her plain wooden chair. A figure suggestive of no drama and certainly of no tragedy, its attitude expectant and waiting, with that alternate hope and fear which is youth at twenty, when all of life lies ahead and every tomorrow may hold some great adventure.

Clare Rossiter walked home that night with Elizabeth. She was a tall blonde girl, lithe and graceful, and with calculated coquetry in her clothes.

"Do you mind going around the block?" she asked. "By Station Street?" There was something furtive and yet candid in her voice, and Elizabeth glanced at her.

"All right. But it's out of your way, isn't it?"

"Yes. I— You're so funny, Elizabeth. It's hard to talk to you. But I've got to talk to somebody. I go around by Station Street every chance I get."

"By Station Street? Why?"

"I should think you could guess why."

She saw that Clare desired to be questioned, and at the

same time she felt a great distaste for the threatened confidence. She loathed arm-in-arm confidences, the indecency of dragging up and exposing, in whispers, things that should have been buried deep in reticence. She hesitated, and Clare slipped an arm through hers.

"You don't know, then, do you? Sometimes I think everyone must know. And I don't care. I've reached that point."

Her confession, naïve and shameless, and yet somehow not without a certain dignity, flowed on. She was mad about Doctor Dick Livingstone. Goodness knew why, for he never looked at her. She might be the dirt under his feet for all he knew. She trembled when she met him in the street, and sometimes he looked past her and never saw her. She didn't sleep well any more.

Elizabeth listened in great discomfort. She did not see in Clare's hopeless passion the joy of the flagellant, or the self-dramatization of a neurotic girl. She saw herself unwillingly forced to peer into the sentimental windows of Clare's soul, and there to see Doctor Dick Livingstone, an unconscious occupant. But she had a certain fugitive sense of guilt, also. Formless as her dreams had been, vague and shy, they had nevertheless centered about some one who should be tall, like Dick Livingstone, and alternately grave, which was his professional manner, and gay, which was his manner when it turned out to be only a cold, and he could take a few minutes to be himself. Generally speaking, they centered about some one who resembled Dick Livingstone, but who did not, as did Doctor Livingstone, assume at times an air of frightful maturity and pretend that in years gone by he had dandled her on his knee.

"Sometimes I think he positively avoids me," Clare wailed. "There's the house, Elizabeth. Do you mind stopping a moment? He must be in his office now. The light's burning."

"I wish you wouldn't, Clare. He'd hate it if he knew."

She moved on and Clare slowly followed her. The Rossiter girl's flow of talk had suddenly stopped. She was thoughtful and impulsively suspicious.

"Look here, Elizabeth, I believe you care for him yourself."

"I? What is the matter with you to-night, Clare?"

"I'm just thinking. Your voice was so queer."

They walked on in silence. The flow of Clare's confidences had ceased, and her eyes were calculating and a trifle hard.

"There's a good bit of talk about him," she jerked out finally. "I suppose you've heard it."

"What sort of talk?"

"Oh, gossip. You'll hear it. Everybody's talking about it. It's doing him a lot of harm."

"I don't believe it," Elizabeth flared. "This town hasn't anything else to do, and so it talks. It makes me sick."

She did not attempt to analyze the twisted motives that made Clare belittle what she professed to love. And she did not ask what the gossip was. Half way up Palmer Lane she turned in at the cement path between borders of early perennials which led to the white Wheeler house. She was flushed and angry, hating Clare for her unsolicited confidence and her malice, hating even Haverly, that smiling, tree-shaded suburb which "talked."

She opened the door quietly and went in. Micky, the Irish terrier, lay asleep at the foot of the stairs, and her father's voice, reading aloud, came pleasantly from the living room.

Suddenly her sense of resentment died. With the closing of the front door the peace of the house enveloped her. What did it matter if, beyond that door, there were unrequited love and petty gossip, and even tragedy? Not that she put all that into conscious thought; she had merely a sensation of sanctuary and peace. Here, within these four walls, were all that one should need, love and security and quiet happiness.

Walter Wheeler, pausing to turn a page, heard her singing as she went up the stairs. In the moment of the turning he too had a flash of content. Twenty-five years of married life and all well; Nina married, Jim out of college, Elizabeth singing her way up the stairs, and here by the lamp his wife quietly knitting while he read to her. He was reading *Paradise Lost:* "The mind is its own place, and in itself can make a Heaven of Hell, a Hell of Heaven."

He did a certain amount of serious reading every year.

On Sunday mornings, during the service, Elizabeth earnestly tried to banish all worldly thoughts. In spite of this resolve, however, she was always conscious of a certain regret that the choir seats necessitated turning her profile to the congregation. At the age of twelve she had decided that her nose was too short, and nothing had happened since to change her conviction.

She seldom so much as glanced at the congregation. During her slow progress up and down the main aisle behind the Courtney boy, who was still a soprano and who carried the great gold cross, she always looked straight ahead. Or rather, although she was unconscious of this, slightly up. She always looked up when she sang, for she had commenced to take singing lessons when the piano music rack was high above her head.

So she still lifted her eyes as she went up the aisle, and was extremly serious over the whole thing. Because it is a solemn matter to take a number of people who have been up to that moment engrossed in thoughts of food or golf or servants or business, and in the twinkling of an eye, as the prayer book said about death, turn their minds to worship.

Nevertheless, although she never looked at the pews, she was always conscious of two of them. The one near the pulpit was the Sayres' and it was the social calendar of the town. When Mrs. Sayre was in it, it was the social season. One never knew when Mrs. Sayre's butler would call up and say: "I am speaking for Mrs. Sayre. Mrs. Sayre would like to have the pleasure of Miss Wheeler's company on Thursday to luncheon, at one-thirty."

When the Sayre pew was empty, the town knew, if it happened to be winter, that the Florida or Santa Barbara season was on; or in summer the Maine coast.

The other pew was at the back of the church. Always it had one occupant; sometimes it had three. But the behavior of this pew was very erratic. Sometimes an elderly and portly gentleman with white hair and fierce eyebrows would come in when the sermon was almost over. Again, a hand would reach through the grill behind it, and a tall young man who had had his eyes fixed in the proper direction, but not always on the rector, would reach for his hat, get up and slip out. On these occasions, however, he would first identify the owner of the hand and then bend over the one permanent occupant of the pew, a little old lady. His speech was as Yea, yea, or Nay, nay, for he either said, "I'll be back for dinner," or "Don't look for me until you see me."

And Mrs. Crosby, without taking her eyes from the sermon, would nod.

Of late years, Doctor David Livingstone had been taking less and less of the "Don't-look-for-me-until-you-see-me" cases, and Doctor Dick had acquired a car, which would not freeze when left outside all night like a forgotten dog, and a sense of philosophy about sleep. That is, that eleven o'clock P. M. was bed-time to some people, but was just eleven o'clock for him.

When he went to church he listened to the sermon, but rather often he looked at Elizabeth Wheeler. When his eyes wandered, as the most faithful eyes will now and then, they were apt to rest on the flag that had hung, ever since the war, beside the altar. He had fought for his country in a sea of mud, never nearer than two hundred miles to the battle line, fought with a surgical kit instead of a gun, but he was content. Not to all the high adventure.

Had he been asked, suddenly, the name of the tall blonde girl who sang among the sopranos, he could not have told it.

The Sunday morning following Clare Rossiter's sentimental confession, Elizabeth tried very hard to banish all worldly thoughts, as usual, and to see the kneeling, rising and sitting congregation as there for worship. But for the first time she wondered. Some of the faces were blank, as though behind the steady gaze the mind had wandered far afield, or slept. Some were intent, some even devout. But for the first time she began to feel that people in the mass might be cruel, too. How many of them, for instance, would sometime during the day pass on, behind their hands, the gossip Clare had mentioned?

She changed her position, and glanced quickly over the church. The Livingstone pew was fully occupied, and well up toward the front, Wallie Sayre was steadfastly regarding her. She looked away quickly.

Came the end of the service. Came down the aisle the Courtney boy, clean and shining and carrying high his glowing symbol. Came the choir, two by two, the women first, sopranos, altos and Elizabeth. Came the men, bass and tenor, neatly shaved for Sunday morning. Came the rector, Mr. Oglethorpe, a trifle wistful, because always he fell so far below the mark he had set. Came the benediction. Came the slow rising from its knees of the congregation and its cheerful bustle of dispersal.

Doctor Dick Livingstone stood up and helped Doctor David into his new spring overcoat. He was very content. It was May, and the sun was shining. It was Sunday, and he would have an hour or two of leisure. And he had made a resolution about a matter that had been in his mind for some time. He was very content.

He looked around the church with what was almost a possessive eye. These people were his friends. He knew them all, and they knew him. They had, against his protest, put his name on the bronze tablet set in the wall on the roll of honor. Small as it was, this was his world.

Half smiling, he glanced about. He did not realize that behind their bows and greetings there was something new that day, something not so much unkind as questioning.

Outside in the street he tucked his aunt, Mrs. Crosby, against the spring wind, and waited at the wheel of the car while David entered with the deliberation of a man accustomed to the sagging of his old side-bar buggy under his weight. Long ago Dick had dropped the titular "uncle," and as David he now addressed him.

"You're going to play some golf this afternoon, David," he said firmly. "Mike had me out this morning to look at your buggy springs."

David chuckled. He still stuck to his old horse, and to the ancient vehicle which had been the signal of distress before so many doors for forty years. "I can trust old Nettie," he would say. "She doesn't freeze her radiator on cold nights, she doesn't skid, and if I drop asleep she'll take me home and into my own barn, which is more then any automobile would do."

"I'm going to sleep," he said comfortably. "Get Wallie Sayre—I see he's back from some place again—or ask a nice girl. Ask Elizabeth Wheeler. I don't think Lucy here expects to be the only woman in your life."

Dick stared into the windshield.

"I've been wondering about that, David," he said, "just how much right——"

"Balderdash!" David snorted. "Don't get any fool notion in your head."

Followed a short silence with Dick driving automatically and thinking. Finally he drew a long breath.

"All right," he said, "how about that golf—you need exercise. You're putting on weight, and you know it. And you smoke too much. It's either less tobacco or more walking, and you ought to know it."

David grunted, but he turned to Lucy Crosby, in the rear seat:

"Lucy, d'you know where my clubs are?"

"You loaned them to Jim Wheeler last fall. If you get three of them back you're lucky." Mrs. Crosby's voice was faintly tart. Long ago she had learned that her brother's belongings were his only by right of purchase, and were by way of being community property. When, early in her widowhood and her return to his home, she had found that her protests resulted only in a sort of clandestine giving or lending, she had exacted a promise from him. "I ask only one thing, David," she had said. "Tell me where the things go. There wasn't a blanket for the guest-room bed at the time of the Diocesan Convention."

"I'll run around to the Wheelers' and get them," Dick observed, in a carefully casual voice. "I'll see the Carter baby, too, David, and that clears the afternoon. Any message?"

Lucy glanced at him, but David moved toward the house.

"Give Elizabeth a kiss for me," he called over his shoulder, and went chuckling up the path.

Chapter Two

MRS. CROSBY stood on the pavement, gazing after the car as it moved off. She had not her brother's simplicity nor his optimism. Her married years had taken her away from the environment which had enabled him to live his busy, uncomplicated life; where, the only medical man in a growing community, he had learned to form his own sturdy decisions and then to abide by them.

Black and white, right and wrong, the proper course and the improper course—he lived in a sort of two-dimensional ethical world. But to Lucy Crosby, between black and white there was a gray no-man's land of doubt and indecision; a half-way house of compromise, and sometimes David frightened her. He was so sure.

She passed the open door into the waiting-room, where sat two or three patient and silent figures, and went back to the kitchen. Minnie, the elderly servant, sat by the table reading, amid the odor of roasting chicken; outside the door on the kitchen porch was the freezer containing the dinner ice-cream. An orderly Sunday peace was in the air, a gesture of homely comfort, order and security.

Minnie got up.

"I'll unpin your veil for you," she offered, obligingly. "You've got time to lie down about ten minutes. Mrs Morgan said she's got to have her ears treated."

"I hope she doesn't sit and talk for an hour."

"She'll talk, all right," Minnie observed, her mouth full of pins. "She'd be talking to me yet if I'd stood there. She's got her nerve, too, that woman."

"I don't like to hear you speak so of the patients who come to the house, Minnie."

"Well, I don't like their asking me questions about the family, either," said Minnie, truculently. "She wanted to know who was Doctor Dick's mother. Said she had had a woman here from Wyoming, and she thought she'd known his people."

Mrs. Crosby stood very still.

"I think she should bring her questions to the family," she said, after a silence. "Thank you, Minnie."

Bonnet in hand, she moved toward the stairs, climbed them and went into her room. Recently life had been growing increasingly calm and less beset with doubts. For the first time, with Dick's coming to live with them ten years before, a boy of twenty-two, she had found a vicarious maternity and gloried in it. Recently she had been very happy. The war was over and he was safely back; again she could sew on his buttons and darn his socks, and turn down his bed at night. He filled the old house with cheer and with vitality. And, as David gave up more and more of the work, he took it on his broad shoulders, efficient, tireless, and increasingly popular.

She put her bonnet away in its box, and suddenly there rose in her frail old body a fierce and unexpected resentment against David. He had chosen a course and abided by it. He had even now no doubt or falterings. Just as in the first anxious days there had been no doubt in him as to the essential rightness of what he was doing. And now——

This was what came of taking a life and moulding it in accordance with a predetermined plan. That was for God to do, not man.

She sat down near her window and rocked slowly, to calm herself. Outside the Sunday movement of the little suburban town went by: the older Wheeler girl, Nina, who had recently married Leslie Ward, in her smart little car; Harrison Miller, the cynical bachelor who lived next door, on his way to the station news stand for the New York papers; young couples taking small babies for the air in a perambulator; younger couples, their eyes on each other and on the future.

That, too, she reflected bitterly! Dick was in love. She had not watched him for that very thing for so long without being fairly sure now. She had caught, as simple David with his celibate heart could never have caught, the tone in Dick's voice when he mentioned the Wheelers. She had watched him for the past few months in church on Sunday mornings, and she knew that as she watched him, so he looked at Elizabeth.

And David was so sure! So sure.

The office door closed and Mrs. Morgan went out, a knitted scarf wrapping her ears against the wind, and following her exit came the slow ascent of David as he climbed the stairs to wash for dinner.

She stopped rocking.

"David!" she called sharply.

He opened the door and came in, a bulky figure, still faintly aromatic of drugs, cheerful and serene.

"D'you call me?" he inquired.

"Yes. Shut the door and come in. I want to talk to you."

He closed the door and went to the hearth-rug. There was a photograph of Dick on the mantel, taken in his uniform, and he looked at it for a moment. Then he turned.

"All right, my dear. Let's have it."

"Did Mrs. Morgan have anything to say?"

He stared at her.

"She usually has," he said. "I never knew you considered it worth repeating. No. Nothing in particular."

The very fact that Mrs. Morgan had limited her inquiry to Minnie confirmed her suspicions. But somehow, face to face with David, she could not see his contentment turned to anxiety.

"I want to talk to you about Dick."

"Yes?"

"I think he's in love, David."

David's heavy body straightened, but his face remained serene.

"We had to expect that, Lucy. Is it Elizabeth Wheeler, do you think?"

"Yes."

For a moment there was silence. The canary in its cage hopped about, a beady inquisitive eye now on one, now on the other of them.

"She's a good girl, Lucy."

"That's not the point, is it?"

"Do you think she cares for him?"

"I don't know. There's some talk of Wallie Sayre. He's there a good bit."

"Wallie Sayre!" snorted David. "He's never done a day's work in his life and never will." He reflected on that with growing indignation. "He doesn't hold a candle to Dick. Of course, if the girl's a fool——"

Hands thrust deep into his pockets David took a turn about the room. Lucy watched him. At last:

"You're evading the real issue, David, aren't you?"

"Perhaps I am," he admitted. "I'd better talk to him. I think he's got an idea he shouldn't marry. That's nonsense."

"I don't mean that, exactly," Lucy persisted. "I mean, won't he want a good many things cleared up before he marries? Isn't he likely to want to go back to Norada?"

Some of the ruddy color left David's face. He stood still, staring at her and silent.

"You know he meant to go three years ago, but the war came, and——"

Her voice trailed off. She could not even now easily recall those days when Dick was drilling on the golf links, and that later period of separation.

"If he does go back——"

"Donaldson is dead," David broke in, almost roughly.

"Maggie Donaldson is still living."

"What if she is? She's loyal to the core, in the first place. In the second, she's criminally liable. As liable as I am."

"There is one thing, David, I ought to know. What has become of the Carlysle girl?"

"She left the stage. There was a sort of general conviction that she was implicated and—I don't know, Lucy. Sometimes I think she was." He sighed. "I read something about her coming back, some months ago, in 'The Valley.' That was the thing she was playing the spring before it happened." He turned on her. "Don't get that in your head. That's gone, with the rest."

"I wonder, sometimes."

"I know it."

Outside the slamming of an automobile door announced Dick's return, and almost immediately Minnie rang the old fashioned gong which hung in the lower hall. Mrs. Crosby got up and placed a leaf of lettuce between the bars of the bird cage.

"Dinner time, Caruso," she said absently. Caruso was

the name Dick had given the bird. And to David: "She must be in her thirties now."

"Probably." Then his anger and anxiety burst out. "What difference can it make about her? About Donaldson's wife? About any hang-over from that rotten time? They're gone, all of them. He's here. He's safe and happy. He's strong and fine. That's gone."

In the lower hall Dick was taking off his overcoat.

"Smells like chicken, Minnie," he said, into the dining room.

"Chicken and biscuits, Mr. Dick."

"Hi, up there!" he called lustily. "Come and feed a starving man. I'm going to muffle the door-bell!"

He stood smiling up at them, very tidy in his Sunday suit, very boyish, for all his thirty-two years. His face, smilingly tender as he watched them, was strong rather than handsome, quietly dependable and faintly humorous.

"In the language of our great ally," he said, *"Madame et Monsieur, le dîner est servi."*

In his eyes there was not only tenderness but a somewhat emphasized affection, as though he meant to demonstrate, not only to them but to himself, that this new thing that had come to him did not touch their old relationship. For the new thing had come. He was still slightly dazed with the knowledge of it, and considerably anxious. Because he had just taken a glance at himself in the mirror of the walnut hat-rack, and had seen nothing there particularly to inspire—well, to inspire what he wanted to inspire.

At the foot of the stairs he drew Lucy's arm through his, and held her hand. She seemed very small and frail beside him.

"Some day," he said, "a strong wind will come along and carry off Mrs. Lucy Crosby, and the Doctors Livingstone will be obliged hurriedly to rent aeroplanes, and to search for her at various elevations!"

David sat down and picked up the old fashioned carving knife.

"Get the clubs?" he inquired.

Dick looked almost stricken.

"I forgot them, David," he said guiltily. "Jim Wheeler went out to look them up, and I—I'll go back after dinner."

It was sometime later in the meal that Dick looked up from his plate and said:

"I'd like to cut office hours on Wednesday night, David. I've asked Elizabeth Wheeler to go into town to the theater."

"What about the baby at the Homer place?"

"Not due until Sunday. I'll leave my seat number at the box office, anyhow."

"What are you going to see, Dick?" Mrs. Crosby asked. "Will you have some dumplings?"

"I will, but David shouldn't. Too much starch. Why, it's called 'The Valley,' I think. An actress named Carlysle, Beverly Carlysle, is starring in it."

He ate on, his mind not on his food, but back in the white house on Palmer Lane, and a girl. Lucy Crosby, fork in air, stared at him, and then glanced at David.

But David did not look up from his plate.

Chapter Three

THE WHEELER house was good, modern and commonplace. Walter Wheeler and his wife were like the house. Just as here and there among the furniture there was a fine thing, an antique highboy, a Sheraton sideboard or some old cut glass, so they had, with a certain mediocrity their own outstanding virtues. They liked music, believed in the home as the unit of the nation, put happiness before undue ambition, and had devoted their lives to their children.

For many years their lives had centered about the children. For years they had held anxious conclave about whooping-cough, about small early disobediences, later about Sunday tennis. They stood united to protect the children against disease, trouble and eternity.

Now that the children were no longer children, they were sometimes lonely and still apprehensive. They feared motor car accidents, and Walter Wheeler had withstood the appeals of Jim for a half dozen years. They feared trains for them, and journeys, and unhappy marriages, and hid their fears from each other. Their nightly prayers were "to keep them safe and happy."

But they saw life reaching out and taking them, one by one. They saw them still as children, but as children determined to bear their own burdens. Jim stayed out late sometimes, and considered his manhood in question if interrogated. Nina was married and out of the home, but there loomed before them the possibility of maternity and its dangers for her. There remained only Elizabeth, and on her they lavished the care formerly divided among the three.

It was their intention and determination that she should never know trouble. She was tenderer than the others, more docile and gentle. They saw her, not as a healthy, normal girl, but as something fragile and very precious.

Nina was different. They had always worried a little about Nina, although they had never put their anxiety to each other. Nina had always overrun her dress allowance, although she had never failed to be sweetly penitent about it, and Nina had always placed an undue emphasis on things. Her bedroom before her marriage was cluttered with odds and ends, cotillion favors and photographs, college pennants and small unwise purchases—trophies of the gayety and conquest which were her life.

And Nina had "come out." It had cost a great deal, and it was not so much to introduce her to society as to put a family recognition on a fact already accomplished, for Nina had brought herself out unofficially at sixteen. There had been the club ballroom, and a great many flowers which withered before they could be got to the hospital; and new clothing for all the family, and a caterer and orchestra. After that, for a cold and tumultuous winter Mrs. Wheeler had sat up with the dowagers night after night until all hours, and the next morning had let Nina sleep, while she went about her household duties. She had aged, rather, and her determined smile had grown a little fixed.

She was a good woman, and she wanted her children's happiness more than anything in the world, but she had a faint and sternly repressed feeling of relief when Nina announced her engagement. Nina did it with characteristic *sangfroid,* at dinner one night.

"Don't ring for Annie for a minute, mother," she said. "I want to tell you all something. I'm going to marry Leslie Ward."

There had been a momentary pause. Then her father said:

"Just a minute. Is that Will Ward's boy?"

"Yes. He's not a boy."

"Well, he'll come around to see me before there's any engagement. Has that occurred to either of you?"

"Oh, he'll be around. He'd have come to-night, but Howard Moore is having his bachelor dinner. I hope he doesn't look shot to pieces to-morrow. These bachelor things—! We'd better have a dinner or something, mother, and announce it."

There had been the dinner, with a silver loving cup bought for the occasion, and thereafter to sit out its useless days on the Sheraton sideboard. And there had been a trousseau and a wedding so expensive that a small frown of anxiety had developed between Walter Wheeler's eyebrows and stayed there.

For Nina's passion for things was inherent, persisting after her marriage. She discounted her birthday and Christmases in advance, coming around to his office a couple of months before the winter holidays and needing something badly.

"It's like this, daddy," she would say. "You're going to give me a check for Christmas anyhow, aren't you? And it would do me more good now. I simply can't go to another ball."

"Where's your trousseau?"

"It's worn out—danced to rags. And out of date, too."

"I don't understand it, Nina. You and Leslie have a good income. Your mother and I——"

"You didn't have any social demands. And wedding presents! If one more friend of mine is married——"

He would get out his checkbook and write a check slowly and thoughtfully. And tearing it off would say:

"Now remember, Nina, this is for Christmas. Don't feel aggrieved when the time comes and you have no gift from us."

But he knew that when the time came Margaret, his wife, would hold out almost to the end, and then slip into a jeweler's and buy Nina something she simply couldn't do without.

It wasn't quite fair, he felt. It wasn't fair to Jim or to Elizabeth. Particularly to Elizabeth.

Sometimes he looked at Elizabeth with a little prayer in his heart, never articulate, that life would be good to her; that she might keep her illusions and her dreams; that the soundness and wholesomeness of her might keep her from unhappiness. Sometimes, as she sat reading or sewing, with the light behind her shining through her soft hair, he saw in her a purity that was almost radiant.

He was in arms at once a night or two before Dick had invited Elizabeth to go to the theater when Margaret Wheeler said:

"The house was gayer when Nina was at home."

"Yes. And you were pretty sick of it. Full of roistering young idiots. Piano and phonograph going at once, pairs of gigglers in the pantry at the refrigerator, pairs on the stairs and on the verandah, cigar-ashes—my cigars—and cigarettes over everything, and more infernal spooning going on than I've ever seen in my life."

He had resumed his newspaper, to put it down almost at once.

"What's that Sayre boy hanging around for?"

"I think he's in love with her, Walter."

"Love? Any of the Sayre tribe? Jim Sayre drank himself to death, and this boy is like him. And Jim Sayre wasn't faithful to his wife. This boy is—well, he's an heir. That's why he was begotten."

Margaret Wheeler stared at him.

"Why, Walter!" she said. "He's a nice boy, and he's a gentleman."

"Why? Because he gets up when you come into the room? Why in heaven's name don't you encourage real men to come here? There's Dick Livingstone. He's a man."

Margaret hesitated.

"Walter, have you ever thought there was anything queer about Dick Livingstone's coming here?"

"Darned good for the town that he did come."

"But—nobody ever dreamed that David and Lucy had a nephew. Then he turns up, and they send him to medical college, and all that."

"I've got some relations I haven't notified the town I possess," he said grimly.

"Well, there's something odd. I don't believe Henry Livingstone, the Wyoming brother, ever had a son."

"What possible foundation have you for a statement like that?"

"Mrs. Cook Morgan's sister-in-law has been visiting her lately. She says she knew Henry Livingstone well years ago in the West, and she never heard he was married. She says positively he was *not* married."

"And trust the Morgan woman to spread the good news," he said with angry sarcasm. "Well, suppose that's true? Suppose Dick is an illegitimate child? That's the worst that's implied, I daresay. That's nothing against Dick himself. I'll tell the world there's good blood on the Livingstone side, anyhow."

"You were very particular about Wallie Sayre's heredity, Walter."

"That's different," he retorted and retired into gloomy silence behind his newspaper. Drat these women anyhow. It was like some fool female to come there and rake up some old and defunct scandal. He'd stand up for Dick, if it ever came to a show-down. He liked Dick. What the devil did his mother matter, anyhow? If this town hadn't had enough evidence of Dick Livingstone's quality the last few years he'd better go elsewhere. He——

He got up and whistled for the dog.

"I'm going to take a walk," he said briefly, and went out. He always took a walk when things disturbed him. . . . . . .

On the Sunday afternoon after Dick had gone Elizabeth was alone in her room upstairs. On the bed lay the sort of gown Nina would have called a dinner dress, and to which Elizabeth referred as her dark blue. Seen thus, in the room which was her own expression, there was a certain nobility about her very simplicity, a steadiness about her eyes that was almost disconcerting.

"She's the saintly-looking sort that would go on the rocks for some man," Nina had said once, rather flippantly, "and never know she was shipwrecked. No man in the world could do that to me."

But just then Elizabeth looked totally unlike shipwreck. Nothing seemed more like a safe harbor than the Wheeler house that afternoon, or all the afternoons. Life went on, the comfortable life of an upper middle-class household. Candles and flowers on the table and a neat waitress to serve; little carefully planned shopping expeditions; fine hand-sewing on dainty undergarments for rainy days; small tributes of books and candy; invitations and consultations as to what to wear; choir practice, a class in the Sunday school, a little work among the poor; the volcano which had been Nina overflowing elsewhere in a smart little house with a butler out on the Ridgely Road.

She looked what she was, faithful and quietly loyal, steady-eyed and serene; not asking greatly but hoping much; full of small unvisualized dreams and little inarticulate prayers; waiting, without knowing that she was waiting.

Sometimes she worried. She thought she ought to "do something." A good many of the girls she knew wanted to do something, but they were vague as to what. She felt at those times that she was not being very useful, and she had gone so far as to lay the matter before her father a couple of years before, when she was just eighteen.

"Just what do you think of doing?" he had inquired.

"That's it," she had said despondently. "I don't know. I haven't any particular talent, you know. But I don't think I ought to go on having you support me in idleness all my life."

"Well, I don't think it likely that I'll have to," he had observed, dryly. "But here's the point, and I think it's important. I don't intend to work without some compensation, and my family is my compensation. You just hang around and make me happy, as you do, and you're fulfilling your economic place in the nation. Don't you forget it, either."

That had comforted her. She had determined then never to marry but to hang around, as he suggested, for the rest of her life. She was quite earnest about it, and resolved. . .

She picked up the blue dress and standing before her mirror, held it up before her. It looked rather shabby, she thought, but the theater was not like a dance, and anyhow it would look better at night. She had been thinking about next Wednesday evening ever since Dick Livingstone had gone. It seemed, somehow, frightfully important. It was frightfully important. For the first time she acknowledged to herself that she had been fond of him, as she put it, for a long time. She had an odd sense, too, of being young and immature, and as though he had stooped to her from some height: such as thirty-two years and being in the war, and having to decide about life and death, and so on.

She hoped he did not think she was only a child.

She heard Nina coming up the stairs. At the click of her high heels on the hard wood she placed the dress on the bed again, and went to the window. Her father was on the path below, clearly headed for a walk. She knew then that Nina had been asking for something.

Nina came in and closed the door. She was smaller than Elizabeth and very pretty. Her eyebrows had been drawn to a tidy line, and from the top of her shining head to her brown *suède* pumps she was exquisite with the hours of careful tending and careful dressing she gave her young body. Exquisitely pretty, too.

She sat down on Elizabeth's bed with a sigh.

"I really don't know what to do with father," she said. "He flies off at a tangent over the smallest things. Elizabeth dear, can you lend me twenty dollars? I'll get my allowance on Tuesday."

"I can give you ten."

"Well, ask mother for the rest, won't you? You needn't say it's for me. I'll give it to you Tuesday."

"I'm not going to mother, Nina. She has had a lot of expenses this month."

"Then I'll borrow it from Wallie Sayre," Nina said, accepting her defeat cheerfully. "If it was an ordinary bill it could wait, but I lost it at bridge last night and it's got to be paid."

"You oughtn't to play bridge for money," Elizabeth said, a bit primly. "And if Leslie knew you borrowed from Wallace Sayre——"

"I forgot! Wallie's downstairs, Elizabeth. Really, if he wasn't so funny, he'd be tragic."

"Why tragic? He has everything in the world."

"If you use a little bit of sense, you can have it too."

"I don't want things."

"Pooh! That's what you think now. Wallie's a nice person. Lots of girls are mad about him. And he has about all the money there is." Getting no response from Elizabeth, she went on: "I was thinking it over last night. You'll have to marry sometime, and it isn't as though Wallie was dissipated, or anything like that. I suppose he knows his way about, but then they all do."

She got up.

"Be nice to him, anyhow," she said. "He's crazy about you, and when I think of you in that house! It's a wonderful house, Elizabeth. She's got a suite waiting for Wallie to be married before she furnishes it."

Elizabeth looked around her virginal little room, with its painted dressing table, its chintz, and its white bed with the blue dress on it.

"I'm very well satisfied as I am," she said.

While she smoothed her hair before the mirror Nina surveyed the room and her eyes lighted on the frock.

"Are you still wearing that shabby old thing?" she demanded. "I do wish you'd get some proper clothes. Are you going somewhere?"

"I'm going to the theater on Wednesday night."

"Who with?" Nina in her family was highly colloquial.

"With Doctor Livingstone."

"Are you joking?" Nina demanded.

"Joking? Of course not."

Nina sat down again on the bed, her eyes on her sister, curious and not a little apprehensive.

"It's the first time it's ever happened, to my knowledge," she declared. "I know he's avoided me like poison. I thought he hated women. You know Clare Rossiter is——"

Elizabeth turned suddenly.

"Clare is ridiculous," she said. "She hasn't any reserve, or dignity, or anything else. And I don't see what my going to the theater with Dick Livingstone has to do with her, anyhow."

Nina raised her carefully plucked eyebrows.

"Really!" she said. "You needn't jump down my throat, you know." She considered, her eyes on her sister. "Don't go and throw yourself away on Dick Livingstone, Sis. You're too good-looking, and he hasn't a cent. A suburban practice, out all night, that tumble-down old house and two old people hung around your necks, for Doctor David is letting go pretty fast. It just won't do. Besides, there's a story going the rounds about him, that——"

"I don't want to hear it, if you don't mind."

She went to the door and opened it.

"I've hardly spoken a dozen words to him in my life. But just remember this. When I do find the man I want to marry, I shall make up my own mind. As you did," she added as a parting shot.

She was rather sorry as she went down the stairs. She had begun to suspect what the family had never guessed, that Nina was not very happy. More and more she saw in Nina's passion for clothes and gaiety, for small possessions, an attempt to substitute them for real things. She even suspected that sometimes Nina was a little lonely.

Wallie Sayre rose from a deep chair as she entered the livingroom.

"Hello," he said, "I was on the point of asking Central

to give me this number so I could get you on the upstairs telephone."

"Nina and I were talking. I'm sorry."

Wallie, in spite of Walter Wheeler's opinion of him, was an engaging youth with a wide smile, an air of careless well-being, and an obstinate jaw. What he wanted he went after and generally secured, and Elizabeth, enlightened by Nina, began to have a small anxious feeling that afternoon that what he wanted just now happened to be herself.

"Nina coming down?" he asked.

"I suppose so. Why?"

"You couldn't pass the word along that you are going to be engaged for the next half hour?"

"I might, but I certainly don't intend to."

"You are as hard to isolate as a—as a germ," he complained. "I gave up a perfectly good golf game to see you, and as your father generally calls the dog the moment I appear and goes for a walk, I thought I might see you alone."

"You're seeing me alone now, you know."

Suddenly he leaned over and catching up her hand, kissed it.

"You're so cool and sweet," he said. "I—I wish you liked me a little." He smiled up at her, rather wistfully. "I never knew any one quite like you."

She drew her hand away. Something Nina had said, that he knew his way about, came into her mind, and made her uncomfortable. Back of him, suddenly, was that strange and mysterious region where men of his sort lived their furtive man-life, where they knew their way about. She had no curiosity and no interest, but the mere fact of its existence as revealed by Nina repelled her.

"There are plenty like me," she said. "Don't be silly, Wallie. I hate having my hand kissed."

"I wonder," he observed shrewdly, "whether that's really true, or whether you just hate having me do it?"

When Nina came in he was drawing a rough sketch of his new power boat, being built in Florida.

Nina's delay was explained by the appearance, a few minutes later, of a rather sullen Annie with a tea tray. Afternoon tea was not a Wheeler institution, but was notoriously a Sayre one. And Nina believed in putting one's best foot foremost, even when that resulted in a state of unstable domestic equilibrium.

"Put in a word for me, Nina," Wallie begged. "I intend to ask Elizabeth to go to the theater this week, and I think she is going to refuse."

"What's the play?" Nina inquired negligently. She was privately determining that her mother needed a tea cart and a new tea service. There were some in old Georgian silver——

" 'The Valley.' Not that the play matters. It's Beverly Carlysle."

"I thought she was dead, or something."

"Or something is right. She retired years ago, at the top of her success. She was a howling beauty, I'm told. I never saw her. There was some queer story. I've forgotten it. I was a kid then. How about it, Elizabeth?"

"I'm sorry. I'm going Wednesday night."

He looked downcast over that, and he was curious, too. But he made no comment save:

"Well, better luck next time."

"Just imagine," said Nina. "She's going with Dick Livingstone. Can you imagine it?"

But Wallace Sayre could and did. He had rather a stricken moment, too. Of course, there might be nothing to it; but on the other hand, there very well might. And Livingstone was the sort to attract the feminine woman; he had gravity and responsibility. He was older too, and that flattered a girl.

"He's not a bit attractive," Nina was saying. "Quiet, and —well, I don't suppose he knows what he's got on."

Wallie was watching Elizabeth.

"Oh, I don't know," he said, with masculine fairness. "He's a good sort, and he's pretty much of a man."

He was quite sure that the look Elizabeth gave him was grateful.

He went soon after that, keeping up an appearance of gaiety to the end, and very careful to hope that Elizabeth would enjoy the play.

"She's a wonder, they say," he said from the doorway. "Take two hankies along, for it's got more tears than 'East Lynne' and 'The Old Homestead' put together."

He went out, holding himself very erect and looking very cheerful until he reached the corner. There however he slumped, and it was a rather despondent young man who stood sometime later, on the center of the deserted bridge over the small river, and surveyed the water with moody eyes.

In the dusky living-room Nina was speaking her mind.

"You treat him like a dog," she said. "Oh, I know you're civil to him, but if any man looked at me the way Wallie looks at you—I don't know, though," she added, thoughtfully. "It may be that that is why he is so keen. It may be good tactics. Most girls fall for him with a crash."

But when she glanced at Elizabeth she saw that she had not heard. Her eyes were fixed on something on the street beyond the window. Nina looked out. With a considerable rattle of loose joints and four extraordinarily worn tires the Livingstone car was going by.

Chapter Four

DAVID DID not sleep well that night. He had not had his golf after all, for the Homer baby had sent out his advance notice early in the afternoon, and had himself arrived on Sunday evening, at the hour when Minnie was winding her clock and preparing to retire early for the Monday washing, and the Sayre butler was announcing dinner. Dick had come in at ten o'clock weary and triumphant, to announce that Richard Livingstone Homer, sex male, color white, weight nine pounds, had been safely delivered into this vale of tears.

David lay in the great walnut bed which had been his mother's, and read his prayer book by the light of his evening lamp. He read the Evening Prayer and the Litany, and then at last he resorted to the thirty-nine articles, which usually had a soporific effect on him. But it was no good.

He got up and took to pacing his room, a portly, solid old figure in striped pajamas and the pair of knitted bedroom slippers which were always Mrs. Morgan's Christmas offering. "To Doctor David, with love and a merry Xmas, from Angeline Morgan."

At last he got his keys from his trousers pocket and padded softly down the stairs and into his office, where he drew the shade and turned on the lights. Around him was the accumulated professional impedimenta of many years; the old-fashioned surgical chair; the corner closet which had been designed for china, and which held his instruments; the bookcase; his framed diplomas on the wall, their signatures faded, their seals a little dingy; his desk, from which Dick had removed the old ledger which had held those erratic records from which, when he needed money, he had been wont—and reluctant—to make out his bills.

Through an open door was Dick's office, a neat place of shining linoleum and small glass stands, highly modern and businesslike. Beyond the office and opening from it was his laboratory, which had been the fruit closet once, and into which Dick on occasion retired to fuss with slides and tubes and stains and a microscope.

Sometimes he called David in, and talked at length and with enthusiasm about such human interest things as the *Staphylococcus pyogenes aureus,* and the Friedländer bacillus. The older man would listen, but his eyes were oftener on Dick than on the microscope or the slide.

David went to the bookcase and got down a large book, much worn, and carried it to his desk. . . . .

An hour or so later he heard footsteps in the hall and closed the book hastily. It was Lucy, a wadded dressing gown over her nightdress and a glass of hot milk in her hand.

"You drink this and come to bed, David," she said peremptorily. "I've been lying upstairs waiting for you to come up, and I need some sleep."

He had no sort of hope that she would not notice the book.

"I just got to thinking things over, Lucy," he explained, his tone apologetic. "There's no use pretending I'm not worried. I am."

"Well, it's in God's hands," she said, quite simply. "Take this up and drink it slowly. If you gulp it down it makes a lump in your stomach."

She stood by while he replaced the book in the bookcase and put out the lights. Then in the darkness she preceded him up the stairs.

"You'd better take the milk yourself, Lucy," he said. "You're not sleeping either."

"I've had some. Good-night."

He went in and sitting on the side of his bed sipped at his milk. Lucy was right. It was not in their hands. He had the feeling all at once of having relinquished a great burden. He crawled into bed and was almost instantly asleep.

So sometime after midnight found David sleeping, and Lucy on her knees. It found Elizabeth dreamlessly unconscious in her white bed, and Dick Livingstone asleep also, but in his clothing, and in a chair by the window. In the light from a street lamp his face showed lines of fatigue and nervous stress, lines only revealed when during sleep a man casts off the mask with which he protects his soul against even friendly eyes.

But midnight found others awake. It found Nina, for instance, in her draped French bed, consulting her jeweled watch and listening for Leslie's return from the country club. An angry and rather heart-sick Nina. And it found the night editor of one of the morning papers drinking a cup of coffee that a boy had brought in, and running through a mass of copy on his desk. He picked up several sheets of paper, with a photograph clamped to them, and ran through them quickly. A man in a soft hat, sitting on the desk, watched him idly.

"Beverly Carlysle," commented the night editor. "Back with bells on!" He took up the photograph. "Doesn't look much older, does she? It's a queer world."

Louis Bassett, star reporter and feature writer of the *Times-Republican*, smiled reminiscently.

"She was a wonder," he said. "I interviewed her once, and I was crazy about her. She had the stage set for me, all right. The papers had been full of the incident of Jud Clark and the night he lined up fifteen Johnnies in the lobby, each with a bouquet as big as a tub, all of them in top hats and Inverness coats, and standing in a row. So she played up the heavy domestic for me; knitting or sewing, I forget."

"Fell for her, did you?"

"Did I? That was ten years ago, and I'm not sure I'm over it yet."

"Probably that's the reason," said the city editor, drily. "Go and see her, and get over it. Get her views on the flapper and bobbed hair, for next Sunday. Smith would be crazy about it."

He finished his coffee.

"You might ask, too, what she thinks has become of Judson Clark," he added. "I have an idea she knows, if any one does."

Bassett stared at him.

"You're joking, aren't you?"

"Yes. But it would make a darned good story."

Chapter Five

WHEN HE finished medical college Dick Livingstone had found, like other men, that the two paths of ambition and duty were parallel and did not meet. Along one lay his desire to focus all his energy in one direction, to follow disease into the laboratory instead of the sick room, and there to fight its unsung battles. And win. He felt that he would win.

Along the other lay David.

It was not until he had completed his course and had come home that he had realized that David was growing old. Even then he might have felt that, by the time David was compelled to relinquish his hold on his practice, he himself would be sufficiently established in his specialty to take over the support of the household. But here there was interposed a new element, one he had not counted on. David was fiercely jealous of his practice; the thought that it might pass into new and alien hands was bitter to him. To hand it down to his adopted son was one thing; to pass it over to "some young whipper-snapper" was another.

Nor were David's motives selfish or unworthy. His patients were his friends. He had a sense of responsibility to them, and very little faith in the new modern methods. He thought there was a great deal of tomfoolery about them, and he viewed the gradual loss of faith in drugs with alarm. When Dick wore rubber gloves during their first obstetric case together he snorted.

"I've delivered about half the population of this town," he said, "and slapped 'em to make 'em breathe with my own bare hands. And I'm still here and so are they."

For by that time Dick had made his decision. He could not abandon David. For him then and hereafter the routine of a general practice in a suburban town, the long hours, the varied responsibilites, the feeling he had sometimes that by doing many things passably he was doing none of them well. But for compensation he had old David's content and greater leisure, and Lucy Crosby's gratitude and love.

Now and then he chafed a little when he read some article in a medical journal by one of his fellow enthusiasts, or when, in France, he saw men younger than himself obtaining an experience in their several specialties that would enable them to reach wide fields at home. But mostly he was content, or at least resigned. He was building up the Livingstone practice, and his one anxiety was lest the time should come when more patients asked for Doctor Dick than for Doctor David. He did not want David hurt.

After ten years the strangeness of his situation had ceased to be strange. Always he meant some time to go back to Norada, and there to clear up certain things, but it was a long journey, and he had very little time. And, as the years went on, the past seemed unimportant compared with the present. He gave little thought to the future.

Then, suddenly, his entire attention became focussed on the future.

Just when he had fallen in love with Elizabeth Wheeler he did not know. He had gone away to the war, leaving her a little girl, apparently, and he had come back to find her a woman. He did not even know he was in love, at first. It was when, one day, he found himself driving past the Wheeler house without occasion that he began to grow uneasy.

The future at once became extraordinarily important and so also, but somewhat less vitally, the past. Had he the right to marry, if he could make her care for him?

He sat in his chair by the window the night after the Homer baby's arrival, and faced his situation. Marriage meant many things. It meant love and companionship, but it also meant, should mean, children. Had he the right to go ahead and live his life fully and happily? Was there any chance that, out of the years behind him, there would come some forgotten thing, some taint or incident, to spoil the carefully woven fabric of his life?

Not his life. Hers.

On the Monday night after he had asked Elizabeth to go to the theater he went into David's office and closed the door. Lucy, alive to every movement in the old house, heard him go in and, rocking in her chair overhead, her hands idle in her lap, waited in tense anxiety for the interview to end. She thought she knew what Dick would ask, and what David would answer. And, in a way, David would be right. Dick, fine, lovable, upstanding Dick, had a right to the things other men had, to love and a home of his own, to children, to his own full life.

But suppose Dick insisted on clearing everying up before he married? For to Lucy it was unthinkable that any girl in her senses would refuse him. Suppose he went back to Norada? He had not changed greatly in ten years. He had been well known there, a conspicuous figure.

Her mind began to turn on the possibility of keeping him away from Norada.

Some time later she heard the office door open and then close with Dick's characteristic slam. He came up the stairs, two at a time as was his custom, and knocked at her door. When he came in she saw what David's answer had been, and she closed her eyes for an instant.

"Put on your things," he said gayly, "and we'll take a ride on the hill-tops. I've arranged for a moon."

And when she hesitated:

"It makes you sleep, you know. I'm going, if I have to ride alone and talk to an imaginary lady beside me."

She rather imagined that that had been his first idea, modified by his thought of her. She went over and put a wrinkled hand on his arm.

"You look happy, Dick," she said wistfully.

"I am happy, Aunt Lucy," he replied, and bending over, kissed her.

On Wednesday he was in a state of alternating high spirits and periods of silence. Even Minnie noticed it.

"Mr. Dick's that queer I hardly know how to take him," she said to Lucy. "He came back and asked for noodle soup, and he put about all the hardware in the kitchen on him and said he was a knight in armor. And when I took the soup in he didn't eat it."

It was when he was ready to go out that Lucy's fears were realized. He came in, as always when anything unusual was afoot, to let her look him over. He knew that she waited for him, to give his tie a final pat, to inspect the laundering of his shirt bosom, to pick imaginary threads off his dinner coat.

"Well?" he said, standing before her, "how's this? Art can do no more, Mrs. Crosby."

"I'll brush your back," she said, and brought the brush. He stooped to her, according to the little ceremony she had established, and she made little dabs at his speckless back. "There, that's better."

He straightened.

"How do you think Uncle David is?" he asked, unexpectedly.

"Better than he has been in years. Why?"

"Because I'm thinking of taking a little trip. Only ten days," he added, seeing her face. "You could house-clean my office while I'm away. You know you've been wanting to."

She dropped the brush, and he stooped to pick it up. That gave her a moment.

"Where?" she managed.

"To Dry River, by way of Norada."

"Why should you go back there?" she asked, in a carefully suppressed voice. "Why don't you go East? You've wanted to go back to Johns Hopkins for months?"

"On the other hand, why shouldn't I go back to Norada?" he asked, with an affectation of lightness. Then he put his hand on her shoulders. "Why shouldn't I go back and clear things up in my own mind? Why shouldn't I find out, for instance, that I am a free man?"

"You *are* free."

"I've got to know," he said, almost doggedly. "I can't take a chance. I believe I am. I believe David, of course. But anyhow I'd like to see the ranch. I want to see Maggie Donaldson."

"She's not at the ranch. Her husband died, you know."

"I have an idea I can find her," he said. "I'll make a good try, anyhow."

When he had gone she got her salts bottle and lay down on her bed. Her heart was hammering wildly. . . . .

Elizabeth was waiting for him in the living-room, in the midst of her family. She looked absurdly young and very pretty, and he had a momentary misgiving that he was old to her, and that—Heaven save the mark!—that she looked up to him. He considered the blue dress the height of fashion and the mold of form, and having taken off his overcoat in the hall, tried to put on Mr. Wheeler's instead in his

excitement. Also, becoming very dignified after the overcoat incident, and making an exit which should conceal his
wild exultation and show only polite pleasure, he stumbled
over Micky, so that they finally departed to a series of stac-
cato yelps.

He felt very hot and slightly ridiculous as he tucked
Elizabeth into the little car, being very particular about her
feet, and starting with extreme care, so as not to jar her.
He had the feeling of being entrusted temporarily with
something infinitely precious, and very, very dear. Something that must never suffer or be hurt.

Chapter Six

ON WEDNESDAY morning David was in an office in the city. He sat forward on the edge of his chair, and from time to time he took out his handkerchief and wiped his face or polished his glasses, quite unconscious of either action. He was in his best suit, with the tie Lucy had given him for Christmas.

Across from him, barricaded behind a great mahogany desk, sat a small man with keen eyes and a neat brown beard. On the desk were a spotless blotter, an inkstand of silver and a pen. Nothing else. The terrible order of the place had at first rather oppressed David.

The small man was answering a question.

"Rather on the contrary, I should say. The stronger the character the greater the smash."

David pondered this.

"I've read all you've written on the subject," he said finally. "Especially since the war."

The psycho-analyst put his finger tips together, judicially.

"Yes. The war bore me out," he observed with a certain complacence. "It added a great deal to our literature, too, although some of the positions are not well taken. Van Alston, for instance——"

"You have said, I think, that every man has a breaking point."

"Absolutely. All of us. We can go just so far. Where the mind is strong and very sound we can go further than when it is not. Some men, for instance, lead lives that would break you or me. Was there—was there such a history in this case?"

"Yes." Doctor David's voice was reluctant.

"The mind is a strange thing," went on the little man, musingly. "It has its censors, that go off duty during sleep.

Our sternest and often unconscious repressions pass them then, and emerge in the form of dreams. But of course you know all that. Dream symbolism. Does the person in this case dream? That would be interesting, perhaps important."

"I don't know," David said unhappily.

"The walling off, you say, followed a shock?"

"Shock and serious illness."

"Was there fear with the shock?"

David hesitated. "Yes," he said finally. "Very great fear, I believe."

Doctor Lauler glanced quickly at David and then looked away.

"I see," he nodded. "Of course the walling off of a part of the past—you said a part——?"

"Practically all of it. I'll tell you about that later. What about the walling off?"

"It is generally the result of what we call the protective mechanism of fear. Back of most of these cases lies fear. Not cowardice, but perhaps we might say the limit of endurance. Fear is a complex, of course. Dislike, in a small way, has the same reaction. We are apt to forget the names of persons we dislike. But if you have been reading on the subject——"

"I've been studying it for ten years."

"Ten years! Do you mean that this condition has persisted for ten years?"

David moistened his dry lips. "Yes," he admitted. "It might not have done so, but the—the person who made this experiment used suggestion. The patient was very ill, and weak. It was desirable that he should not identify himself with his past. The loss of memory of the period immediately preceding was complete, but of course, gradually, the cloud began to lift over the earlier periods. It was there that suggestion was used, so that such memories as came back were,—well, the patient adapted them to fit what he was told."

Again Doctor Lauler shot a swift glance at David, and looked away.

"An interesting experiment," he commented. "It must have taken courage."

"A justifiable experiment," David affirmed stoutly. "And it took courage. Yes."

David got up and reached for his hat. Then he braced himself for the real purpose of his visit.

"What I have been wondering about," he said, very carefully, "is this: this mechanism of fear, this wall—how strong is it?"

"Strong?"

"It's like a dam, I take it. It holds back certain memories, like a floodgate. Is anything likely to break it down?"

"Possibly something intimately connected with the forgotten period might do it. I don't know, Livingstone. We've only commenced to dig into the mind, and we have many theories and a few established facts. For instance, the primal instincts——"

He talked on, with David nodding now and then in apparent understanding, but with his thoughts far away. He knew the theories; a good many of them he considered poppycock. Dreams might come from the subconscious mind, but a good many of them came from the stomach. They might be safety valves for the mind, but also they might be *rarebit*. He didn't want dreams; what he wanted was facts. Facts and hope.

The office attendant came in. She was as tidy as the desk, as obsessed by order, as wooden. She placed a pad before the small man and withdrew. He rose.

"Let me know if I can be of any further assistance, Doctor," he said. "And I'll be glad to see your patient at any time. I'd like the record for my files."

"Thank you," David said. He stood fingering his hat.

"I suppose there's nothing to do? The dam will either break, or it won't."

"That's about it. Of course since the conditions that produced the setting up of the defensive machinery were unhappy, I'd say that happiness will play a large part in the situation. That happiness and a normal occupation will do a great deal to maintain the *status quo*. Of course I would advise no return to the unhappy environment, and no shocks. Nothing, in other words, to break down the wall."

Outside, in the corridor, David remembered to put on his hat. Happiness and a normal occupation, yes. But no shock.

Nevertheless, he felt vaguely comforted, and as though it had helped to bring the situation out into the open and discuss it. He had carried his burden alone for ten years, or with only the additional weight of Lucy's apprehensions. He wandered out into the city streets, and found himself, some time later, at the railway station, without remembering how he got there.

Across from the station was a large billboard, and on it the name of Beverly Carlysle and her play, "The Valley." He stood for some time and looked at it, before he went in to buy his ticket. Not until he was in the train did he realize that he had forgotten to get his lunch.

He attended to his work that evening as usual, but he felt very tired, and Lucy, going in at nine o'clock, found him dozing in his chair, his collar half choking him and his face deeply suffused. She wakened him and then, sitting down across from him, joined him in the vigil that was to last until they heard the car outside.

She had brought in her sewing, and David pretended to read. Now and then he looked at his watch.

At midnight they heard the car go in, and the slamming of the stable door, followed by Dick's footsteps on the walk outside. Lucy was very pale, and the hands that held her sewing twitched nervously. Suddenly she stood up and put a hand on David's shoulder.

Dick was whistling on the kitchen porch.

Chapter Seven

LOUIS BASSETT was standing at the back of the theater, talking to the publicity man of The Valley company, Fred Gregory. Bassett was calm and only slightly interested. By the end of the first act he had realized that the star was giving a fine performance, that she had even grown in power, and that his sentimental memory of her was considerably dearer than the reality.

"Going like a house afire," he said, as the curtain fell.

Beside his robust physique, Gregory, the publicity man, sank into insignificance. Even his pale spats, at which Bassett had shot a contemptuous glance, his highly expensive tailoring, failed to make him appear more than he was, a little, dapper man, with a pale cold eye and a rather too frequent smile. "She's the best there is," was his comment. He hesitated, then added: "She's my sister, you know. Naturally, for business reasons, I don't publish the relationship."

Bassett glanced at him.

"That so? Well, I'm glad she decided to come back. She's too good to bury."

But if he expected Gregory to follow the lead he was disappointed. His eyes, blank and expressionless, were wandering over the house as the lights flashed up.

"This whole tour has been a triumph. She's the best there is," Gregory repeated, "and they know it."

"Does *she* know it?" Bassett inquired.

"She doesn't throw any temperament, if that's what you mean. She——"

He checked himself suddenly, and stood, clutching the railing, bent forward and staring into the audience. Bassett watched him, considerably surprised. It took a great deal to startle a theatrical publicity man, yet here was one who looked as though he had seen a ghost.

After a time Gregory straightened and moistened his dry lips.

"There's a man sitting down there—see here, the sixth row, next the aisle; there's a girl in a blue dress beside him. See him? Do you know who he is?"

"Never saw him before."

For perhaps two minutes Gregory continued to stare. Then he moved over to the side of the house and braced against the wall continued his close and anxious inspection. After a time he turned away and, passing behind the boxes, made his way into the wings. Bassett's curiosity was aroused, especially when, shortly after, Gregory reappeared, bringing with him a small man in an untidy suit who was probably, Bassett surmised, the stage manager.

He saw the small man stare, nod, stand watching, and finally disappear, and Gregory resume his former position and attitude against the side wall. Throughout the last act Gregory did not once look at the stage. He continued his steady, unwavering study of the man in the sixth row, seat next the aisle, and Bassett continued his study of the little man.

His long training made him quick to scent a story. He was not sure, of course, but the situation appeared to him at least suggestive. With the end of the play he wandered out with the crowd, edging his way close to the man and girl who had focussed Gregory's attention, and following them into the street. He saw only a tall man with a certain quiet distinction of bearing, and a young and pretty girl, still flushed and excited, who went up the street a short distance and got into a small and shabby car. Bassett noted, carefully, the license number of the car.

Then, still curious and extremely interested, he walked briskly around to the stage entrance, nodded to the door-keeper, and went in.

Gregory was not in sight, but the stage manager was there, directing the striking of the last set.

"I'm waiting for Gregory," Bassett said. "Hasn't fainted, has he?"

"What d'you mean, fainted?" inquired the stage manager, with a touch of hostility.

"I was with him when he thought he recognized somebody. You know who. You can tell him I got his automobile number."

The stage manager's hostility faded, and he fell into the trap. "You know about it, then?"

"I was with him when he saw him. Unfortunately I couldn't help him out."

"It's just possible it's a chance resemblance. I'm darned if I know. Look at the facts! He's supposed to be dead. Ten years dead. His money's been split up a dozen ways from the ace. Then—I knew him, you know—I don't think even he would have the courage to come here and sit through a performance. Although," he added reflectively, "Jud Clark had the nerve for anything."

Bassett gave him a cigar and went out into the alley way that led to the street. Once there, he stood still and softly whistled. Jud Clark! If that was Judson Clark, he had the story of a lifetime.

For some time he walked the deserted streets of the city, thinking and puzzling over the possibility of Gregory's being right. Sometime after midnight he went back to the office and to the filing room. There, for two hours, he sat reading closely old files of the paper, going through them methodically and making occasional brief notes in a memorandum. Then, at two o'clock he put away the files, and sitting back, lighted a cigar.

It was all there; the enormous Clark fortune inherited by a boy who had gone mad about this same Beverly Carlysle; her marriage to her leading man, Howard Lucas; the subsequent killing of Lucas by Clark at his Wyoming ranch, and Clark's escape into the mountains. The sensational details of Clark's infatuation, the drama of a crime and Clark's subsequent escape, and the later certainty of his death in a mountain storm had filled the newspapers of the time for weeks. Judson Clark had been famous, notorious, infamous and dead, all in less than two years. A shameful and somehow a pitiful story.

But if Judson Clark had died, the story still lived. Every so often it came up again. Three years before he had been declared legally dead, and his vast estates, as provided by the will of old Elihu Clark, had gone to universities and hospitals. But now and then came a rumor. Jud Clark was living in India; he had a cattle ranch in Venezuela; he had been seen on the streets of New Orleans.

Bassett ran over the situation in his mind.

First then, grant that Clark was still living and had been in the theater that night. It became necessary to grant other things. To grant, for instance, that Clark was capable of sitting, with a girl beside him, through a performance by the woman for whom he had wrecked his life, of a play he had once known from the opening line to the tag. To grant that he could laugh and applaud, and at the drop of the curtain go calmly away, with such memories behind him as must be his. To grant, too, that he had survived miraculously his sensational disappearance, found a new identity and a new place for himself; even, witness the girl, possible new ties.

At half past two Bassett closed his memorandum book, stuffed it into his pocket, and started for home. As he passed the Ardmore Hotel he looked up at its windows. Gregory would have told her, probably. He wondered, half amused, whether the stage manager had told him of his inquiries, and whether in that case they might not fear him more than Clark himself. After all, they had nothing to fear from Clark, if this were Clark.

No. What they might see and dread, knowing he had had a hint of a possible situation, was the revival of the old story she had tried so hard to live down. She was ambitious, and a new and rigid morality was sweeping the country. What once might have been an asset stood now to be a bitter liability.

He slowed down, absorbed in deep thought. It was a queer story. It might be even more queer than it seemed. Gregory had been frightened rather than startled. The man had even gone pale.

Motive, motive, that was the word. What motive lay behind action. Conscious and unconscious, every volitional act was the result of motive.

He wondered what she had done when Gregory had told her. . . . .

As a matter of fact, Beverly Carlysle had shown less anxiety than her brother. Still pale and shocked, he had gone directly to her dressing-room when the curtain was rung down, had tapped and gone in. She was sitting wearily in a chair, a cigarette between her fingers. Around was the usual litter of a stage dressing-room after the play, the long shelf beneath the mirror crowded with powders, rouge and pencils, a bunch of roses in the corner washstand basin, a wardrobe trunk, and a maid covering with cheesecloth bags the evening's costumes.

"It went all right, I think, Fred."

"Yes," he said absently. "Go on out, Alice. I'll let you come back in a few minutes."

He waited until the door closed.

"What's the matter?" she asked rather indifferently. "If it's more quarreling in the company I don't want to hear it. I'm tired." Then she took a full look at him, and sat up.

"Fred! What is it?"

He gave her the truth, brutally and at once.

"I think Judson Clark was in the house to-night."

"I don't believe it."

"Neither would I, if somebody told me," he agreed sullenly. "I saw him. Don't you suppose I know him? And if you don't believe me, call Saunders. I got him out front. He knows."

"You called Saunders!"

"Why not? I tell you, Bev, I was nearly crazy. I'm nearly crazy now."

"What did Saunders say?"

"If he didn't know Clark was dead, he'd say it was Clark."

She was worried by that time, but far more collected than he was. She sat, absently tapping the shelf with a nail file, and reflecting.

"All right," she said. "Suppose he was? What then? He has been in hiding for ten years. Why shouldn't he continue to hide? What would bring him out now? Unless he needed money. Was he shabby?"

"No," he said sulkily. "He was with a girl. He was dressed all right."

"You didn't say anything, except to Saunders?"

"No. I'm not crazy."

"I'd better see Joe," she reflected. "Go and get him, Fred. And tell Alice she needn't wait."

She got up and moved about the room, putting things away and finding relief in movement, a still beautiful woman, with rather accentuated features and an easy carriage. Without her make-up the stage illusion of her youth was gone, and she showed past suffering and present strain. Just then she was uneasy and resentful, startled but not particularly alarmed. Her reason told her that Judson Clark, even if he still lived and had been there that night, meant to leave the dead past to care for itself, and wished no more than she to revive it. She was surprised to find, as she moved about, that she was trembling.

Her brother came back, and she turned to meet him. To her surprise he was standing inside the door, white to the lips and staring at her with wild eyes.

"Saunders!" he said chokingly, "Saunders, the damned fool! He's given it away."

He staggered to a chair, and ran a handkerchief across his shaking lips.

"He told Bassett, of the *Times-Republican*," he managed to say. "Do you—do you know what that means? And Bassett got Clark's automobile number. He said so."

He looked up at her, his face twitching. "They're hound dogs on a scent, Bev. They'll get the story, and blow it wide open."

"You know I'm prepared for that. I have been for ten years."

"I know." He was suddenly emotional. He reached out and took her hand. "Poor old Bev!" he said. "After the way you've come back, too. It's a damned shame."

She was calmer than he was, less convinced for one thing, and better balanced always. She let him stroke her hand, standing near him with her eyes absent and a little hard.

"I'd better make sure that was Jud first," he offered, after a time, "and then warn him."

"Why?"

"Bassett will be after him."

"No!" she commanded sharply. "No, Fred. You let the thing alone. You've built up an imaginary situation, and you're not thinking straight. Plenty of things might happen. What probably has happened is that this Bassett is at home and in bed."

She sent him out for a taxi soon after, and they went back to the hotel. But, alone later on in her suite in the Ardmore she did not immediately go to bed. She put on a dressing gown and stood for a long time by her window, looking out. Instead of the city lights, however, she saw a range of snow-capped mountains, and sheltered at their foot the Clark ranch house, built by the old millionaire as a place of occasional refuge from the pressure of his life. There he had raised his fine horses, and trained them for the track. There, when late in life he married, he had taken his wife for their honeymoon and two years later, for the birth of their son. And there, when she died, he had returned with the child, himself broken and prematurely aged, to be killed by one of his own stallions when the boy was fifteen.

Six years his own master, Judson had been twenty-one to her twenty, when she first met him. Going the usual pace, too, and throwing money right and left. He had financed her as a star, ransacking Europe for her stage properties, and then he fell in love with her. She shivered as she remembered it. It had been desperate and terrible, because she had cared for some one else.

Standing by the window, she wondered as she had done over and over again for ten years, what would have happened if, instead of marrying Howard, she had married Judson Clark? Would he have settled down? She had felt sometimes that in his wildest moments he was only playing a game that amused him; that the hard-headed part of him inherited from his father sometimes stood off and watched, with a sort of interested detachment, the follies of the other. That he played his wild game with his tongue in his cheek.

She left the window, turned out the lights and got into her bed. She was depressed and lonely, and she cried a little. After a time she remembered that she had not put any cream on her face. She crawled out again and went through the familiar motions in the dark.

Chapter Eight

DICK ROSE the next morning with a sense of lightness and content that sent him singing into his shower. In the old stable which now housed both Nettie and the little car Mike was washing them both with indiscriminate wavings of the hose nozzle, his old pipe clutched in his teeth. From below there came up the odors of frying sausages and of strong hot coffee.

The world was a good place. A fine old place. It had work and play and love. It had office hours and visits and the golf links, and it had soft feminine eyes and small tender figures to be always cared for and looked after.

She liked him. She did not think he was old. She thought his profession was the finest in the world. She had wondered if he would have time to come and see her, some day. Time! He considered very seriously, as he shaved before the slighly distorted mirror in the bathroom, whether it would be too soon to run in that afternoon, just to see if she was tired, or had caught cold or anything? Perhaps to-morrow would look better. No, hang it all, to-day was to-day.

On his way from the bathroom to his bedroom he leaned over the staircase.

"Aunt Lucy!" he called.

"Yes, Dick?"

"The top of the morning to you. D'you think Minnie would have time to press my blue trousers this morning?"

There was the sound of her chair being pushed back in the dining-room, of a colloquy in the kitchen, and Minnie herself appeared below him.

"Just throw them down, Doctor Dick," she said. "I've got an iron hot now."

"Some day, Minnie," he announced, "you will wear a halo and with the angels sing."

This mood of unreasoning happiness continued all morning. He went from house to house, properly grave and responsible but with a small song in his heart, and about eleven o'clock he found time to stop at the village haberdasher's and to select a new tie, which he had wrapped and stuffed in his pocket. And which, inspected in broad day later on a country road, gave him uneasy qualms as to its brilliance.

At the luncheon table he was almost hilarious, and David played up to him, albeit rather heavily. But Lucy was thoughtful and quiet. She had a sense of things somehow closing down on them, of hands reaching out from the past, and clutching; Mrs. Morgan, Beverly Carlysle, Dick in love and possibly going back to Norada. Unlike David, who was content that one emergency had passed, she looked ahead and saw their common life a series of such chances, with their anxieties and their dangers.

She could not eat.

Nevertheless when she herself admitted a new patient for Dick that afternoon, she had no premonition of trouble. She sent him into the waiting-room, a tall, robust and youngish man, perhaps in his late thirties, and went quietly on her way to her sitting-room, and to her weekly mending.

On the other hand, Louis Bassett was feeling more or less uncomfortable. There was an air of peace and quiet respectability about the old house, a domestic odor of baking cake, a quietness and stability that somehow made his errand appear absurd. To connect it with Judson Clark and his tumultuous past seemed ridiculous.

His errand, on the surface, was a neuralgic headache.

When, hat in hand, he walked into Dick's consulting room, he had made up his mind that he would pay the price of an overactive imagination for a prescription, walk out again, and try to forget that he had let a chance resemblance carry him off his feet.

But, as he watched the man who sat across from him, tilted back in his swivel chair, he was not so sure. Here was the same tall figure, the heavy brown hair, the features and boyish smile of the photograph he had seen the night before. As Judson Clark might have looked at thirty-two this man looked.

He made his explanation easily. Was in town for the

day. Subject to these headaches. Worse over the right eye. No, he didn't wear glasses; perhaps he should.

It wasn't Clark. It couldn't be. Jud Clark sitting there tilted back in an old chair and asking questions as to the nature of his fictitious pain! Impossible. Nevertheless he was of a mind to clear the slate and get some sleep that night, and having taken his prescription and paid for it, he sat back and commenced an apparently casual interrogation.

"Two names on your sign, I see. Father and son, I suppose?"

"Doctor David Livingstone is my uncle."

"I should think you'd be in the city. Limitations to this sort of thing, aren't there?"

"I like it," said Dick, with an eye on the office clock.

"Patients are your friends, of course. Born and raised here, I suppose?"

"Not exactly. I was raised on a ranch in Wyoming. My father had a ranch out there."

Bassett shot a glance at him, but Dick was calm and faintly smiling.

"Wyoming!" the reporter commented. "That's a long way from here. Anywhere near the new oil fields?"

"Not far from Norada. That's the oil center," Dick offered, good-naturedly. He rose, and glanced again at the clock. "If those headaches continue you'd better have your eyes examined."

Bassett was puzzled. It seemed to him that there had been a shade of evasion in the other man's manner, slightly less frankness in his eyes. But he showed no excitement, nothing furtive or alarmed. And the open and unsolicited statement as to Norada baffled him. He had to admit to himself either that a man strongly resembling Judson Clark had come from the same neighborhood, or——

"Norada?" he said. "That's where the big Clark ranch was located, wasn't it? Ever happen to meet Judson Clark?"

"Our place was very isolated."

Bassett found himself being politely ushered out, considerably more at sea than when he went in and slightly irritated. His annoyance was not decreased by the calm voice behind him which said:

"Better drink considerable water when you take that stuff. Some stomachs don't tolerate it very well."

The door closed. The reporter stood in the waiting-room for a moment. Then he clapped on his hat.

"Well, I'm a damned fool," he muttered, and went out into the street.

He was disappointed and a trifle sheepish. Life was full of queer chances, that was all. No resemblance on earth, no coincidence of birthplace, could make him believe that Judson Clark, waster, profligate and fugitive from the law was now sitting up at night with sick children, or delivering babies.

After a time he remembered the prescription in his hand, and was about to destroy it. He stopped and examined it, and then carefully placed it in his pocket-book. After all, there were things that looked queer. The fellow had certainly evaded that last question of his.

He made his way, head bent, toward the station.

He had ten minutes to wait, and he wandered to the newsstand. He made a casual inspection of its display, bought a newspaper and was turning away, when he stopped and gazed after a man who had just passed him from an out-bound train.

The reporter looked after him with amused interest. Gregory, too! The Livingstone chap had certainly started something. But it was odd, too. How had Gregory traced him? Wasn't there something more in Gregory's presence there than met the eye? Gregory's visit might be, like his own, the desire to satisfy himself that the man was or was not Clark. Or it might be the result of a conviction that it was Clark, and a warning against himself. But if he had traced him, didn't that indicate that Clark himself had got into communication with him? In other words, that the chap was Clark, after all?

Gregory, having made an inquiry of a hackman, had started along the street, and, after a moment's thought, Bassett fell into line behind him. He was extremely interested and increasingly cheerful. He remained well behind, and with his newspaper rolled in his hand assumed the easy yet brisk walk of the commuters around him, bound for home and their early suburban dinners.

Half-way along Station Street Gregory stopped before the Livingstone house, read the sign, and rang the doorbell. The reporter slowed down, to give him time for admission, and then slowly passed. In front of Harrison Miller's

house, however, he stopped and waited. He lighted a cigarette and made a careful survey of the old place. Strange,
if this were to prove the haven where Judson Clark had
taken refuge, this old brick two-story dwelling, with its
ramshackle stable in the rear, its small vegetable garden, its
casual beds of simple garden flowers set in a half acre or so
of ground.

A doctor. A pill shooter. Jud Clark!

Chapter Nine

ELIZABETH had gone about all day with a smile on her lips and a sort of exaltation in her eyes. She had, girl fashion, gone over and over the totally uneventful evening they had spent together, remembering small speeches and gestures; what he had said and she had answered.

She had, for instance, mentioned Clare Rossiter, very casually. Oh very, very casually. And he had said: "Clare Rossiter? Oh, yes, the tall blonde girl, isn't she?"

She was very happy. He had not seemed to find her too young or particularly immature. He had asked her opinion on quite important things, and listened carefully when she replied. She felt, though, that she knew about one-tenth as much as he did, and she determined to read very seriously from that time on. Her mother, missing her that afternoon, found her curled up in the library, beginning the first volume of Gibbon's "Rome" with an air of determined concentration, and wearing her best summer frock.

She did not intend to depend purely on Gibbon's "Rome," evidently.

"Are you expecting any one, Elizabeth?" she asked, with the frank directness characteristic of mothers, and Elizabeth, fixing a date in her mind with terrible firmness, looked up absently and said:

"No one in particular."

At three o'clock, with a slight headache from concentration, she went upstairs and put up her hair again; rather high this time to make her feel taller. Of course, it was not likely he would come. He was very busy. So many people depended on him. It must be wonderful to be like that, to have people needing one, and looking out of the door and saying: "I think I see him coming now."

Nevertheless when the postman rang her heart gave a

small leap and then stood quite still. When Annie slowly mounted the stairs she was already on her feet, but it was only a card announcing: "Mrs. Sayre, Wednesday, May fifteenth, luncheon at one-thirty."

However, at half past four the bell rang again, and a masculine voice informed Annie, a moment later, that it would put its overcoat here, because lately a dog had eaten a piece out of it and got most awful indigestion.

The time it took Annie to get up the stairs again gave her a moment so that she could breathe more naturally, and she went down very deliberately and so dreadfully poised that at first he thought she was not glad to see him.

"I came, you see," he said. "I intended to wait until to-morrow, but I had a little time. But if you're doing anything——"

"I was reading Gibbon's 'Rome,' " she informed him. "I think every one should know it. Don't you?"

"Good heavens, what for?" he inquired.

"I don't know." They looked at each other, and suddenly they laughed.

"I wanted to improve my mind," she explained. "I felt, last night, that you—that you know so many things, and that I was frightfully stupid."

"Do you mean to say," he asked, aghast, "that I——! Great Scott!"

Settled in the living-room, they got back rather quickly to their status of the night before, and he was moved to confession.

"I didn't really intend to wait until to-morrow," he said. "I got up with the full intention of coming here to-day, if I did it over the wreck of my practice. At eleven o'clock this morning I held up a consultation ten minutes to go to Yardsleys and buy a tie, for this express purpose. Perhaps you have noticed it already."

"I have indeed. It's a wonderful tie."

"Neat but not gaudy, eh?" He grinned at her, happily. "You know, you might steer me a bit about my ties. I have the taste of an African savage. I nearly bought a purple one, with red stripes. And Aunt Lucy thinks I should wear white lawn, like David!"

They talked, those small, highly significant nothings which are only the barrier behind which go on the eager questionings and unspoken answers of youth and love.

They had known each other for years, had exchanged the same give and take of neighborhood talk when they met as now. To-day nothing was changed, and everything.

Then, out of a clear sky, he said:

"I may be going away before long, Elizabeth."

He was watching her intently. She had a singular feeling that behind this, as behind everything that afternoon, was something not spoken. Something that related to her. Perhaps it was because of his tone.

"You don't mean—not to stay?"

"No. I want to go back to Wyoming. Where I was born. Only for a few weeks."

And in that "only for a few weeks" there lay some of the unspoken things. That he would miss her and come back quickly to her. That she would miss him, and that subconsciously he knew it. And behind that, too, a promise. He would come back to her.

"Only for a few weeks," he repeated. "I thought perhaps, if you wouldn't mind my writing to you, now and then—I write a rotten hand, you know. Most medical men do."

"I should like it very much," she said, primly

She felt suddenly very lonely, as though he had already gone, and slightly resentful, not at him but at the way things happened. And then, too, everyone knew that once a Westerner always a Westerner. The West always called its children. Not that she put it that way. But she had a sort of vision, gained from the moving pictures, of a country of wide spaces and tall mountains, where men wore quaint clothing and the women rode wild horses and had the dash she knew she lacked. She was stirred by vague jealousy.

"You may never come back," she said, casually. "After all, you were born there, and we must seem very quiet to you."

"Quiet!" he exclaimed. "You are heavenly restful and comforting. You——" he checked himself and got up. "Then I'm to write, and you are to make out as much of my scrawl as you can and answer. Is that right?"

"I'll write you all the town gossip."

"If you do——!" he threatened her. "You're to write me what you're doing, and all about yourself. Remember, I'll be counting on you."

And, if their voices were light, there was in both of them

the sense of a pact made, of a bond that was to hold them, like clasped hands, against their coming separation. It was rather anti-climactic after that to have him acknowledge that he didn't know exactly when he could get away!

She went with him to the door and stood there, her soft hair blowing, as he got into the car. When he looked back, as he turned the corner, she was still there. He felt very happy and affable, and he picked up an elderly village woman with her basket and went considerably out of his way to take her home. . . . .

He got back to the office at half past six to find a red-eyed Minnie in the hall.

Chapter Ten

AT HALF PAST five that afternoon David had let himself into the house with his latch key, hung up his overcoat on the old walnut hat rack, and went into his office. The strain of the days before had told on him, and he felt weary and not entirely well. He had fallen asleep in his buggy, and had wakened to find old Nettie drawing him slowly down the main street of the town, pursuing an erratic but homeward course, while the people on the pavements watched and smiled.

He went into his office, closed the door, and then, on the old leather couch with its sagging springs he stretched himself out to finish his nap.

Almost immediately, however, the doorbell rang, and a moment later Minnie opened his door.

"Gentleman to see you, Doctor David."

He got up clumsily and settled his collar. Then he opened the door into his waiting-room.

"Come in," he said resignedly.

A small, dapper man, in precisely the type of clothes David most abominated, and wearing light-colored spats, rose from his chair and looked at him with evident surprise.

"I'm afraid I've made a mistake. A Doctor Livingstone left his seat number for calls at the box office of the Annex Theater last night—the Happy Valley company—but he was a younger man. I——"

David stiffened, but he surveyed his visitor impassively from under his shaggy white eyebrows.

"I haven't been in a theater for a dozen years, sir."

Gregory was convinced that he had made a mistake. Like Louis Bassett, the very unlikeliness of Jud Clark being connected with the domestic atmosphere and quiet respectability of the old house made him feel intrusive and absurd. He was about to apologize and turn away, when he thought of something.

"There are two names on your sign. The other one, was he by any chance at the theater last night?"

"I think I shall have to have a reason for these inquiries," David said slowly.

He was trying to place Gregory, to fit him into the situation; straining back over ten years of security, racking his memory, without result.

"Just what have you come to find out?" he asked, as Gregory turned and looked around the room.

"The other Doctor Livingstone is your brother?"

"My nephew."

Gregory shot a sharp glance at him, but all he saw was an elderly man, with heavy white hair and fierce shaggy eyebrows, a portly and dignified elderly gentleman, rather resentfully courteous.

"Sorry to trouble you," he said. "I suppose I've made a mistake. I—is your nephew at home?"

"No."

"May I see a picture of him, if you have one?"

David's wild impulse was to smash Gregory to the earth, to annihilate him. His collar felt tight, and he pulled it away from his throat.

"Not unless I know why you want to see it."

"He is tall, rather spare? And he took a young lady to the theater last night?" Gregory persisted.

"He answers that description. What of it?"

"And he is your nephew?"

"My brother's son," David said steadily.

Somehow it began to dawn on him that there was nothing inimical in this strange visitor, that he was anxious and ill at ease. There was, indeed, something almost beseeching in Gregory's eyes, as though he stood ready to give confidence for confidence. And, more than that, a sort of not unfriendly stubbornness, as though he had come to do something he meant to do.

"Sit down," he said, relaxing somewhat. "Certainly my nephew is making no secret of the fact that he went to the theater last night. If you'll tell me who you are——"

But Gregory did not sit down. He stood where he was, and continued to eye David intently.

"I don't know just what it conveys to you, Doctor, but I am Beverly Carlysle's brother."

David lowered himself into his chair. His knees were suddenly weak under him. But he was able to control his voice.

"I see," he said. And waited.

"Something happened last night at the theater. It may be important. I'd have to see your nephew, in order to find out if it is. I can't afford to make a mistake."

David's ruddy color had faded. He opened a drawer of his desk and produced a copy of the photograph of Dick in his uniform. "Maybe this will help you."

Gregory studied it carefully, carrying it to the window to do so. When he confronted David again he was certain of himself and his errand for the first time, and his manner had changed.

"Yes," he said, significantly. "It does."

He placed the photograph on the desk, and sitting down, drew his chair close to David's. "I'll not use any names, Doctor. I think you know what I'm talking about. I was sure enough last night. I'm certain now."

David nodded. "Go on."

"We'll start like this. God knows I don't want to make any trouble. But I'll put a hypothetical case. Suppose that a man when drunk commits a crime and then disappears; suppose he leaves behind him a bad record and an enormous fortune; suppose then he reforms and becomes a useful citizen, and everything is buried."

Doctor David listened stonily. Gregory lowered his voice.

"Suppose there's a woman mixed up in that situation. Not guiltily, but there's a lot of talk. And suppose she lives it down, for ten years, and then goes back to her profession, in a play the families take the children to see, and makes good. It isn't hard to suppose that neither of those two people wants the thing revived, is it?"

David cleared his throat.

"You mean, then, that there is danger of such a revival?"

"I think there is," Gregory said bitterly. "I recognized this man last night, and called a fellow who knew him in the old days, Saunders, our stage manager. And a newspaper man named Bassett wormed it out of Saunders. You know what that means."

David heard him clearly, but as though from a great distance.

"You can see how it appears to Bassett. If he's found it, it's the big story of a lifetime. I thought *he'd* better be warned."

When David said nothing, but sat holding tight to the arms of his old chair, Gregory reached for his hat and got up.

"The thing for him to do," he said, "is to leave town for a while. This Bassett is a hound-hog on a scent. They all are. He is Bassett of the *Times-Republican*. And he took Jud—he took your nephew's automobile license number."

Still David sat silent, and Gregory moved to the door.

"Get him away, to-night if you can."

"Thank you," David said. His voice was thick. "I appreciate your coming."

He got up dizzily, as Gregory said, "Good-evening" and went out. The room seemed very dark and unsteady, and not quite familiar. So this was what had happened, after all the safe years! A man could work and build and pray, but if his house was built on the sand—

As the outer door closed David fell to the floor with a crash.

Chapter Eleven

BASSETT lounged outside the neat privet hedge which it was Harrison Miller's custom to clip with his own bachelor hands, and waited. And as he waited he tried to imagine what was going on inside, behind the neatly curtained windows of the old brick house.

He was tempted to ring the bell again, pretend to have forgotten something, and perhaps happen in on what might be drama of a rather high order; what, supposing the man was Clark after all, was fairly sure to be drama. He discarded the idea, however, and began again his interested survey of the premises. Whoever conceived this sort of haven for Clark, if it were Clark, had shown considerable shrewdness. The town fairly smelt of respectability; the tree-shaded streets, the children in socks and small crisp-laundered garments, the houses set back, each in its square of shaved lawn, all peaceful, middle class and unexciting. The last town in the world for Judson Clark, the last profession, the last house, this shabby old brick before him.

He smiled rather grimly as he reflected that if Gregory had been right in his identification, he was, beyond those windows at that moment, very possibly warning Clark against himself. Gregory would know his type, that he never let go. He drew himself up a little.

The house door opened, and Gregory came out, turning toward the station. Bassett caught up with him and put a hand on his arm.

"Well?" he said cheerfully. "It was, wasn't it?"

Gregory stopped dead and stared at him. Then:

"Old dog Tray!" he said sneeringly. "If your brain was as good as your nose, Bassett, you'd be a whale of a newspaper man."

"Don't bother about my brain. It's working fine to-day, anyhow. Well, what had he to say for himself?"

Gregory's mind was busy, and he had had a moment to pull himself together.

"We both get off together," he said, more amiably. "That fellow isn't Jud Clark and never was. He's a doctor, and the nephew of the old doctor there. They're in practice together."

"Did you see them both?"

"Yes."

Bassett eyed him. Either Gregory was a good actor, or the whole trail ended there after all. He himself had felt, after his interview, with Dick, that the scent was false. And there was this to be said: Gregory had been in the house scarcely ten minutes. Long enough to acknowledge a mistake, but hardly long enough for any dramatic identification. He was keenly disappointed, but he had had long experience of disappointment, and after a moment he only said:

"Well, that's that. He certainly looked like Clark to me."

"I'll say he did."

"Rather surprised him, didn't you?"

"Oh, he was all right," Gregory said. "I didn't tell him anything, of course."

Bassett looked at his watch.

"I was after you, all right," he said, cheerfully. "But if I was barking up the wrong tree, I'm done. I don't have to be hit on the head to make me stop. Come and have a soda-water on me," he finished amiably. "There's no train until seven."

But Gregory refused.

"No, thanks. I'll wander on down to the station and get a paper."

The reporter smiled. Gregory was holding a grudge against him, for a bad night and a bad day.

"All right," he said affably. "I'll see you at the train. I'll walk about a bit."

He turned and started back up the street again, walking idly. His chagrin was very real. He hated to be fooled, and fooled he had been. Gregory was not the only one who had lost a night's sleep. Then, unexpectedly, he was hailed from the curbstone, and he saw with amazement that it was Dick Livingstone.

"Take you anywhere?" Dick asked. "How's the headache?"

"Better, thanks." Bassett stared at him. "No, I'm just walking around until train-time. Are you starting out or going home, at this hour?"

"Going home. Well, glad the head's better."

He drove on, leaving the reporter gazing after him. So Gregory had been lying. He hadn't seen this chap at all. Then why—? He walked on, turning this new phase of the situation over in his mind. Why this elaborate fiction, if Gregory had merely gone in, waited for ten minutes, and come out again?

It wasn't reasonable. It wasn't logical. Something had happened inside the house to convince Gregory that he was right. He had seen somebody, or something. He hadn't needed to lie. He could have said frankly that he had seen no one. But no, he had built up a fabric carefully calculated to throw Bassett off the scent.

He saw Dick stop in front of the house, get out and enter. And coming to a decision, he followed him and rang the doorbell. For a long time no one answered. Then the maid of the afternoon opened the door, her eyes red with crying, and looked at him with hostility.

"Doctor Richard Livingstone?"

"You can't see him."

"It's important."

"Well, you can't see him. Doctor David has just had a stroke. He's in the office now, on the floor."

She closed the door on him, and he turned and went away. It was all clear to him; Gregory had seen, not Clark, but the older man; had told him and gone away. And under the shock the older man had collapsed. That was sad. It was very sad. But it was also extremely convincing.

He sat up late that night again, running over the entries in his notebook. The old story, as he pieced it out, ran like this:

It had been twelve years ago, when, according to the old files, Clark had financed Beverly Carlysle's first starring venture. He had, apparently, started out in the beginning only to give her the publicity she needed. In devising it, however, he had shown a sort of boyish recklessness and ingenuity that had caught the interest of the press, and set newspaper men to chuckling wherever they got together.

He had got together a dozen or so of young men like himself, wealthy, idle and reckless with youth, and, headed by him, they had made the exploitation of the young star an occupation. The newspapers referred to the star and her constellation as Beverly Carlysle and her Broadway Beauties. It had been unvicious, young, and highly entertaining, and it had cost Judson Clark his membership in his father's conservative old clubs.

For a time it livened the theatrical world with escapades that were harmless enough, if sensational. Then, after a time, newspaper row began to whisper that young Clark was in love with the girl. The Broadway Beauties broke up, after a wild farewell dinner. The audiences ceased to expect a row of a dozen youths, all dressed alike with gardenias in their buttonholes and perhaps red neckties with their evening suits, to rise in their boxes on the star's appearance and solemnly bow. And the star herself lost a little of the anxious look she frequently wore.

The story went, after a while, that Judson Clark had been refused, and was taking his refusal badly. Reporters saw him, carelessly dressed, outside the stage door waiting, and the story went that the girl had thrown him over, money and all, for her leading man. One thing was clear; Clark, not a drinker before, had taken to drinking hard, and after a time, and some unpleasant scenes probably, she refused to see him any more.

When the play closed in June, 1911, she married Howard Lucas, her leading man; his third wife. Lucas had been not a bad chap, a good-looking, rather negligible man, given to all-day Sunday poker, carefully valeted, not very keen mentally, but amiable. They had bought a house on East Fifty-sixth Street, and were looking for a new play with Lucas as co-star, when he unaccountably went to pieces nervously, stopped sleeping, and developed a slight twitching of his handsome, rather vacuous face.

Judson Clark had taken his yacht and gone to Europe, and was reported from here and there not too favorably. But when he came back, in early September, he had apparently recovered from his infatuation, was his old, carefully dressed self again, and when interviewed declared his intention of spending the winter on his Wyoming ranch.

Of course he must have heard of Lucas's breakdown, and equally, of course, he must have seen them both. What happened at that interview, by what casual attitude he allayed Lucas's probable jealousy and the girl's own nervousness, Bassett had no way of discovering. It was clear that he convinced them both of his good faith, for the next note in the reporter's book was simply a date, September 12, 1911.

That was the day they had all started West together, travelling in Clark's private car, with Lucas, twitching slightly, smiling and waving farewell from a window.

The big smash did not come until the middle of October.

Bassett sat back and considered. He had a fairly clear idea of the conditions at the ranch; daily riding, some little reading, and a great deal too much of each other. A sick man, too, unhappy in his exile, chafing against his restrictions, lonely and irritable. The girl, early seeing her mistake, and Clark's jealousy of her husband. The door into their apartment closing, the thousand and one unconscious intimacies between man and wife, the breakfast for two going up the stairs, and below that hot-eyed boy, agonized and passionately jealous, yet meeting them and looking after them, their host and a gentleman.

Lucas took to drinking, after a time, to allay his sheer boredom. And Jud Clark drank with him. At the end of three weeks they were both drinking heavily, and were politely quarrelsome. Bassett could fill that in also. He could see the girl protesting, watching, increasingly anxious as she saw that Clark's jealousy was matched by her husband's.

A queer picture, he reflected, the three of them shut away on the great ranch, and every day some new tension, some new strain.

Then, one night at dinner, they quarreled, and Beverly left the table. She was going to pack her things and go back to New York. She had felt, probably, that something was bound to snap. And while she was upstairs Clark had shot and killed Howard Lucas, and himself disappeared.

He had run, testimony at the inquest revealed, to the corral, and saddled a horse. Although it was only October, it was snowing hard, but in spite of that he had turned his horse toward the mountains. By midnight a posse from Norada had started out, and another up the Dry River Canyon, but the storm turned into a blizzard in the mountains, and they were obliged to turn back. A few inches more snow, and they could not have got their horses out. A

week or so later, with a crust of ice over it, a few of them
began again, with no expectation, however, of finding
Clark alive. They came across his horse on the second day,
but they did not find him, and there were some among
them who felt that, after all, old Elihu Clark's boy had
chosen the better way.

Bassett closed his notebook and lighted a cigar.

There was a big story to be had for the seeking, a whale
of a story. He could go to the office, give them a hint, draw
expense money and start for Norada the next night. He
knew well enough that he would have to begin there, and
that it would not be easy. Witnesses of the affair at the
ranch would be missing now, or when found the first accuracy of their statements would either be dulled by time or
have been added to with the passing years. The ranch itself
might have passed into other hands. To reconstruct the
events of ten years ago might be impossible, or nearly so.
But that was not his problem. He would have to connect
Norada with Haverly, Clark with Livingstone. One thing
only was simple. If he found Livingstone's story was correct, that he had lived on a ranch near Norada before the
crime and as Livingstone, then he would acknowledge that
two men could look precisely alike and come from the
same place, and yet not be the same. If not——

But, after he had turned out his light and got into bed,
he began to feel a certain distaste for his self-appointed
task. If Livingstone were Clark, if after years of effort he
had pulled himself up by his own boot-straps, had made
himself a man out of the reckless boy he had been, a decent and useful citizen, why pull him down? After all, the
world hadn't lost much in Lucas; a sleek, not over-intelli-
gent big animal, that had been Howard Lucas.

He decided to sleep over it, and by morning he found
himself not only disinclined to the business, but firmly resolved to let it drop. Things were well enough as they were.
The woman in the case was making good. Jud was making
good. And nothing would restore Howard Lucas to that
small theatrical world of his which had waved him good-
bye at the station so long ago.

He shaved and dressed, his resolution still holding. He
had indeed almost a conscious glow of virtue, for he was
making one of those inglorious and unsung sacrifices which
ought to bring a man credit in the next world, because they

certainly got him nowhere in this. He was quite affable to the colored waiter who served his breakfasts in the bachelor apartment house, and increased his weekly tip to a dollar and a half. Then he sat down and opened the *Times-Republican,* skimming over it after his habit for his own space, and frowning over a row of exclamation and interrogation points unwittingly set behind the name of the mayor.

On the second page, however, he stopped, coffee cup in air.

"Is Judson Clark alive? Wife of former ranch manager makes confession."

A woman named Margaret Donaldson, it appeared, fatally injured by an automobile near the town of Norada, Wyoming, had made a confession on her deathbed. In it she stated that, afraid to die without shriving her soul, she had sent for the sheriff of Dallas County and had made the following confession:

That following the tragedy at the Clark ranch her husband, John Donaldson, since dead, had immediately following the inquest, where he testified, started out into the mountains in the hope of finding Clark alive, as he knew of a deserted ranger's cabin where Clark sometimes camped when hunting. It was his intention to search for Clark at his cabin and effect his escape. He carried with him food and brandy.

That, owing to the blizzard, he was very nearly frozen; that he was obliged to abandon his horse, shooting it before he did so, and that, close to death himself, he finally reached the cabin and there found Judson Clark, the fugitive, who was very ill.

She further testified that her husband cared for Clark for four days, Clark being delirious at the time, and that on the fifth day he started back on foot for the Clark ranch, having left Clark locked in the cabin, and that on the following night he took three horses, two saddled, and one packed with food and supplies. That accompanied by herself they went back to the cabin in the mountains and that she remained there to care for Clark, while her husband returned to the ranch, to prevent suspicion.

That, a day or so later, looking out of her window, she had perceived a man outside in the snow coming toward the cabin, and that she had thought it one of the searching party. That her first instinct had been to lock him outside, but that she had finally admitted him, and that thereafter he had remained and had helped her to care for the sick man.

Unfortunately for the rest of the narrative it appeared that the injured woman had here lapsed into a coma, and had subsequently died, carrying her further knowledge with her.

But, the article went on, the story opened a field of infinite surmise. In all probability Judson Clark was still alive, living under some assumed identity, free of punishment, outwardly respectable. Three years before he had been adjudged legally dead, and the estate divided, under bond of the legatees.

Close to a hundred million dollars had gone to charities, and Judson Clark, wherever he was, would be dependent on his own efforts for existence. He could have summoned all the legal talent in the country to his defense, but instead he had chosen to disappear.

The whole situation turned on the deposition of Mrs. Donaldson, now dead. The local authorities at Norada maintained that the woman had not been sane for several years. On the other hand, the cabin to which she referred was well known, and no search of it had been made at the time. Clark's horse had been found not ten miles from the town, and the cabin was buried in snow twenty miles further away. If Clark had made that journey on foot he had accomplished the impossible.

Certain facts, according to the local correspondent, bore out Margaret Donaldson's confession. Inquiry showed that she was supposed to have spent the winter following Judson Clark's crime with relatives in Omaha. She had returned to the ranch the following spring.

A detailed description of Judson Clark, and a photograph of him accompanied the story. Bassett re-read the article carefully, and swore a little, under his breath. If he had needed confirmation of his suspicions, it lay to his hand. But the situation had changed over night. There would be a search for Clark now, as wide as the knowledge of his disappearance. Local police authorities would turn him up in every city from Maine to the Pacific coast. Even Europe would be on the lookout and South America.

But it was not the police he feared so much as the press.

Not all of the papers, but some of them, would go after that story, and send their best men on it. It offered not so much a chance of solution as an opportunity to revive the old dramatic story. He could see, when he closed his eyes, the local photographers climbing to that cabin and later sending its pictures broadcast, and divers gentlemen of the press, eager to pit their wits against ten years of time and the ability of a once conspicuous man to hide from the law, packing their suitcases for Norada.

No, he couldn't stop now. He would go on, like the others, and with this advantage, that he was morally certain he could lay his hands on Clark at any time. But he would have to prove his case, connect it. Who, for instance, was the other man in the cabin? He must have known who the boy was who lay in that rough bunk, delirious. Must have suspected, anyhow. That made him, like the Donaldsons, accessory after the fact, and criminally liable. Small chance of him coming out with any confession. Yet he was the connecting link. Must be.

On his third reading the reporter began to visualize the human elements of the fight to save the boy; he saw moving before him the whole pitiful struggle; the indomitable ranch manager, his heart-breaking struggle with the blizzard, the shooting of his horse, the careful disarming of suspicion, and later the intrepid woman, daring that night ride through snow that had sent the posse back to its firesides to the boy, locked in the cabin and raving.

His mind was busy as he packed his suitcase. Already he had forgotten his compunctions of the early morning; he moved about methodically, calculating roughly what expense money he would need, and the line of attack, if any, required at the office. Between Norada and that old brick house at Haverly lay his story. Ten years of it. He was closing his bag when he remembered the little girl in the blue dress, at the theater. He straightened and scowled. After a moment he snapped the bag shut. Damn it all, if Clark had chosen to tie up with a girl, that was on Clark's conscience, not his.

But he was vaguely uncomfortable.

"It's a queer world, Joe," he observed to the waiter, who had come in for the breakfast dishes.

"Yes, sir. It is *that*," said Joe.

Chapter Twelve

DURING ALL the long night Dick sat by David's bedside. Earlier in the evening there had been a consultation; David had suffered a light stroke, but there was no paralysis, and the prognosis was good. For this time, at least, David had escaped, but there must be no other time. He was to be kept quiet and free from worry, his diet was to be carefully regulated, and with care he still had long years before him.

David slept, his breathing heavy and slow. In the morning there would be a nurse, but that night Dick, having sent Lucy to bed, himself kept watch. On the walnut bed lay Doctor David's portly figure, dimly outlined by the shaded lamp, and on a chair drawn close sat Dick.

He was wide-awake and very anxious, but as time went on and no untoward symptoms appeared, as David's sleep seemed to grow easier and more natural, Dick's thoughts wandered. They went to Elizabeth first, and then on and on from that starting point, through the years ahead. He saw the old house with Elizabeth waiting in it for his return; he saw both their lives united and flowing on together, with children, with small cares, with the routine of daily living, and behind it all the two of them, hand in hand.

Then his mind turned on himself. How often in the past ten years it had done that! He had sat off, with a sort of professional detachment, and studied his own case. With the entrance into his world of the new science of psycho-analysis he had made now and then small, not very sincere, attempts to penetrate the veil of his own unconscious devising. Not very sincere, for with the increase of his own knowledge of the mind he had learned that behind such conditions as his lay generally, deeply hidden, the desire to forget. And that behind that there lay, acknowledged or not, fear.

"But to forget what?" he used to say to David, when the first text-books on the new science appeared, and he and David were learning the new terminology, Dick eagerly and David with contemptuous snorts of derision. "To forget what?"

"You had plenty to forget," David would say, stolidly. "I think this man's a fool, but at that—you'd had your father's death, for one thing. And you'd gone pretty close to the edge of eternity yourself. You'd fought single-handed the worst storm of ten years, you came out of it with double pneumonia, and you lay alone in that cabin about fifty-six hours. Forget! You had plenty to forget."

It had never occurred to Dick to doubt David's story. It did not, even now. He had accepted it unquestioningly from the first, supplemented the shadowy childish memories that remained to him with it, and gradually co-ordinating the two had built out of them his house of the past.

Thus, the elderly man whom he dimly remembered was not only his father; he was David's brother. And he had died. It was the shock of that death, according to David, that had sent him into the mountains, where David had followed and nursed him back to health.

It was quite simple, and even explicable by the new psychology. Not that he had worried about the new psychology in those early days. He had been profoundly lethargic, passive and incurious. It had been too much trouble even to think.

True, he had brought over from those lost years certain instincts and a few mental pictures. He had had a certain impatience at first over the restrictions of comparative poverty; he had had to learn the value of money. And the pictures he retained had had a certain opulence which the facts appeared to contradict. Thus he remembered a large ranch house, and innumerable horses, grazing in meadows or milling in a corral. But David had warned him early that there was no estate; that his future depended entirely on his own efforts.

Then the new life had caught and held him. For the first time he had mothering and love. Lucy was his mother, and David the pattern to which he meant to conform. He was happy and contented.

Now and then, in the early days, he had been conscious

of a desire to go back and try to reconstruct his past again. Later on he knew that if he were ever to fill up the gap in his life, it would be easier in that environment of once familiar things. But in the first days he had been totally dependent on David, and money was none too plentiful. Later on, as the new life took hold, as he went to medical college and worked at odd clerical jobs in vacations to help pay his way, there had been no chance. Then the war came, and on his return there had been the practice, and his knowledge that David's health was not what it should have been.

But as time went on he was more and more aware that there was in him a peculiar shrinking from going back, an almost apprehension. He knew more of the mind than he had before, and he knew that not physical hardship, but mental stress, caused such lapses as his. But what mental stress had been great enough for such a smash? His father's death?

Strain and fear, said the new psychology. Fear? He had never found himself lacking in courage. Certainly he would have fought a man who called him a coward. But there was cowardice behind all such conditions as his; a refusal of the mind to face reality. It was weak. Weak. He hated himself for that past failure of his to face reality. . . . . .

But that night, sitting by David's bed, he faced reality with a vengeance. He was in love, and he wanted the things that love should bring to a normal man. He felt normal. He felt, strengthened by love, that he could face whatever life had to bring, so long as also it brought Elizabeth.

Painfully he went back over his talk with David the preceding Sunday night.

"Don't be a fool," David had said. "Go ahead and take her, if she'll have you. And don't be too long about it. I'm not as young as I used to be."

"What I feel," he had replied, "is this: I don't know, of course, if she cares." David had grunted. "I do know I'm going to try to make her care, if it—if it's humanly possible. But I'd like to go back to the ranch again, David, before things go any further."

"Why?"

"I'd like to fill the gap. Attempt it anyhow."

What he was thinking about, as he sat by David's bedside, was David's attitude toward that threatened return of

his. For David had opposed it, offering a dozen trivial, almost puerile reasons. Had shown indeed, a dogged obstina-
cy and an irritability that were somehow oddly like fear.
David afraid! David, whose life and heart were open
books! David, whose eyes never wavered, nor his courage!

"You let well enough alone, Dick," he had finished.
"You've got everything you want. And a medical man
can't afford to go gadding about. When people want him
they want him."

But he had noticed that David had been different, since.
He had taken to following him with his faded old eyes, had
even spoken once of retiring and turning all the work over
to him. Was it possible that David did not want him to go
back to Norada?

He bent over and felt the sick man's pulse. It was
stronger, not so rapid. The mechanical act took him back
to his first memory of David.

He had been lying in a rough bunk in the mountain cabin, and David, beside him on a wooden box, had been
bending forward and feeling his pulse. He had felt weak
and utterly inert, and he knew now that he had been very
ill. The cabin had been a small and lonely one, with
snow-peaks not far above it, and it had been very cold.
During the day a woman kept up the fire. Her name was
Maggie, and she moved about the cabin like a thin ghost.
At night she slept in a lean-to shed and David kept the fire
going. A man who seemed to know him well—John Donaldson, he learned, was his name—was Maggie's husband,
and every so often he came, about dawn, and brought food
and supplies.

After a long time, as he grew stronger, Maggie had gone
away, and David had fried the bacon and heated the
canned tomatoes or the beans. Before she left she had written out a recipe for biscuits, and David would study over it
painstakingly, and then produce a panful of burned and
blackened lumps, over which he would groan and agonize.

He himself had been totally incurious. He had lived a
sort of animal life of food and sleep, and later on of small
tentative excursions around the room on legs that shook
when he walked. The snows came and almost covered the
cabin, and David had read a great deal, and talked at intervals. David had tried to fill up the gap in his mind. That

was how he learned that David was his father's brother, and that his father had recently died.

Going over it all now, it had certain elements that were not clear. They had, for instance, never gone back to the ranch at all. With the first clearing of the snow in the spring John Donaldson had appeared again, leading two saddled horses and driving a pack animal, and they had started off, leaving him standing in the clearing and gazing after them. But they had not followed Donaldson's trail. They had started West, over the mountains, and David did not know the country. Once they were lost for three days.

He looked at the figure on the bed. Only ten years, and yet at that time David had been vigorous, seemed almost young. He had aged in that ten years. On the bed he was an old man, a tired old man at that. On that long ride he had been tireless. He had taken the burden of the nightly camps, and had hacked a trail with his hatchet across snow fields while Dick, still weak but furiously protesting, had been compelled to stand and watch.

Now, with the perspective of time behind him, and with the clearly defined issue of David's protest against his return to the West, he went again over the details of that winter and spring. Why had they not taken Donaldson's trail? Or gone back to the ranch? Why, since Donaldson could make it, had not other visitors come? Another doctor, the night he almost died, and David sat under the lamp behind the close-screened windows, and read the very pocket prayer-book that now lay on the stand beside the bed? Why had they burned his clothes, and Donaldson brought a new outfit? Why did Donaldson, for all his requests, never bring a razor, so that when they struck the railroad, miles from anywhere, they were both full bearded?

He brought himself up sharply. He had allowed his imagination to run away with him. He had been depicting a flight, and no one who knew David could imagine him in flight.

Nevertheless he was conscious of a new uneasiness and anxiety. When David recovered sufficiently he would go to Norada, as he had told Elizabeth, and there he would find the Donaldsons, and clear up the things that bothered him. After that . . . .

He thought of Elizabeth, of her sweetness and sanity. He

remembered her at the theater the evening before, lost in its fictitious emotions, its counterfeit drama. He had felt moved to comfort her, when he found her on the verge of tears.

"Just remember, they're only acting," he had said.

"Yes. But life does do things like that to people."

"Not often. The theater deals in the dramatic exceptions to life. You and I, plain bread and butter people, come to see these things because we get a sort of vicarious thrill out of them."

"Doesn't anything ever happen to the plain bread and butter people?"

"A little jam, sometimes. Or perhaps they drop it, butter side down, on the carpet."

"But that is tragedy, isn't it?"

He had had to acknowledge that it might be. But he had been quite emphatic over the fact that most people didn't drop it.

After a long time he slept in his chair. The spring wind came in through the opened window, and fluttered the leaves of the old prayer-book on the stand.

Chapter Thirteen

THE WEEK that followed was
an anxious one. David's physical condition slowly improved.
The slight thickness was gone from his speech, and he
sipped resignedly at the broths Lucy or the nurse brought
at regular intervals. Over the entire house there hung all
day the odor of stewing chicken or of beef tea in the making, and above the doorbell was a white card which said:
"Don't ring. Walk in."

As it happened, no one in the old house had seen
Maggie Donaldson's confession in the newspaper. Lucy
was saved that anxiety, at least. Appearing, as it did, the
morning after David's stroke, it came in with the morning
milk, lay about unnoticed, and passed out again, to start a
fire or line a pantry shelf. Harrison Miller, next door, read
it over his coffee. Walter Wheeler in the eight-thirty train
glanced at it and glanced away. Nina Ward read it in bed.
And that was all.

There came to the house a steady procession of inquirers
and bearers of small tribute, flowers and jellies mostly, but
other things also. A table in David's room held a steadily
growing number of bedroom slippers, and Mrs. Morgan
had been seen buying soles for still others. David, propped
up in his bed, would cheer a little at these votive offerings,
and then relapse again into the heavy troubled silence that
worried Dick and frightened Lucy Crosby. Something had
happened, she was sure. Something connected with Dick.
She watched David when Dick was in the room, and she
saw that his eyes followed the younger man with something very like terror.

And for the first time since he had walked into the house
that night so long ago, followed by the tall young man for
whose coming a letter had prepared her, she felt that David had withdrawn himself from her. She went about her

daily tasks a little hurt, and waited for him to choose his
own time. But, as the days went on, she saw that whatever
this new thing might be, he meant to fight it out alone, and
that the fighting it out alone was bad for him. He improved
very slowly.

She wondered, somtimes, if it was after all because of
Dick's growing interest in Elizabeth Wheeler. She knew
that he was seeing her daily, although he was too busy now
for more than a hasty call. She felt that she could even tell
when he had seen her; he would come in, glowing and almost exalted, and, as if to make up for the moments stolen
from David, would leap up the stairs two at a time and
burst into the invalid's room like a cheerful cyclone.
Wasn't it possible that David had begun to feel as she did,
that the girl was entitled to a clean slate before she pledged
herself to Dick? And the slate—poor Dick!—could never
be cleaned.

Then, one day, David astonished them both. He was
propped up in his bed, and he had demanded a cigar, and
been very gently but firmly refused. He had been rather
sulky about it, and Dick had been attempting to rally him
into better humor when he said suddenly:

"I've had time to think things over, Dick. I haven't been
fair to you. You're thrown away here. Besides—" he hesitated. Then: "We might as well face it. The day of the general practitioner has gone."

"I don't believe it," Dick said stoutly. "Maybe we are
only signposts to point the way to the other fellows, but the
world will always need signposts."

"What I've been thinking of," David pursued his own
train of thought, "is this: I want you to go to Johns Hopkins and take up the special work you've been wanting to
do. I'll be up soon and—"

"Call the nurse, Aunt Lucy," said Dick. "He's raving."

"Not at all," David retorted testily. "I've told you. This
whole town only comes here now to be told what specialist
to go to, and you know it."

"I don't know anything of the sort."

"If you don't, it's because you won't face the facts."

Dick chuckled, and threw an arm over David's
shoulder.

"You old hypocrite!" he said. "You're trying to get rid

of me, for some reason. Don't tell me you're going to get married!"

But David did not smile. Lucy, watching him from her post by the window, saw his face and felt a spasm of fear. At the most, she had feared a mental conflict in David. Now she saw that it might be something infinitely worse, something impending and immediate. She could hardly reply when Dick appealed to her.

"Are you going to let him get rid of me like this, Aunt Lucy?" he demanded. "Sentenced to Johns Hopkins, like Napoleon to St. Helena! Are you with me, or forninst me?"

"I don't know, Dick," she said, with her eyes on David. "If it's for your good——"

She went out after a time, leaving them at it hammer and tongs. David was vanquished in the end, but Dick, going down to the office later on, was puzzled. Somehow it was borne in on him that behind David's insistence was a reason, unspoken but urgent, and the only reason that occurred to him as possible was that David did not, after all, want him to marry Elizabeth Wheeler. He put the matter to the test that night, wandering in in dressing-gown and slippers, as was his custom before going to bed, for a brief chat. The nurse was downstairs, and Dick moved about the room restlessly. Then he stopped and stood by the bed, looking down.

"A few nights ago, David, I asked you if you thought it would be right for me to marry; if my situation justified it, and if to your knowledge there was any other reason why I could not or should not. You said there was not."

"There is no reason, of course. If she'll have you."

"I don't know that. I know that whether she will or not is a pretty vital matter to me, David."

David nodded, silently.

"But now you want me to go away. To leave her. You're rather urgent about it. And I feel—well, I begin to think you have a reason for it."

David clenched his hands under the bed-clothing, but he returned Dick's gaze steadily.

"She's a good girl," he said. "But she's entitled to more than you can give her, the way things are."

"That is presupposing that she cares for me. I haven't an

idea that she does. That she may, in time— Then, that's the reason for this Johns Hopkins thing, is it?"

"That's the reason," David said stoutly. "She would wait for you. She's that sort. I've known her all her life. She's as steady as a rock. But she's been brought up to have a lot of things. Walter Wheeler is well off. You do as I want you to; pack your things and go to Baltimore. Bring Reynolds down here to look after the work until I'm around again."

But Dick evaded the direct issue thus opened and followed another line of thought.

"Of course you understand," he observed, after a renewal of his restless pacing, "that I've got to tell her my situation first. I don't need to tell you that I funk doing it, but it's got to be done."

"Don't be a fool," David said querulously. "You'll set a lot of women cackling, and what they don't know they'll invent. I know 'em."

"Only herself and her family."

"Why?"

"Because they have a right to know it."

But when he saw David formulating a further protest he dropped the subject.

"I'll not do it until we've gone into it together," he promised. "There's plenty of time. You settle down now and get ready for sleep."

When the nurse came in at eleven o'clock she found Dick gone and David, very still, with his face to the wall.

It was the end of May before David began to move about his upper room. The trees along the shaded streets had burst into full leaf by that time, and Mike was enjoying that gardener's interval of paradise when flowers grow faster than the weeds among them. Harrison Miller, having rolled his lawn through all of April, was heard abroad in the early mornings with the lawn mower or hoe in hand was to be seen behind his house in his vegetable patch.

Cars rolled through the streets, the rear seats laden with blossoming loot from the country lanes, and the Wheeler dog was again burying bones in the soft warm ground under the hedge.

Elizabeth Wheeler was very happy. Her look of expectant waiting, once vague, had crystallized now into definite form. She was waiting, timidly and shyly but with infinite content. In time, everything would come. And in the meantime there was to-day, and some time to-day a shabby car would stop at the door, and there would be five minutes, or ten. And then Dick would have to hurry to work, or back to David. After that, of course, to-day was over, but there would always be to-morrow.

Now and then, at choir practice or at service, she saw Clare Rossiter. But Clare was very cool to her, and never on any account sought her, or spoke to her alone. She was rather unhappy about Clare, when she remembered her. Because it must be so terrible to care for a man who only said, when one spoke of Clare, "Oh, the tall blonde girl?"

Once or twice, too, she had found Clare's eyes on her, and they were hostile eyes. It was almost as though they said: "I hate you because you *know*. But don't dare to pity me."

Yet, somehow, Elizabeth found herself not entirely believing that Clare's passion was real. Because the real thing you hid with all your might, at least until you were sure it was wanted. After that, of course, you could be so proud of it that you might become utterly shameless. She was afraid sometimes that she was the sort to be utterly shameless.

Yet, for all her halcyon hours, there were little things that worried her. Wallie Sayre, for instance, always having to be kept from saying things she didn't want to hear. And Nina. She wasn't sure that Nina was entirely happy. And, of course, there was Jim.

Jim was difficult. Sometimes he was a man, and then again sometimes he was a boy, and one never knew just which he was going to be. He was too old for discipline and too young to manage himself. He was spending almost all his evenings away from home now, and her mother always drew an inaudible sigh when he was spoken of.

Elizabeth had waited up for him one night, only a short time before, and beckoning him into her room, had talked to him severely.

"You ought to be ashamed, Jim," she said. "You're simply worrying mother sick."

"Well, why?" he demanded defiantly. "I'm old enough to take care of myself."

"You ought to be taking care of her, too."

He had looked rather crestfallen at that, and before he

went out he offered a half-sheepish explanation.

"I'd tell them where I go," he said, "but you'd think a pool room was on the direct road to hell. Take to-night, now. I can't tell them about it, but it was all right. I met Wallie Sayre and Leslie at the club before dinner, and we got a fourth and played bridge. Only half a cent a point. I swear we were going on playing, but somebody brought in a chap named Gregory for a cocktail. He turned out to be a brother of Beverly Carlysle, the actress, and he took us around to the theater and gave us a box. Not a thing wrong with it, was there?"

"Where did you go from there?" she persisted, inexorably. "It's half past one."

"Went around and met her. She's wonderful, Elizabeth. But do you know what would happen if I told them? They'd have a fit."

She felt rather helpless, because she knew he was right from his own standpoint.

"I know. I'm surprised at Les, Jim."

"Oh, Les! He just trailed along. He's all right."

She kissed him and he went out, leaving her to lie awake for a long time. She would have had all her world happy those days, and all her world good. She didn't want anybody's bread and butter spilled on the carpet.

So the days went on, and the web slowly wove itself into its complicated pattern: Bassett speeding West, and David in his quiet room; Jim and Leslie Ward seeking amusement, and finding it in the littered dressing-room of a woman star at a local theater; Clare Rossiter brooding, and the little question being whispered behind hands, figuratively, of course—the village was entirely well-bred; Gregory calling round to see Bassett, and turning away with the information that he had gone away for an indefinite time; and Maggie Donaldson, lying in the cemetery at the foot of the mountains outside Norada, having shriven her soul to the limit of her strength so that she might face her Maker.

Out of all of them it was Clare Rossiter who made the first conscious move of the shuttle; Clare, affronted and not a little malicious, but perhaps still dramatizing herself, this time as the friend who feels forced to carry bad tidings. Behind even that, however, was an unconscious desire to see Dick again, and this time so to impress herself on him that never again could he pass her in the street unnoticed.

On the day, then, that David first sat up in bed Clare went to the house and took her place in the waiting-room. She was dressed with extreme care, and she carried a parasol. With it, while she waited, she drilled small nervous indentations in the old office carpet, and formulated her line of action.

Nevertheless she found it hard to begin.

"I don't want to keep you, if you're busy," she said, avoiding his eyes. "If you are in a hurry——"

"This is my business," he said patiently. And waited.

"I wonder if you are going to understand me, when I do begin?"

"You sound alarmingly ominous." He smiled at her, and she had a moment of panic. "You don't look like a young lady with anything eating at her damask cheek, or however it goes."

"Doctor Livingstone," she said suddenly, "people are saying something about you that you ought to know."

He stared at her, amazed and incredulous.

"About me? What can they say? That's absurd."

"I felt you ought to know. Of course I don't believe it. Not for a moment. But you know what this town is."

"I know it's a very good town," he said steadily. "However, let's have it. I daresay it is not very serious."

She was uneasy enough by that time, and rather frightened when she had finished. For he sat, quiet and rather pale, not looking at her at all, but gazing fixedly at an old daguerreotype of David that stood on his desk. One that Lucy had shown him one day and which he had preëmpted; David at the age of eight, in a small black velvet suit and with very thin legs.

"I thought you ought to know," she justified herself, nervously.

Dick got up.

"Yes," he said. "I ought to know, of course. Thank you."

When she had gone he went back and stood before the picture again. From Clare's first words he had had a stricken conviction that the thing was true; that, as Mrs. Cook Morgan's visitor from Wyoming had insisted, Henry Livingstone had never married, never had a son. He stood and gazed at the picture. His world had collapsed about him, but he was steady and very erect.

"David, David!" he thought. "Why did you do it? And what am I? And who?"

Characteristically his first thought after that was of David himself. Whatever David had done, his motive had been right. He would have to start with that. If David had built for him a false identity it was because there was a necessity for it. Something shameful, something he was to be taken away from. Wasn't it probable that David had heard the gossip, and had then collapsed? Wasn't the fear that he himself would hear it behind David's insistence that he go to Baltimore?

His thoughts flew to Elizabeth. Everything was changed now, as to Elizabeth. He would have to be very certain of that past of his before he could tell her that he loved her, and he had a sense of immediate helplessness. He could not go to David, as things were. To Lucy?

Probably he would have gone to Lucy at once, but the telephone rang. He answered it, got his hat and bag and went out to the car. Years with David had made automatic the subordination of self to the demands of the practice.

At half past six Lucy heard him come in and go into his office. When he did not immediately reappear and take his flying run up the stairs to David's room, she stood outside the office door and listened. She had a premonition of something wrong, something of the truth, perhaps. Anyhow, she tapped at the door and opened it, to find him sitting very quietly at his desk with his head in his hands.

"Dick!" she exclaimed. "Is anything wrong?"

"I have a headache," he said. He looked at his watch and got up. "I'll take a look at David, and then we'll have dinner. I didn't know it was so late."

But when she had gone out he did not immediately move. He had been going over again, painfully and carefully, the things that puzzled him, that he had accepted before without dispute. David and Lucy's reluctance to discuss his father; the long days in the cabin, with David helping him to reconstruct his past; the spring, and that slow progress which now he felt, somehow, had been an escape.

He ate very little dinner, and Lucy's sense of dread increased. When, after the meal, she took refuge in her sitting-room on the lower floor and picked up her knitting, it was with a conviction that it was only a temporary reprieve. She did not know from what.

She heard him, some time later, coming down from David's room. But he did not turn into his office. Instead, he came on to her door, stood for a moment like a man undecided, then came in. She did not look up, even when very gently he took her knitting from her and laid it on the table.

"Aunt Lucy?"

"Yes, Dick."

"Don't you think we'd better have a talk?"

"What about?" she asked, with her heart hammering.

"About me." He stood above her, and looked down, still with the tenderness with which he always regarded her, but with resolution in his very attitude. "First of all, I'll tell you something. Then I'll ask you to tell me all you can."

She yearned over him as he told her, for all her terror. His voice, for all its steadiness, was strained.

"I have felt for some time," he finished, "that you and David were keeping something from me. I think, now, that this is what it was. Of course, you realize that I shall have to know."

"Dick! Dick!" was all she could say.

"I was about," he went on, with his almost terrible steadiness, "to ask a girl to take my name. I want to know if I have a name to offer her. I have, you see, only two alternatives to believe about myself. Either I am Henry Livingstone's illegitimate son, and in that case I have no right to my name, or to offer it to any one, or I am—"

He made a despairing gesture.

"—or I am some one else, some one who was smuggled out of the mountains and given an identity that makes him a living lie."

Always she had known that this might come some time, but always too she had seen David bearing the brunt of it. He should bear it. It was not of her doing or of her approving. For years the danger of discovery had hung over her like a cloud.

"Do you know which?" he persisted.

"Yes, Dick."

"Would you have the unbelievable cruelty not to tell me?"

She got up, a taut little figure with a dignity born of her fear and of her love for him.

"I shall not betray David's confidence," she said. "Long ago I warned him that this time would come. I was never in favor of keeping you in ignorance. But it is David's problem, and I cannot take the responsibility of telling you."

He knew her determination and her obstinate loyalty. But he was fairly desperate.

"You know that if you don't tell me, I shall go to David?"

"If you go now you will kill him."

"It's as bad as that, is it?" he asked grimly. "Then there is something shameful behind it, is there?"

"No, no, Dick. Not that. And I want you, always, to remember this. What David did was out of love for you. He has made many sacrifices for you. First he saved your life, and then he made you what you are. And he has had a great pride in it. Don't destroy his work of years."

Her voice broke and she turned to go out, her chin quivering, but half way to the door he called to her.

"Aunt Lucy!" he said gently.

She heard him behind her, felt his strong arms as he turned her about. He drew her to him and stooping, kissed her cheek.

"You're right," he said. "Always right. I'll not worry him with it. My word of honor. When the time comes he'll tell me, and until it comes, I'll wait. And I love you both. Don't ever forget that."

He kissed her again and let her go.

But long after David had put down his prayer-book that night, and after the nurse had rustled down the stairs to the night supper on the dining-room table, Lucy lay awake and listened to Dick's slow pacing of his bedroom floor.

He was very gentle with David from that time on, and tried to return to his old light-hearted ways. On the day David was to have his first broiled sweetbread he caught the nurse outside, borrowed her cap and apron and carried in the tray himself.

"I hope your food is to your taste, Doctor David," he said, in a high falsetto which set the nurse giggling in the hall. "I may not be much of a nurse, but I *can* cook."

Even Lucy was deceived at times. He went his customary round, sent out the monthly bills, opened and answered David's mail, bore the double burden of David's work and his own ungrudgingly, but off guard he was grave and abstracted. He began to look very thin, too, and Lucy often heard him pacing the floor at night. She thought that he seldom or never went to the Wheeler's.

And so passed the tenth day of David's illness, with the smile on Elizabeth's face growing a trifle fixed as three days went by without the shabby car rattling to the door; with "The Valley" playing its second and final week before going into New York; and with Leslie Ward unconsciously taking up the shuttle Clare had dropped, and carrying the pattern one degree further toward completion.

Chapter Fourteen

JUST HOW Leslie Ward had drifted into his innocuous affair with the star of "The Valley" he was not certain himself. Innocuous it certainly was. Afterwards, looking back, he was to wonder sometimes if it had not been precisely for the purpose it served. But that was long months after. Not until the pattern was completed and he was able to recognize his own work in it.

The truth was that he was not too happy at home. Nina's smart little house on the Ridgely Road had at first kept her busy. She had spent unlimited time with decorators, had studied and rejected innumerable water-color sketches of interiors, had haunted auction rooms and bid recklessly on things she felt at the moment she could not do without, later on to have to wheedle Leslie into straightening her bank balance. Thought, too, and considerable energy had gone into training and outfitting her servants, and still more into inducing them to wear the expensive uniforms and livery she provided.

But what she made, so successfully, was a house rather than a home. There were times, indeed, when Leslie began to feel that it was not even a house, but a small hotel. They almost never dined alone, and when they did Nina would explain that everybody was tied up. Then, after dinner, restlessness would seize her, and she would want to run in to the theater, or to make a call. If he refused, she nursed a grievance all evening.

And he did not like her friends. Things came to a point where, when he knew one of the gay evenings was on, he would stay in town, playing billiards at his club, or occasionally wandering into a theater, where he stood or sat at the back of the house and watched the play with cynical, discontented eyes.

The casual meeting with Gregory and the introduction to his sister brought a new interest. Perhaps the very novelty was what first attracted him, the oddity of feeling that he was on terms of friendship, for it amounted to that with surprising quickness, with a famous woman, whose face smiled out at him from his morning paper or, huge and shockingly colored, from the sheets on the bill boards.

He formed the habit of calling on her in the afternoons at her hotel, and he saw that she liked it. It was often lonely, she explained. He sent her flowers and cigarettes, and he found her poised and restful, and sometimes, when she was off guard, with the lines of old suffering in her face.

She sat still. She didn't fidget, as Nina did. She listened, too. She was not as beautiful as she appeared on the stage, but she was attractive, and he stilled his conscience with the knowledge that she placed no undue emphasis on his visits. In her world men came and went, brought or sent small tribute, and she was pleased and grateful. No more. The next week, or the week after, and other men in other places would be doing the same things.

But he wondered about her, sometimes. Did she ever think of Judson Clark, and the wreck he had made of her life? What of resentment and sorrow lay behind her quiet face, or the voice with its careful intonations which was so unlike Nina's?

Now and then he saw her brother. He neither liked nor disliked Gregory, but he suspected him of rather bullying Beverly. On the rare occasions when he saw them together there was a sort of nervous tension in the air, and although Leslie was not subtle he sensed some hidden difference between them. A small incident one day almost brought this concealed dissension to a head. He said to Gregory:

"By the way, I saw you in Haverly yesterday afternoon."

"Must have seen somebody else. Haverly? Where's Haverly?"

Leslie Ward had been rather annoyed. There had been no mistake about the recognition. But he passed it off with that curious sense of sex loyalty that will actuate a man even toward his enemies.

"Funny," he said. "Chap looked like you. Maybe a little heavier."

Nevertheless he had a conviction that he had said some-

thing better left unsaid, and that Beverly Carlysle's glance
at her brother was almost hostile. He had that instan-
taneous picture of the two of them, the man defiant and
somehow frightened, and the woman's eyes anxious and
yet slightly contemptuous. Then, in a flash, it was gone.

He had meant to go home that evening, would have,
probably, for he was not ignorant of where he was drifting.
But when he went back to the office Nina was on the wire,
with the news that they were to go with a party to a country inn.

"For chicken and waffles, Les," she said. "It will be
oceans of fun. And I've promised the cocktails."

"I'm tired," he replied, sulkily. "And why don't you let
some of the other fellows come over with the drinks? It
seems to me I'm always the goat."

"Oh, if that's the way you feel!" Nina said, and hung up
the receiver.

He did not go home. He went to the theater and stood at
the back, with his sense of guilt deadened by the knowledge that Nina was having what she would call a heavenly
time. After all, it would soon be over. He counted the
days. "The Valley" had only four more before it moved
on.

He had already played his small part in the drama that
involved Dick Livingstone, but he was unaware of it. He
went home that night, to find Nina settled in bed and very
sulky, and he retired himself in no pleasant frame of mind.
But he took a firmer hold of himself that night before he
slept. He didn't want a smash, and yet they might be headed
that way. He wouldn't see Beverly Carlysle again.

He lived up to his resolve the next day, bought his flowers as usual, but this time for Nina and took them with
him. And went home with the orchids which were really an
offering to his own conscience.

But Nina was not at home. The butler reported that she
was dining at the Wheelers', and he thought the man eyed
him with restrained commiseration.

"Did she say I am expected there?" he asked.

"She ordered dinner for you here, sir."

Even for Nina that sounded odd. He took his coat and
went out again to the car; after a moment's hesitation he
went back and got the orchids.

Dick Livingstone's machine was at the curb before the

Wheeler house, and in the living-room he found Walter Wheeler, pacing the floor. Mr. Wheeler glanced at him and looked away.

"Anybody sick?" Leslie asked, his feeling of apprehension growing.

"Nina is having hysterics upstairs," Mr. Wheeler said, and continued his pacing.

"Nina! Hysterics?"

"That's what I said," replied Mr. Wheeler, suddenly savage. "You've made a nice mess of things, haven't you?"

Leslie placed the box of orchids on the table and drew off his gloves. His mind was running over many possibilities.

"You'd better tell me about it, hadn't you?"

"Oh, I will. Don't worry. I've seen this coming for months. I'm not taking her part. God knows I know her, and she has as much idea of making a home as—as"—he looked about—"as that poker has. But that's the worst you can say of her. As to you———"

"Well?"

Mr. Wheeler's anxiety was greater than his anger. He lowered his voice.

"She got a bill to-day for two or three boxes of flowers, sent to some actress." And when Leslie said nothing, "I'm not condoning it, mind you. You'd no business to do it. But," he added fretfully, "why the devil, if you've got to act the fool, don't you have your bills sent to your office?"

"I suppose I don't need to tell you that's all there was to it? Flowers, I mean."

"I'm taking that for granted. But she says she won't go back."

Leslie was aghast and frightened. Not at the threat; she would go back, of course. But she would always hold it against him. She cherished small grudges faithfully. And he knew she would never understand, never see her own contribution to his mild defection, nor comprehend the actual innocence of those afternoons of tea and talk.

There was no sound from upstairs. Mr. Wheeler got his hat and went out, calling to the dog. Jim came in whistling, looked in and said: "Hello, Les," and disappeared. He sat in the growing twilight and cursed himself for a fool. After all, where had he been heading? A man couldn't eat his cake and have it. But he was resentful, too; he stressed rather hard his own innocence, and chose to ignore the less innocent impulse that lay behind it.

After a half hour or so he heard some one descending and Dick Livingstone appeared in the hall. He called to him, and Dick entered the room. Before he sat down he lighted a cigarette and in the flare of the match Leslie got an impression of fatigue and of something new, of trouble. But his own anxieties obsessed him.

"She's told you about it, I suppose?"

"Yes."

"I was a fool, of course. But it was only a matter of a few flowers and some afternoon calls. She's a fine woman, Livingstone, and she is lonely. The women have given her a pretty cold deal since the Clark story. They copy her clothes and her walk, but they don't ask her into their homes."

"Isn't the trouble more fundamental than that, Ward? I was thinking about it upstairs. Nina was pretty frank. She says you've had your good time and want to settle down, and that she is young and now is her only chance. Later on there may be children, you know. She blames herself, too, but she has a fairly clear idea of how it happened."

"Do you think she'll go back home?"

"She promised she would."

They sat smoking in silence. In the dining-room Annie was laying the table for dinner, and a most untragic odor of new garden peas began to steal along the hall. Dick suddenly stirred and threw away his cigarette.

"I was going to talk to you about something else," he said, "but this is hardly the time. I'll get on home." He rose. "She'll be all right. Only I'd advise very tactful handling and—the fullest explanation you can make."

"What is it? I'd be glad to have something to keep my mind occupied. It's eating itself up just now."

"It's a personal matter."

Ward glanced up at him quickly.

"Yes?"

"Have you happened to hear a story that I believe is going round? One that concerns me?"

"Well, I have," Leslie admitted. "I didn't pay much attention. Nobody is taking it very seriously."

"That's not the point," Dick persisted. "I don't mind idle

gossip. I don't give a damn about it. It's the statement itself."

"I should say that you are the only person who knows anything about it."

Dick made a restless, impatient gesture.

"I want to know one thing more," he said. "Nina told you, I suppose. Does—I suppose Elizabeth knows it, too?"

"I rather think she does."

Dick turned abruptly and went out of the room, and a moment later Leslie heard the front door slam.

Elizabeth, standing at the head of the stairs, heard it also, and turned away, with a new droop to her usually valiant shoulders. Her world, too, had gone awry, that safe world of protection and cheer and kindliness. First had come Nina, white-lipped and shaken, and Elizabeth had had to face the fact that there were such things as treachery and the queer hidden things that men did, and that came to light and brought horrible suffering.

And that afternoon she had had to acknowledge that there was something wrong with Dick. No. Between Dick and herself. There was a formality in his speech to her, an aloofness that seemed to ignore utterly their new intimacy. He was there, but he was miles away from her. She tried hard to feel indignant, but she was only hurt.

Peace seemed definitely to have abandoned the Wheeler house. Then late in the evening a measure of it was restored when Nina and Leslie effected a reconciliation. It followed several bad hours when Nina had locked her door against them all, but at ten o'clock she sent for Leslie and faced him with desperate calmness.

To Elizabeth, putting cold cloths on her mother's head as she lay on the bed, there came a growing conviction that the relation between men and women was a complicated and baffling thing, and that love and hate were sometimes close together.

Love, and habit perhaps, triumphed in Nina's case, however, for at eleven o'clock they heard Leslie going down the stairs and later on moving about the kitchen and pantry while whistling softly. The servants had gone, and the air was filled with the odor of burning bread. Some time later Mrs. Wheeler, waiting uneasily in the upper hall, beheld her son-in-law coming up and carrying proudly a tray on which was toast of an incredible blackness, and a pot which smelled feebly of tea.

"The next time you're out of a cook just send for me," he said cheerfully.

Mrs. Wheeler, full and overflowing with indignation and the piece of her mind she had meant to deliver, retired vanquished to her bedroom.

Late that night when Nina had finally forgiven him and had settled down for sleep, Leslie went downstairs for a cigar, to find Elizabeth sitting there alone, a book on her knee, face down, and her eyes wistful and with a question in them.

"Sitting and thinking, or just sitting?" he inquired.

"I was thinking."

"Air-castles, eh? Well, be sure you put the right man into them!" He felt more or less a fool for having said that, for it was extremely likely that Nina's family was feeling some doubt about Nina's choice.

"What I mean is," he added hastily, "don't be a fool and take Wallie Sayre. Take a *man*, while you're about it."

"I would, if I could do the taking."

"That's piffle, Elizabeth." He sat down on the arm of a chair and looked at her. "Look here, what about this story the Rossiter girl and a few others are handing around about Dick Livingstone? You're not worrying about it, are you?"

"I don't believe it's true, and it wouldn't matter to me, anyhow."

"Good for you," he said heartily, and got up. "You'd better go to bed, young lady. It's almost midnight."

But although she rose she made no further move to go.

"What I am worrying about is this, Leslie. He may hear it."

"He has heard it, honey."

He had expected her to look alarmed, but instead she showed relief.

"I'll tell you the truth, Les," she said. "I *was* worrying. I'm terribly fond of him. It just came all at once, and I couldn't help it. And I thought he liked me, too, that way." She stopped and looked up at him to see if he understood, and he nodded gravely. "Then to-day, when he came to see Nina, he avoided me. He—I was waiting in the hall upstairs, and he just said a word or two and went on down."

"Poor devil!" Leslie said. "You see, he's in an unpleasant position, to say the least. But here's a thought to go to sleep on. If you ask me, he's keeping out of your way, not because he cares too little, but because he cares too much."

Long after a repentant and chastened Leslie had gone to sleep, his arm over Nina's unconscious shoulder, Elizabeth stood wide-eyed on the tiny balcony outside her room. From it in daylight she could see the Livingstone house. Now it was invisible, but an upper window was outlined in the light. Very shyly she kissed her finger tips to it.

"Good-night, dear," she whispered.

Chapter Fifteen

LOUIS BASSETT had left for Norada the day after David's sudden illness, but ten days later found him only as far as Chicago, and laid up in his hotel with a sprained knee. It was not until the day Nina went back to the little house in the Ridgely Road, having learned the first lesson of married life, that men must not only be captured but also held, that he was able to resume his journey.

He had chafed wretchedly under the delay. It was true that nothing in the way of a story had broken yet. The *Tribune* had carried a photograph of the cabin where Clark had according to the Donaldson woman spent the winter following the murder, and there were the usual reports that he had been seen recently in spots as diverse as Seattle and New Orleans. But when the following Sunday brought nothing further he surmised that the pack, having lost the scent, had been called off.

He confirmed this before starting West by visiting some of the offices of the leading papers and looking up old friends. The Clark story was dead for the time. They had run a lot of pictures of him, however, and some one might turn him up eventually, but a scent was pretty cold in ten years. The place had changed, too. Oil had been discovered five years ago, and the old settlers had, a good many of them, cashed in and moved away. The town had grown like all oil towns.

Bassett was fairly content. He took the night train out of Chicago and spent the next day crossing Nebraska, fertile, rich and interesting. On the afternoon of the second day he left the train and took a branch line toward the mountains and Norada, and from that time on he became an urbane, interested and generally cigar-smoking interrogation point.

"Railroad been here long?" he asked the conductor.

"Four years."

"Norada must have been pretty isolated before that."

"Thirty miles in a coach or a Ford car."

"I was reading the other day," said Bassett, "about the Judson Clark case. Have a cigar? Got time to sit down?"

"You a newspaper man?"

"Oil well supplies," said Bassett easily. "Well, in this article it seemed some woman or other had made a confession. It sounded fishy to me."

"Well, I'll tell you about that." The conductor sat down and bit off the end of his cigar. "I knew the Donaldsons well, and Maggie Donaldson was an honest woman. But I'll tell you how I explain the thing. Donaldson died, and that left her pretty much alone. The executors of the Clark estate kept her on the ranch, but when the estate was settled three years ago she had to move. That broke her all up. She's always said he wasn't dead. She kept the house just as it was, and my wife says she had his clothes all ready and everything."

"That rather sounds as though the story is true, doesn't it?"

"Not necessarily. It's my idea she got from hoping to moping, so to speak. She went in to town regular for letters for ten years, and the postmaster says she never got any. She was hurt in front of the post office. The talk around here is that she's been off her head for the last year or two."

"But they found the cabin."

"Sure they did," said the conductor equably. "The cabin was no secret. It was an old fire station before they put the new one on Goat Mountain. I spent a month in it myself, once, with a dude who wanted to take pictures of bear. We found a bear, but it charged the camera and I'd be running yet if I hadn't come to civilization."

When he had gone Bassett fell into deep thought. So Maggie Donaldson had gone to the post office for ten years. He tried to visualize those faithful, wearisome journeys, through spring mud and winter snow, always futile and always hopeful. He did not for a moment believe that she had "gone off her head." She had been faithful to the end, as some women were, and in the end, too, as had happened before, her faith had killed her.

And again he wondered at the curious ability of some men to secure loyalty. They might go through life, tearing down ideals and destroying illusions to the last, but always there was some faithful hand to rebuild, some faithful soul to worship.

He was somewhat daunted at the size and bustling activity of Norada. Its streets were paved and well-lighted, there were a park and a public library, and the clerk at the Commercial Hotel asked him if he wished a private bath! But the development was helpful in one way. In the old Norada a newcomer might have been subjected to a friendly but inquisitive interest. In this grown-up and self-centered community a man might come and go unnoticed.

And he had other advantages. The pack, as he cynically thought of them, would have started at the Clark ranch and the cabin. He would get to them, of course, but he meant to start on the outside of the circle and work in.

"Been here long?" he asked the clerk at the desk, after a leisurely meal.

The clerk grinned.

"I came here two years ago. I never saw Jud Clark. To get to the Clark place take the road north out of the town and keep straight about eight miles. The road's good now. You fellows have worn it smooth."

"Must have written that down and learned it off," Bassett said admiringly. "What the devil's the Clark place? And why should I go there? Unless," he added, "they serve a decent meal."

"Sorry." The clerk looked at him sharply, was satisfied, and picked up a pen. "You'll hear the story if you stay around here any time. Anything I can do for you?"

"Yes. Fire the cook," Bassett said, and moved away.

He spent the evening in going over his notes and outlining a campaign, and the next day he stumbled on a bit of luck. His elderly chambermaid had lived in and around the town for years.

"Ever hear of any Livingstones in these parts?" he asked.

"Why, yes. There used to be a Livingstone ranch at Dry River," she said, pausing with her carpet sweeper, and looking at him. "It wasn't much of a place. Although you can't tell these days. I sold sixty acres eight years ago for two thousand dollars, and the folks that bought it are getting a thousand a day out of it."

She sighed. She had touched the hem of fortune's garment and passed on; for some opportunity knocked but faintly, and for others it burst open the door and forced its way in.

"I'd be a millionaire now if I'd held on," she said somberly.

That day Bassett engaged a car by the day, he to drive it himself and return it in good condition, the garage to furnish tires.

"I'd just like to say one thing," the owner said, as he tried the gears. "I don't know where you're going, and it's not exactly my business. Here in the oil country, where they're cutting each other's throats for new leases, we let a man alone. But if you've any idea of taking that car by the back road to the old fire station where Jud Clark's supposed to have spent the winter, I'll just say this: we've had two stuck up there for a week, and the only way I see to get them back is a cyclone."

"I'm going to Dry River," Bassett said shortly.

"*Dry* River's right, if you're looking for oil! Go easy on the brakes, old man. We need 'em in our business."

Dry River was a small settlement away from the railroad. It consisted of two intersecting unpaved streets, a dozen or so houses, a closed and empty saloon and two general stores. He chose one at random and found that the old Livingstone place had been sold ten years ago, on the death of its owner, Henry Livingstone.

"His brother from the East inherited it," said the storekeeper. "He came and sold out, lock, stock and barrel. Not that there was much. A few cattle and horses, and the stuff in the ranch house, which wasn't valuable. There were a lot of books, and the brother gave them for a library, but we haven't any building. The railroad isn't built this far yet, and unless we get oil here it won't be."

"The brother inherited it, eh? Do you know the brother's name?"

"David, I think. He was a doctor back East somewhere."

"Then this Henry Livingstone wasn't married? Or at least had no children?"

"He wasn't married. He was a sort of hermit. He'd been dead two days before any one knew it. My wife went out when they found him and got him ready for the funeral. He was buried before the brother got here." He glanced at

Bassett shrewdly. "The place has been prospected for oil, and there's a dry hole on the next ranch. I tell my wife nature's like the railroad. It quit before it got this far."

Bassett's last scruple had fled. The story was there, ready for the gathering. So ready, indeed, that he was almost suspicious of his luck.

And that conviction, that things were coming too easy, persisted through his interview with the storekeeper's wife, in the small house behind the store. She was a talkative woman, eager to discuss the one drama in a drab life, and she showed no curiosity as to the reason for his question.

"Henry Livingstone!" she said. "Well, I should say so. I went out right away when we got the word he was dead, and there I stayed until it was all over. I guess I know as much about him as any one around here does, for I had to go over his papers to find out who his people were."

The papers, it seemed, had not been very interesting; cancelled checks and receipted bills, and a large bundle of letters, all of them from a brother named David and a sister who signed herself Lucy. There had been a sealed one, too, addressed to David Livingstone, and to be opened after his death. She had had her husband wire to "David" and he had come out, too late for the funeral.

"Do you remember when that was?"

"Let me see. Henry Livingstone died about a month before the murder at the Clark ranch. We date most things around here from that time."

"How long did 'David' stay?" Bassett had tried to keep his tone carefully conversational, but he saw that it was not necessary. She was glad of a chance to talk.

"Well, I'd say about three or four weeks. He hadn't seen his brother for years, and I guess there was no love lost. He sold everything as quick as he could, and went back East." She glanced at the clock. "My husband will be in soon for dinner. I'd be glad to have you stay and take a meal with us."

The reporter thanked her and declined.

"It's an interesting story," he said. "I didn't tell your husband, for I wasn't sure I was on the right trail. But the David and Lucy business eliminates this man. There's a piece of property waiting in the East for a Henry Livingstone who came to this state in the 80's, or for his heirs. You can say positively that this man was not married?"

"No. He didn't like women. Never had one on the place. Two ranch hands that are still at the Wassons', and himself, that was all. The Wassons are the folks who bought the ranch."

No housekeeper then, and no son born out of wedlock, so far as any evidence went. All that glib lying in the doctor's office, all that apparent openness and frankness, gone by the board! The man in the cabin, reported by Maggie Donaldson, had been David Livingstone. Somehow, some way, he had got Judson Clark out of the country and spirited him East. Not that the how mattered just yet. The essential fact was there, that David Livingstone had been in this part of the country at the time Maggie Donaldson had been nursing Judson Clark in the mountains.

Bassett sat back and chewed the end of his cigar thoughtfully. The sheer boldness of the scheme which had saved Judson Clark compelled his admiration, but the failure to cover the trail, the ease with which he had picked it up, made him suspicious.

He rose and threw away his cigar.

"You say this David went East, when he had sold out the place. Do you remember where he lived?"

"Some town in eastern Pennsylvania. I've forgotten the name."

"I've got to be sure I'm wrong, and then go ahead," he said, as he got his hat. "I'll see those men at the ranch, I guess, and then be on my way. How far is it?"

It was about ten miles, along a bad road which kept him too much occupied for any connected thought. But his sense of exultation persisted. He had found Judson Clark.

Chapter Sixteen

DICK'S DECISION to cut himself off from Elizabeth was born of his certainty that he could not see her and keep his head. He was resolutely determined to keep his head, until he knew what he had to offer her. But he was very unhappy. He worked sturdily all day and slept at night out of sheer fatigue, only to rouse in the early morning to a conviction of something wrong before he was fully awake. Then would come the uncertainty and pain of full consciousness, and he would lie with his arms under his head, gazing unblinkingly at the ceiling and preparing to face another day.

There was no prospect of early relief, although David had not again referred to his going away. David was very feeble. The look of him sometimes sent an almost physical pain through Dick's heart. But there were times when he roused to something like his old spirit, shouted for tobacco, frowned over his diet tray, and fought Harrison Miller when he came in to play cribbage in much his old tumultuous manner.

Then, one afternoon late in May, when for four days Dick had not seen Elizabeth, suddenly he found the decision as to their relation taken out of his hands, and by Elizabeth herself.

He opened the door one afternoon to find her sitting alone in the waiting-room, clearly very frightened and almost inarticulate. He could not speak at all at first, and when he did his voice, to his dismay, was distinctly husky.

"Is anything wrong?" he asked, in a tone which was fairly sepulchral.

"That's what I want to know, Dick."

Suddenly he found himself violently angry. Not at her, of course. At everything.

"Wrong?" he said, savagely. "Yes. Everything is wrong!"

Then he *was* angry! She went rather pale.

"What have I done, Dick?"

As suddenly as he had been fierce he was abject and ashamed. Startled, too.

"You?" he said. "What have *you* done? You're the only thing that's right in a wrong world. You——"

He checked himself, put down his bag—he had just come in—and closed the door into the hall. Then he stood at a safe distance from her, and folded his arms in order to be able to keep his head—which shows how strange the English language is.

"Elizabeth," he said gravely. "I've been a self-centered fool. I stayed away because I've been in trouble. I'm still in trouble, for that matter. But it hasn't anything to do with you. Not directly, anyhow."

"Don't you think it's possible that I know what it is?"

"You do know."

He was too absorbed to notice the new maturity in her face, the brooding maternity born of a profound passion. To Elizabeth just then he was not a man, her man, daily deciding matters of life and death, but a worried boy, magnifying a trifle into importance.

"There is always gossip," she said, "and the only thing one can do is to forget it at once. You ought to be too big for that sort of thing."

"But—suppose it is true?"

"What difference would it make?"

He made a quick movement toward her.

"There may be more than that. I don't know, Elizabeth," he said, his eyes on hers. "I have always thought—I can't go to David now."

He was moved to go on. To tell her of his lost youth, of that strange trick by which his mind had shut off those hidden years. But he could not. He had a perfectly human fear of being abnormal in her eyes, precisely but greatly magnified, the same instinct which had made him inspect his new tie in daylight for fear it was too brilliant. But greater than that was his new fear that something neither happy nor right lay behind him under lock and key in his memory.

"I want you to know this, Dick," she said. "That nothing, no gossip or anything, can make any difference to me. And I've been terribly hurt. We've been such friends. You—I've been lying awake at night, worrying."

That went to his heart first, and then to his head. This might be all, all he was ever to have. This hour, and this precious and tender child, so brave in her declaration, so simple and direct; all his world in that imitation mahogany chair.

"You're all I've got," he said. "The one real thing in a world that's going to smash. I think I love you more than God." . . . .

The same mood, of accepting what he had without question and of refusing to look ahead, actuated him for the next few days. He was incredibly happy.

He went about his work with his customary care and thoroughness, for long practice had made it possible for him to go on as though nothing had happened, to listen to querulous complaints and long lists of symptoms, and to write without error those scrawled prescriptions which were, so hopefully, to cure. Not that Dick himself believed greatly in those empirical doses, but he considered that the expectation of relief was half the battle. But that was the mind of him, which went about clothed in flesh, of course, and did its daily and nightly work, and put up a very fair imitation of Doctor Richard Livingstone. But hidden away was a heart that behaved in a highly unprofessional manner, and sang and dreamed, and jumped at the sight of a certain small figure on the street, and generally played hob with systole and diastole, and the vagus and accelerator nerves. Which are all any doctor really knows about the heart, until he falls in love.

He even began to wonder if he had read into the situation something that was not there, and in this his consciousness of David's essential rectitude helped him. David could not do a wrong thing, or an unworthy one. He wished he were more like David.

The new humility extended to his love for Elizabeth. Sometimes, in his room or shaving before the bathroom mirror, he wondered what she could see in him to care about. He shaved twice a day now, and his face was so sore that he had to put cream on it at night, to his secret humiliation. When he was dressed in the morning he found himself once or twice taking a final survey of the ensemble, and at those times he wished very earnestly that he had some outstanding quality of appearance that she might admire.

He refused to think. He was content for a time simply to feel, to be supremely happy, to live each day as it came and not to look ahead. And the old house seemed to brighten with him. Never had Lucy's window boxes been so bright, or Minnie's bread so light; the sun poured into David's sick room and turned the nurse so dazzling white in her uniform that David declared he was suffering from snow-blindness.

And David himself was improving rapidly. With the passage of each day he felt more secure. The reporter from the *Times-Republican*—if he were really on the trail of Dick he would have come to see him, would have told him the story. No. That bridge was safely crossed. And Dick was happy. David, lying in his bed, would listen and smile faintly when Dick came whistling into the house or leaped up the stairs two at a time; when he sang in his shower, or tormented the nurse with high-spirited nonsense. The boy was very happy. He would marry Elizabeth Wheeler, and things would be as they should be; there would be the fullness of life, young voices in the house, toys on the lawn. He himself would pass on, in the fullness of time, but Dick . . . .

On Decoration Day they got him out of bed, making a great ceremony of it, and when he was settled by the window in his big chair with a blanket over his knees, Dick came in with a great box. Unwrapping it he disclosed a mass of paper and a small box, and within that still another.

"What fol-de-rol is all this?" David demanded fiercely, with a childish look of expectation in his eyes. "Give me that box. Some more slippers, probably!"

He worked eagerly, and at last he came to the small core of the mass. It was a cigar!

It was somewhat later, when the peace of good tobacco had relaxed him into a sort of benignant drowsiness, and when Dick had started for his late afternoon calls, that Lucy came into the room.

"Elizabeth Wheeler's downstairs," she said. "I told her you wanted to see her. She's brought some chicken jelly, too."

She gathered up the tissue paper that surrounded him, and gave the room a critical survey. She often felt that the nurse was not as tidy as she might be. Then she went over to him and put a hand on his shoulder.

"I don't want to worry you, David. Not now. But if he's going to marry her—"

"Well, why shouldn't he?" he demanded truculently. "A good woman would be one more anchor to windward."

She found that she could not go on. David was always incomprehensible to her when it came to Dick. Had been incomprehensible from the first. But she could not proceed without telling him that the village knew something, and what that something was; that already she felt a change in the local attitude toward Dick. He was, for one thing, not quite so busy as he had been.

She went out of the room, and sent Elizabeth to David.

In her love for Dick, Elizabeth now included everything that pertained to him, his shabby coats, his rattling car, and his people. She had an inarticulate desire for their endorsement, to be liked by them and wanted by them. Not that there could be any words, because both she and Dick were content just then with love, and were holding it very secret between them.

"Well, well!" said David. "And here we are reversed and I'm the patient and you're the doctor! And good medicine you are, my dear."

He looked her over with approval, and with speculation, too. She was a small and fragile vessel on which to embark all the hopes that, out of his own celibate and unfulfilled life, he had dreamed for Dick. She was even more than that. If Lucy was right, from now on she was a part of that experiment in a human soul which he had begun with only a professional interest, but which had ended by becoming a vital part of his own life.

She was a little shy with him, he saw; rather fluttered and nervous, yet radiantly happy. The combination of these mixed emotions, plus her best sick-room manner, made her slightly prim at first. But soon she was telling him the small news of the village, although David rather suspected her of listening for Dick's car all the while. When she got up to go and held out her hand he kept it, between both of his.

"I haven't been studying symptoms for all these years for nothing, my dear," he said. "And it seems to me somebody is very happy."

"I am, Doctor David."

He patted her hand.

"Mind you," he said, "I don't know anything and I'm not asking any questions. But if the Board of Trade, or the Chief of Police, had come to me and said, 'Who is the best wife for—well, for a young man who is an important part of his community?' I'd have said in reply, 'Gentlemen, there is a Miss Elizabeth Wheeler who—' "

Suddenly she bent down and kissed him.

"Oh, do you think so?" she asked, breathlessly. "I love him so much, Doctor David. And I feel so unworthy."

"So you are," he said. "So's he. So are all of us, when it comes to a great love, child. That is, we are never quite what the other fellow thinks we are. It's when we don't allow for what the scientist folk call a margin of error that we come our croppers. I wonder"—he watched her closely—"if you young people ever allow for a margin of error?"

"I only know this," she said steadily. "I can't imagine ever caring any less. I've never thought about myself very much, but I do know that. You see, I think I've cared for a long time."

When she had gone he sat in his chair staring ahead of him and thinking. Yes. She would stick. She had loyalty, loyalty and patience and a rare humility. It was up to Dick then. And again he faced the possibility of an opening door into the past, of crowding memories, of confusion and despair and even actual danger. And out of that, what?

Habit. That was all he had to depend on. The brain was a thing of habits, like the body; right could be a habit, and so could evil. As a man thought, so he was. For all of his childhood, and for the last ten years, Dick's mental habits had been right; his environment had been love, his teaching responsibility. Even if the door opened, then, there was only the evil thinking of two or three reckless years to combat, and the door might never open. Happiness, Lauler had said, would keep it closed, and Dick was happy. . . . .

When at five o'clock the nurse came in with a thermometer he was asleep in his chair, his mouth slightly open, and snoring valiantly. Hearing Dick in the lower hall, she went to the head of the stairs, her finger to her lips.

Dick nodded and went into the office. The afternoon

mail was lying there, and he began mechanically to open it. His thoughts were elsewhere.

Now that he had taken the step he had so firmly determined not to take, certain things, such as Clare Rossiter's story, David's uneasiness, his own doubts, no longer involved himself alone, nor even Elizabeth and himself. They had become of vital importance to her family.

There was no evading the issue. What had once been only his own misfortune, mischance, whatever it was, had now become of vital importance to an entire group of hitherto disinterested people. He would have to put his situation clearly before them and let them judge. And he would have to clarify that situation for them and for himself.

He had had a weak moment or two. He knew that some men, many men, went to marriage with certain reticences, meaning to wipe the slate clean and begin again. He had a man's understanding of such concealments. But he did not for a moment compare his situation with theirs, even when the temptation to seize his happiness was strongest. No mere misconduct, but something hidden and perhaps terrible lay behind David's strange new attitude. Lay, too, behind the break in his memory which he tried to analyze with professional detachment. The mind in such cases set up its defensive machinery of forgetfulness, not against the trivial but against the unbearable.

For the last day or two he had faced the fact that, not only must he use every endeavor to revive his past, but that such revival threatened with cruelty and finality to separate him from the present.

With an open and unread letter in his hand he stared about the office. This place was his; he had fought for it, worked for it. He had an almost physical sense of unseen hands reaching out to drag him away from it; from David and Lucy, and from Elizabeth. And of himself holding desperately to them all, and to the believed commonplaceness of his surroundings.

He shook himself and began to read the letter.

Dear Doctor: I have tried to see you, but understand you are laid up. Burn this as soon as you've read it. Louis Bassett has started for Norada, and I advise your getting the person we discussed out of town as soon as possible. Bassett is up to mischief. I'm not signing this fully, for obvious reasons. G.

Chapter Seventeen

THE SAYRE house stood on the hill behind the town, a long, rather low white house on Italian lines. In summer, until the family exodus to the Maine Coast, the brilliant canopy which extended out over the terrace indicated, as Harrison Miller put it, that the family was "in residence." Originally designed as a summer home, Mrs. Sayre now used it the year round. There was nothing there, as there was in the town house, to remind her of the bitter days before her widowhood.

She was a short, heavy woman, of fine taste in her house and of no taste whatever in her clothing.

"I never know," said Harrison Miller, "when I look up at the Sayre place, whether I'm seeing Ann Sayre or an awning."

She was not a shrewd woman, nor a clever one, but she was kindly in the main, tolerant and maternal. She liked young people, gave gay little parties to which she wore her outlandish clothes of all colors and all cuts, lavished gifts on the girls she liked, and was anxious to see Wallie married to a good steady girl and settled down. Between her son and herself was a quiet but undemonstrative affection. She viewed him through eyes that had lost their illusion about all men years ago, and she had no delusions about him. She had no idea that she knew all that he did with his time, and no desire to penetrate the veil of his private life.

"He spends a great deal of money," she said one day to her lawyer. "I suppose in the usual ways. But he is not quite like his father. He has real affections, which his father hadn't. If he marries the right girl she can make him almost anything."

She had her first inkling that he was interested in Elizabeth Wheeler one day when the head gardener reported that Mr. Wallace had ordered certain roses cut and sent to the Wheeler house. She was angry at first, for the roses were being saved for a dinner party. Then she considered.

"Very well, Phelps," she said. "Do it. And I'll select a plant also, to go to Mrs. Wheeler."

After all, why not the Wheeler girl? She had been carefully reared, if the Wheeler house was rather awful in spots, and she was a gentle little thing; very attractive, too, especially in church. And certainly Wallie had been seeing a great deal of her.

She went to the greenhouses, and from there upstairs and into the rooms that she had planned for Wallie and his bride, when the time came. She was more content than she had been for a long time. She was a lonely woman, isolated by her very grandeur from the neighborliness she craved; when she wanted society she had to ask for it, by invitation. Standing inside the door of the boudoir, her thoughts already at work on draperies and furniture, she had a vague dream of new young life stirring in the big house, of no more lonely evenings, of the bustle and activity of a family again.

She wanted Wallie to settle down. She was tired of paying his bills at his clubs and at various hotels, tired and weary of the days he lay in bed all morning while his valet concocted various things to enable him to pull himself together. He had been four years sowing his wild oats, and now at twenty-five she felt he should be through with them.

The south room could be the nursery. . . . .

On Decoration Day, as usual, she did her dutiful best by the community, sent flowers to the cemetery and even stood through a chilly hour there while services were read and taps sounded over the graves of those who had died in three wars. She felt very grateful that Wallie had come back safely, and that if only now he would marry and settle down all would be well.

The service left her emotionally untouched. She was one of those women who saw in war, politics, even religion, only their reaction on herself and her affairs. She had taken the German deluge as a personal affliction. And she stood only stoically enduring while the village soprano sang "The Star Spangled Banner." By the end of the service she had decided that Elizabeth Wheeler was the answer to her problem.

Rather under pressure, Wallie lunched with her at the country club, but she found him evasive and not particularly happy.

"You're twenty-five, you know," she said, toward the end of a discussion. "By thirty you'll be too set in your habits, too hard to please."

"I'm not going to marry for the sake of getting married, mother."

"Of course not. But you have a good bit of money. You'll have much more when I'm gone. And money carries responsibility with it."

He glanced at her, looked away, rapped a fork on the table cloth.

"It takes two to make a marriage, mother."

He closed up after that, but she had learned what she wanted.

At three o'clock that afternoon the Sayre limousine stopped in front of Nina's house, and Mrs. Sayre, in brilliant pink and a purple hat, got out. Leslie, lounging in a window, made the announcement.

"Here's the Queen of Sheba," he said. "I'll go upstairs and have a headache, if you don't mind."

He kissed Nina and departed hastily. He was feeling extremely gentle toward Nina those days and rather smugly virtuous. He considered that his conscience had brought him back and not a very bad fright, which was the fact, and he fairly exuded righteousness.

It was the great lady's first call, and Nina was considerably uplifted. It was for such moments as this one trained servants and put Irish lace on their aprons, and had decorators who stood off with their heads a little awry and devised backgrounds for one's personality.

"What a delightful room!" said Mrs. Sayre. "And *how* do you keep a maid as trim as that?"

"I must have service," Nina replied. "The butler's marching in a parade or something. How nice of you to come and see our little place. It's a band-box, of course."

Mrs. Sayre sat down, a gross disharmony in the room, but a solid and not unkindly woman for all that.

"My dear," she said, "I am not paying a call. Or not only that. I came to talk to you about something. About Wallace and your sister."

Nina was gratified and not a little triumphant.

"I see," she said. "Do you mean that they are fond of one another?"

"Wallace is. Of course, this talk is between ourselves, but —I'm going to be frank, Nina. I want Wallie to marry, and I want him to marry soon. You and I know that the life of an unattached man about town is full of temptations. I want him to settle down. I'm lonely, too, but that's not so important."

Nina hesitated.

"I don't know about Elizabeth. She's fond of Wallie, as who isn't? But lately—"

"Yes?"

"Well, for the last few days I have been wondering. She doesn't talk, you know. But she has been seeing something of Dick Livingstone."

"Doctor Livingstone! She'd be throwing herself away!"

"Yes, but she's like that. I mean, she isn't ambitious. We've always expected her to throw herself away; at least I have."

A half hour later Leslie, upstairs, leaned over the railing to see if there were any indications of departure. The door was open, and Mrs. Sayre evidently about to take her leave. She was saying:

"It's very close to my heart, Nina dear, and I know you will be tactful. I haven't stressed the material advantages, but you might point them out to her."

A few moments later Leslie came downstairs. Nina was sitting alone, thinking, with a not entirely pleasant look of calculation on her face.

"Well?" he said. "What were you two plotting?"

"Plotting? Nothing, of course."

He looked down at her. "Now see here, old girl," he said, "you keep your hands off Elizabeth's affairs. If I know anything she's making a damn good choice, and don't you forget it."

Chapter Eighteen

DICK STOOD with the letter in his hand, staring at it. Who was Bassett? Who was "G"? What had the departure of whoever Bassett might be for Norada to do with David? And who was the person who was to be got out of town?

He did not go upstairs. He took the letter into his private office, closed the door, and sitting down at his desk turned his reading lamp on it, as though that physical act might bring some mental light.

Reread, the cryptic sentences began to take on meaning. An unknown named Bassett, whoever he might be, was going to Norada bent on "mischief," and another unknown who signed himself "G" was warning David of that fact. But the mischief was designed, not against David, but against a third unknown, some one who was to be got out of town.

David had been trying to get him out of town. . . . The warning referred to himself.

His first impulse was to go to David, and months later he was to wonder what would have happened had he done so. How far could Bassett have gone? What would have been his own decision when he learned the truth? . . . . .

For a little while, then, the shuttle was in Dick's own hand. He went up to David's room, and with his hand on the letter in his pocket, carried on behind his casual talk the debate that was so vital. But David had a headache and a slightly faster pulse, and that portion of the pattern was never woven.

The association between anxiety and David's illness had always been apparent in Dick's mind, but now he began to surmise a concrete shock, a person, a telegram, or a telephone call. And after dinner that night he went back to the kitchen.

"Minnie," he inquired, "do you remember the afternoon Doctor David was taken sick?"

"I'll never forget it."

"Did he receive a telegram that day?"

"Not that I know of. He often answers the bell himself."

"Do you know whether he had a visitor, just before you heard him fall?"

"He had a patient, yes. A man."

"Who was it?"

"I don't know. He was a stranger to me."

"Do you remember what he looked like?"

Minnie reflected.

"He was a smallish man, maybe thirty-five or so," she said. "I think he had gaiters over his shoes, or maybe light tops. He was a nice appearing person."

"How soon after that did you hear Doctor David fall?"

"Right away. First the door slammed, and then he dropped."

Poor old David! Dick had not the slightest doubt now that David had received some unfortunate news, and that up there in his bedroom ever since, alone and helpless, he had been struggling with some secret dread he could not share with any one. Not even with Lucy, probably.

Nevertheless, Dick made a try with Lucy that evening.

"Aunt Lucy," he said, "do you know of anything that could have caused David's collapse?"

"What sort of thing?" she asked guardedly.

"A letter, we'll say, or a visitor?"

When he saw that she was only puzzled and thinking back, he knew she could not help him.

"Never mind," he said. "I was feeling about for some cause. That's all."

He was satisfied that Lucy knew no more than he did of David's visitor, and that David had kept his own counsel ever since. But the sense of impending disaster that had come with the letter did not leave him. He went through his evening office hours almost mechanically, with a part of his mind busy on the puzzle. How did it affect the course of action he had marked out? Wasn't it even more necessary than ever now to go to Walter Wheeler and tell him how things stood?

He hated mystery. He liked to walk in the middle of the road in the sunlight. But even stronger than that was a growing feeling that he needed a sane and normal judgment on his situation; a fresh viewpoint and some unprejudiced advice.

He visited David before he left, and he was very gentle with him. In view of this new development he saw David from a different angle, facing and dreading something imminent, and it came to him with a shock that he might have to clear things up to save David. The burden, whatever it was, was breaking him.

He had telephoned, and Mr. Wheeler was waiting for him. Walter Wheeler thought he knew what was coming, and he had well in mind what he was going to say. He had thought it over, pacing the floor alone, with the dog at his heels. He would say:

"I like and respect you, Livingstone. If you're worrying about what these damned gossips say, let's call it a day and forget it. I know a man when I see one, and if it's all right with Elizabeth it's all right with me."

Things, however, did not turn out just that way. Dick came in, grave and clearly preoccupied, and the first thing he said was:

"I have a story to tell you, Mr. Wheeler. After you've heard it, and given me your opinion on it, I'll come to a matter that—well, that I can't talk about now."

"If it's the silly talk that I daresay you've heard—"

"No. I don't give a damn for talk. But there is something else. Something I haven't told Elizabeth, and that I'll have to tell you."

Walter Wheeler drew himself up rather stiffly. Leslie's defection was still in his mind.

"Don't tell me you're tangled up with another woman."

"No. At least I think not. I don't know."

It is doubtful if Walter Wheeler grasped many of the technicalities that followed. Dick talked and he listened, nodding now and then, and endeavoring very hard to get the gist of the matter. It seemed to him curious rather than serious. Certainly the mind was a strange thing. He must read up on it. Now and then he stopped Dick with a question, and Dick would break in on his narrative to reply. Thus, once:

"You've said nothing to Elizabeth at all? About the walling off, as you call it?"

"No. At first I was simply ashamed of it. I didn't want her to get the idea that I wasn't normal."

"I see."

"Now, as I tell you, I begin to think— I've told you that this walling off is an unconscious desire to forget something too painful to remember. It's practically always that. I can't go to her with just that, can I? I've got to know first what it is."

"I'd begun to think there was an understanding between you."

Dick faced him squarely.

"There is. I didn't intend it. In fact, I was trying to keep away from her. I didn't mean to speak to her until I'd cleared things up. But it happened anyhow; I suppose the way those things always happen."

It was Walter Wheeler's own decision, finally, that he go to Norada with Dick as soon as David could be safely left. It was the letter which influenced him. Up to that he had viewed the situation with a certain detachment; now he saw that it threatened the peace of two households.

"It's a warning, all right."

"Yes. Undoubtedly."

"You don't recognize the name Bassett?"

"No. I've tried, of course."

The result of some indecision was finally that Elizabeth should not be told anything until they were ready to tell it all. And in the end a certain resentment that she had become involved in an unhappy situation died in Walter Wheeler before Dick's white face and sunken eyes.

At ten o'clock the house-door opened and closed, and Walter Wheeler got up and went out into the hall.

"Go on upstairs, Margaret," he said to his wife. "I've got a visitor." He did not look at Elizabeth. "You settle down and be comfortable," he added, "and I'll be up before long. Where's Jim?"

"I don't know. He didn't go to Nina's."

"He started with you, didn't he?"

"Yes. But he left us at the corner."

They exchanged glances. Jim had been worrying them lately. Strange how a man could go along for years, his only worries those of business, his track a single one through comfortable fields where he reaped only what he sowed. And then his family grew up, and involved him without warning in new perplexities and new troubles. Nina first, then Jim, and now this strange story which so inevitably involved Elizabeth.

He put his arm around his wife and held her to him.

"Don't worry about Jim, mother," he said. "He's all right fundamentally. He's going through the bad time between being a boy and being a man. He's a good boy."

He watched her moving up the stairs, his eyes tender and solicitous. To him she was just "mother." He had never thought of another woman in all their twenty-four years together.

Elizabeth waited near him, her eyes on his face.

"Is it Dick?" she asked in a low tone.

"Yes."

"You don't mind, daddy, do you?"

"I only want you to be happy," he said rather hoarsely. "You know that, don't you?"

She nodded, and turned up her face to be kissed. He knew that she had no doubt whatever that this interview was to seal her to Dick Livingstone for ever and ever. She fairly radiated happiness and confidence. He left her standing there and going back to the living-room closed the door.

Chapter Nineteen

LOUIS BASSETT, when he started to the old Livingstone ranch, now the Wasson place, was carefully turning over in his mind David's participation in the escape of Judson Clark. Certain phases of it were quite clear, provided one accepted the fact that, following a heavy snowfall, an Easterner and a tenderfoot had gone into the mountains alone, under conditions which had caused the posse after Judson Clark to turn back and give him up for dead.

Had Donaldson sent him there, knowing he was a medical man? If he had, would Maggie Donaldson not have said so? She had said "a man outside that she had at first thought was a member of the searching party." Evidently, then, Donaldson had not prepared her to expect medical assistance.

Take the other angle. Say David Livingstone had not been sent for. Say he knew nothing of the cabin or its occupants until he stumbled on them. He had sold the ranch, distributed his brother's books, and apparently the townspeople at Dry River believed that he had gone back home. Then what had taken him, clearly alone and having certainly given the impression of a departure for the East, into the mountains? To hunt? To hunt what, that he went about it secretly and alone?

Bassett was inclined to the Donaldson theory, finally. John Donaldson would have been wanting a doctor, and not wanting one from Norada. He might have heard of this Eastern medical man at Dry River, have gone to him with his story, even have taken him part of the way. The situation was one that would have a certain appeal. It was possible, anyhow. . . . .

But instead of clarifying the situation Bassett's visit at the Wasson place brought forward new elements which fitted neither of the hypotheses in his mind.

To Wasson himself, whom he met on horseback on the road into the ranch, he gave the same explanation he had given to the store-keeper's wife. Wasson was a tall man in chaps and a Stetson, and he was courteously interested.

"Bill and Jake are still here," he said. "They're probably in for dinner now, and I'll see you get a chance to talk to them. I took them over with the ranch. Property, you say? Well, I hope it's better land than he had here."

He turned his horse and rode beside the car to the house.

"Comes a little late to do Henry Livingstone much good," he said. "He's been lying in the Dry River graveyard for about ten years. Not much mourned either. He was about as close-mouthed and uncompanionable as they make them."

The description Wasson had applied to Henry Livingstone, Bassett himself applied to the two ranch hands later on, during their interview. It could hardly have been called an interview at all, indeed, and after a time Bassett realized that behind their taciturnity was suspicion. They were watching him, undoubtedly; he rather thought, when he looked away, that once or twice they exchanged glances. He was certain, too, that Wasson himself was puzzled.

"Speak up, Jake," he said once, irritably. "This gentleman has come a long way. It's a matter of some property."

"What sort of property?" Jake demanded. Jake was the spokesman of the two.

"That's not important," Bassett observed, easily. "What we want to know is if Henry Livingstone had any family."

"He had a brother."

"No one else?"

"No."

"Then it's up to me to trail the brother," Bassett observed. "Either of you remember where he lived?"

"Somewhere in the East."

Bassett laughed.

"That's a trifle vague," he commented good-humoredly. "Didn't you boys ever mail any letters for him?"

He was certain again that they exchanged glances, but they continued to present an unbroken front of ignorance. Wasson was divided between irritation and amusement.

"What'd I tell you?" he asked. "Like master like man. I've been here ten years, and I've never got a word about the Livingstones out of either of them."

"I'm a patient man." Bassett grinned. "I suppose you'll

admit that one of you drove David Livingstone to the train, and that you had a fair idea then of where he was going?"

He looked directly at Jake, but Jake's face was a solid mask. He made no reply whatever.

From that moment on Bassett was certain that David had not been driven away from the ranch at all. What he did not know, and was in no way to find out, was whether the two ranch hands knew that he had gone into the mountains, or why. He surmised back of their taciturnity a small mystery of their own, and perhaps a fear. Possibly David's going was as much a puzzle to them as to him. Conceivably, during the hours together on the range, or during the winter snows, for ten years they had wrangled and argued over a disappearance as mysterious in its way as Judson Clark's.

He gave up at last, having learned certain unimportant facts: that the recluse had led a lonely life; that he had never tried to make the place more than carry itself; that he was a student, and that he had no other peculiarities.

"Did he ever say anything that would lead you to believe that he had any family, outside of his brother and sister? That is, any direct heir?" Bassett asked.

"He never talked about himself," said Jake. "If that's all, Mr. Wasson, I've got a steer bogged down in the north pasture and I'll be going."

On the Wassons' invitation he remained to lunch, and when the ranch owner excused himself and rode away after the meal he sat for some time on the verandah, with Mrs. Wasson sewing and his own eyes fixed speculatively on the mountain range, close, bleak and mysterious.

"Strange thing," he commented. "Here's a man, a book-lover and student, who comes out here, not to make a living and be a useful member of the community, but apparently to bury himself alive. I wonder why."

"A great many come out here to get away from something, Mr. Bassett."

"Yes, to start again. But this man never started again. He apparently just quit."

Mrs. Wasson put down her sewing and looked at him thoughtfully.

"Did the boys tell you anything about the young man who visited Henry Livingstone now and then?"

"No. They were not very communicative."

"I suppose they wouldn't tell. Yet I don't see, unless——"

She stopped, lost in some field of speculation where he could not follow her. "You know, we haven't much excitement here, and when this boy was first seen around the place— he was here mostly in the summer—we decided that he was a relative. I don't know why we considered him mysterious, unless it was because he was hardly ever seen. I don't even know that that was deliberate. For that matter Mr. Livingstone wasn't much more than a name to us."

"You mean, a son?"

"Nobody knew. He was here only now and then."

Bassett moved in his chair and looked at her.

"How old do you suppose this boy was?" he asked.

"He was here at different times. When Mr. Livingstone died I suppose he was in his twenties. The thing that makes it seem odd to me is that the men didn't mention him to you."

"I didn't ask about him, of course."

She went on with her sewing, apparently intending to drop the matter; but the reporter felt that now and then she was subjecting him to a sharp scrutiny, and that, in some shrewd woman-fashion, she was trying to place him.

"You said it was a matter of some property?"

"Yes."

"But it's rather late, isn't it? Ten years?"

"That's what makes it difficult."

There was another silence, during which she evidently made her decision.

"I have never said this before, except to Mr. Wasson. But I believe he was here when Henry Livingstone died."

Her tone was mysterious, and Bassett stared at her.

"You don't think Livingstone was murdered!"

"No. He died of heart failure. There was an autopsy. But he had a bad cut on his head. Of course, he may have fallen—Bill and Jake were away. They'd driven some cattle out on the range. It was two days before he was found, and it would have been longer if Mr. Wasson hadn't ridden out to talk to him about buying. He found him dead in his bed, but there was blood on the floor in the next room. I washed it up myself."

"Of course," she added, when Bassett maintained a puzzled silence, "I may be all wrong. He might have fallen in the next room and dragged himself to bed. But he was very neatly covered up."

"It's your idea, then, that this boy put him into the bed?"

"I don't know. He wasn't seen about the place. He's never been here since. But the posse found a horse with the Livingstone brand, saddled, dead in Dry River Canyon when it was looking for Judson Clark. Of course, that was a month later. The men here, Bill and Jake, claimed it had wandered off, but I've often wondered."

After a time Bassett got up and took his leave. He was confused and irritated. Here, whether creditably or not, was Dick Livingstone accounted for. There was a story there, probably, but not the story he was after. This unknown had been at the ranch when Henry Livingstone died, had perhaps been indirectly responsible for his death. He had, witness the horse, fled after the thing happened. Later on, then, David Livingstone had taken him into his family. That was all.

Except for that identification of Gregory's, and for the photograph of Judson Clark. . . . For a moment he wondered if the two, Jud Clark and the unknown, could be the same. But Dry River would have known Clark. That couldn't be.

He almost ditched the car on his way back to Norada, so deeply was he engrossed in thought.

Chapter Twenty

ON THE SEVENTH of June David and Lucy went to the seashore, went by the order of various professional gentlemen who had differed violently during the course of David's illness, but who now suddenly agreed with an almost startling unanimity. Which unanimity was the result of careful coaching by Dick.

He saw in David's absence his only possible chance to go back to Norada without worry to the sick man, and he felt, too, that a change, getting away from the surcharged atmosphere of the old house, would be good for both David and Lucy.

For days before they started Lucy went about in a frenzy of nervous energy, writing out menus for Minnie for a month ahead, counting and recounting David's collars and handkerchiefs, cleaning and pressing his neckties. In the harness room in the stable Mike polished boots until his arms ached, and at the last moment with trunks already bulging, came three gift dressing-gowns for David, none of which he would leave behind.

"I declare," Lucy protested to Dick, "I don't know what's come over him. Every present he's had since he was sick he's taking along. You'd think he was going to be shut up on a desert island."

But Dick thought he understood. In David's life his friends had had to take the place of wife and children; he clung to them now, in his age and weakness, and Dick knew that he had a sense of deserting them, of abandoning them after many faithful years.

So David carried with him the calendars and slippers, dressing-gowns and bed-socks which were at once the tangible evidence of their friendliness and Lucy's despair.

Watching him, Dick was certain nothing further had come to threaten his recovery. Dick carefully inspected the mail, but no suspicious letter had arrived, and as the days went on David's peace seemed finally re-established. He made no more references to Johns Hopkins, slept like a child, and railed almost pettishly at his restricted diet.

"When we get away from Dick, Lucy," he would say, "we'll have beef again, and roast pork and sausage."

Lucy would smile absently and shake her head.

"You'll stick to your diet, David," she would say. "David, it's the strangest thing about your winter underwear. I'm sure you had five suits, and now there are only three."

Or it was socks she missed, or night-clothing. And David, inwardly chuckling, would wonder with her, knowing all the while that they had clothed some needy body.

On the night before the departure David went out for his first short walk alone, and brought Elizabeth back with him.

"I found a rose walking up the street, Lucy," he bellowed up the stairs, "and I brought it home for the dinner table."

Lucy came down, flushed from her final effort over the trunks, but gently hospitable.

"It's fish night, Elizabeth," she said. "You know Minnie's a Catholic, so we always have fish on Friday. I hope you eat it." She put her hand on Elizabeth's arm and gently patted it, and thus was Elizabeth taken into the old brick house as one of its own. . . . .

Elizabeth was finding this period of her tacit engagement rather puzzling. Her people puzzled her. Even Dick did, at times. And nobody seemed anxious to make plans for the future, or even to discuss the wedding. She was a little hurt about that, remembering the excitement over Nina's.

But what chiefly bewildered her was the seeming necessity for secrecy. Even Nina had not been told, nor Jim. She did not resent that, although it bewildered her. Her own inclination was to shout it from the house-tops. Her father had simply said: "I've told your mother, honey, and we'd better let it go at that, for a while. There's no hurry. And I don't want to lose you yet."

But there were other things. Dick himself varied. He was always gentle and very tender, but there were times when he seemed to hold himself away from her, would seem aloof and remote, but all the time watching her almost fiercely. But after that, as though he had tried an experiment in separation and failed with it, he would catch her to him savagely and hold her there. She tried, very meekly, to meet his mood; was submissive to his passion and acquiescent to those intervals when he withdrew himself and sat or stood near her, not touching her but watching her intently.

She thought men in love were very queer and quite incomprehensible. Because he varied in other ways, too. He was boyish and gay sometimes, and again silent and almost brooding. She thought at those times that perhaps he was tired, what with David's work and his own, and sometimes she wondered if he were still worrying about that silly story. But once or twice, after he had gone, she went upstairs and looked carefully into her mirror. Perhaps she had not looked her best that day. Girl-like, she set great value on looks in love. She wanted frightfully to be beautiful to him. She wished she could look like Beverly Carlysle, for instance.

Two days before David and Lucy's departure he had brought her her engagement ring, a square-cut diamond set in platinum. He kissed it first and then her finger, and slipped it into place. It became a rite, done as he did it, and she had a sense of something done that could never be undone. When she looked up at him he was very pale.

"Forsaking all others, so long as we both shall live," he said, unsteadily.

"So long as we both shall live," she repeated.

However she had to take it off later, for Mrs. Wheeler, it developed, had very pronounced ideas of engagement rings. They were put on the day the notices were sent to the newspapers, and not before. So Elizabeth wore her ring around her neck on a white ribbon, inside her camisole, until such time as her father would consent to announce that he was about to lose her.

Thus Elizabeth found her engagement full of unexpected turns and twists, and nothing precisely as she had expected. But she accepted things as they came, being of the type around which the dramas of life are enacted, while remaining totally undramatic herself. She lived her quiet days, worried about Jim on occasion, hemmed table napkins for her linen chest, and slept at night with her ring on her finger and a sense of being wrapped in protecting love that was no longer limited to the white Wheeler house, but now extended two blocks away and around the corner to a shabby old brick building in a more or less shabby yard. . . . .

They were very gay in the old brick house that night before the departure, very noisy over the fish and David's broiled lamb chop. Dick demanded a bottle of Lucy's home-made wine, and even David got a little of it. They toasted the seashore, and the departed nurse, and David quoted Robert Burns at some length and in a horrible Scotch accent. Then Dick had a trick by which one read the date on one of three pennies while he was not looking, and he could tell without failing which one it was. It was most mysterious. And after dinner Dick took her into his laboratory, and while she squinted one eye and looked into the finder of his microscope he kissed the white nape of her neck.

When they left the laboratory there were patients in the waiting-room, but he held her in his arms in the office for a moment or two, very quietly, and because the door was thin they made a sort of game of it, and pretended she was a patient.

"How did you sleep last night?" he said, in a highly professional and very distinct voice. Then he kissed her.

"Very badly, doctor," she said, also very clearly, and whispered, "I lay awake and thought about you, dear."

"I'd better give you this sleeping powder." Oh, frightfully professional, but the powder turned out to be another kiss. It was a wonderful game.

When she slipped out into the hall she had to stop and smooth her hair, before she went to Lucy's tidy sitting-room.

Chapter Twenty-one

IT WAS Jim Wheeler's turn to take up the shuttle. A girl met in some casual fashion, his own youth and the urge of it, perhaps the unconscious family indulgence of an only son—and Jim wove his bit and passed on.

There had been mild contention in the Wheeler family during all the spring. Looking out from his quiet windows Walter Wheeler saw the young world going by a-wheel, and going fast. Much that legitimately belonged to it, and much that did not in the laxness of the new code, he laid to the automobile. And doggedly he refused to buy one.

"We can always get a taxicab," was his imperturbable answer to Jim. "I pay pretty good-sized taxi bills without unpleasant discussion. I know you pretty well too, Jim. Better than you know yourself. And if you had a car, you'd try your best to break your neck in it."

Now and then Jim got a car, however. Sometimes he rented one, sometimes he cajoled Nina into lending him hers.

"A fellow looks a fool without one," he would say to her. "Girls expect to be taken out. It's part of the game."

And Nina, always reached by that argument of how things looked, now and then reluctantly acquiesced. But a night or two after David and Lucy had started for the seashore Nina came in like a whirlwind, and routed the family peace immediately.

"Father," she said, "you just must speak to Jim. He's taken our car twice at night without asking for it, and last night he broke a spring. Les is simply crazy."

"Taken your car!" Mrs. Wheeler exclaimed.

"Yes. I hate telling on him, but I spoke to him after the first time, and he did it anyhow."

Mrs. Wheeler glanced at her husband uneasily. She often felt he was too severe with Jim.

"Don't worry," he said grimly. "He'll not do it again."

"If we only had a car of our own——" Mrs. Wheeler protested.

"You know what I think about that, mother. I'm not going to have him joy-riding over the country, breaking his neck and getting into trouble. I've seen him driving Wallace Sayre's car, and he drives like a fool or a madman."

It was an old dispute and a bitter one. Mr. Wheeler got up, whistled for the dog, and went out. His wife turned on Nina.

"I *wish* you wouldn't bring these things to your father, Nina," she said. "He's been very nervous lately, and he isn't always fair to Jim."

"Well, it's time Jim was fair to Leslie," Nina said, with family frankness. "I'll tell you something, mother. Jim has a girl somewhere, in town probably. He takes her driving. I found a glove in the car. And he must be crazy about her, or he'd never do what he's done."

"Do you know who it is?"

"No. Somebody's he's ashamed of, probably, or he wouldn't be so clandestine about it."

"Nina!"

"Well, it looks like it. Jim's a man, mother. He's not a little boy. He'll go through his shady period, like the rest."

That night it was Mrs. Wheeler's turn to lie awake. Again and again she went over Nina's words, and her troubled mind found a basis in fact for them. Jim had been getting money from her, to supplement his small salary; he had been going out a great deal at night, and returning very late; once or twice, in the morning, he had looked ill and his eyes had been bloodshot, as though he had been drinking.

Anxiety gripped her. There were so many temptations for young men, so many who waited to waylay them. A girl. Not a good girl, perhaps.

She raised herself on her elbow and looked at her sleeping husband. Men were like that; they begot children and then forgot them. They never looked ahead or worried. They were taken up with business, and always they forgot that once they too had been young and liable to temptation.

She got up, some time later, and tiptoed to the door of

Jim's room. Inside she could hear his heavy, regular breathing. Her boy. Her only son.

She went back and crawled carefully into the bed.

There was an acrimonious argument between Jim and his father the next morning, and Jim slammed out of the house, leaving chaos behind him. It was then that Elizabeth learned that her father was going away. He said:

"Maybe I'm wrong, mother. I don't know. Perhaps, when I come back, I'll look around for a car. I don't want him driven to doing underhand things."

"Are you going away?" Elizabeth asked, surprised.

It appeared that he was. More than that, that he was going West with Dick. It was all arranged and nobody had told her anything about it.

She was hurt and a trifle offended, and she cried a little about it. Yet, as Dick explained to her later that day, it was simple enough. Her father needed a rest, and besides, it was right that he should know all about Dick's life before he came to Haverly.

"He's going to make me a present of something highly valuable, you know."

"But it looks as though he didn't trust you!"

"He's being very polite about it; but, of course, in his eyes I'm a common thief, stealing—"

She would not let him go on. . . . .

A certain immaturity, the blind confidence of youth in those it loves, explains Elizabeth's docility at that time. But underneath her submission that day was a growing uneasiness, fiercely suppressed. Buried deep, the battle between absolute trust and fear was beginning, a battle which was so rapidly to mature her.

Nina, shrewd and suspicious, sensed something of nervous strain in her when she came in, later that day, to borrow a hat.

"Look here, Elizabeth," she began, "I want to talk to you. Are you going to live in this—this hole all your life?"

"Hole nothing," Elizabeth said, hotly. "Really, Nina, I do think you might be more careful of what you say."

"Oh, it's a dear old hole," Nina said negligently. "But hole it is, nevertheless. Why in the world mother don't *manage* her servants—but no matter about that now. Elizabeth, there's a lot of talk about you and Dick Livingstone, and it makes me furious. When I think that you can have Wallie Sayre by lifting your finger——"

"And that I don't intend to lift my finger," Elizabeth interrupted.

"Then you're a fool. And it is Dick Livingstone!"

"It is, Nina."

Nina's ambitious soul was harrowed.

"That stodgy old house," she said, "and two old people! A general house-work girl, and you cooking on her Thursdays out! I wish you joy of it."

"I wonder," Elizabeth said calmly, "whether it ever occurs to you that I may put love above houses and servants? Or that my life is my own, to live exactly as I please? Because that is what I intend to do."

Nina rose angrily.

"Thanks," she said. "I wish you joy of it." And went out, slamming the door behind her.

Then, with only a day or so remaining before Dick's departure, and Jim's hand already reaching for the shuttle, Elizabeth found herself the object of certain unmistakable advances from Mrs. Sayre herself, and that at a rose luncheon at the house on the hill.

The talk about Dick and Elizabeth had been slow in reaching the house on the hill. When it came, *via* a little group on the terrace after the luncheon, Mrs. Sayre was upset and angry and inclined to blame Wallie. Everything that he wanted had come to him, all his life, and he did not know how to go after things. He had sat by, and let this shabby-genteel doctor, years older than the girl, walk away with her.

Not that she gave up entirely. She knew the town, and its tendency toward over-statement. And so she made a desperate attempt, that afternoon, to tempt Elizabeth. She took her through the greenhouses, and then through the upper floors of the house. She showed her pictures of their boat at Miami, and of the house at Marblehead. Elizabeth was politely interested and completely unresponsive.

"When you think," Mrs. Sayre said at last, "that Wallie will have to assume a great many burdens one of these days, you can understand how anxious I am to have him marry the right sort of girl."

She thought Elizabeth flushed slightly.

"I am sure he will, Mrs. Sayre."

Mrs. Sayre tried a new direction.

"He will have all I have, my dear, and it is a great responsibility. Used properly, money can be an agent of great good. Wallie's wife can be a power, if she so chooses. She can look after the poor. I have a long list of pensioners, but I am too old to add personal service."

"That would be wonderful," Elizabeth said gravely. For a moment she wished Dick were rich. There was so much to be done with money, and how well he would know how to do it. She was thoughtful on the way downstairs, and Mrs. Sayre felt some small satisfaction. Now if Wallie would only do his part—. . . . .

It was that night that Jim brought the tragedy on the Wheeler house that was to lie heavy on it for many a day.

There had been a little dinner, one of those small informal affairs where Mrs. Wheeler, having found in the market the first of the broiling chickens and some fine green peas, bought them first and then sat down to the telephone to invite her friends. Mr. Oglethorpe, the clergyman, and his wife accepted cheerfully; Harrison Miller, resignedly. Then Mrs. Wheeler drew a long, resolute breath and invited Mrs. Sayre. When that lady accepted with alacrity Mrs. Wheeler hastily revised her menu, telephoned the florist for flowers, and spent a long half-hour with Annie over plates and finger bowls.

Jim was not coming home, and Elizabeth was dining with Nina. Mrs. Wheeler bustled about the house contentedly. Everything was going well, after all. Before long there would be a car, and Jim would spend more time at home. Nina and Leslie were happy again. And Elizabeth —not a good match, perhaps, but a marriage for love, if ever there was one.

She sat at the foot of her table that night, rather too watchful of Annie, but supremely content. She had herself scoured the loving cup to the last degree of brightness and it stood, full of flowers, in the center of the cloth.

At Nina's was a smaller but similar group. All over the village at that time in the evening were similar groups, gathered around flowers and candles; neatly served, cheerful and undramatic groups, with the house doors closed and dogs waiting patiently outside in the long spring twilight.

Elizabeth was watching Nina. Just so, she was deciding,

would she some day preside at her own board. Perhaps before so very long, too. A little separation, letters to watch for and answer, and then. . . . .

The telephone rang, and Leslie answered it. He did not come back; instead they heard the house door close, and soon after the rumble of the car as it left the garage. It stopped at the door, and Leslie came in.

"I'm sorry," he said, "but I guess Elizabeth will have to go home. You'd better come along, Nina."

"What is it? Is somebody sick?" Elizabeth gasped.

"Jim's been in an automobile accident. Steady now, Elizabeth! He's hurt, but he's going to be all right."

The Wheeler house, when they got there, was brightly lighted. Annie was crying in the hall, and in the living-room Mrs. Sayre stood alone, a strange figure in a gaudy dress, but with her face strong and calm.

"They've gone to the hospital in my car," she said. "They'll be there now any minute, and Mr. Oglethorpe will telephone at once. You are to wait before starting in."

They all knew what that meant. It might be too late to start in. Nina was crying hysterically, but Elizabeth could not cry. She stood dry-eyed by the telephone, listening to Mrs. Sayre and Leslie, but hardly hearing them. They had got Dick Livingstone and he had gone on in. Mrs. Sayre was afraid it had been one of Wallie's cars. She had begged Wallie to tell Jim to be careful in it. It had too much speed.

The telephone rang and Leslie took the receiver and pushed Elizabeth gently aside. He listened for a moment.

"Very well," he said. Then he hung up and stood still before he turned around:

"It isn't very good news," he said. "I wish I could— Elizabeth!"

Elizabeth had crumpled up in a small heap on the floor.

All through the long night that followed, with the movement of feet through the halls, with her mother's door closing and the ghastly silence that followed it, with the dawn that came through the windows, the dawn that to Jim meant not a new day, but a new life beyond their living touch, all through the night Elizabeth was aware of two figures that came and went. One was Dick, quiet, tender and watchful. And one was of a heavy woman in a gaudy dress, her face old and weary in the morning light, who tended her with gentle hands.

She fell asleep as the light was brightening in the East, with Dick holding her hands and kneeling on the floor beside her bed. . . . .

It was not until the next day that they knew that Jim had not been alone. A girl who was with him had been pinned under the car and had died instantly.

Jim had woven his bit in the pattern and passed on. The girl was negligible; she was, she had been. That was all. But Jim's death added the last element to the impending catastrophe. It sent Dick West alone.

Chapter Twenty-two

FOR SEVERAL days after his visit to the Livingstone ranch Louis Bassett made no move to go to the cabin. He wandered around the town, made promiscuous acquaintances and led up, in careful conversations with such older residents as he could find, to the Clark and Livingstone families. Of the latter he learned nothing; of the former not much that he had not known before.

One day he happened on a short, heavy-set man, the sheriff, who had lost his office on the strength of Jud Clark's escape, and had now recovered it. Bassett had brought some whisky with him, and on the promise of a drink lured Wilkins to his room. Over his glass the sheriff talked.

"All this newspaper stuff lately about Jud Clark being alive is dead wrong," he declared, irritably. "Maggie Donaldson was crazy. You can ask the people here about her. They all know it. Those newspaper fellows descended on us here with a tooth-brush apiece and a suitcase full of liquor, and thought they'd get something. Seemed to think we'd hold out on them unless we got our skins full. But there isn't anything to hold out. Jud Clark's dead. That's all."

"Sure he's dead," Bassett agreed, amiably. "You found his horse, didn't you?"

"Yes. Dead. And when you find a man's horse dead in the mountains in a blizzard, you don't need any more evidence. It was five months before you could see a trail up the Goat that winter."

Bassett nodded, rose and poured out another drink.

"I suppose," he observed casually, "that even if Clark turned up now, it would be hard to convict him, wouldn't it?"

The sheriff considered that, holding up his glass.

"Well, yes and no," he said. "It was circumstantial evidence, mostly. Nobody saw it done. The worst thing against him was his running off."

"How about witnesses?"

"Nobody actually saw it done. John Donaldson came the nearest, and he's dead. Lucas's wife was still alive, the last I heard, and I reckon the valet is floating around somewhere."

"I suppose if he did turn up you'd make a try for it." Bassett stared at the end of his cigar.

"We'd make a try for it, all right," Wilkins said somberly. "There are some folks in this country still giving me the laugh over that case."

The next day Bassett hired a quiet horse, rolled in his rain-coat two days' supply of food, strapped it to the cantle of his saddle, and rode into the mountains. He had not ridden for years, and at the end of the first hour he began to realize that he was in for a bad time. By noon he was so sore that he could hardly get out of the saddle, and so stiff that once out, he could barely get back again. All morning the horse had climbed, twisting back and forth on a narrow canyon trail, grunting occasionally, as is the way of a horse on a steep grade. All morning they had followed a roaring mountain stream, descending in small cataracts from the ice fields far above. And all morning Bassett had been mentally following that trail as it had been ridden ten years ago by a boy maddened with fear and drink, who drove his horse forward through the night and the blizzard, with no objective and no hope.

He found it practically impossible to connect this frenzied fugitive with the quiet man in his office chair at Haverly, the man who was or was not Judson Clark. He lay on a bank at noon and faced the situation squarely, while his horse, hobbled, grazed with grotesque little forward jumps in an upland meadow. Either Dick Livingstone was Clark, or he was the unknown occasional visitor at the Livingstone Ranch. If he were Clark, and if that could be proved, there were two courses open to Bassett. He could denounce him to the authorities and then spring the big story of his career. Or he could let things stand. From a professional standpoint the first course attracted him, as a man he began to hate it. The last few days had shed a new light on Judson Clark. He had been immensely popular; there were men in the town who told about trying to save him from himself. He had been extravagant, but he had also been generous. He had been "a good kid," until liberty and money got hold of him. There had been more than one man in the sheriff's posse who hadn't wanted to find him.

He was tempted to turn back. The mountains surrounded him, somber and majestically still. They made him feel infinitely small and rather impertinent, as though he had come to penetrate the secrets they never yielded. He had almost to fight a conviction that they were hostile.

After an hour or so he determined to go on. Let them throw him over a gorge if they so determined. He got up, grunting, and leading the horse beside a boulder, climbed painfully into the saddle. To relieve his depression he addressed the horse:

"It would be easier on both of us if you were two feet narrower in the beam, old dear," he said.

Nevertheless, he made good time. By six o'clock he knew that he must have made thirty odd miles, and that he must be near the cabin. Also that it was going to be bitterly cold that night, under the snow fields, and that he had brought no wood axe. The deep valley was purple with twilight by seven, and he could scarcely see the rough-drawn trail map he had been following. And the trail grew increasingly bad. For the last mile or two the horse took its own way.

It wandered on, through fords and out of them, under the low-growing branches of scrub pine, brushing his bruised legs against rocks. He had definitely decided that he had missed the cabin when the horse turned off the trail, and he saw it.

It was built of rough logs, the chinks once closed with mud which had fallen away. The door stood open, and his entrance into its darkness was followed by the scurrying of many little feet. Bassett unstrapped his raincoat from the saddle with fingers numb with cold, and flung it to the ground. He uncinched and removed the heavy saddle, hobbled his horse and removed the bridle, and turned him loose with a slap on the flank.

"For the love of Mike, don't go far, old man," he besought him. And was startled by the sound of his own voice.

By the light of his candle lantern the prospects were extremely poor. The fir branches in the double-berthed bunk were dry and useless, the floor was crumbling under his feet, and the roof of the lean-to had fallen in and crushed the rusty stove. In the cabin itself some one had recently placed a large flat stone in a corner for a fireplace, with two slabs to back it, and above it had broken out a corner of the roof as a chimney. Bassett thought he saw the handwork of some enterprising journalist, and smiled grimly.

He set to work with the resource of a man who had learned to take what came, threw the dry bedding onto the slab and set a match to it, brought in portions of the lean-to roof for further supply for the fire, opened a can of tomatoes and set it on the edge of the hearth to heat, and sliced bacon into his diminutive frying-pan.

It was too late for any examination that night. He ate his supper from the rough table, drawing up to it a broken chair, and afterwards brought in more wood for his fire. Then, with a lighted cigar, and with his boots steaming on the hearth, he sat in front of the blaze and fell into deep study.

He was aching in every muscle when he finally stretched out on the bare boards of the lower bunk. While he slept small furry noses appeared in the openings in the broken floor, to be followed by little bodies that moved cautiously out into the open. He roused once and peered over the edge of the bunk. Several field mice were basking in front of the dying embers of the fire, and two were sitting on his boots. He grinned at them and lay back again, but he found himself fully awake and very uncomfortable. He lay there, contemplating his own folly, and demanding of himself almost fiercely what he had expected to get out of all this effort and misery. For ten days or so men had come here. Wilkins had come, for one, and there had been others. And had found nothing, and had gone away. And now he was there, the end of the procession, to look for God knows what.

He pulled the raincoat up around his shoulders, and lay back stiffly. Then—he was not an imaginative man—he began to feel that eyes were staring at him, furtive, hidden eyes, intently watching him.

Without moving he began to rake the cabin with his eyes, wall to wall, corner to corner. He turned, cautiously, and glanced at the door into the lean-to. It gaped, cavernous and empty. But the sense of being watched persisted, and when he looked at the floor the field mice had disappeared.

He began gradually to see more clearly as his eyes grew accustomed to the semi-darkness, and he felt, too, that he could almost locate the direction of the menace. For as a menace he found himself considering it. It was the broken, windowless East wall, opposite the bunk.

After a time the thing became intolerable. He reached for his revolver, and getting quickly out of the bunk, ran to the doorway and threw open the door, to find himself peering into a blackness like a wall, and to hear a hasty crunching of the underbrush that sounded like some animal in full flight.

With the sounds, and his own movement, the terror died. The cold night air on his face, the feel of the pine needles under his stockinged feet, brought him back to sense and normality. Some creature of the wilderness, a deer or a bear, perhaps, had been moving stealthily outside the cabin, and it was sound he had heard, not a gaze he had felt. He was rather cynically amused at himself. He went back into the cabin, closed the door, and stooped to turn his boots over before the fire.

It was while he was stooping that he heard a horse galloping off along the trail.

He did not go to sleep again. Now and then he considered the possibility of its having been his own animal, somehow freed of the rope and frightened by the same thing that had frightened him. But when with the first light he went outside, his horse, securely hobbled, was grazing on the scant pasture not far away.

Before he cooked his breakfast he made a minute examination of the ground beneath the East wall, but the earth was hard, and a broken branch or two might have been caused by his horse. He had no skill in woodcraft, and in the broad day his alarm seemed almost absurd. Some free horse on the range had probably wandered into the vicinity of the cabin, and had made off again on a trot. Nevertheless, he made up his mind not to remain over another night, but to look about after breakfast, and then to start down again.

He worked on his boots, dry and hard after yesterday's wetting, fried his bacon and dropped some crackers into the sizzling fat, and ate quickly. After that he went out to the trail and inspected it. He had an idea that range horses were mostly unshod, and that perhaps the trail would reveal something. But it was unused and overgrown. Not until he had gone some distance did he find anything. Then in a small bare spot he found in the dust the imprints of a horse's shoes, turned down the trail up which he had come.

Even then he was slow to read into the incident anything that related to himself or to his errand. He went over the various contingencies of the trail: a ranger, on his way to town; a forest fire somewhere; a belated hound from the newspaper pack. He was convinced now that human eyes had watched him for some time through the log wall the night before, but he could not connect them with the business in hand.

He set resolutely about his business, which was to turn up, somehow, some way, a proof of the truth of Maggie Donaldson's dying statement. To begin with then he accepted that statement, to find where it would lead him, and it led him, eventually, to the broken-down stove under the fallen roof of the lean-to.

He deliberately set himself to work, at first, to reconstruct the life in the cabin. Jud would have had the lower bunk, David the upper. The skeleton of a cot bed in the lean-to would have been Maggie's. But none of them yielded anything.

Very well. Having accepted that they lived here, it was from here that the escape was made. They would have started the moment the snow was melted enough to let them get out, and they would have taken, not the trail toward the town, but some other and circuitous route toward the railroad. But there had been things to do before they left. They would have cleared the cabin of every trace of occupancy; the tin cans, Clark's clothing, such bedding as they could not carry. The cans must have been a problem; the clothes, of course, could have been burned. But there were things, like buttons, that did not burn easily. Clark's watch, if he wore one, his cuff links. Buried?

It occurred to him that they might have disposed of some of the unburnable articles under the floor, and he lifted a rough board or two. But to pursue the search systematically he would have needed a pickaxe, and reluctantly he gave it up and turned his attention to the lean-to and the buried stove.

The stove lay in a shallow pit, filled with ancient ashes and crumbled bits of wood from the roof. It lay on its side, its sheet-iron sides collapsed, its long chimney disintegrated. He was in a heavy sweat before he had uncovered it and was able to remove it from its bed of ashes and pine needles. This done, he brought his candle-lantern and settled himself cross-legged on the ground.

His first casual inspection of the ashes revealed nothing. He set to work more carefully then, picking them up by handfuls, examining and discarding. Within ten minutes he had in a pile beside him some burned and blackened metal buttons, the eyelets and a piece of leather from a shoe, and the almost unrecognizable nib of a fountain pen.

He sat with them in the palm of his hand. Taken alone, each one was insignificant, proved nothing whatever. Taken all together, they assumed vast proportions, became convincing, became evidence.

Late that night he descended stiffly at the livery stable, and turned his weary horse over to a stableman.

"Looks dead beat," said the stableman, eyeing the animal.

"He's got nothing on me," Bassett responded cheerfully. "Better give him a hot bath and put him to bed. That's what I'm going to do."

He walked back to the hotel, glad to stretch his aching muscles. The lobby was empty, and behind the desk the night clerk was waiting for the midnight train. Bassett was wide awake by that time, and he went back to the desk and lounged against it.

"You look as though you'd struck oil," said the night clerk.

"Oil! I'll tell you what I have struck. I've struck a livery stable saddle two million times in the last two days."

The clerk grinned, and Bassett idly pulled the register toward him.

"J. Smith, Minneapolis," he read. Then he stopped and stared. Richard Livingstone was registered on the next line above.

Chapter Twenty-three

DICK HAD found it hard to leave Elizabeth, for she clung to him in her grief with childish wistfulness. He found, too, that her family depended on him rather than on Leslie Ward for moral support. It was to him that Walter Wheeler looked for assurance that the father had had no indirect responsibility for the son's death; it was to him that Jim's mother, lying gray-faced and listless in her bed or on her couch, brought her anxious questionings. Had Jim suffered? Could they have avoided it? And an insistent demand to know who and what had been the girl who was with him.

In spite of his own feeling that he would have to go to Norada quickly, before David became impatient over his exile, Dick took a few hours to find the answer to that question. But when he found it he could not tell them. The girl had been a dweller in the shady byways of life, had played her small unmoral part and gone on, perhaps to some place where men were kinder and less urgent. Dick did not judge her. He saw her, as her kind had been through all time, storm centers of the social world, passively and unconsciously blighting, at once the hunters and the prey.

He secured her former address from the police, a three-story brick rooming-house in the local tenderloin, and waited rather uncomfortably for the mistress of the place to see him. She came at last, a big woman, vast and shapeless and with an amiable loose smile, and she came in with the light step of the overfleshed, only to pause in the doorway and to stare at him.

"My God!" she said. "I thought you were dead!"

"I'm afraid you're mistaking me for some one else, aren't you?"

She looked at him carefully.

"I'd have sworn——" she muttered, and turning to the

button inside the door she switched on the light. Then she surveyed him again.

"What's your name?"

"Livingstone. Doctor Livingstone. I called——"

"Is that for me, or for the police?"

"Now see here," he said pleasantly. "I don't know who you are mistaking me for, and I'm not hiding from the police. Here's my card, and I have come from the family of a young man named Wheeler, who was killed recently in an automobile accident."

She took the card and read it, and then resumed her intent scrutiny of him.

"Well, you fooled me all right," she said at last. "I thought you were—well, never mind that. What about this Wheeler family? Are they going to settle with the undertaker? Because I tell you flat, I can't and won't. She owed me a month's rent, and her clothes won't bring over seventy-five or a hundred dollars."

As he left he was aware that she stood in the doorway looking after him. He drove home slowly in the car, and on the way he made up a kindly story to tell the family. He could not let them know that Jim had been seeking love in the byways of life. And that night he mailed a check in payment of the undertaker's bill, carefully leaving the stub empty.

On the third day after Jim's funeral he started for Norada. An *interne* from a local hospital, having newly finished his service there, had agreed to take over his work for a time. But Dick was faintly jealous when he installed Doctor Reynolds in his office, and turned him over to a mystified Minnie to look after.

"Is he going to sleep in your bed?" she demanded belligerently.

She was only partially mollified when she found Doctor Reynolds was to have the spare room. She did not like the way things were going, she confided to Mike. Why wasn't she to let on to Mrs. Crosby that Doctor Dick had gone away? Or to the old doctor? Both of them away, and that little upstart in the office ready to steal their patients and hang out his own sign the moment they got back!

Unused to duplicity as he was, Dick found himself floundering along an extremely crooked path. He wrote a half dozen pleasant, non-committal letters to David and Lucy, spending an inordinate time on them, and gave them to Walter Wheeler to mail at stated intervals. But his chief difficulty was with Elizabeth. Perhaps he would have told her; there were times when he had to fight his desire to have her share his anxiety as well as know the truth about him. But she was already carrying the burden of Jim's tragedy, and her father, too, was insistent that she be kept in ignorance.

"Until she can have the whole thing," he said, with the new heaviness which had crept into his voice.

Beside that real trouble Dick's looked dim and nebulous. Other things could be set right; there was always a fighting chance. It was only death that was final.

Elizabeth went to the station to see him off, a small slim thing in a black frock, with eyes that persistently sought his face, and a determined smile. He pulled her arm through his, so he might hold her hand, and when he found that she was wearing her ring he drew her even closer, with a wave of passionate possession.

"You are mine. My little girl."

"I am yours. For ever and ever."

But they assumed a certain lightness after that, each to cheer the other. As when she asserted that she was sure she would always know the moment he stopped thinking about her, and he stopped, with any number of people about, and said:

"That's simply terrible! Suppose, when we are married, my mind turns on such a mundane thing as beefsteak and onions? Will you simply walk out on me?"

He stood on the lowest step of the train until her figure was lost in the darkness, and the porter expostulated. He was, that night, a little drunk with love, and he did not read the note she had thrust into his hand at the last moment until he was safely in his berth, his long figure stretched diagonally to find the length it needed.

"Darling, darling Dick," she had written. "I wonder so often how you can care for me, or what I have done to deserve you. And I cannot write how I feel, just as I cannot say it. But, Dick dear, I have such a terrible fear of losing you, and you are my life now. You will be careful and not run any risks, won't you? And just remember this always. Wherever you are and wherever I am, I am thinking of you and waiting for you."

He read it three times, until he knew it by heart, and he slept with it in the pocket of his pajama coat.

Three days later he reached Norada, and registered at the Commercial Hotel. The town itself conveyed nothing to him. He found it totally unfamiliar, and for its part the town passed him by without a glance. A new field had come in, twenty miles from the old one, and had brought with it a fresh influx of prospectors, riggers, and lease buyers. The hotel was crowded.

That was his first disappointment. He had been nursing the hope that surroundings which he must once have known well would assist him in finding himself. That was the theory, he knew. He stood at the window of his hotel room, with its angular furniture and the Gideon Bible, and for the first time he realized the difficulty of what he had set out to do. Had he been able to take David into his confidence he would have had the names of one or two men to go to, but as things were he had nothing.

The almost morbid shrinking he felt from exposing his condition was increased, rather than diminished, in the new surroundings. He would, of course, go to the ranch at Dry River, and begin his inquiries from there, but not until now had he realized what that would mean; his recognition by people he could not remember, the questions he could not answer.

He knew the letter to David from beginning to end, but he got it out and read it again. Who was this Bassett, and what mischief was he up to? Why should he himself be got out of town quickly and the warning burned? Who was "G"? And why wouldn't the simplest thing be to locate this Bassett himself?

The more he considered that the more obvious it seemed as a solution, provided of course he could locate the man. Whether Bassett were friendly or inimical, he was convinced that he knew or was finding out something concerning himself which David was keeping from him.

He was relieved when he went down to the desk to find that his man was registered there, although the clerk reported him out of town. But the very fact that only a few hours or days separated him from a solution of the mystery heartened him.

He ate his dinner alone, unnoticed, and after dinner, in the writing room, with its mission furniture and its traveling men copying orders, he wrote a letter to Elizabeth. Into it he put some of the things that lay too deep for speech when he was with her, and because he had so much to say and therefore wrote extremely fast, a considerable portion of it was practically illegible. Then, as though he could hurry the trains East, he put a special delivery stamp on it.

With that off his mind, and the need of exercise after the trip insistent, he took his hat and wandered out into the town. The main street was crowded; moving picture theaters were summoning their evening audiences with bright lights and colored posters, and automobiles lined the curb. But here and there an Indian with braids and a Stetson hat, or a cowpuncher from a ranch in boots and spurs reminded him that after all this was the West, the horse and cattle country. It was still twilight, and when he had left the main street behind him he began to have a sense of the familiar. Surely he had stood here before, had seen the court-house on its low hill, the row of frame houses in small gardens just across the street. It seemed infinitely long ago, but very real. He even remembered dimly an open place at the other side of the building where the ranchmen tied their horses. To test himself he walked around. Yes, it was there, but no horses stood there now, heads drooping, bridle reins thrown loosely over the rail. Only a muddy automobile, without lights, and a dog on guard beside it.

He spoke to the dog, and it came and sniffed at him. Then it squatted in front of him, looking up into his face.

"Lonely, old chap, aren't you?" he said. "Well, you've got nothing on me."

He felt a little cheered as he turned back toward the hotel. A few encounters with the things of his youth, and perhaps the cloud would clear away. Already the court-house had stirred some memories. And on turning back down the hill he had another swift vision, photographically distinct but unrelated to anything that had preceded or followed it. It was like a few feet cut from a moving picture film.

He was riding down that street at night on a small horse, and his father was beside him on a tall one. He looked up at his father, and he seemed very large. The largest man in the world. And the most important.

It began and stopped there, and his endeavor to follow it further resulted in its ultimately leaving him. It faded,

became less real, until he wondered if he had not himself
conjured it. But that experience taught him something.
Things out of the past would come or they would not
come, but they could not be forced. One could not will to revive them.

He stood at a window facing north that night, under the
impression it was east, and sent his love and an inarticulate
sort of prayer to Elizabeth, for her safety and happiness, in
the general direction of the Arctic Circle.

Bassett had not returned in the morning, and he found
himself with a day on his hands. He decided to try the experiment of visiting the Livingstone ranch, or at least of view-
ing it from a safe distance, with the hope of a repetition of
last night's experience. Of all his childish memories the ranch
house, next to his father, was most distinct. When he had at
various times tried to analyze what things he recalled he
had found that what they lacked of normal memory was
connection. They stood out, like the one the night before,
each complete in itself, brief, and having no apparent relation to what had gone before or what came after.

But the ranch house had been different. The pictures were
mostly superimposed on it; it was their background. Himself
standing on the mountain looking down at it, and his father
pointing to it; the tutor who was afraid of horses, sitting at a
big table in a great wood-ceiled and wood-paneled room; a
long gallery or porch along one side of the building and
rooms added on to the house so that one had to go along
the gallery to reach them; a gun-room full of guns.

When, much later, Dick was able calmly to review that
day, he found his recollection of it confused by the events
that followed, but one thing stood out as clearly as his later
knowledge of the almost incredible fact that for one entire
day and for the evening of another, he had openly appeared
in Norada and had not been recognized. That fact was his
discovery that the Livingstone ranch house had no place in
his memory whatever.

He had hired a car and a driver, a driver who asserted
that this was the old Livingstone ranch house. And it bore
no resemblance, not the faintest, to the building he remembered. It did not lie where it should have lain. The mountains
were too far behind it. It was not the house. The fields were
not the proper fields. It was wrong, all wrong.

He went no closer than the highway, because it was not

necessary. He ordered the car to turn and go back, and for the first and only time he was filled with bitter resentment against David. David had fooled him. He sat beside the driver, his face glowering and his eyes hot, and let his indignation burn in him like a flame.

Hours afterwards he had, of course, found excuses for David. Accepted them, rather, as a part of the mystery which wrapped him about. But they had no effect on the decision he made during that miserable ride back to Norada, when he determined to see the man Bassett and get the truth out of him if he had to choke it out.

Chapter Twenty-four

BASSETT WAS astounded when he saw Dick's signature on the hotel register. It destroyed, in one line, every theory he held. That Judson Clark should return to Norada after his flight was incredible. Ten years was only ten years after all. It was not a lifetime. There were men in the town who had known Clark well.

Nevertheless for a time he held to his earlier conviction, even fought for it. He went so far as to wonder if Clark had come back for a tardy surrender. Men had done that before this, had carried a burden for years, had reached the breaking point, had broken. But he dismissed that. There had been no evidence of breaking in the young man in the office chair. He found himself thrown back, finally, on the story of the Wasson woman, and wondering if he would have to accept it after all.

The reaction from his certainty in the cabin to uncertainty again made him fretful and sleepless. It was almost morning before he relaxed on his hard hotel bed enough to sleep.

He wakened late, and telephoned down for breakfast. His confusion had not decreased with the night, and while he got painfully out of bed and prepared to shave and dress, his thoughts were busy. There was no doubt in his mind that, in spite of the growth of the town, the newcomer would be under arrest almost as soon as he made his appearance. A resemblance that could deceive Beverly Carlysle's brother could deceive others, and would. That he had escaped so long amazed him.

By the time he had bathed he had developed a sort of philosophic acceptance of the new situation. There would be no exclusive story now, no scoop. The events of the next few hours were for every man to read. He shrugged his shoulders as, partially dressed, he carried his shaving materials into the better light of his bedroom.

With his face partially lathered he heard a knock at the door, and sang out a not uncheerful "Come in." It happened, then, that it was in his mirror that he learned that his visitor was not the waiter, but Livingstone himself. He had an instant of stunned amazement before he turned.

"I beg your pardon," Dick said. "I was afraid you'd get out before I saw you. My name's Livingstone, and I want to talk to you, if you don't mind. If you like I'll come back later."

Bassett perceived two things simultaneously; that owing probably to the lather on his face he had not been recognized, and that the face of the man inside the door was haggard and strained.

"That's all right. Come in and sit down. I'll get this stuff off my face and be with you in a jiffy."

But he was very deliberate in the bathroom. His astonishment grew, rather than decreased. Clearly Livingstone had not known him. How, then, had he known that he was in Norada? And when he recognized him, as he would in a moment, what then? He put on his collar and tied his tie slowly. Gregory might be the key. Gregory might have found out that he had started for Norada and warned him. Then, if that were true, this man was Clark after all. But if he were Clark he wouldn't be there. It was like a kitten after its tail. It whirled in a circle and got nowhere.

The waiter had laid his breakfast and gone when he emerged from the bathroom, and Dick was standing by the window looking out. He turned.

"I'm here, Mr. Bassett, on rather a peculiar——" He stopped and looked at Bassett. "I see. You were in my office about a month ago, weren't you?"

"For a headache, yes." Bassett was very wary and watchful, but there was no particular unfriendliness in his visitor's eyes.

"It never occurred to me that you might be Bassett," Dick said gravely. "Never mind about that. Eat your breakfast. Do you mind if I talk while you do it?"

"Will you have some coffee? I can get a glass from the bathroom. It takes a week to get a waiter here."

"Thanks. Yes."

The feeling of unreality grew in the reporter's mind. It increased still further when they sat opposite each other, the small table with its Bible on the lower shelf between them, while he made a pretense at breakfasting.

"First of all," Dick said, at last, "I was not sure I had found the right man. You are the only Bassett in the place, however, and you're registered from my town. So I took a chance. I suppose that headache was not genuine."

Bassett hesitated.

"No," he said at last.

"What you really wanted to do was to see me, then?"

"In a way, yes."

"I'll ask you one more question. It may clear the air. Does this mean anything to you? I'll tell you now that it doesn't, to me."

From his pocketbook he took the note addressed to David, and passed it over the table. Bassett looked at him quickly and took it.

"Before you read it, I'll explain something. It was not sent to me. It was sent to my—to Doctor David Livingstone. It happened to fall into my hands. I've come a long way to find out what it means."

He paused, and looked the reporter straight in the eyes. "I am laying my cards on the table, Bassett. This 'G,' whoever he is, is clearly warning my uncle against you. I want to know what he is warning him about."

Bassett read the note carefully, and looked up.

"I suppose you know who 'G' is?"

"I do not. Do you?"

"I'll give you another name, and maybe you'll get it. A name that I think will mean something to you. Beverly Carlysle."

"The actress?"

Bassett had an extraordinary feeling of unreality, followed by one of doubt. Either the fellow was a very good actor, or—

"Sorry," Dick said slowly. "I don't seem to get it. I don't know that 'G' is as important as his warning. That note's a warning."

"Yes. It's a warning. And I don't think you need me to tell you what about."

"Concerning my uncle, or myself?"

"Are you trying to put it over on me that you don't know?"

"That's what I'm trying to do," Dick said, with a sort of grave patience.

The reporter liked courage when he saw it, and he was compelled to a sort of reluctant admiration.

"You've got your courage with you," he observed. "How long do you suppose it will be after you set foot on the streets of this town before you're arrested? How do you know I won't send for the police myself?"

"I know damned well you won't," Dick said grimly. "Not before I'm through with you. You've chosen to interest yourself in me. I suppose you don't deny the imputation in that letter. You'll grant that I have a right to know who and what you are, and just what you are interested in."

"Right-o," the reporter said cheerfully, glad to get to grips; and to stop a fencing that was getting nowhere. "I'm connected with the *Times-Republican*, in your own fair city. I was in the theater the night Gregory recognized you. *Verbum sap.*"

"This Gregory is the 'G'?"

"Oh, quit it, Clark," Bassett said, suddenly impatient. "That letter's the last proof I needed. Gregory wrote it after he'd seen David Livingstone. He wouldn't have written it if he and the old man hadn't come to an understanding. I've been to the cabin. My God, man, I've even got the parts of your clothing that wouldn't burn! You can thank Maggie Donaldson for that."

"Donaldson," Dick repeated. "That was it. I couldn't remember her name. The woman in the cabin. Maggie. And Jack. Jack Donaldson."

He got up, and was apparently dizzy, for he caught at the table.

"Look here," Bassett said, "let me give you a drink. You look all in."

But Dick shook his head.

"No, thanks just the same. I'll ask you to be plain with me, Bassett. I am—I have become engaged to a girl, and—well, I want the story. That's all."

And, when Bassett only continued to stare at him:

"I suppose I've begun wrong end first. I forgot about how it must seem to you. I dropped a block out of my life about ten years ago. Can't remember it. I'm not proud of it, but it's the fact. What I'm trying to do now is to fill in the gap. But I've got to, somehow. I owe it to the girl."

When Bassett could apparently find nothing to say he went on:

"You say I may be arrested if I go out on the street. And you rather more than intimate that a woman named Beverly Carlysle is mixed up in it somehow. I take it that I knew her."

"Yes. You knew her," Bassett said slowly. At the intimation in his tone Dick surveyed him for a moment without speaking. His face, pale before, took on a grayish tinge.

"I wasn't—married to her?"

"No. You didn't marry her. See here, Clark, this is straight goods, is it? You're not trying to put something over on me? Because if you are, you needn't. I'd about made up my mind to follow the story through for my own satisfaction, and then quit cold on it. When a man's pulled himself out of the mud as you have it's not my business to pull him down. But I don't want you to pull any bunk."

Dick winced.

"Out of the mud!" he said. "No. I'm telling you the truth, Bassett. I have some fragmentary memories, places and people, but no names, and all of them, I imagine from my childhood. I pick up at a cabin in the mountains, with snow around, and David Livingstone feeding me soup with a tin spoon." He tried to smile and failed. His face twitched. "I could stand it for myself," he said, "but I've tied another life to mine, like a cursed fool, and now you speak of a woman, and of arrest. Arrest! For what?"

"Suppose," Bassett said after a moment, "suppose you let that go just now, and tell me about this—this gap. You're a medical man. You've probably gone into your own case pretty thoroughly. I'm accepting your statement, you see. As a matter of fact it must be true, or you wouldn't be here. But I've got to know what I'm doing before I lay my cards on the table. Make it simple, if you can. I don't know your medical jargon."

Dick did his best. The mind closed down now and then, mainly from a shock. No, there was no injury required. He didn't think he had had an injury. A mental shock would do it, if it were strong enough. And fear. It was generally fear. He had never considered himself braver than the other fellow, but no man liked to think that he had a cowardly mind. Even if things hadn't broken as they had, he'd have come back before he went to the length of marriage, to find out what it was he had been afraid of. He paused then, to give Bassett a chance to tell him, but the reporter only said: "Go on. You put your cards on the table, and then I'll lay mine out."

Dick went on. He didn't blame Bassett. If there was something that was in his line of work, he understood. At the same time he wanted to save David anything unpleasant. (The word "unpleasant" startled Bassett, by its very inadequacy.) He knew now that David had built up for him an identity that probably did not exist, but he wanted Bassett to know that there could never be doubt of David's high purpose and his essential fineness.

"Whatever I was before," he finished simply, "and I'll get that from you now, if I am any sort of a man at all it is his work."

He stood up and braced himself. It had been clear to Bassett for ten minutes that Dick was talking against time, against the period of revelation. He would have it, but he was mentally bracing himself against it.

"I think," he said, "I'll have that whisky now."

Bassett poured him a small drink, and took a turn about the room while he drank it. He was perplexed and apprehensive. Strange as the story was, he was convinced that he had heard the truth. He had, now and then, run across men who came back after a brief disappearance, with a cock and bull story of forgetting who they were, and because nearly always these men vanished at the peak of some crisis they had always been open to suspicion. Perhaps, poor devils, they had been telling the truth after all. So the mind shut down, eh? Closed like a grave over the unbearable!

His own part in the threatening catastrophe began to obsess him. Without the warning from Gregory there would have been no return to Norada, no arrest. It had all been dead and buried, until he himself had revived it. And a girl, too! The girl in the blue dress at the theater, of course.

Dick put down the glass.

"I'm ready, if you are."

"Does the name of Clark recall anything to you?"

"Nothing."

"Judson Clark? Jud Clark?"

Dick passed his hand over his forehead wearily.

"I'm not sure," he said. "It sounds familiar, and then it doesn't. It doesn't *mean* anything to me, if you get that. If it's a key, it doesn't unlock. That's all. Am I Judson Clark?"

Oddly enough, Bassett found himself now seeking for hope of escape in the very situation that had previously irritated him, in the story he had heard at Wasson's. He considered, and said, almost violently:

"Look here, I may have made a mistake. I came out here pretty well convinced I'd found the solution to an old mystery, and for that matter I think I have. But there's a twist in it that isn't clear, and until it is clear I'm not going to saddle you with an identity that may not belong to you. You are one of two men. One of them is Judson Clark, and I'll be honest with you; I'm pretty sure you're Clark. The other I don't know, but I have reason to believe that he spent part of his time with Henry Livingstone at Dry River."

"I went to the Livingstone ranch yesterday. I remember my early home. That wasn't it. Which one of these two men will be arrested if he is recognized?"

"Clark."

"For what?"

"I'm coming to that. I suppose you'll have to know. Another drink? No? All right. About ten years ago, or a little less, a young chap called Judson Clark got into trouble here and headed into the mountains in a blizzard. He was supposed to have frozen to death. But recently a woman named Donaldson made a confession on her deathbed. She said that she had helped to nurse Clark in a mountain cabin, and that with the aid of some one unnamed he had got away."

"Then I'm Clark. I remember her, and the cabin."

There was a short silence following that admission. To Dick, it was filled with the thought of Elizabeth, and of her relation to what he was about to hear. Again he braced himself for what was coming.

"I suppose," he said at last, "that if I ran away I was in pretty serious trouble. What was it?"

"We've got no absolute proof that you are Clark, remember. You don't know, and Maggie Donaldson was considered not quite sane before she died. I've told you there's a chance you are the other man."

"All right. What had Clark done?"

"He had shot a man."

The reporter was instantly alarmed. If Dick had been haggard before, he was ghastly now. He got up slowly and held to the back of his chair.

"Not—murder?" he asked, with stiff lips.

"No," Bassett said quickly. "Not at all. See here, you've had about all you can stand. Remember, we don't even know you are Clark. All I said was——"

"I understand that. It was murder, wasn't it?"

"Well, there had been a quarrel, I understand. The law allows for that, I think."

Dick went slowly to the window, and stood with his back to Bassett. For a long time the room was quiet. In the street below long lines of cars in front of the hotel denoted the luncheon hour. An Indian woman with a child in the shawl on her back stopped in the street, looked up at Dick and extended a beaded belt. With it still extended she continued to stare at his white face.

"The man died, of course?" he asked at last, without turning.

"Yes. I knew him. He wasn't any great loss. It was at the Clark ranch. I don't believe a conviction would be possible, although they would try for one. It was circumstantial evidence."

"And I ran away?"

"Clark ran away," Bassett corrected him. "As I've told you, the authorities here believe he is dead."

After an even longer silence Dick turned.

"I told you there was a girl. I'd like to think out some way to keep the thing from her, before I surrender myself. If I can protect her, and David——"

"I tell you, you don't even know you are Clark."

"All right. If I'm not, they'll know. If I am—I tell you I'm not going through the rest of my life with a thing like that hanging over me. Maggie Donaldson was sane enough. Why, when I look back, I know our leaving the cabin was a flight. I'm not Henry Livingstone's son, because he never had a son. I can tell you what the Clark ranch house looks like." And after a pause: "Can you imagine the reverse of a dream when you've dreamed you are guilty of something, and wake up to find you are innocent? Who was the man?"

Bassett watched him narrowly.

"His name was Lucas. Howard Lucas."

"All right. Now we have that, where does Beverly Carlysle come in?"

"Clark was infatuated with her. The man he shot was the man she had married."

Chapter Twenty-five

SHORTLY after that Dick said he would go to his room. He was still pale, but his eyes looked bright and feverish, and Bassett went with him, uneasily conscious that something was not quite right. Dick spoke only once on the way.

"My head aches like the mischief," he said, and his voice was dull and lifeless.

He did not want Bassett to go with him, but Bassett went, nevertheless. Dick's statement, that he meant to surrender himself, had filled him with uneasiness. He determined, following him along the hall, to keep a close guard on him for the next few hours, but beyond that, just then, he did not try to go. If it were humanly possible he meant to smuggle him out of the town and take him East. But he had an uneasy conviction that Dick was going to be ill. The mind did strange things with the body.

Dick sat down on the edge of the bed.

"My head aches like the mischief," he repeated. "Look in that grip and find me some tablets, will you? I'm dizzy."

He made an effort and stretched out on the bed. "Good Lord," he muttered, "I haven't had such a headache since——"

His voice trailed off. Bassett, bending over the army kit bag in the corner, straightened and looked around. Dick was suddenly asleep and breathing heavily.

For a long time the reporter sat by the side of the bed, watching him and trying to plan some course of action. He was overcome by his own responsibility, and by the prospect of tragedy that threatened. That Livingstone was Clark, and that he would insist on surrendering himself when he wakened, he could no longer doubt. His mind wandered back to that day when he had visited the old house as a patient, and from that along the strange road they had both come since then. He reflected, not exactly in those terms, that life, any man's life, was only one thread in a pattern woven of an infinite number of threads, and that to tangle the one thread was to interfere with all the others. David Livingstone, the girl in the blue dress, the man twitching uneasily on the bed, Wilkins the sheriff, himself, who could tell how many others, all threads.

He swore in a whisper.

The maid tapped at the door. He opened it an inch or so and sent her off. In view of his new determination even the maid had become a danger. She was the same elderly woman who looked after his own bedroom, and she might have known Clark. Just what Providence had kept him from recognition before this he did not know, but it could not go on indefinitely.

After an hour or so Bassett locked the door behind him and went down to lunch. He was not hungry, but he wanted to get out of the room, to think without that quiet figure before him. Over the pretence of food he faced the situation. Lying ready to his hand was the biggest story of his career, but he could not carry it through. It was characteristic of him that, before abandoning it, he should follow through to the end the result of its publication. He did not believe, for instance, that either Dick's voluntary surrender or his own disclosure of the situation necessarily meant a conviction for murder. To convict a man of a crime he did not know he had committed would be difficult. But, with his customary thoroughness he followed that through also. Livingstone acquitted was once again Clark, would be known to the world as Clark. The new place he had so painfully made for himself would be gone. The story would follow him, never to be lived down. And in his particular profession confidence and respect were half the game. All that would be gone.

Thus by gradual stages he got back to David, and he struggled for the motive which lay behind every decisive human act. A man who followed a course by which he had nothing to gain and everything to lose was either a fool or was actuated by some profound unselfishness. To save a life? But with all the resources Clark could have commanded, added to his personal popularity, a first degree sentence would have been unlikely. Not a life, then, but perhaps something greater than a life. A man's soul.

It came to him, then, in a great light of comprehension, the thing David had tried to do; to take this waster and fugitive, the slate of his mind wiped clean by shock and illness, only his childish memories remaining, and on it to lead him to write a new record. To take the body he had found, and the always untouched soul, and from them to make a man.

And with that comprehension came the conviction, too, that David had succeeded. He had indeed made a man.

He ate absently, consulting his railroad schedule and formulating the arguments he meant to use against Dick's determination to give himself up. He foresaw a struggle there, but he himself held one or two strong cards—the ruthless undoing of David's work, the involving of David for conspiring against the law. And Dick's own obligation to the girl at home.

He was more at ease in the practical arrangements. An express went through on the main line at midnight, and there was a local on the branch line at eight. But the local train, the railway station, too, were full of possible dangers. After some thought he decided to get a car, drive down to the main line with Dick, and then send the car back.

He went out at once and made an arrangement for a car, and on returning notified the clerk that he was going to leave, and asked to have his bill made out. After some hesitation he said: "I'll pay three-twenty too, while I'm at it. Friend of mine there, going with me. Yes, up to to-night."

As he turned away he saw the short, heavy figure of Wilkins coming in. He stood back and watched. The sheriff went to the desk, pulled the register toward him and ran over several pages of it. Then he shoved it away, turned and saw him.

"Been away, haven't you?" he asked.

"Yes. I took a little horseback trip into the mountains. My knees are still not on speaking terms."

The Sheriff chuckled. Then he sobered.

"Come and sit down," he said. "I'm going to watch who goes in and out of here for a while."

Bassett followed him unwillingly to two chairs that faced the desk and the lobby. He had the key of Dick's room in his pocket, but he knew that if he wakened he could easily telephone and have his door unlocked. But that was not his only anxiety. He had a sudden conviction that the Sheriff's watch was connected with Dick himself. Wilkins, from a friendly and gregarious fellow-being, had suddenly grown to sinister proportions in his mind.

And, as the minutes went by, with the Sheriff sitting forward and watching the lobby and staircase with intent, unblinking eyes, Bassett's anxiety turned to fear. He found his heart leaping when the room bells rang, and the clerk, with a glance at the annunciator, sent boys hurrying off. His hands shook, and he felt them cold and moist. And all the time Wilkins was holding him with a flow of unimportant chatter.

"Watching for any one in particular?" he managed, after five minutes or so.

"Yes. I'll tell you about it as soon as—Bill! Is Alex outside?"

Bill stopped in front of them, and nodded.

"All right. Now get this—I want everything decent and in order. No excitement. I'll come out behind him, and you and Bill stand by. Outside I'll speak to him, and when we walk off, just fall in behind. But keep close."

Bill wandered off, to take up a stand of extreme nonchalance inside the entrance. When Wilkins turned to him again Bassett had had a moment to adjust himself, and more or less to plan his own campaign.

"Somebody's out of luck," he commented. "And speaking of being out of luck, I've got a sick man on my hands. Friend of mine from home. We've got to catch the midnight, too."

"Too bad," Wilkins commented rather absently. Then, perhaps feeling that he had not shown proper interest, "Tell you what I'll do. I've got some business on hand now, but it'll be cleared up one way or another pretty soon. I'll bring my car around and take him to the station. These hacks are the limit to ride in."

The disaster to his plans thus threatened steadied the reporter, and he managed to keep his face impassive.

"Thanks," he said. "I'll let you know if he's able to travel. Is this—is this business you're on confidential?"

"Well, it is and it isn't. I've talked some to you, and as you're leaving anyhow—it's the Jud Clark case again."

"Sort of hysteria, I suppose. He'll be seen all over the country for the next six months."

"Yes. But I never saw a hysterical Indian. Well, a little

while ago an Indian woman named Lizzie Lazarus blew into my office. She's a smart woman. Her husband was a breed, dairy hand on the Clark ranch for years. Lizzie was the first Indian woman in these parts to go to school, and besides being smart, she's got Indian sight. You know these Indians. When they aren't blind with trachoma they can see further and better than a telescope."

Bassett made an effort.

"What's that got to do with Jud Clark?" he asked.

"Well, she blew in. You know there was a reward out for him, and I guess it still stands. I'll have to look it up, for if Maggie Donaldson wasn't crazy some one will turn him up some day, probably. Well, Lizzie blew in, and she said she'd seen Jud Clark. Saw him standing at a second story window of this hotel. Can you beat that?"

"Not for pure invention. Hardly."

"That's what I said at first. But I don't know. In some ways it would be like him. He wouldn't mind coming back and giving us the laugh, if he thought he could get away with it. He didn't know fear. Only time he ever showed funk was when he beat it after the shooting, and then he was full of hootch, and on the edge of D. T.'s."

"A man doesn't play jokes with the hangman's rope," Bassett commented, dryly. He looked at his watch and rose. "It's a good story, but I wouldn't wear out any trouser-seats sitting here watching for him. If he's living he's taken pretty good care for ten years not to put his head in the noose; and I'd remember this, too. Wherever he is, if he is anywhere, he's probably so changed his appearance that Telescope Lizzie wouldn't know him. Or you either."

"Probably," the Sheriff said, comfortably. "Still I'm not taking any chances. I'm up for reëlection this fall, and that Donaldson woman's story nearly queered me. I've got a fellow at the railroad station, just for luck."

Bassett went up the stairs and along the corridor, deep in dejected thought. The trap of his own making was closing, and his active mind was busy with schemes for getting Dick away before it shut entirely.

It might be better, in one way, to keep Livingstone there in his room until the alarm blew over. On the other hand, Livingstone himself had to be dealt with, and that he would remain quiescent under the circumstances was unlikely. The motor to the main line seemed to be the best thing. True, he would have first to get Livingstone to agree to go. That done, and he did not underestimate its difficulty, there was the question of getting him out of the hotel, now that the alarm had been given.

When he found Dick still sleeping he made a careful survey of the second floor. There was a second staircase, but investigation showed that it led into the kitchens. He decided finally on a fire-escape from a rear hall window, which led into a courtyard littered with the untidy rubbish of an overcrowded and undermanned hotel, and where now two or three saddled horses waited while their riders ate within.

When he had made certain that he was not observed he unlocked and opened the window, and removed the wire screen. There was a red fire-exit lamp in the ceiling nearby, but he could not reach it, nor could he find any wall switch. Nevertheless he knew by that time that through the window lay Dick's only chance of escape. He cleared the grating of a broken box and an empty flower pot, stood the screen outside the wall, and then, still unobserved, made his way back to his own bedroom and packed his belongings.

Dick was still sleeping, stretched on his bed, when he returned to three-twenty. And here Bassett's careful plans began to go awry, for Dick's body was twitching, and his face was pale and covered with a cold sweat. From wondering how they could get away, Bassett began to wonder whether they would get away at all. The sleep was more like a stupor than sleep. He sat down by the bed, closer to sheer fright than he had ever been before, and wretched with the miserable knowledge of his own responsibility.

As the afternoon wore on, it became increasingly evident that somehow or other he must get a doctor. He turned the subject over in his mind, pro and con. If he could get a new man, one who did not remember Jud Clark, it might do. But he hesitated until, at seven, Dick opened his eyes and clearly did not know him. Then he knew that the matter was out of his hands, and that from now on whatever it was that controlled the affairs of men, David's God or his own vague Providence, was in charge.

He got his hat and went out, and down the stairs again. Wilkins had disappeared, but Bill still stood by the entrance, watching the crowd that drifted in and out. In his state of tension he felt that the hotel clerk's eyes were suspicious as he retained the two rooms for another day, and that Bill watched him out with more than casual interest. Even the matter of cancelling the order for the car loomed large and suspicion-breeding before him, but he accomplished it, and then set out to find medical assistance.

There, however, chance favored him. The first doctor's sign led him to a young man, new to the town, and obviously at leisure. Not that he found that out at once. He invented a condition for himself, as he had done once before, got a prescription and paid for it, learned what he wanted, and then mentioned Dick. He was careful to emphasize his name and profession, and his standing "back home."

"I'll admit he's got me worried," he finished. "He saw me registered and came to my room this morning to see me, and got sick there. That is, he said he had a violent headache and was dizzy. I got him to his room and on the bed, and he's been sleeping ever since. He looks pretty sick to me."

He was conscious of Bill's eyes on him as they went through the lobby again, but he realized now that they were unsuspicious. Bassett himself was in a hot sweat. He stopped outside the room and mopped his face.

"Look kind of shot up yourself," the doctor commented. "Watch this sun out here. Because it's dry here you Eastern people don't notice the heat until it plays the deuce with you."

He made a careful examination of the sleeping man, while Bassett watched his face.

"Been a drinking man? Or do you know?"

"No. But I think not. I gave him a small drink this morning, when he seemed to need it."

"Been like this all day?"

"Since noon. Yes."

Once more the medical man stooped. When he straightened it was to deliver Bassett a body blow.

"I don't like his condition, or that twitching. If these were the good old days in Wyoming I'd say he is on the verge of delirium tremens. But that's only snap judgment. He might be on the verge of a good many things. Anyhow, he'd better be moved to the hospital. This is no place for him."

And against this common-sense suggestion Bassett had nothing to offer. If the doctor had been looking he would have seen him make a gesture of despair.

"I suppose so," he said, dully. "Is it near? I'll go my-self and get a room."

"That's my advice. I'll look in later, and if the stupor continues I'll have in a consultant." He picked up his bag and stood looking down at the bed. "Big fine-looking chap, isn't he?" he commented. "Married?"

"No."

"Well, we'll get the ambulance, and later on we'll go over him properly. I'd call a maid to sit with him, if I were you."

In the grip of a situation that was too much for him, Bas-sett rang the ball. It was answered by the elderly maid who took care of his own bedroom.

Months later, puzzling over the situation, Bassett was to wonder, and not to know, whether chance or design brought the Thorwald woman to the door that night. At the time, and for weeks, he laid it to tragic chance, the same chance which had placed in Dick's hand the warning letter that had brought him West. But as months went on, the part played in the tragedy by that faded woman with her tired disspirited voice and her ash colored hair streaked with gray, assumed other proportions, loomed large and mys-terious.

There were times when he wished that some prescience of danger had made him throttle her then and there, so she could not have raised her shrill, alarming voice! But he had no warning. All he saw was a woman in a washed-out blue calico dress and a fresh white apron, raising incurious eyes to his.

"I suppose it's all right if she sits in the hall?" Bassett in-quired, still fighting his losing fight. "She can go in if he stirs."

"Right-o," said the doctor, who had been to France and had brought home some British phrases.

Bassett walked back from the hospital alone. The game was up and he knew it. Sooner or later— In a way he tried to defend himself to himself. He had done his best. Two or three days ago he would have been exultant over the developments. After all, mince things as one would, Clark was a murderer. Other men killed and paid the penalty. And the game was not up entirely, at that. The providence which had watched over him for so long might continue to.

The hospital was new. (It was, ironically enough, the Clark Memorial hospital.) There was still a chance.

He was conscious of something strange as he entered the lobby. The constable was gone, and there was no clerk behind the desk. At the foot of the stairs stood a group of guests and loungers, looking up, while a bell-boy barred the way.

Even then Bassett's first thought was of fire. He elbowed his way to the foot of the stairs, and demanded to be allowed to go up, but he was refused.

"In a few minutes," said the boy. "No need of excitement."

"Is it a fire?"

"I don't know myself. I've got my orders. That's all."

Wilkins came hurrying in. The crowd, silent and respectful before the law, opened to let him through and closed behind him.

Bassett stood at the foot of the stairs, looking up.

Chapter Twenty-six

TO ELIZABETH the first days of Dick's absence were unbelievably dreary. She seemed to live only from one visit of the postman to the next. She felt sometimes that only a part of her was at home in the Wheeler house, slept at night in her white bed, donned its black frocks and took them off, and made those sad daily pilgrimages to the cemetery above the town, where her mother tidied with tender hands the long narrow mound, so fearfully remindful of Jim's tall slim body.

That part of her grieved sorely, and spent itself in small comforting actions and little caressing touches on bowed heads and grief-stooped shoulders. It put away Jim's clothing, and kept immaculate the room where now her mother spent most of her waking hours. It sent her on her knees at night to pray for Jim's happiness in some young-man heaven which would please him. But the other part of her was not there at all. It was off with Dick in some mysterious place of mountains and vast distance called Wyoming.

And because of this division in herself, because she felt that her loyalty to her people had wavered, because she knew that already she had forsaken her father and her mother and would follow her love through the rest of her life, she was touchingly anxious to comfort and to please them.

"She's taking Dick's absence very hard," Mrs. Wheeler said one night, when she had kissed them and gone upstairs to bed. "She worries me sometimes."

Mr. Wheeler sighed. Why was it that a man could not tell his children what he had learned,—that nothing was so great as one expected; that love was worth living for, but not dying for. The impatience of youth for life! It had killed Jim. It was hurting Nina. It would all come, all come, in God's good time. The young did not live to-day, but always

to-morrow. There seemed no time to live to-day, for any
one. First one looked ahead and said, "I will be so happy."
And before one knew it one was looking back and saying:
"I was so happy."

"She'll be all right," he said aloud.

He got up and whistled for the dog.

"I'll take him around the block before I lock up," he
said heavily. He bent over and kissed his wife. She was a
sad figure to him in her black dress. He did not say to her
what he thought sometimes; that Jim had been saved a
great deal. That to live on, and to lose the things one loved,
one by one, was harder than to go quickly, from a joyous
youth.

He had not told her what he knew about Jim's com-
panion that night. She would never have understood. In her
simple and child-like faith she knew that her boy sat that
day among the blessed company of heaven. He himself
believed that Jim had gone forgiven into whatever lay behind the veil we call death, had gone shriven and clean before the Judge who knew the urge of youth and life. He did
not fear for Jim. He only missed him.

He walked around the block that night, a stooped com-
mon-place figure, the dog at his heels. Now and then he
spoke to him, for companionship. At the corner he stopped
and looked along the side street toward the Livingstone
house. And as he looked he sighed. Jim and Nina, and now
Elizabeth. Jim and Nina were beyond his care now. He
could do no more. But what could he do for Elizabeth?
That, too, wasn't that beyond him? He stood still, facing
the tragedy of his helplessness, beset by vague apprehensions. Then he went on doggedly, his hands clasped behind
him, his head sunk on his breast.

He lay awake for a long time that night, wondering
whether he and Dick had been quite fair to Elizabeth. She
should, he thought, have been told. Then, if Dick's apprehensions were justified, she would have some preparation.
As it was— Suppose something turned up out there, something that would break her heart?

He had thought Margaret was sleeping, but after a time
she moved and slipped her hand into his. It comforted him.
That, too, was life. Very soon now they would be alone
together again, as in the early days before the children came.
All the years and the struggle, and then back where they

started. But still, thank God, hand in hand. . . . .

Ever since the night of Jim's death Mrs. Sayre had been a constant visitor to the house. She came in, solid, practical, and with an everyday manner neither forcedly cheerful nor too decorously mournful, which made her very welcome. After the three first days, when she had practically lived at the house, there was no necessity for small pretensions with her. She knew the china closet and the pantry, and the kitchen. She had even penetrated to Mr. Wheeler's shabby old den on the second floor, and had slept a part of the first night there on the leather couch with broken springs which he kept because it fitted his body.

She was a kindly woman, and she had ached with pity. And, because of her usual detachment from the town and its affairs, the feeling that she was being of service gave her a little glow of content. She liked the family, too, and particularly she liked Elizabeth. But after she had seen Dick and Elizabeth together once or twice she felt that no plan she might make for Wallace could possibly succeed. Lying on the old leather couch that first night, between her frequent excursions among the waking family, she had thought that out and abandoned it.

But, during the days that followed the funeral, she was increasingly anxious about Wallace. She knew that rumors of the engagement had reached him, for he was restless and irritable. He did not care to go out, but wandered about the house or until late at night sat smoking alone on the terrace, looking down at the town with sunken, unhappy eyes. Once or twice in the evening he had taken his car and started out, and lying awake in her French bed she would hear him coming in hours later. In the morning his eyes were suffused and his color bad, and she knew that he was drinking in order to get to sleep.

On the third day after Dick's departure for the West she got up when she heard him coming in, and putting on her dressing gown and slippers, knocked at his door.

"Come in," he called ungraciously.

She found him with his coat off, standing half defiantly with a glass of whisky and soda in his hand. She went up to him and took it from him.

"We've had enough of that in the family, Wallie," she said. "And it's a pretty poor resource in time of trouble."

"I'll have that back, if you don't mind."

"Nonsense," she said briskly, and flung it, glass and all, out of the window. She was rather impressive when she turned.

"I've been a fairly indulgent mother," she said. "I've let you alone, because it's a Sayre trait to run away when they feel a pull on the bit. But there's a limit to my patience, and it is reached when my son drinks to forget a girl."

He flushed and glowered at her in somber silence, but she moved about the room calmly, giving it a housekeeper's critical inspection, and apparently unconscious of his anger.

"I don't believe you ever cared for any one in all your life," he said roughly. "If you had, you would know."

She was straightening a picture over the mantel, and she completed her work before she turned.

"I care for you."

"That's different."

"Very well, then. I cared for your father. I cared terribly. And he killed my love."

She padded out of the room, her heavy square body in its blazing kimono a trifle rigid, but her face still and calm. He remained staring at the door when she had closed it, and for some time after. He knew what message for him had lain behind that emotionless speech of hers, not only understanding, but a warning. She had cared terribly, and his father had killed that love. He had drunk and played through his gay young life, and then he had died, and no one had greatly mourned him.

She had left the decanter on its stand, and he made a movement toward it. Then, with a half smile, he picked it up and walked to the window with it. He was still smiling, half boyishly, as he put out his light and got into bed. It had occurred to him that the milkman's flivver, driving in at the break of dawn, would encounter considerable glass.

By morning, after a bad night, he had made a sort of double-headed resolution, that he was through with booze, as he termed it, and that he would find out how he stood with Elizabeth. But for a day or two no opportunity presented itself. When he called there was always present some grave-faced sympathizing visitor, dark clad and low of voice, and over the drawing-room would hang the indescribable hush of a house in mourning. It seemed to touch Elizabeth, too, making her remote and beyond earthly things. He would go in, burning with impatience, hungry for the mere sight of her, fairly overcharged with emotion, only to face that strange new spirituality that made him ashamed of the fleshly urge in him.

Once he found Clare Rossiter there, and was aware of something electric in the air. After a time he identified it. Behind the Rossiter girl's soft voice and sympathetic words, there was a veiled hostility. She was watching Elizabeth, was over-conscious of her. And she was, for some reason, playing up to himself. He thought he saw a faint look of relief on Elizabeth's face when Clare at last rose to go.

"I'm on my way to see the man Dick Livingstone left in his place," Clare said, adjusting her veil at the mirror. "I've got a cold. Isn't it queer, the way the whole Livingstone connection is broken up?"

"Hardly queer. And it's only temporary."

"Possibly. But if you ask me, I don't believe Dick will come back. Mind, I don't defend the town, but it doesn't like to be fooled. And he's fooled it for years. I know a lot of people who'd quit going to him." She turned to Wallie. "He isn't David's nephew, you know. The question is, who is he? Of course I don't say it, but a good many are saying that when a man takes a false identity he has something to hide."

She gave them no chance to reply, but sauntered out with her sex-conscious, half-sensuous walk. Outside the door her smile faded, and her face was hard and bitter. She might forget Dick Livingstone, but never would she forgive herself for her confession to Elizabeth, nor Elizabeth for having heard it.

Wallie turned to Elizabeth when she had gone, slightly bewildered.

"What's got into her?" he inquired. And then, seeing Elizabeth's white face, rather shrewdly: "That was one for him and two for you, was it?"

"I don't know. Probably."

"I wonder if you would look like that if any one attacked me!"

"No one attacks you, Wallie."

"That's not an answer. You wouldn't, would you? It's different, isn't it?"

"Yes. A little."

He straightened, and looked past her, unseeing, at the wall. "I guess I've known it for quite a while," he said at last. "I didn't want to believe it, so I wouldn't. Are you engaged to him?"

"Yes. It's not to be known just yet, Wallie."

"He's a good fellow," he said, after rather a long silence. "Not that that makes it easier," he added with a twisted smile. Then, boyishly and unexpectedly he said, "Oh, my God!"

He sat down, and when the dog came and placed a head on his knee he patted it absently. He wanted to go, but he had a queer feeling that when he went he went for good.

"I've cared for you for years," he said. "I've been a poor lot, but I'd have been a good bit worse, except for you."

And again:

"Only last night I made up my mind that if you'd have me, I'd make something out of myself. I suppose a man's pretty weak when he puts a responsibility like that on a girl."

She yearned over him, rather. She made little tentative overtures of friendship and affection. But he scarcely seemed to hear them, wrapped as he was in the selfish absorption of his disappointment. When she heard the postman outside and went to the door for the mail, she thought he had not noticed her going. But when she returned he was watching her with jealous, almost tragic eyes.

"I suppose you hear from him by every mail."

"There has been nothing to-day."

Something in her voice or her face made him look at her closely.

"Has he written at all?"

"The first day he got there. Not since."

He went away soon, and not after all with the feeling of going for good. In his sceptical young mind, fed by Clare's malice, was growing a comforting doubt of Dick's good faith.

Chapter Twenty-seven

WHEN WILKINS had disappeared around the angle of the staircase Bassett went to a chair and sat down. He felt sick, and his knees were trembling. Something had happened, a search for Clark room by room perhaps, and the discovery had been made.

He was totally unable to think or to plan. With Dick well they could perhaps have made a run for it. The fire-escape stood ready. But as things were—

The murmuring among the crowd at the foot of the stairs ceased, and he looked up. Wilkins was on the staircase, searching the lobby with his eyes. When he saw Bassett he came quickly down and confronted him, his face angry and suspicious.

"You're mixed up in this somehow," he said sharply. "You might as well come over with the story. We'll get him. He can't get out of this town."

With the words, and the knowledge that in some incredible fashion Dick had made his escape, Bassett's mind reacted instantly.

"What's eating you, Wilkins?" he demanded. "Who got away? I couldn't get that tongue-tied bell-hop to tell me. Thought it was a fire."

"Don't stall, Bassett. You've had Jud Clark hidden upstairs in three-twenty all day."

Bassett got up and towered angrily over the Sheriff. The crowd had turned and was watching.

"In three-twenty?" he said. "You're crazy. Jud Clark! Let me tell you something. I don't know what you've got in your head, but three-twenty is a Doctor Livingstone from near my home town. Well known and highly respected, too. What's more, he's a sick man, and if he's got away, as you say, it's because he is delirious. I had a doctor in to see him an hour ago. I've just arranged for a room at the hospital for him. Does that look as though I've been hiding him?"

The positiveness of his identification and his indignation resulted in a change in Wilkins' manner.

"I'll ask you to stay here until I come back." His tone was official, but less suspicious. "We'll have him in a half hour. It's Clark all right. I'm not saying you knew it was Clark, but I want to ask you some questions."

He went out, and Bassett heard him shouting an order in the street. He went to the street door, and realized that a search was going on, both by the police and by unofficial volunteers. Men on horseback clattered by to guard the borders of the town, and in the vicinity of the hotel searchers were investigating yards and alleyways.

Bassett himself was helpless. He stood by, watching the fire of his own igniting, conscious of the curious scrutiny of the few hotel loungers who remained, and expecting momentarily to hear of Dick's capture. It must come eventually, he felt sure. As to how Dick had been identified, or by what means he had escaped, he was in complete ignorance; and an endeavor to learn by establishing the former *entente cordiale* between the room clerk and himself was met by a suspicious glance and what amounted to a snub. He went back to his chair against the wall and sat there, waiting for the end.

It was an hour before the Sheriff returned, and he came in scowling.

"I'll see you now," he said briefly, and led the way back to the hotel office behind the desk. Bassett's last hope died when he saw sitting there, pale but composed, the elderly maid. The Sheriff lost no time.

"Now I'll tell you what we know about your connection with this case, Bassett," he said. "You engaged a car to take you both to the main line to-night. You paid off Clark's room as well as your own this afternoon. When you found he was sick you cancelled your going. That's true, isn't it?"

"It is. I've told you I knew him at home, but not as Clark."

"I'll let that go. You intended to take the midnight on the main line, but you ordered a car instead of using the branch road."

"Livingstone was sick. I thought it would be easier. That's all." His voice sharpened. "You can't drag me into this, Sheriff. In the first place I don't believe it was Clark, or he wouldn't have come here, of all places on the earth. I didn't even know he was here, until he came into my room this morning."

"Why did he come into your room?"

"He had seen that I was registered. He said he felt sick. I took him back and put him to bed. To-night I got a doctor."

The Sheriff felt in his pocket and produced a piece of paper. Bassett's *morale* was almost destroyed when he saw that it was Gregory's letter to David.

"I'll ask you to explain this. It was on Clark's bed."

Bassett took it and read it slowly. He was thinking hard.

"I see," he said. "Well, that explains why he came here. He was too sick to talk when I saw him. You see, this is not addressed to him, but to his uncle, David Livingstone. David Livingstone is a brother of Henry Livingstone, who died some years ago at Dry River. This refers to a personal matter connected with the Livingstone estate."

The Sheriff took the letter and reread it. He was puzzled.

"You're a good talker," he acknowledged grudgingly. He turned to the maid.

"All right, Hattie," he said. "We'll have that story again. But just a minute." He turned to the reporter. "Mrs. Thorwald here hasn't seen Lizzie Lazarus, the squaw. Lizzie has been sitting in my office ever since noon. Now, Hattie."

Hattie moistened her dry lips.

"It was Jud Clark, all right," she said. "I knew him all his life, off and on. But I wish I hadn't screamed. I don't believe he killed Lucas, and I never will. I hope he gets away."

She eyed the Sheriff vindictively, but he only smiled grimly.

"What did I tell you?" he said to Bassett. "Hell with the women—that was Jud Clark. And we'll get him, Hattie. Don't worry. Go on."

She looked at Bassett.

"When you left me, I sat outside the door, as you said. Then I heard him moving, and I went in. The room was not very light, and I didn't know him at first. He sat up in bed and looked at me, and he said, 'Why, hello, Hattie Thorwald.' That's my name. I married a Swede. Then he looked again, and he said, 'Excuse me, I thought you were a Mrs. Thorwald, but I see now you're older.' I recognized him then, and I thought I was going to faint. I knew he'd be arrested the moment it was known he was here. I said, 'Lie down, Mr. Jud. You're not very well.' And I closed the door and locked it. I was scared."

Her voice broke; she fumbled for a handkerchief. The Sheriff glanced at Bassett.

"Now where's your Livingstone story?" he demanded. "All right, Hattie. Let's have it."

"I said, 'For God's sake, Mr. Jud, lie still, until I think what to do. The Sheriff's likely downstairs this very minute.' And then he went queer and wild. He jumped off the bed and stood listening and staring, and shaking all over. 'I've got to get away,' he said, very loud. 'I won't let him take me. I'll kill myself first!' When I put my hand on his arm he threw it off, and he made for the door. I saw then that he was delirious with fever, and I stood in front of the door and begged him not to go out. But he threw me away so hard that I fell, and I screamed."

"And then what?"

"That's all. If I hadn't been almost out of my mind I'd never have told that it was Jud Clark. That'll hang on me to my dying day."

An hour or so later Bassett went back to his room in a state of mental and nervous exhaustion. He knew that from that time on he would be under suspicion and probably under espionage, and he proceeded methodically, his door locked, to go over his papers. His notebook and the cuttings from old files relative to the Clark case he burned in his wash basin and then carefully washed the basin. That done, his attendance on a sick man, and the letter found on the bed was all the positive evidence they had to connect him with the case. He had had some thought of slipping out by the fire-escape and making a search for Dick on his own account, but his lack of familiarity with his surroundings made that practically useless.

At midnight he stretched out on his bed without undressing, and went over the situation carefully. He knew nothing of the various neuroses which affect the human mind, but he had a vague impression that memory when lost did eventually return, and Dick's recognition of the chambermaid pointed to such a return. He wondered what a man would feel under such conditions, what he would think. He could not do it. He abandoned the effort finally, and lay frowning at the ceiling while he considered his own part in the catastrophe. He saw himself, following his training and his instinct, leading the inevitable march toward this night's tragedy, planning, scheming, searching, and now that it had come, lying helpless on his bed while the procession of events went on past him and beyond his control.

When an automobile engine back-fired in the street below he went sick with fear.

He made the resolution then that was to be the guiding motive for his life for the next few months, to fight the thing of his own creating to a finish. But with the resolution newly made he saw the futility of it. He might fight, would fight, but nothing could restore to Dick Livingstone the place he had made for himself in the world. He might be saved from his past, but he could not be given a future.

All at once he was aware that some one was working stealthily at the lock of the door which communicated with a room beyond. He slid cautiously off the bed and went to the light switch, standing with a hand on it, and waited. The wild thought that it might be Livingstone was uppermost in his mind, and when the door creaked open and closed again, that was the word he breathed into the darkness.

"No," said a woman's voice in a whisper. "It's the maid, Hattie. Be careful. There's a guard at the top of the stairs."

He heard her moving to his outer door, and he knew that she stood there, listening, her head against the panel. When she was satisfied she slipped, with the swiftness of familiarity with her surroundings, to the stand beside his bed, and turned on the lamp. In the shaded light he saw that she wore a dark cape, with its hood drawn over her head. In some strange fashion the maid, even the woman, was lost, and she stood, strange, mysterious, and dramatic in the little room.

"If you found Jud Clark, what would you do with him?" she demanded. From beneath the hood her eyes searched his face. "Turn him over to Wilkins and his outfit?"

"I think you know better than that."

"Have you got any plan?"

"Plan? No. They've got every outlet closed, haven't they? Do you know where he is?"

"I know where he isn't, or they'd have him by now. And I know Jud Clark. He'd take to the mountains, same as he did before. He's got a good horse."

"A horse!"

"Listen. I haven't told this, and I don't mean to. They'll learn it in a couple of hours, anyhow. He got out by a back fire-escape—they know that. But they don't know he took Ed Rickett's black mare. They think he's on foot. I've been down there now, and she's gone. Ed's shut up in a room on the top floor, playing poker. They won't break up until about three o'clock and he'll miss his horse then. That's two hours yet."

Bassett tried to see her face in the shadow of the hood. He was puzzled and suspicious at her change of front, more than half afraid of a trap.

"How do I know you are not working with Wilkins?" he demanded. "You could have saved the situation to-night by saying you weren't sure."

"I was upset. I've had time to think since."

He was forced to trust her, eventually, although the sense of some hidden motive, some urge greater than compassion, persisted in him.

"You've got some sort of plan for me, then? I can't follow him haphazard into the mountains at night, and expect to find him."

"Yes. He was delirious when he left. That thing about the Sheriff being after him—he wasn't after him then. Not until I gave the alarm. He's delirious, and he thinks he's back to the night he—you know. Wouldn't he do the same thing again, and make for the mountains and the cabin? He went to the cabin before."

Bassett looked at his watch. It was half past twelve.

"Even if I could get a horse I couldn't get out of the town."

"You might, on foot. They'll be trailing Rickett's horse by dawn. And if you can get out of town I can get you a horse. I can get you out, too, I think. I know every foot of the place."

A feeling of theatrical unreality was Bassett's chief emotion during the trying time that followed. The cloaked and shrouded figure of the woman ahead, the passage through two dark and empty rooms by pass key to an unguarded corridor in the rear, the descent of the fire-escape, where they stood flattened against the wall while a man, possibly one of the posse, rode in, tied his horse and stamped in high heeled boots into the building, and always just ahead the sure movement and silent tread of the woman, kept his nerves taut and increased his feeling of the unreal.

At the foot of the fire-escape the woman slid out of sight noiselessly, but under Bassett's feet a tin can rolled and clattered. Then a horse snorted close to his shoulder, and he was frozen with fright. After that she gave him her hand, and led him through an empty outbuilding and another yard into a street.

At two o'clock that morning Bassett, waiting in a lonely road near what he judged to be the camp of a drilling crew, heard a horse coming toward him and snorting nervously as it came, and drew back into the shadows until he recognized the shrouded silhouette leading him.

"It belongs to my son," she said. "I'll fix it with him tomorrow. But if you're caught you'll have to say you came out and took him, or you'll get us all in trouble."

She gave him careful instructions as to how to find the trail, and urged him to haste.

"If you get him," she advised, "better keep right on over the range."

He paused, with his foot in the stirrup.

"You seem pretty certain he's taken to the mountains."

"It's your only chance. They'll get him anywhere else."

He mounted and prepared to ride off. He would have shaken hands with her, but the horse was still terrified at her shrouded figure and veered and snorted when she approached. "However it turns out," he said, "you've done your best, and I'm grateful."

The horse moved off and left her standing there, her cowl drawn forward and her hands crossed on her breast. She stood for a moment, facing toward the mountains, oddly monkish in outline and posture. Then she turned back toward the town.

Chapter Twenty-eight

DICK HAD picked up life again where he had left it off so long before. Gone was David's house built on the sands of forgetfulness. Gone was David himself, and Lucy. Gone—not even born into his consciousness was Elizabeth. The war, his work, his new place in the world, were all obliterated, drowned in the flood of memories revived by the shock of Bassett's revelations.

Not that the breaking point had revealed itself as such at once. There was confusion first, then stupor and unconsciousness, and out of that, sharply and clearly, came memory. It was not ten years ago, but an hour ago, a minute ago, that he had stood staring at Howard Lucas on the floor of the billiard room, and had seen Beverly run in through the door.

"Bev!" he was saying. "Bev! Don't look like that!"

He moved and found he was in bed. It had been a dream. He drew a long breath, looked about the room, saw the woman and greeted her. But already he knew he had not been dreaming. Things were sharpening in his mind. He shuddered and looked at the floor, but nobody lay there. Only the horror in his mind, and the instinct to get away from it. He was not thinking at all, but rising in him was not only the need for flight, but the sense of pursuit. *They* were after him. *They* would get him. *They* must never get him alive.

Instinct and will took the place of thought, and whatever closed chamber in his brain had opened, it clearly influenced his physical condition. He bore all the stigmata of prolonged and heavy drinking; his nerves were gone; he twitched and shook. When he got down the fire-escape his legs would scarcely hold him.

The discovery of Ed Rickett's horse in the courtyard, saddled and ready, fitted in with the brain pattern of the past.

Like one who enters a room for the first time, to find it already familiar, for a moment he felt that this thing that he was doing he had done before. Only for a moment. Then partial memory ceased, and he climbed into the saddle, rode out and turned toward the mountains and the cabin. By that strange quality of the brain which is called habit, although the habit be of only one emphatic precedent, he followed the route he had taken ten years before. How closely will never be known. Did he stop at this turn to look back, as he had once before? Did he let his horse breathe there? Not the latter, probably, for as, following the blind course that he had followed ten years before, he left the town and went up the canyon trail, he was riding as though all the devils of hell were behind him.

One thing is certain. The reproduction of the conditions of the earlier flight, the familiar associations of the trail, must have helped rather than hindered his fixation in the past. Again he was Judson Clark, who had killed a man, and was flying from himself and from pursuit.

Before long his horse was in acute distress, but he did not notice it. At the top of the long climb the animal stopped, but he kicked him on recklessly. He was as unaware of his own fatigue, or that he was swaying in the saddle, until galloping across a meadow the horse stumbled and threw him.

He lay still for some time; not hurt but apparently lacking the initiative to get up again. He had at that period the alternating lucidity and mental torpor of the half drunken man. But struggling up through layers of blackness at last there came again the instinct for flight, and he got on the horse and set off.

The torpor again overcame him and he slept in the saddle. When the horse stopped he roused and kicked it on. Once he came up through the blackness to the accompaniment of a great roaring, and found that the animal was saddle deep in a ford, and floundering badly among the rocks. He turned its head upstream, and got it out safely.

Toward dawn some of the confusion was gone, but he was firmly fixed in the past. The horse wandered on, head down, occasionally stopping to seize a leaf as it passed, and once to drink deeply at a spring. Dick was still not thinking—there was something that forbade him to think—but he was weak and emotional. He muttered:

"Poor Bev! Poor old Bev!"

A great wave of tenderness and memory swept over him.
Poor Bev! He had made life hell for her, all right. He
had an almost uncontrollable impulse to turn the horse
around, go back and see her once more. He was gone anyhow. They would get him. And he wanted her to know that
he would have died rather than do what he had done.

The flight impulse died; he felt sick and very cold, and
now and then he shook violently. He began to watch the
trail behind him for the pursuit, but without fear. He
seemed to have been wandering for a thousand black nights
through deep gorges and over peaks as high as the stars,
and now he wanted to rest, to stop somewhere and sleep,
to be warm again. Let them come and take him, anywhere
out of this nightmare. . . .

With the dawn still gray he heard a horse behind and
below him on the trail up the cliff face. He stopped and sat
waiting, twisted about in his saddle, his expression ugly
and defiant, and yet touchingly helpless, the look of a boy
in trouble and at bay. The horseman came into sight on the
trail below, riding hard, a middle-aged man in a dark sack
suit and a straw hat, an oddly incongruous figure and
manifestly weary. He rode bent forward, and now and
again he raised his eyes from the trail and searched the
wall above with bloodshot, anxious eyes.

On the turn below Dick, Bassett saw him for the first
time, and spoke to him in a quiet voice.

"Hello, old man," he said. "I began to think I was going
to miss you after all."

His scrutiny of Dick's face had rather reassured him. The
delirium had passed, apparently. Dishevelled although he
was, covered with dust and with sweat from the horse,
Livingstone's eyes were steady enough. As he rode up to
him, however, he was not so certain. He found himself surveyed with a sort of cool malignity that startled him.

"Miss me!" Livingstone sneered bitterly. "With every
damned hill covered by this time with your outfit! I'll tell
you this. If I'd had a gun you'd never have got me alive."

Bassett was puzzled and slightly ruffled.

"*My* outfit! I'll tell you this, son, I've risked my neck
half the night to get you out of this mess."

"God Almighty couldn't get me out of this mess," Dick
said somberly.

It was then that Bassett saw something not quite normal in his face, and he rode closer.

"See here, Livingstone," he said, in a soothing tone, "nobody's going to get you. I'm here to keep them from getting you. We've got a good start, but we'll have to keep moving."

Dick sat obstinately still, his horse turned across the trail, and his eyes still suspicious and unfriendly.

"I don't know you," he said doggedly. "And I've done all the running away I'm going to do. You go back and tell Wilkins I'm here and to come and get me. The sooner the better." The sneer faded, and he turned on Bassett with a depth of tragedy in his eyes that frightened the reporter. "My God," he said, "I killed a man last night! I can't go through life with that on me. I'm done, I tell you."

"Last night!" Some faint comprehension began to dawn in Bassett's mind, a suspicion of the truth. But there was no time to verify it. He turned and carefully inspected the trail to where it came into sight at the opposite rim of the valley. When he was satisfied that the pursuit was still well behind them he spoke again.

"Pull yourself together, Livingstone," he said, rather sharply. "Think a bit. You didn't kill anybody last night. Now listen," he added impressively. "You are Livingstone, Doctor Richard Livingstone. You stick to that, and think about it."

But Dick was not listening, save to some bitter inner voice, for suddenly he turned his horse around on the trail. "Get out of the way," he said, "I'm going back to give myself up."

He would have done it, probably, would have crowded past Bassett on the narrow trail and headed back toward capture, but for his horse. It balked and whirled on the ledge, but it would not pass Bassett. Dick swore and kicked it, his face ugly and determined, but it refused sullenly. He slid out of the saddle then and tried to drag it on, but he was suddenly weak and sick. He staggered. Bassett was off his horse in a moment and caught him. He eased him onto a boulder, and he sat there, his shoulders sagging and his whole body twitching.

"Been drinking my head off," he said at last. "If I had a drink now I'd straighten out." He tried to sit up. "That's what's the matter with me. I'm funking, of course, but that's not all. I'd give my soul for some whisky."

"I can get you a drink, if you'll come on about a mile," Bassett coaxed. "At the cabin you and I talked about yesterday."

"Now you're talking." Dick made an effort and got to his feet, shaking off Bassett's assisting arm. "For God's sake keep your hands off me," he said irritably. "I've got a hangover, that's all."

He got into his saddle without assistance and started off up the trail. Bassett once more searched the valley, but it was empty save for a deer drinking at the stream far below. He turned and followed.

He was fairly hopeless by that time, what with Dick's unexpected resistance and the change in the man himself. He was dealing with something he did not understand, and the hypothesis of delirium did not hold. There was a sort of desperate sanity in Dick's eyes. That statement, now, about drinking his head off—he hadn't looked yesterday like a drinking man. But now he did. He was twitching, his hands shook. On the rock his face had been covered with a cold sweat. What was that the doctor yesterday had said about delirium tremens? Suppose he collapsed? That meant capture.

He did not need to guide Dick to the cabin. He turned off the trail himself, and Bassett, following, saw him dismount and survey the ruin with a puzzled face. But he said nothing. Bassett waiting outside to tie the horses came in to find him sitting on one of the dilapidated chairs, staring around, but all he said was:

"Get me that drink, won't you? I'm going to pieces."

Bassett found his tin cup where he had left it on a shelf and poured out a small amount of whisky from his flask.

"This is all we have," he explained. "We'll have to go slow with it."

It had an almost immediate effect. The twitching grew less, and a faint color came into Dick's face. He stood up and stretched himself. "That's better," he said. "I was all in. I must have been riding that infernal horse for years."

He wandered about while the reporter made a fire and set the coffee pot to boil. Bassett, glancing up once, saw him surveying the ruined lean-to from the doorway, with an expression he could not understand. But he did not say anything, nor did he speak again until Bassett called him to get some food. Even then he was laconic, and he seemed to be listening and waiting.

Once something startled the horses outside, and he sat up and listened.

"They're here!" he said.

"I don't think so," Bassett replied, and went to the doorway. "No," he called back over his shoulder, "you go on and finish. I'll watch."

"Come back and eat," Dick said surlily.

He ate very little, but drank of the coffee. Bassett too ate almost nothing. He was pulling himself together for the struggle that was to come, marshaling his arguments for flight, and trying to fathom the extent of the change in the man across the small table.

Dick put down his tin cup and got up. He was strong again, and the nightmare confusion of the night had passed away. Instead of it there was a desperate lucidity and a courage born of desperation. He remembered it all distinctly; he had killed Howard Lucas the night before. Before long Wilkins or some of his outfit would ride up to the door, and take him back to Norada. He was not afraid of that. They would always think he had run away because he was afraid of capture, but it was not that. He had run away from Bev's face. Only he had not got away from it. It had been with him all night, and it was with him now.

But he would have to go back. He couldn't be caught like a rat in a trap. The Clarks didn't run away. They were fighters. Only the Clarks didn't kill. They fought, but they didn't murder.

He picked up his hat and went to the door.

"Well, you've been mighty kind, old man," he said. "But I've got to go back. I ran last night like a scared kid, but I'm through with that sort of foolishness."

"I'd give a good bit," Bassett said, watching him, "to know what made you run last night. You were safe where you were."

"I don't know what you are talking about," Dick said drearily. "I didn't run from *them*. I ran to get away from something." He turned away irritably. "You wouldn't understand. Say I was drunk. I was, for that matter. I'm not over it yet."

Bassett watched him.

"I see," he said quietly. "It was last night, was it, that this thing happened?"

"You know it, don't you?"

"And, after it happened, do you remember what followed?"

"I've been riding all night. I didn't care what happened. I knew I'd run into a whale of a blizzard, but I——"

He stopped and stared outside, to where the horses grazed in the upland meadow, knee deep in mountain flowers. Bassett, watching him, saw the incredulity in his eyes, and spoke very gently.

"My dear fellow," he said, "you are right. Try to understand what I am saying, and take it easy. You rode into a blizzard, right enough. But that was not last night. *It was ten years ago.*"

Chapter Twenty-nine

HAD BASSETT had some wider knowledge of Dick's condition he might have succeeded better during that bad hour that followed. Certainly, if he had hoped that the mere statement of fact and its proof would bring results, he failed. And the need for haste, the fear of the pursuit behind them, made him nervous and incoherent.

He had first to accept the incredible, himself—that Dick Livingstone no longer existed, that he had died and was buried deep in some chamber of an unconscious mind. He made every effort to revive him, to restore him into the field of consciousness, but without result. And his struggle was increased in difficulty by the fact that he knew so little of Dick's life. David's name meant nothing, apparently, and it was the only name he knew. He described the Livingstone house; he described Elizabeth as he had seen her that night at the theater. Even Minnie. But Dick only shook his head. And until he had aroused some instinct, some desire to live, he could not combat Dick's intention to return and surrender.

"I understand what you are saying," Dick would say. "I'm trying to get it. But it doesn't *mean* anything to me."

He even tried the war.

"War? What war?" Dick asked. And when he heard about it he groaned.

"A war!" he said. "And I've missed it!"

But soon after that he got up, and moved to the door. "I'm going back," he said.

"Why?"

"They're after me, aren't they?"

"You're forgetting again. Why should they be after you now, after ten years?"

"I see. I can't get it, you know. I keep listening for them."

Bassett too was listening, but he kept his fears to himself.

"Why did you do it?" he asked finally.

"I was drunk, and I hated him. He married a girl I was crazy about."

Bassett tried new tactics. He stressed the absurdity of surrendering for a crime committed ten years before and forgotten.

"They won't convict you anyhow," he urged. "It was a quarrel, wasn't it? I mean, you didn't deliberately shoot him?"

"I don't remember. We quarreled. Yes. I don't remember shooting him."

"What do you remember?"

Dick made an effort, although he was white to the lips.

"I saw him on the floor," he said slowly, and staggered a little.

"Then you don't even know you did it."

"I hated him."

But Bassett saw that his determination to surrender himself was weakening. Bassett fought it with every argument he could summon, and at last he brought forward the one he felt might be conclusive.

"You see, you've not only made a man's place in the world, Clark, as I've told you. You've formed associations you can't get away from. You've got to think of the Livingstones, and you told me yesterday a shock would kill the old man. But it's more than that. There's a girl back in your town. I think you were engaged to her."

But if he had hoped to pierce the veil with that statement he failed. Dick's face flushed, and he went to the door of the cabin, much as he had gone to the window the day before. He did not look around when he spoke.

"Then I'm an unconscionable cad," he said. "I've only cared for one woman in my life. And I've shipwrecked her for good."

"You mean——"

"You know who I mean."

Sometime later Bassett got on his horse and rode out to a ledge which commanded a long stretch of trail in the valley below. Far away horsemen were riding along it, one behind the other, small dots that moved on slowly but steadily. He turned and went back to the cabin.

"We'd better be moving," he said, "and it's up to you to say where. You've got two choices. You can go back to Norada and run the chance of arrest. You know what that means. Without much chance of a conviction you will stand trial and bring wretchedness to the people who stood by you before and who care for you now. Or you can go on over the mountains with me and strike the railroad somewhere to the West. You'll have time to think things over, anyhow. They've waited ten years. They can wait longer."

To his relief Dick acquiesced. He had become oddly passive; he seemed indeed not greatly interested. He did not even notice the haste with which Bassett removed the evidences of their meal, or extinguished the dying fire and scattered the ashes. Nor, when they were mounted, the care with which they avoided the trail. He gave, when asked, information as to the direction of the railroad at the foot of the western slope of the range, and at the same instigation found a trail for them some miles beyond their starting point. But mostly he merely followed, in a dead silence.

They made slow progress. Both horses were weary and hungry, and the going was often rough and even dangerous. But for Dick's knowledge of the country they would have been hopelessly lost. Bassett, however, although tortured with muscular soreness, felt his spirits rising as the miles were covered, and there was no sign of the pursuit.

By mid-afternoon they were obliged to rest their horses and let them graze, and the necessity of food for themselves became insistent. Dick stretched out and was immediately asleep, but the reporter could not rest. The magnitude of his undertaking obsessed him. They had covered perhaps twenty miles since leaving the cabin, and the railroad was still sixty miles away. With fresh horses they could have made it by dawn of the next morning, but he did not believe their jaded animals could go much farther. The country grew worse instead of better. A pass ahead, which they must cross, was full of snow.

He was anxious, too, as to Dick's physical condition. The twitching was gone, but he was very pale and he slept like a man exhausted and at his physical limit. But the necessity of crossing the pass before nightfall or of waiting until dawn to do it drove Bassett back from an anxious reconnoitering of the trail at five o'clock, to rouse the sleeping man and start on again.

Near the pass, however, Dick roused himself and took the lead.

"Let me ahead, Bassett," he said peremptorily. "And give your horse his head. He'll take care of you if you give him a chance."

Bassett was glad to fall back. He was exhausted and nervous. The trail frightened him. It clung to the side of a rocky wall, twisting and turning on itself; it ran under milky waterfalls of glacial water, and higher up it led over an ice field which was a glassy bridge over a rushing stream beneath. To add to their wretchedness mosquitoes hung about them in voracious clouds, and tiny black gnats which got into their eyes and their nostrils and set the horses frantic.

Once across the ice field Dick's horse fell and for a time could not get up again. He lay, making ineffectual efforts to rise, his sides heaving, his eyes rolling in distress. They gave up then, and prepared to make such camp as they could.

With the setting of the sun it had grown bitterly cold, and Bassett was forced to light a fire. He did it under the protection of the mountain wall, and Dick, after unsaddling his fallen horse, built a rough shelter of rocks against the wind. After a time the exhausted horse got up, but there was no forage, and the two animals stood disconsolate, or made small hopeless excursions, noses to the ground, among the moss and scrub pines.

Before turning in Bassett divided the remaining contents of the flask between them, and his last cigarettes. Dick did not talk. He sat, his back to the shelter, facing the fire, his mind busy with what Bassett knew were bitter and conflicting thoughts. Once, however, as the reporter was dozing off, Dick spoke.

"You said I told you there was a girl," he said. "Did I tell you her name?"

"No."

"All right. Go to sleep. I thought if I heard it it might help."

Bassett lay back and watched him.

"Better get some sleep, old man," he said.

He dozed, to waken again cold and shivering. The fire had burned low, and Dick was sitting near it, unheeding, and in a deep study. He looked up, and Bassett was shocked at the quiet tragedy in his face.

"Where is Beverly Carlysle now?" he asked. "Or do you know?"

"Yes. I saw her not long ago."

"Is she married again?"

"No. She's revived 'The Valley,' and she's in New York with it."

Dick slept for only an hour or so that night, but as he slept he dreamed. In his dream he was at peace and happy, and there was a girl in a black frock who seemed to be a part of that peace. When he roused, however, still with the warmth of his dream on him, he could not summon her. She had slipped away among the shadows of the night.

He sat by the fire in the grip of a great despair. He had lost ten years out of his life, his best years. And he could not go back to where he had left off. There was nothing to go back to but shame and remorse. He looked at Bassett, lying by the fire, and tried to fit him into the situation. Who was he, and why was he here? Why had he ridden out at night alone, into unknown mountains, to find him?

As though his intent gaze had roused the sleeper, Bassett opened his eyes, at first drowsily, then wide awake. He raised himself on his elbow and listened, as though for some far-off sound, and his face was strained and anxious. But the night was silent, and he relaxed and slept again.

Something that had been forming itself in Dick's mind suddenly crystallized into conviction. He rose and walked to the edge of the mountain wall and stood there listening. When he went back to the fire he felt in his pockets, found a small pad and pencil, and bending forward to catch the light, commenced to write. . . . .

At dawn Bassett wakened. He was stiff and wretched, and he grunted as he moved. He turned over and surveyed the small plateau. It was empty, except for his horse, making its continuous, hopeless search for grass.

Chapter Thirty

DAVID WAS enjoying his holiday. He lay in bed most of the morning, making the most of his one after-breakfast cigar and surrounded by newspaper and magazines. He had made friends of the waiter who brought his breakfast, and of the little chambermaid who looked after his room, and such conversations as this would follow:

"Well, Nellie," he would say, "and did you go to the dance on the pier last night?"

"Oh, yes, doctor."

"Your gentleman friend showed up all right, then?"

"Oh, yes. He didn't telephone because he was on a job out of town."

Here perhaps David would lower his voice, for Lucy was never far away.

"Did you wear the flowers?"

"Yes, violets. I put one away to remember you by. It was funny at first. I wouldn't tell him who gave them to me."

David would chuckle delightedly.

"That's right," he would say. "Keep him guessing, the young rascal. We men are kittle cattle, Nellie, kittle cattle!"

Even the valet unbent to him, and inquired if the doctor needed a man at home to look after him and his clothes. David was enormously tickled.

"Well," he said, with a twinkle in his eye. "I'll tell you how I manage now, and then you'll see. When I want my trousers pressed I send them downstairs and then I wait in my bathrobe until they come back. I'm a trifle better off for boots, but you'd have to knock Mike, my hired man, unconscious before he'd let you touch them."

The valet grinned understandingly.

"Of course, there's my nephew," David went on, a little

note of pride in his voice. "He's become engaged recently, and I notice he's bought some clothes. But still I don't think even he will want anybody to hold his trousers while he gets into them."

David chuckled over that for a long time after the valet had gone.

He was quite happy and contented. He spent all afternoon in a roller chair, conversing affably with the man who pushed him, and now and then when Lucy was out of sight getting out and stretching his legs. He picked up lost children and lonely dogs, and tried his eye in a shooting gallery, and had hard work keeping off the roller coasters and out of the sea.

Then, one day, when he had been gone some time, he was astonished on entering his hotel to find Harrison Miller sitting in the lobby. David beamed with surprise and pleasure.

"You old humbug!" he said. "Off on a jaunt after all! And the contempt of you when I was shipped here!"

Harrison Miller was constrained and uncomfortable. He had meant to see Lucy first. She was a sensible woman, and she would know just what David could stand, or could not. But David did not notice his constraint; took him to his room, made him admire the ocean view, gave him a cigar, and then sat down across from him, beaming and hospitable.

"Suffering Crimus, Miller," he said. "I didn't know I was homesick until I saw you. Well, how's everything? Dick's letters haven't been much, and we haven't had any for several days."

Harrison Miller cleared his throat. He knew that David had not been told of Jim Wheeler's death, but that Lucy knew. He knew too from Walter Wheeler that David did not know that Dick had gone west. Did Lucy know that, or not? Probably yes. But he considered the entire benevolent conspiracy an absurdity and a mistake. It was making him uncomfortable, and most of his life had been devoted to being comfortable.

He decided to temporize.

"Things are about the same," he said. "They're going to pave Chisholm Street. And your Mike knocked down the night watchman last week. I got him off with a fine."

"I hope he hasn't been in my cellar. He's got a weakness, but then——How's Dick? Not overworking?"

"No. He's all right."

But David was no man's fool. He began to see something strange in Harrison's manner, and he bent forward in his chair.

"Look here, Harrison," he said, "there's something the matter with you. You've got something on your mind."

"Well, I have and I haven't. I'd like to see Lucy, David, if she's about."

"Lucy's gadding. You can tell me if you can her. What is it? Is it about Dick?"

"In a way, yes."

"He's not sick?"

"No. He's all right, as far as I know. I guess I'd better tell you, David. Walter Wheeler has got some sort of bee in his bonnet, and he got me to come on. Dick was pretty tired and——well, one or two things happened to worry him. One was that Jim Wheeler——you'll get this sooner or later——was in an automobile accident, and it did for him."

David had lost some of his ruddy color. It was a moment before he spoke.

"Poor Jim," he said hoarsely. "He was a good boy, only full of life. It will be hard on the family."

"Yes," Harrison Miller said simply.

But David was resentful, too. When his friends were in trouble he wanted to know about it. He was somewhat indignant and not a little hurt. But he soon reverted to Dick.

"I'll go back and send him off for a rest," he said. "I'm as good as I'll ever be, and the boy's tired. What's the bee in Wheeler's bonnet?"

"Look here, David, you know your own business best, and Wheeler didn't feel at liberty to tell me very much. But he seemed to think you were the only one who could tell us certain things. He'd have come himself, but it's not easy for him to leave the family just now. Dick went away just after Jim's funeral. He left a young chap named Reynolds in his place, and, I believe, in order not to worry you, some letters to be mailed at intervals."

"*Went where?*" David asked, in a terrible voice.

"To a town called Norada, in Wyoming. Near his old home somewhere. And the Wheelers haven't heard anything from him since the day he got there. That's three weeks ago.

He wrote Elizabeth the night he got there, and wired her at the same time. There's been nothing since."

David was gripping the arms of his chair with both hands, but he forced himself to calmness.

"I'll go to Norada at once," he said. "Get a time-table, Harrison, and ring for the valet."

"Not on your life you won't. I'm here to do that, when I've got something to go on. Wheeler thought you might have heard from him. If you hadn't, I was to get all the information I could and then start. Elizabeth's almost crazy. We wired the chief of police of Norada yesterday."

"Yes!" David said thickly. "Trust your friends to make every damned mistake possible! You've set the whole pack on his trail." And then he fell back in his chair, and gasped, "Open the window!"

When Lucy came in, a half hour later, she found David on his bed with the hotel doctor beside him, and Harrison Miller in the room. David was fighting for breath, but he was conscious and very calm. He looked up at her and spoke slowly and distinctly.

"They've got Dick, Lucy," he said.

He looked aged and pinched, and entirely hopeless. Even after his heart had quieted down and he lay still among his pillows, he gave no evidence of his old fighting spirit. He lay with his eyes shut, relaxed and passive. He had done his best, and he had failed. It was out of his hands now, and in the hands of God. Once, as he lay there, he prayed. He said that he had failed, and that now he was too old and weak to fight. That God would have to take it on, and do the best He could. But he added that if God did not save Dick and bring him back to happiness, that he, David, was through.

Toward morning he wakened from a light sleep. The door into Lucy's room was open and a dim light was burning beyond it. David called her, and by her immediate response he knew she had not been sleeping.

"Yes, David," she said, and came padding in in her bedroom slippers and wadded dressing-gown, a tragic figure of apprehension, determinedly smiling. "What do you want?"

"Sit down, Lucy."

When she had done so he put out his hand, fumbling for hers. She was touched and alarmed, for it was a long while

since there had been any open demonstration of affection
between them. David was silent for a time, absorbed in
thought. Then:

"I'm not in very good shape, Lucy. I suppose you know
that. This old pump of mine has sprung a leak or something. I don't want you to worry if anything happens. I've
come to the time when I've got a good many over there,
and it will be like going home."

Lucy nodded. Her chin quivered. She smoothed his hand,
with its high twisted veins.

"I know, David," she said. "Mother and father, and
Henry, and a good many friends. But I need you, too.
You're all I have, now that Dick——"

"That's why I called you. If I can get out there, I'll go.
And I'll put up a fight that will make them wish they'd
never started anything. But if I can't, if I——" She felt his
fingers tighten on her hand. "If Hattie Thorwald is still
living, we'll put her on the stand. If I can't go, for any
reason, I want you to see that she is called. And you know
where Henry's statement is?"

"In your box, isn't it?"

"Yes. Have the statement read first, and then have her
called to corroborate it. Tell the story I have told you—or
no, I'll dictate it to you in the morning, and sign it before
witnesses. Jake and Bill will testify too."

He felt easier in his mind after that. He had marshalled
his forces and begun his preparations for battle. He felt less
apprehension now in case he fell asleep, to waken among
those he had loved long since and lost awhile. After a few
moments his eyes closed, and Lucy went back to her bed
and crawled into it.

It was, however, Harrison Miller who took the statement
that morning. Lucy's cramped old hand wrote too slowly
for David's impatience. Harrison Miller took it, on hotel
stationery, covering the carefully numbered pages with his
neat, copper-plate writing. He wrote with an impressive
face, but with intense interest, for by that time he knew
Dick's story.

Never, in his orderly bachelor life, of daily papers and a
flower garden and political economy at night, had he been
so close to the passions of men to love and hate and the
disorder they brought with them.

Chapter Thirty-one

"MY BROTHER, Henry Livingstone, was not a strong man," David dictated. "He had the same heart condition I have, but it developed earlier. After he left college he went to Arizona and bought a ranch, and there he met and chummed with Elihu Clark, who had bought an old mine and was reworking it. Henry loaned him a small amount of money at that time, and a number of years later in return for that, when Henry's health failed Clark, who had grown wealthy, bought him a ranch in Wyoming at Dry River, not far from Clark's own property.

"Henry had been teaching in an Eastern university, and then taken up tutoring. We saw little of him. He was a student, and he became almost a recluse. I saw less of him than ever after Clark gave him the ranch.

"In the spring of 1910 Henry wrote me that he was not well, and I went out to see him. He seemed worried and was in bad shape physically. Elihu Clark had died five years before, and left him a fair sum of money, fifty thousand dollars, but he was living in a way which made me think he was not using it. The ranch buildings were dilapidated, and there was nothing but the barest necessities in the house.

"I taxed Henry with miserliness, and he then told me that the money was not his, but left to him to be used for an illegitimate son of Clark's, born before his marriage, the child of a small rancher's daughter named Hattie Burgess. The Burgess girl had gone to Omaha for its birth, and the story was not known. In early years Clark had paid the child's board through his lawyer to an Omaha woman named Hines, and had later sent him to college. The Burgess girl married a Swede named Thorwald. The boy was eight years older than Judson, Clark's legitimate son.

"After the death of his wife Elihu Clark began to think

about the child, especially after Judson became a fair-sized boy. He had the older boy, who went by the name of Hines, sent to college, and in summer he stayed at Henry's tutoring school. Henry said the boy was like the Burgess family, blonde and excitable and rather commonplace. He did not get on well at college, and did not graduate. So far as he knew, Clark never saw him.

"The boy himself believed that he was an orphan, and that the Hines woman had adopted him as a foundling. But on the death of the woman he found that she had no estate, and that a firm of New York attorneys had been paying his college bills.

"He had spent considerable time with Henry, one way and another, and he began to think that Henry knew who he was. He thought at first that Henry was his father, and there was some trouble. In order to end it Henry finally acknowledged that he knew who the father was, and after that he had no peace. Clifton—his name was Clifton Hines —attacked Henry once, and if it had not been for the two men on the place he would have hurt him.

"Henry began to give him money. Clark had left the fifty thousand for the boy with the idea that Henry should start him in business with it. But he only turned up wildcat schemes that Henry would not listen to. He did not know how Henry got the money, or from where. He thought for a long time that Henry had saved it.

"I'd better say here that Henry was fond of Clifton, although he didn't approve of him. He'd never married, and the boy was like a son to him for a good many years. He didn't have him at the ranch much, however, for he was a Burgess through and through and looked like them. And he was always afraid that somehow the story would get out.

"Then Clifton learned, somehow or other, of Clark's legacy to Henry, and he put two and two together. There was a bad time, but Henry denied it and they went upstairs to bed. That night Clifton broke into Henry's desk and found some letters from Elihu Clark that told the story.

"He almost went crazy. He took the papers up to Henry's bedroom and wakened him, standing over Henry with them in his hand, and shaking all over. I think they had a struggle, too. All Henry told me was that he took them from him and threw them in the fire.

"That was a year before Henry died, and at the time

young Jud Clark's name was in all the newspapers. He had left college after a wild career there, and although Elihu had tied up the property until Jud was twenty-one, Jud had his mother's estate and a big allowance. Then, too, he borrowed on his prospects, and he lost a hundred thousand dollars at Monte Carlo within six weeks after he graduated.

"One way and another he was always in the newspapers, and when he saw how Jud was throwing money away Clifton went wild.

"As Henry had burned the letters he had no proofs. He didn't know who his mother was, but he set to work to find out. He ferreted into Elihu's past life, and he learned something about Hattie Burgess, or Thorwald. She was married by that time, and lived on a little ranch near Norada. He went to see her, and he accused her downright of being his mother. It must have been a bad time for her, for after all he was her son, and she had to disclaim him. She had a husband and a boy by that husband, however, by that time, and she was desperate. She threw him off the track somehow, lied and talked him down, and then went to bed in collapse. She sent for Henry later and told him.

"The queer thing was that as soon as she saw him she wanted him. He was her son. She went to Henry one night, and said she had perjured her soul, and that she wanted him back. She wasn't in love with Thorwald. I think she'd always cared for Clark. She went away finally, however, after promising Henry she would keep Clark's secret. But I have a suspicion that later on she acknowledged the truth to the boy.

"What he wanted, of course, was a share of the Clark estate. Of course he hadn't a chance in law, but he saw a chance to blackmail young Jud Clark and he tried it. Not personally, for he hadn't any real courage, but by mail. Clark's attorneys wrote back saying they would jail him if he tried it again, and he went back to Dry River and after Henry again.

"That was in the spring of 1911. Henry was uneasy, for Clifton was not like himself. He had spells of brooding, and he took to making long trips on his horse into the mountains, and coming in with the animal run to death. Henry thought, too, that he was seeing the Thorwald woman, the mother. Thorwald had died, and she was living with the son on their ranch and trying to sell it. He thought Hines was trying to have her make a confession which would give him a hold on Jud Clark.

"Henry was not well, and in the early fall he knew he hadn't long to live. He wrote out the story and left it in his desk for me to read after he had gone, and as he added to it from time to time, when I got it it was almost up to date.

"Judson came back to the Clark ranch in September, bringing along an actress named Beverly Carlysle, and her husband, Howard Lucas. There was considerable talk, because it was known Jud had been infatuated with the woman. But no one saw much of the party, outside of the ranch. The Carlysle woman seemed to be a lady, but the story was that both men were drinking a good bit, especially Jud.

"Henry wrote that Hines had been in the East for some months at that time, and that he had not heard from him. But he felt it was only a truce, and that he would turn up again, hell bent for trouble. He made a will and left the money to me, with instructions to turn it over to Hines. It is still in the bank, and amounts to about thirty-five thousand dollars. It is not mine, and I will not touch it. But I have never located Clifton Hines.

"In the last entry in his record I call attention to my brother's statement that he did not regard Clifton Hines as entirely sane on this one matter, and to his conviction that the hatred Hines then bore him, amounting to a delusion of persecution, might on his death turn against Judson Clark. He instructed me to go to Clark, tell him the story, and put him on his guard.

"Clark and his party had been at the ranch only a day or two when one night Hines turned up at Dry River. He wanted the fifty thousand, or what was left of it, and when he failed to move Henry he attacked him. The two men on the place heard the noise and ran in, but Hines got away. Henry swore them to secrecy, and told them the story. He felt he might need help.

"From what the two men at the ranch told me when I got there, I think Hines stayed somewhere in the mountains for the next day or two, and that he came down for food the night Henry died.

"Just what he contributed to Henry's death I do not know. Henry fell in one room, and was found in bed in another when the hands had been taking the cattle to the winter range, and he'd been alone in the house.

"When I got there the funeral was over. I read the letter he had left, and then I talked to the two hands, Bill Ardary and Jake Mazetti. They would not talk at first, but I showed them Henry's record and then they were free enough. The autopsy had shown that Henry died from heart disease, but he had a cut on his head also, and they believed that Hines had come back, had quarreled with him again, and had knocked him down.

"As Henry had in a way handed over to me his responsibility for the boy, and as I wanted to transfer the money, I waited for three weeks at the ranch, hoping he would turn up again. I saw the Thorwald woman, but she protested that she did not know where he was. And I made two attempts to see and warn Jud Clark, but failed both times. Then one night the Thorwald woman came in, looking like a ghost, and admitted that Hines had been hiding in the mountains since Henry's death, that he insisted he had killed him, and that he blamed Jud Clark for that, and for all the rest of his troubles. She was afraid he would kill Clark. The three of us, the two men at the ranch and myself, prepared to go into the mountains and hunt for him, before he got snowed in.

"Then came the shooting at the Clark place, and I rode over that night in a howling storm and helped the coroner and a Norada doctor in the examination. All the evidence was against Clark, especially his running away. But I happened on Hattie Thorwald outside on a verandah—she'd been working at the house—and I didn't need any conversation to tell me what she thought. All she said was:

"He didn't do it, doctor. He's still in the mountains."

"He's been here to-night, Hattie, and you know it. He shot the wrong man."

"But she swore he hadn't been, and at the end I didn't know. I'll say right now that I don't know. But I'll say, too, that I believe that is what happened, and that Hines probably stayed hidden that night on Hattie Thorwald's place. I went there the next day, but she denied it all, and said he was still in the mountains. She carried on about the blizzard and his being frozen to death, until I began to think she was telling the truth.

"The next day I did what only a tenderfoot would do, started into the mountains alone. Bill and Jake were out with a posse after Clark, and I packed up some food and started. I'll not go into the details of that trip. I went in from the Dry River Canyon, and I guess I faced death a dozen times the first day. I had a map, but I lost myself in six hours. I had food and blankets and an axe along, and I built a shelter and stayed there overnight. I had to cut up one of my blankets the next morning and tie up the horse's feet, so he wouldn't sink too deep in the snow. But it stayed cold and the snow hardened, and we got along better after that.

"I'd have turned back more than once, but I thought I'd meet up with some of the Sheriff's party. I didn't do that, but I stumbled on a trail on the third day, toward evening. It was the trail made by John Donaldson, as I learned later. I followed it, but I concluded after a while that whoever made it was lost, too. It seemed to be going in a circle. I was in bad shape and had frozen a part of my right hand, when I saw a cabin, and there was smoke coming out of the chimney."

From that time on David's statement dealt with the situation in the cabin; with Jud Clark and the Donaldsons, and with the snow storm, which began again and lasted for days. He spoke at length of his discovery of Clark's identity, and of the fact that the boy had lost all memory of what had happened, and even of who he was. He went into that in detail; the peculiar effect of fear and mental shock on a high-strung nature, especially where the physical condition was lowered by excess and wrong-living; his early attempts, as the boy improved, to pierce the veil, and then his slow-growing conviction that it were an act of mercy not to do so. The Donaldsons' faithfulness, the cessation of the search under the conviction that Clark was dead, both were there, and also David's growing liking for Judson himself. But David's own psychology was interesting and clearly put.

"First of all," he dictated, in his careful old voice, "it must be remembered that I was not certain that the boy had committed the crime. I believed, and I still believe, that Lucas was shot by Clifton Hines, probably through an open window. There were no powder marks on the body. I believed, too, and still believe, that Hines had fled after the crime, either to Hattie Thorwald's house or to the mountains. In one case he had escaped and could not be brought to justice, and in the other he was dead, and beyond conviction.

"But there is another element which I urge, not in defense but in explanation. The boy Judson Clark was a new slate to write on. He had never had a chance. He had had too much money, too much liberty, too little responsibility. His errors had been wiped away by the loss of his memory, and he had, I felt, a chance for a new and useful life.

"I did not come to my decision quickly. It was a long fight for his life, for he had contracted pneumonia, and he had the drinker's heart. But in the long days of his convalescence while Maggie worked in the lean-to, I had time to see what might be done. If in making an experiment with a man's soul I usurped the authority of my Lord and Master, I am sorry. But he knows that I did it for the best.

"I deliberately built up for Judson Clark a new identity. He was my nephew, my brother Henry's son. He had the traditions of an honorable family to carry on, and those traditions were honor, integrity, clean living and work. I did not stress love, for that I felt must be experienced, not talked about. But love was to be the foundation on which I built. The boy had had no love in his life.

"It had worked out. I may not live to see it at its fullest, but I defy the world to produce today a finer or more honorable gentleman, a more useful member of the community. And it will last. The time may come when Judson Clark will again be Judson Clark. I have expected it for many years. But he will never again be the Judson Clark of ten years ago. He may even will to return to the old reckless ways, but as I lie here, perhaps never to see him, I say this: *he cannot go back*. His character and habits of thought are established.

"To convict Judson Clark of the murder of Howard Lucas is to convict a probably or at least possibly innocent man. To convict Richard Livingstone of that crime is to convict a different man, innocent of the crime, innocent of its memory, innocent of any single impulse to lift his hand against a law of God or the state."

Chapter Thirty-two

FOR A MONTH Haverly had buzzed with whispered conjectures. It knew nothing, and yet somehow it knew everything. Doctor David was ill at the seashore, and Dick was not with him. Harrison Miller, who was never known to depart farther from his comfortable hearth than the railway station in one direction and the Sayre house in the other, had made a trip East and was now in the far West. Doctor Reynolds, who might or might not know something, had joined the country club and sent for his golf bag.

And Elizabeth Wheeler was going around with a drawn white face and a determined smile that faded the moment one looked away.

The village was hurt and suspicious. It resented its lack of knowledge, and turned cynical where, had it been taken into confidence, it would have been solicitous. It believed that Elizabeth had been jilted, for it knew, via Annie and the Oglethorpe's laundress, that no letters came from Dick. And against Dick its indignation was directed, in a hot flame of mainly feminine anger.

But it sensed a mystery, too, and if it hated a jilt it loved a mystery.

Nina had taken to going about with her small pointed chin held high, and angrily she demanded that Elizabeth do the same.

"You know what they are saying, and yet you go about looking *crushed*."

"I can't act, Nina. I do go about."

And Nina had a softened moment.

"Don't think about him," she said. "He isn't sick, or he would have had some one wire or write, and he isn't dead, or they'd have found his papers and let us know."

"Then he's in some sort of trouble. I want to go out there. *I want to go out there!*"

That, indeed, had been her constant cry for the last two weeks. She would have done it probably, packed her bag and slipped away, but she had no money of her own, and even Leslie, to whom she appealed, had refused her when he knew her purpose.

"We're following him up, little sister," he said. "Harrison Miller has gone out, and there's enough talk as it is."

She thought, lying in her bed at night, that they were all too afraid of what people might say. It seemed so unimportant to her. And she could not understand the conspiracy of silence. Other men went away and were not heard from, and the police were notified and the papers told. It seemed to her, too, that every one, her father and Nina and Leslie and even Harrison Miller, knew more than she did.

There had been that long conference behind closed doors, when Harrison Miller came back from seeing David, and before he went west. Leslie had been there, and even Doctor Reynolds, but they had shut her out. And her father had not been the same since.

He seemed, sometimes, to be burning with a sort of inner anger. Not at her, however. He was very gentle with her.

And here was a curious thing. She had always felt that she knew when Dick was thinking of her. All at once, and without any warning, there would come a glow of happiness and warmth, and a sort of surrounding and encircling sense of protection. Rather like what she had felt as a little girl when she had run home through the terrors of twilight, and closed the house door behind her. She was in the warm and lighted house, safe and cared for.

That was completely gone. It was as though the warm and lighted house of her love had turned her out and locked the door, and she was alone outside, cold and frightened.

She avoided the village, and from a sense of delicacy it left her alone. The small gaieties of the summer were on, dinners, dances and picnics, but her mourning made her absence inconspicuous. She could not, however, avoid Mrs. Sayre. She tried to, at first, but that lady's insistence and her own apathy made it easier to accept than to refuse. Then, after a time, she found the house rather a refuge. She seldom saw Wallie, and she found her hostess tactful, kindly and uninquisitive.

"Take the scissors and a basket, child, and cut your mother some roses," she would say. Or they would loot the green houses and, going in the car to the cemetery, make of Jim's grave a thing of beauty and remembrance.

Now and then, of course, she saw Wallie, but he never reverted to the day she had told him of her engagement. Mother and son, she began to feel that only with them could she be herself. For the village, her chin high as Nina had said. At home, assumed cheerfulness. Only at the house on the hill could she drop her pose.

She waited with a sort of desperate courage for word from Harrison Miller. What she wanted that word to be she did not know. There were, of course, times when she had to face the possibility that Dick had deliberately cut himself off from her. After all, there had never been any real reason why he should care for her. She was not clever and not beautiful. Perhaps he had been disappointed in her, and this was the thing they were concealing. Perhaps he had gone back to Wyoming and had there found some one more worthy of him, some one who understood when he talked about the things he did in his laboratory, and did not just sit and listen with loving, rather bewildered eyes.

Then, one night at dinner, a telegram was brought in, and she knew it was the expected word. She felt her mother's eyes on her, and she sat very still with her hands clenched in her lap. But her father did not read it at the table; he got up and went out, and some time later he came to the door. The telegram was not in sight.

"That was from Harrison Miller," he said. "He has traced Dick to a hotel at Norada, but he had left the hotel, and he hasn't got in touch with him yet."

He went away then, and they heard the house door close.

Then, some days later, she learned that Harrison Miller was coming home, and that David was being brought back. She saw that telegram from Mr. Miller, and read into it failure and discouragement, and something more ominous than either.

"Reach home Tuesday night. Nothing definite. Think safe."

"Think safe?" she asked, breathlessly. "Then he has been in danger? What are you keeping from me?" And when no one spoke: "Oh, don't you see how cruel it is? You are all trying to protect me, and you are killing me instead."

"Not danger," her father said, slowly. "So far as we know, he is well. Is all right." And seeing her face: "It is nothing that affects his feeling for you, dear. He is thinking of you and loving you, wherever he is. Only, we don't know where he is."

But when he came back on Tuesday, after seeing Harrison Miller, he was discouraged and sick at heart. He went directly upstairs to his wife, and shut the bedroom door.

"Not a trace," he said, in reply to the question in her eyes. "The situation is as he outlined it in the letter. He elaborated, of course. The fact is, and David will have to see it, that that statement of his doesn't help at all, unless he can prove there is a Clifton Hines. And even then it's all supposition. There's a strong sentiment out there that Dick either killed himself or met with an accident and died in the mountains. The horse wandered into town last week. I'll have to tell her."

Over this possibility they faced each other, a tragic middle-aged pair, helpless as is the way of middle-age before the attacks of life on their young.

"It will kill her, Walter."

"She's young," he said sturdily. "She'll get over it."

But he did not think so, and she knew it.

"There is a rather queer element in it," he observed, after a time. "Another man, named Bassett, disappeared the same night. His stuff is at the hotel, but no papers to identify him. He had looked after Dick that day when he was sick, and he simply vanished. He didn't take the train. He was under suspicion for being with Dick, and the station was being watched."

But she was not interested in Bassett. The name meant nothing to her. She harked back to the question that had been in both their minds since they had read, in stupefied amazement, David's statement.

"In a way, Walter, it would be better, if he . . . ."

"Why?"

"My little girl, and—Judson Clark!"

But he fought that sturdily. They had ten years of knowledge and respect to build on. The past was past. All he prayed for was Dick's return, an end to this long waiting. There would be no reservations in *his* welcome, if only . . .

Some time later he went downstairs, to where Elizabeth sat waiting in the library. He went like a man to his execution, and his resolution nearly gave way when he saw her, small in her big chair and pathetically patient. He told her the story as guardedly as he could. He began with Dick's story to him, about his forgotten youth, and went on carefully to Dick's own feeling that he must clear up that past before he married. She followed him carefully, bewildered a little and very tense.

"But why didn't he tell me?"

"He saw it as a sort of weakness. He meant to when he came back."

He fought Dick's fight for him valiantly, stressing certain points that were to prepare her for others to come. He plunged, indeed, rather recklessly into the psychology of the situation, and only got out of the unconscious mind with an effort. But behind it all was his overwhelming desire to save her pain.

"You must remember," he said, "that Dick's life before this happened, and since, are two different things. Whatever he did then should not count against him now."

"Of course not," she said. "Then he—had done something?"

"Yes. Something that brought him into conflict with the authorities."

She did not shrink from that, and he was encouraged to go on.

"He was young then, remember. Only twenty-one or so. And there was a quarrel with another man. The other man was shot."

"You mean Dick shot him?"

"Yes. You understand, don't you," he added anxiously, "that he doesn't remember doing it?"

In spite of his anxiety he was forced to marvel at the sublime faith with which she made her comment, through lips that had gone white.

"Then it was either an accident, or he deserved shooting," she said. But she inquired, he thought with difficulty, "Did he die?"

He could not lie to her. "Yes," he said.

She closed her eyes, but a moment later she was fighting her valiant fight again for Dick.

"But they let him go," she protested. "Men do shoot in the West, don't they? There must have been a reason for it. You know Dick as well as I do. He couldn't do a wrong thing."

He let that pass. "Nothing was done about it at the time," he said. "And Dick came here and lived his useful life among us. He wouldn't have known the man's name if he heard it. But do you see, sweetheart, where this is taking us? He went back, and they tried to get him, for a thing he didn't remember doing."

"Father!" she said, and went very white. "Is that where he is? In prison?"

He tried to steady his voice.

"No, dear. He escaped into the mountains. But you can understand his silence. You can understand, too, that he may feel he cannot come back to us, with this thing hanging over him. What we have to do now is to find him, and to tell him that it makes no difference. That he has his place in the world waiting for him, and that we are waiting too."

When it was all over, her questions and his sometimes stumbling replies, he saw that out of it all the one thing that mattered vitally to her was that Dick was only a fugitive, and not dead. But she said, just before they went, arm in arm, up the stairs:

"It is queer in one way, father. It isn't like him to run away."

He told Margaret, later, and she listened carefully.

"Then you didn't tell her about the woman in the case?"

"Certainly not. Why should I?"

Mrs. Wheeler looked at him, with the eternal surprise of woman at the lack of masculine understanding.

"Because, whether you think it or not, she will resent and hate that as she hates nothing else. Murder will be nothing, to that. And she will have to know it some time."

He pondered her flat statement unhappily, standing by the window and looking out into the shaded street, and a man who had been standing, cigar in mouth, on a pavement across withdrew into the shadow of a tree box.

"It's all a puzzle to me," he said, at last. "God alone knows how it will turn out. Harrison Miller seems to think this Bassett, whoever he is, could tell us something. I don't know."

He drew the shade and wound his watch. "I don't know," he repeated. . . . .

Outside, on the street, the man with the cigar struck a match and looked at his watch. Then he walked briskly toward the railway station. A half hour later he walked into the offices of the *Times-Republican* and to the night editor's desk.

"Hello, Bassett," said that gentleman. "We thought you were dead. Well, how about the sister in California? It was the Clark story, wasn't it?"

"Yes," said Bassett, noncommittally.

"And it blew up on you! Well, there were others who were fooled, too. You had a holiday, anyhow."

"Yes, I had a holiday," said Bassett, and going over to his own desk began to sort his vast accumulation of mail. Sometime later he found the night editor at his elbow.

"Did you get anything on the Clark business at all?" he asked. "Williams thinks there's a page in it for Sunday, anyhow. You've been on the ground, and there's a human interest element in it. The last man who talked to Clark; the ranch to-day. That sort of thing."

Bassett went on doggedly sorting his mail.

"You take it from me," he said, "the story's dead, and so is Clark. The Donaldson woman was crazy. That's all."

Chapter Thirty-three

DAVID WAS brought home the next day, a shrivelled and aged David, but with a fighting fire in his eyes and a careful smile at the station for the group of friends who met him.

David had decided on a course and meant to follow it. That course was to protect Dick's name, and to keep the place he had made in the world open for him. Not even to Lucy had he yet breathed the terror that was with him day and night, that Dick had reached the breaking point and had gone back. But he knew it was possible. Lauler had warned him against shocks and trouble, and looking back David could see the gradually accumulating pressure against that mental wall of Dick's subconscious building; overwork and David's illness, his love affair and Jim Wheeler's tragedy, and coming on top of that, in some way he had not yet learned, the knowledge that he was Judson Clark and a fugitive from the law. The work of ten years perhaps undone.

Both David and Lucy found the home-coming painful. Harrison Miller rode up with them from the station, and between him and Doctor Reynolds David walked into his house and was assisted up the stairs. At the door of Dick's room he stopped and looked in, and then went on, his face set and rigid. He would not go to bed, but sat in his chair while about him went on the bustle of the return, the bringing up of trunks and bags; but the careful smile was gone, and his throat, now so much too thin for his collar, worked convulsively.

He had got Harrison Miller's narrative from him on the way from the station, and it had only confirmed his suspicions.

"He had been in a stupor all day," Miller related, "and was being cared for by a man named Bassett. I daresay

that's the man Gregory had referred to. He may have become suspicious of Bassett. I don't know. But a chambermaid recognized him as he was making his escape, and
raised an alarm. He got a horse out of the courtyard of the
hotel, and not a sign of him has been found since."

"It wasn't Bassett who raised the alarm?"

"No, apparently not. The odd thing is that this Bassett
disappeared, too, the same night. I called up his paper yesterday, but he hasn't shown up."

And with some small amplifications, that is all there
was to it.

Before Harrison Miller and Doctor Reynolds left him
to rest, David called Lucy in, and put his plea to all of them.

"It is my hope," he said, "to carry on exactly as though
Dick might walk in to-morrow and take his place again.
As I hold to my belief in God, so I hold to my conviction
that he will come back, and that before I—before long. But
our friends will be asking where he is and what he is doing,
and we would better agree on that beforehand. What we'd
better say is simply that Dick was called away on business
connected with some property in the West. They may not believe it, but they'll hardly disprove it."

So the benevolent conspiracy to protect Dick Livingstone's name was arranged, and from that time on the
four of them who were a party to it turned to the outside
world an unbroken front of loyalty and courage. Even to
Minnie, anxious and red-eyed in her kitchen, Lucy gave
the same explanation while she arranged David's tray.

"He has been detained in the West on business," Lucy
said.

"He might have sent me a postcard. And he hasn't
written Doctor Reynolds at all."

"He has been very busy. Get the sugar bowl, Minnie.
He'll be back soon, I'm sure."

But Minnie did not immediately move.

"He'd better come soon if he wants to see Doctor David,"
she said, with twitching lips. "And I'll just say this, Mrs.
Crosby. The talk that's going on in this town is something
awful."

"I don't want to hear it," Lucy said firmly.

She ate alone, painfully remembering that last gay little
feast before they started away. But before she sat down

she did a touching thing. She rang the bell and called Minnie.

"After this, Minnie," she said, "we will always set Doctor Richard's place. Then, when he comes——"

Her voice broke and Minnie, scenting a tragedy but ignorant of it, went back to her kitchen to cry into the roller towel. Her world was gone to pieces. By years of service to the one family she had no other world, no home, no ties. She was with the Livingstones, but not one of them. Alone in her kitchen she felt lonely and cut off. She thought that David, had he not been ill, would have told her.

Lucy found David moving about upstairs some time later, and when she went up she found him sitting in Dick's room, on a stiff chair inside the door. She stood beside him and put her hand on his shoulder, but he did not say anything, and she went away.

That night David had a caller. All evening the bell had been ringing, and the little card tray on the hatrack was filled with visiting cards. There were gifts, too, flowers and jellies and some squab from Mrs. Sayre. Lucy had seen no one, excusing herself on the ground of fatigue, but the man who came at nine o'clock was not inclined to be turned away.

"You take this card up to Doctor Livingstone, anyhow," he said. "I'll wait."

He wrote in pencil on the card, placing it against the door post to do so, and passed it to Minnie. She calmly read it, and rather defiantly carried it off. But she came down quickly, touched by some contagion of expectation from the room upstairs.

"Hang your hat on the rack and go on up."

So it was that David and the reporter met, for the first time, in David's old fashioned chamber, with its walnut bed and the dresser with the marble top, and Dick's picture in his uniform on the mantle.

Bassett was shocked at the sight of David, shocked and alarmed. He was uncertain at first as to the wisdom of telling his startling story to an obviously sick man, but David's first words reassured him.

"Come in," he said. "You are the Bassett who was with Doctor Livingstone at Norada?"

"Yes. I see you know about it."

"We know something, not everything." Suddenly David's pose deserted him. He got up and stood very straight, searching eyes on his visitor. "Is he living?" he asked, in a low voice.

"I think so. I'm not certain."

"Then you don't know where he is?"

"No. He got away—but you know that. Sit down, doctor. I've got a long story to tell."

"I'll get you to call my sister first," David said. "And tell her to get Harrison Miller. Mr. Miller is our neighbor, and he very kindly went west when my health did not permit me to go."

While they waited David asked only one question.

"The report we have had is that he was in a stupor in the hotel, and the doctor who saw him—you got him, I think—said he appeared to have been drinking heavily. Is that true? He was not a drinking man."

"I am quite sure he had not."

There was another question in David's mind, but he did not put it. He sat, with the patience of his age and his new infirmity, waiting for Lucy to bring Harrison Miller, and had it not been for the trembling of his hands Bassett would have thought him calm and even placid.

During the recital that followed somewhat later David did not move. He sat silent, his eyes closed, his face set.

"That's about all," Bassett finished. "He had been perfectly clear in his head all day, and it took headwork to get over the pass. But as I say, he had simply dropped ten years, and was back to the Lucas trouble. I tried everything I knew, used your name and would have used the young lady's, because sometimes that sort of thing strikes pretty deep, but I didn't know it. He was convinced after a while, but he was dazed, of course. He knew it, that is, but he couldn't comprehend it.

"I was done up, and I've cursed myself for it since, but I must have slept like the dead. I wakened once, early in the night, and he was still sitting by the fire, staring at it. I've forgotten to say that he had been determined all day to go back and give himself up, and the only way I prevented it was by telling him what a blow it would be to you and to the girl. I wakened once and said to him, 'Better get some sleep, old man.' He did not answer at once, and then he said, 'All right.' I was dozing off when he spoke again. He said, 'Where is Beverly Carlysle now? Has she married again?' 'She's revived "The Valley," and she's in New York with it,' I told him.

"When I wakened in the morning he was gone, but he'd left a piece of paper in a cleft stick beside me, with directions for reaching the railroad, and—well, here it is."

Bassett took from his pocket-book a note, and passed it over to David, who got out his spectacles with shaking hands and read it. It was on Dick's prescription paper, with his name at the top of the familiar ℞ below it. David read it aloud, his voice husky.

"Many thanks for everything, Bassett," he read. "I don't like to leave you, but you'll get out all right if you follow the map on the back of this. I've had all night to think things out, and I'm leaving you because you are safer without me. I realize now what you've known all day and kept from me. That woman at the hotel recognized me, and they are after me.

"I can't make up my mind what to do. Ultimately I think I'll go back and give myself up. I am a dead man, anyhow, to all who might have cared, but I've got to do one or two things first, and I want to think things over. One thing you've got a right to know. I hated Lucas, but it never entered my head to kill him. How it happened God only knows. I don't."

It was signed "J.C."

Bassett broke the silence that followed the reading.

"I made every effort to find him. I had to work alone, you understand, and from the west side of the range, not to arouse suspicion. They were after me, too, you know. His horse, I heard, worked its way back a few days ago, It's a forsaken country, and if he lost his horse he was in it on foot and without food. Of course there's a chance——"

His voice trailed off. In the stillness David sat, touching with tender tremulous fingers what might be Dick's last message, and gazing at the picture of Dick in his uniform. He knew what they all thought, that Dick was dead and that he held his final words in his hands, but his militant old spirit refused to accept that silent verdict. Dick might be dead to them, but he was living. He looked around the room defiantly, resentfully. Of all of them he was the only one to have faith, and he was bound to a chair. He knew them. They would sit down supinely and grieve, while time passed and Dick fought his battle alone.

. No, by God, he would not be bound to a chair. He raised himself and stood, swaying on his shaking legs.

"You've given up," he said scornfully. "You make a few days' search, and then you quit. It's easy to say he's dead, and so you say he's dead. I'm going out there myself, and I'll make a search——"

He collapsed into the chair again, and looked at them with shamed, appealing eyes. Bassett was the first to break the silence, speaking in a carefully emotionless tone.

"I haven't given up for a minute. I've given up the search, because he's beyond finding just now. Either he's got away, or he is—well, beyond help. We have to go on the hypothesis that he got away, and in that case sooner or later you'll hear from him. He's bound to remember you in time. The worst thing is this charge against him."

"He never killed Howard Lucas," David said, in a tone of conviction. "Harrison, read Mr. Bassett my statement to you." . . . .

Bassett took the statement home with him that night, and studied it carefully. It explained a great deal that had puzzled him before; Mrs. Wasson's story and David's arrival at the mountain cabin. But most of all it explained why the Thorwald woman had sent him after Dick. She knew then, in spite of her protests to David, that Jud Clark had not killed Lucas.

He paced the floor for an hour or two, sunk in thought, and then unlocked a desk drawer and took out his bankbook. He had saved a little money. Not much, but it would carry him over if he couldn't get another leave of absence. He thought, as he put the book away and prepared for bed, that it was a small price to pay for finding Clifton Hines and saving his own soul.

Chapter Thirty-four

DICK HAD written his note, and placed it where Bassett would be certain to see it. Then he found his horse and led him for the first half mile or so of level ground before the trail began to descend. He mounted there, for he knew the animal could find its way in the darkness where he could not.

He felt no weariness and no hunger, although he had neither slept nor eaten for thirty-odd hours, and as contrasted with the night before his head was clear. He was able to start a train of thought and to follow it through consecutively for the first time in hours. Thought, however, was easier than realization, and to add to his perplexity, he struggled to place Bassett and failed entirely. He remained a mysterious and incomprehensible figure, beginning and ending with the trail.

Then he had an odd thought, that brought him up standing. He had only Bassett's word for the story. Perhaps Bassett was lying to him, or mad. He rode on after a moment, considering that, but there was something, not in Bassett's circumstantial narrative but in himself, that refused to accept that loophole of escape. He could not have told what it was.

And, with his increasing clarity, he began to make out the case for Bassett and against himself; the unfamiliar clothing he wore, the pad with the name of Livingstone on it and the sign ℞, the other contents of his pockets.

He tried to orient himself in Bassett's story. A doctor. The devil's irony of it! Some poor hack, losing sleep and bringing babies. Peddling pills. Leading what Bassett had called a life of usefulness! That was a career for you, a pill peddler. God!

But underlying all his surface thinking was still the need of flight, and he was continually confusing it with the earlier one. One moment he was looking about for the snow of that earlier escape, and the next he would remember, and the sense of panic would leave him. After all he meant to surrender eventually. It did not matter if they caught him.

But, like the sense of flight, there was something else in his mind, something that he fought down and would not face. When it came up he thrust it back fiercely. That something was the figure of Beverly Carlysle, stooping over her husband's body. He would have died to save her pain, and yet last night—no, it wasn't last night. It was years and years ago, and all this time she had hated him.

It was unbearable that she had gone on hating him, all this time.

He was very thirsty, and water did not satisfy him. He wanted a real drink. He wanted alcohol. Suddenly he wanted all the liquor in the world. The craving came on at dawn, and after that he kicked his weary horse on recklessly, so that it rocked and stumbled down the trail. He had only one thought after the frenzy seized him, and that was to get to civilization and whisky. It was as though he saw in drunkenness his only escape from the unbearable. In all probability he would have killed both his horse and himself in the grip of that sudden madness, but deliverance came in the shape of a casual rider, a stranger who for a moment took up the shuttle, wove his bit of the pattern and passed on, to use his blow-pipe, his spirit lamp and his chemicals in some prospector's paradise among the mountains.

When Dick heard somewhere ahead the creaking of saddle leather and the rattle of harness he drew aside on the trail and waited. He had lost all caution in the grip of his craving, and all fear. A line of loaded burrows rounded a point ahead and came toward him, picking their way delicately with small deliberate feet and walking on the outer edge of the trail, after the way of pack animals the world over. Behind them was a horseman, rifle in the scabbard on his saddle and spurs jingling. Dick watched him with thirsty, feverish eyes as he drew near. He could hardly wait to put his question.

"Happen to have a drink about you, partner?" he called.

The man stopped his horse and grinned.

"Pretty early in the morning for a drink, isn't it?" he inquired. Then he saw Dick's eyes, and reached reluctantly into his saddle bag. "I've got a quart here," he said. "I've traveled forty miles and spent nine dollars to get it, but I guess you need some."

"You wouldn't care to sell it, I suppose?"

"The bottle? Not on your life."

He untied a tin cup from his saddle and carefully poured a fair amount into it, steadying the horse the while.

"Here," he said, and passed it over. "But you'd better cut it out after this. It's bad medicine. You've got two good drinks there. Be careful."

Dick took the cup and looked at the liquor. The odor assailed him, and for a queer moment he felt a sudden distaste for it. He had a revulsion that almost shook him. But he drank it down and passed the cup back.

"You've traveled a long way for it," he said, "and I needed it, I guess. If you'll let me pay for it——"

"Forget it," said the man amiably, and started his horse. "But better cut it out, first chance you get. It's bad medicine."

He rode on after his vanishing pack, and Dick took up the trail again. But before long he began to feel sick and dizzy. The aftertaste of the liquor in his mouth nauseated him. The craving had been mental habit, not physical need, and his body fought the poison rebelliously. After a time the sickness passed, and he slept in the saddle. He roused once, enough to know that the horse had left the trail and was grazing in a green meadow. Still overcome with his first real sleep he tumbled out of the saddle and stretched himself out on the ground. He slept all day, lying out in the burning sun, his face upturned to the sky.

When he wakened it was twilight, and the horse had disappeared. His face burned from the sun, and his head ached violently. He was weak, too, from hunger, and the morning's dizziness persisted. Connected thought was impossible, beyond the fact that if he did not get out soon, he would be too weak to travel. Exhausted and on the verge of sunstroke, he set out on foot to find the trail.

He traveled all night, and the dawn found him still moving, a mere automaton of a man, haggard and shambling, no longer willing his progress, but somehow incredibly advancing. He found water and drank it, fell, got up, and still, right foot, left foot, he went on. Some time during that advance he had found a trail, and he kept to it automatically.

He felt no surprise and no relief when he saw a cabin in a clearing and a woman in the doorway, watching him with curious eyes. He pulled himself together and made a final effort, but without much interest in the result.

"I wonder if you could give me some food?" he said. "I have lost my horse and I've been wandering all night."

"I guess I can," she replied, not unamiably. "You look as though you need it, and a wash, too. There's a basin and a pail of water on that bench."

But when she came out later to call him to breakfast she found him sitting on the bench and the pail overturned on the ground.

"I'm sorry," he said, dully, "I tried to lift it, but I'm about all in."

"You'd better come in. I've made some coffee."

He could not rise. He could not even raise his hands.

She called her husband from where he was chopping wood, off in the trees, and together they got him into the house. It was days before he so much as spoke again....

So it happened that the search went on. Wilkins from the east of the range, and Bassett from the west, hunted at first with furious energy, then spasmodically, then not at all, while Dick lay in a mountain cabin, on the bed made of young trees, and for the second time in his life watched a woman moving in a lean-to kitchen, and was fed by a woman's hand.

He forced himself to think of this small panorama of life that moved before him, rather than of himself. The woman was young, and pretty in a slovenly way. The man was much older, and silent. He was of better class than the woman, and underlying his assumption of crudity there were occasional outcroppings of some cultural background. Not then, nor at any subsequent time, did he learn the story, if story there was. He began to see them, however, not so much pioneers as refugees. The cabin was, he thought, a haven to the man and a prison to the woman.

But they were uniformly kind to him, and for weeks he stayed there, slowly readjusting. In his early convalescence he would sit paring potatoes or watching a cooking pot for her. As he gained in strength he cut a little firewood. Always he sought something to keep him from thinking.

Two incidents always stood out afterwards in his memory of the cabin. One was the first time he saw himself in a mirror. He knew by that time that Bassett's story had been true, and that he was ten years older than he remembered himself to be. He thought he was in a measure prepared. But he saw in the glass a man whose face was lined and whose hair was streaked with gray. The fact that his beard had grown added to the terrible maturity of the reflection he saw, and he sent the mirror clattering to the ground.

The other incident was later, and when he was fairly strong again. The man was caught under a tree he was felling, and badly hurt. During the hour or so that followed, getting the tree cut away, and moving the injured man to the cabin on a wood sledge, Dick had the feeling of helplessness of any layman in an accident. He was solicitous but clumsy. But when they had got the patient into his bed, quite automatically he found himself making an investigation and pronouncing a verdict.

Later he was to realize that this was the first peak of submerged memory, rising about the flood. At the time all he felt was a great certainty. He must act quickly or the man would not live. And that night, with such instruments as he could extemporize, he operated. There was no time to send to a town.

All night, after the operation, Dick watched by the bedside, the woman moving back and forth restlessly. He got his only knowledge of the story, such as it was, then when she said once:

"I deserve this, but he didn't. I took him away from his wife."

He had to stay on after that, for the woman could not be left alone. And he was glad of the respite, willing to drift until he got his bearings. Certain things had come back, more as pictures than realities. Thus he saw David clearly, Lucy dimly, Elizabeth not at all. But David came first; David in the buggy with the sagging springs, David's loud voice and portly figure, David, steady and upright and gentle as a woman. But there was something wrong about David. He puzzled over that, but he was learning not to try to force things, to let them come to the surface themselves.

It was two or three days later that he remembered that David was ill, and was filled with a sickening remorse and anxiety. For the first time he made plans to get away, for whatever happened after that he knew he must see David again. But all his thought led him to an *impasse* at that time, and that *impasse* was the feeling that he was a criminal and a fugitive, and that he had no right to tie up innocent lives with his. Even a letter to David might incriminate him.

Coupled with his determination to surrender, the idea of atonement was strong in him. An eye for an eye, and a tooth for a tooth. That had been his father's belief, and well he remembered it. But during the drifting period he thrust it back, into that painful niche where he held Beverly, and the thing he would not face.

That phase of his readjustment, then, when he reached it, was painful and confused. There was the necessity for atonement, which involved surrender, and there was the call of David, and the insistent desire to see Beverly again, which was the thing he would not face. Of the three, the last, mixed up as it was with the murder and its expiation, was the strongest. For by the very freshness of his released memories, it was the days before his flight from the ranch that seemed most recent, and his life with David that was long ago, and blurred in its details as by the passing of infinite time.

When Elizabeth finally came back to him it was as something very gentle and remote, out of the long-forgotten past. Even his image of her was blurred and shadowy. He could not hear the tones of her voice, or remember anything she had said. He could never bring her at will, as he could David, for instance. She only came clearly at night, while he slept. Then the guard was down, and there crept into his dreams a small figure, infinitely loving and tender; but as he roused from sleep she changed gradually into Beverly. It was Beverly's arms he felt around his neck. Nevertheless he held to Elizabeth more completely than he knew, for the one thing that emerged from his misty recollection of her was that she cared for him. In a world of hate and bitterness she cared.

But she was never real to him, as the other woman was real. And he knew that she was lost to him, as David was lost. He could never go back to either of them.

As time went on he reached the point of making practical plans. He had lost his pocketbook somewhere, probably during his wanderings afoot, and he had no money. He knew that the obvious course was to go to the nearest settlement and surrender himself and he played with the thought, but even as he did so he knew that he would not do it. Surrender he would, eventually, but before he did that he would satisfy a craving that was in some ways like his desire for liquor that morning on the trail. A reckless, mad, and irresistible impulse to see Beverly Lucas again.

In August he started for the railroad, going on foot and without money, his immediate destination the harvest fields of some distant ranch, his object to earn his train fare to New York.

Chapter Thirty-five

THE SUMMER passed slowly. To David and Elizabeth it was a long waiting, but with this difference, that David was kept alive by hope, and that Elizabeth felt sometimes that hope was killing her. To David each day was a new day, and might hold Dick. To Elizabeth, after a time, each day was but one more of separation.

Doctor Reynolds had become a fixture in the old house, but he was not like Dick. He was a heavy, silent young man, shy of intruding into the family life and already engrossed in a budding affair with the Rossiter girl. David tolerated him, but with a sort of smouldering jealousy increased by the fact that he had introduced innovations David resented; had for instance moved Dick's desk nearer the window, and instead of doing his own laboratory work had what David considered a damnably lazy fashion of sending his little tubes, carefully closed with cotton, to a hospital in town.

David found the days very long and infinitely sad. He wakened each morning to renewed hope, watched for the postman from his upper window, and for Lucy's step on the stairs with the mail. His first glimpse of her always told him the story. At the beginning he had insisted on talking about Dick, but he saw that it hurt her, and of late they had fallen into the habit of long silences.

The determination to live on until that return which he never ceased to expect only carried him so far, however. He felt no incentive to activity. There were times when he tried Lucy sorely, when she felt that if he would only move about, go downstairs and attend to his office practice, get out into the sun and air, he would grow stronger. But there were times, too, when she felt that only the will to live was carrying him on.

Nothing further had developed, so far as they knew. The search had been abandoned. Lucy was no longer so sure as

she had been that the house was under surveillance, against
Dick's possible return. Often she lay in her bed and faced
the conviction that Dick was dead. She had never understood
the talk that at first had gone on about her, when Bassett and
Harrison Miller, and once or twice the psycho-analyst David
had consulted in town, had got together in David's bedroom.
The mind was the mind, and Dick was Dick. This thing
about habit, over which David pored at night when he should
have been sleeping, or brought her in to listen to, with an
air of triumphant vindication, meant nothing to her.

A man properly trained in right habits of thinking and of
action could not think wrong and go wrong, David argued.
He even went further. He said that love was a habit, and
that love would bring Dick back to him. That he could not
forget them.

She believed that, of course, if he still lived. But hadn't
Mr. Bassett, who seemed so curiously mixed in the affair,
been out again to Norada without result? No, it was all
over, and she felt that it would be a comfort to know where
he lay, and to bring him back to some well-loved and tended
grave.

Elizabeth came often to see them. She looked much the
same as ever, although she was very slender and her smile
rather strained, and she and David would have long talks
together. She always felt rather like an empty vessel when
she went in, but David filled her with hope and sent her away
cheered and visibly brighter to her long waiting. She rather
avoided Lucy, for Lucy's fears lay in her face and were like
a shadow over her spirit. She came across her one day putting
Dick's clothing away in camphor, and the act took on an
air of finality that almost crushed her.

So far they had kept from her Dick's real identity, but
certain things they had told her. She knew that he had gone
back, in some strange way, to the years before he came to
Haverly, and that he had temporarily forgotten everything
since. But they had told her too, and seemed to believe themselves, that it was only temporary.

At first the thought had been more than she could bear.
But she had to live her life, and in such a way as to hide her
fears. Perhaps it was good for her, the necessity of putting
up a bold front, to join the conspiracy that was to hold Dick's
place in the world against the hope of his return. And she
still went to the Sayre house, sure that there at least there

would be no curious glances, no too casual questions. She could not be sure of that even at home, for Nina was constantly conjecturing.

"I sometimes wonder——" Nina began one day, and stopped.

"Wonder what?"

"Oh, well, I suppose I might as well go on. Do you ever think that if Dick had gone back, as they say he has, that there might be somebody else?"

"Another girl, you mean?"

"Yes. Some one he knew before."

Nina was watching her. Sometimes she almost burst with the drama she was suppressing. She had been a small girl when Judson Clark had disappeared, but even at twelve she had known something of the story. She wanted frantically to go about the village and say to them: "Do you know who has been living here, whom you used to patronize? Judson Clark, one of the richest men in the world!" She built day dreams on that foundation. He would came back, for of course he would be found and acquitted, and buy the Sayre place perhaps, or build a much larger one, and they would all go to Europe in his yacht. But she knew now that the woman Leslie had sent his flowers to had loomed large in Dick's past, and she both hated and feared her. Not content with having given her, Nina, some bad hours, she saw the woman now possibly blocking her ambitions for Elizabeth.

"What I'm getting at is this," she said, examining her polished nails critically. "If it does turn out that there was somebody, you'd have to remember that it was all years and years ago, and be sensible."

"I only want him back," Elizabeth said. "I don't care how he comes, so he comes." . . . .

Louis Bassett had become a familiar figure in the village life by that time. David depended on him with a sort of wistful confidence that set him to grinding his teeth occasionally in a fury at his own helplessness. And, as the extent of the disaster developed, as he saw David failing and Lucy ageing, and when in time he met Elizabeth, the feeling of his own guilt was intensified.

He spent hours studying the case, and he was chiefly instrumental in sending Harrison Miller back to Norada in September. He had struck up a friendship with Miller over their common cause, and the night he was to depart that small inner group which was fighting David's battle for him formed a board of strategy in Harrison's tidy living-room; Walter Wheeler and Bassett, Miller and, tardily taken into their confidence, Doctor Reynolds.

The same group met him on his return, sat around with expectant faces while he got out his tobacco and laid a sheaf of papers on the table, and waited while their envoy, laying Bassett's map on the table, proceeded carefully to draw in a continuation of the trail beyond the pass, some sketchy mountains, and a small square.

"I've got something," he said at last. "Not much, but enough to work on. Here's where you lost him, Bassett." He pointed with his pencil. "He went on for a while on the horse. Then somehow he must have lost the horse, for he turned up on foot, date unknown, in a state of exhaustion at a cabin that lies here. I got lost myself, or I'd never have found the place. He was sick there for weeks, and he seems to have stayed on quite a while after he recovered, as though he couldn't decide what to do next."

Walter Wheeler stirred and looked up.

"What sort of condition was he in when he left?"

"Very good, they said."

"You're sure it was Livingstone?"

"The man there had a tree fall on him. He operated. I guess that's the answer."

"It's the answer to more than that," Reynolds said slowly. "It shows he had come back to himself. If he hadn't he couldn't have done it."

"And after that?" some one asked.

"I lost him. He left to hike to the railroad, and he said nothing of his plans. If I'd been able to make open inquiries I might have turned up something, but I couldn't. It's a hard proposition. I had trouble finding Hattie Thorwald, too. She'd left the hotel, and is living with her son. She swears she doesn't know where Clifton Hines is, and hasn't seen him for years."

Bassett had been listening intently, his head dropped forward.

"I suppose the son doesn't know about Hines?"

"No. She warned me. He was surly and suspicious. The Sheriff had sent for him and questioned him about how you got his horse, and I gathered that he thought I was a detective. When I told him I was a friend of yours, he sent you a message. You may be able to make something out of it. I can't. He said: 'You can tell him I didn't say anything about the other time.' "

Bassett sat forward.

"The other time?"

"He is under the impression that his mother got the horse for you once before, about ten days before Clark escaped. At night, also."

"Not for me," Bassett said decisively. "Ten days before that I was——" he got out his notebook and consulted it. "I was on my way to the cabin in the mountains, where the Donaldsons had hidden Jud Clark. I hired a horse at a livery stable."

"Could the Thorwald woman have followed you?"

"Why the devil should she do that?" he asked irritably. "She didn't know who I was. She hadn't a chance at my papers, for I kept them on me. If she did suspect I was on the case, a dozen fellows had preceded me, and half of them had gone to the cabin."

He considered the situation.

"Nevertheless," he finished, "I believe she did. She or Hines himself. There was some one on a horse outside the cabin that night."

There was silence in the room, Harrison Miller thoughtfully drawing at random on the map before him. Each man was seeing the situation from his own angle; to Reynolds, its medical interest, and the possibility of his permanency in the town; to Walter Wheeler, Elizabeth's spoiled young life; to Harrison Miller, David; and to the reporter a conviction that the clues he now held should lead him somewhere, and did not.

Before the meeting broke up Miller took a folded manuscript from the table and passed it to Bassett.

"Copy of the Coroner's inquiry, after the murder," he said. "Thought it might interest you. . . ."

Then, for a time, that was all. Bassett, poring at home over the inquest records, and finding them of engrossing interest, saw the futility of saving a man who could not be found. And even Nina's faith, that the fabulously rich could not die obscurely, began to fade as the summer waned. She restored some of her favor to Wallie Sayre, and even listened again to his alternating hopes and fears.

And by the end of September he felt that he had gained

real headway with Elizabeth. He had come to a point where she needed him more than she realized, where the call in her of youth for youth, even in trouble, was insistent. In return he felt his responsibility and responded to it. In the vernacular of the town he had "settled down," and the general trend of opinion, which had previously disapproved him, was now that Elizabeth might do worse.

On a crisp night early in October he had brought her home from Nina's, and because the moon was full they sat for a time on the steps of the veranda, Wallie below her, stirring the dead leaves on the walk with his stick, and looking up at her with boyish adoring eyes when she spoke. He was never very articulate with her, and her trouble had given her a strange new aloofness that almost frightened him. But that night, when she shivered a little, he reached up and touched her hand.

"You're cold," he said almost roughly. He was sometimes rather savage, for fear he might be tender.

"I'm not cold. I think it's the dead leaves."

"Dead leaves?" he repeated, puzzled. "You're a queer girl, Elizabeth. Why dead leaves?"

"I hate the fall. It's the death of the year."

"Nonsense. It's going to bed for a long winter's nap. That's all. I'll bring you a wrap."

He went in, and came out in a moment with her father's overcoat.

"Here," he said peremptorily, "put this on. I'm not going to be called on the carpet for giving you a sniffle."

She stood up obediently and he put the big coat around her. Then, obeying an irresistible impulse, he caught her to him. He released her immediately, however, and stepped back.

"I love you so," he stammered. "I'm sorry. I'll not do it again."

She was startled, but not angry.

"I don't like it," was all she said. And because she did not want him to think she was angry, she sat down again. But the boy was shaken. He got out a cigarette and lighted it, his hands trembling. He could not think of anything to say. It was as though by that one act he had cut a bridge behind him and on the other side lay all the platitudes, the small give and take of their hours together. What to her was a regrettable incident was to him a great dramatic climax. Boy-like, he refused to recognize its unimportance to her. He wanted to talk about it.

"When you said just now that you didn't like what I did just then, do you mean you didn't like *me* to do it? Or that you don't care for that sort of thing? Of course I know," he added hastily, "you're not that kind of girl. I——"

He turned and looked at her.

"You know I'm still in love with you, don't you, Elizabeth?"

She returned his gaze frankly.

"I don't see how you can be when you know what you do know."

"I know how you feel now. But I know that people don't go on loving hopelessly all their lives. You're young. You've got"—he figured quickly—"you've got about fifty-odd years to live yet, and some of these days you'll be—not forgetting," he changed, when he saw her quick movement. "I know you'll not forget him. But remembering and loving are different."

"I wonder," she said, her eyes on the moon, and full of young tragedy. "If they are, if one can remember without loving, then couldn't one love without remembering?"

He stared at her.

"You're too deep for me sometimes," he said. "I'm not subtle, Elizabeth. I daresay I'm stupid in lots of things. But I'm not stupid about this. I'm not trying to get a promise, you know. I only want you to know how things are. I don't want to know why he went away, or why he doesn't come back. I only want you to face the facts. I'd be good to you," he finished, in a low tone. "I'd spend my life thinking of ways to make you happy."

She was touched. She reached down and put her hand on his shoulder.

"You deserve the best, Wallie. And you're asking for a second best. Even that—I'm just not made that way, I suppose. Fifty years or a hundred, it would be all the same."

"You'd always care for him, you mean?"

"Yes. I'm afraid so."

When he looked at her her eyes had again that faraway and yet flaming look which he had come to associate with her thoughts of Dick. She seemed infinitely removed from him, traveling her lonely road past loving outstretched hands and facing ahead toward—well, toward fifty years of spinsterhood. The sheer waste of it made him shudder.

"You're cold, too, Wallie," she said gently. "You'd better go home."

He was about to repudiate the idea scornfully, when he sneezed! She got up at once and held out her hand.

"You are very dear to feel about me the way you do," she said, rather rapidly. "I appreciate your telling me. And if you're chilly when you get home, you'd better take some camphor."

He saw her in, hat in hand, and then turned and stalked up the street. Camphor, indeed! But so stubborn was hope in his young heart that before he had climbed the hill he was finding comfort in her thought for him.

Mrs. Sayre had been away for a week, visiting in Michigan, and he had not expected her for a day or so. To his surprise he found her on the terrace, wrapped in furs, and evidently waiting for him.

"I wasn't enjoying it," she explained, when he had kissed her. "It's a summer place, not heated to amount to anything, and when it turned cold—where have you been to-night?"

"Dined at the Wards', and then took Elizabeth home."

"How is she?"

"She's all right."

"And there's no news?"

He knew her very well, and he saw then that she was laboring under suppressed excitement.

"What's the matter, mother? You're worried about something, aren't you?"

"I have something to tell you. We'd better go inside."

He followed her in, unexcited and half smiling. Her world was a small one, of minor domestic difficulties, of not unfriendly gossip, of occasionally money problems, investments and what not. He had seen her hands tremble over a matter of a poorly served dinner. So he went into the house, closed the terrace window and followed her to the library.

When she closed the door he recognized her old tactics when the servants were in question.

"Well?" he inquired. "I suppose——" Then he saw her face. "Sorry, mother. What's the trouble?"

"Wallie, I saw Dick Livingstone in Chicago."

Chapter Thirty-six

DURING AUGUST Dick had labored in the alfalfa fields of Central Washington, a harvest hand or "working stiff" among other migratory agricultural workers. Among them, but not entirely of them. Recruited from the lowest levels as men grade, gathered in at a slave market on the coast, herded in bunk houses alive with vermin, fully but badly fed, overflowing with blasphemy and filled with sullen hate for those above them in the social scale, the "stiffs" regarded him with distrust from the start.

In the beginning he accepted their sneers with a degree of philosophy. His physical condition was poor. At night he ached intolerably, collapsing into his wooden bunk to sleep the dreamless sleep of utter exhaustion. There were times when he felt that it would be better to return at once to Norada and surrender, for that he must do so eventually he never doubted. It was as well perhaps that he had no time for brooding, but he gained sleep at the cost of super-human exertion all day.

A feeling of unreality began to obsess him, so that at times he felt like a ghost walking among sweating men, like a resurrection into life, but without life. And more than once he tried to sink down to the level of the others, to unite himself again with the crowd, to feel again the touch of elbows, the sensation of fellowship. The primal instinct of the herd asserted itself, the need of human companionship of any sort.

But he failed miserably, as Jud Clark could never have failed. He could not drink with them. He could not sink to their level of degradation. Their oaths and obscenity sickened and disgusted him, and their talk of women drove him into the fresh air.

The fact that he could no longer drink himself into a stupor puzzled him. Bad whiskey circulated freely among the hay stacks and bunk houses where the harvest hands were quartered, and at ruinous prices. The men clubbed together to buy it, and he put in his share, only to find that it not only sickened him, but that he had a mental inhibition against it.

They called him the "Dude," and put into it gradually all the class hatred of their wretched sullen lives. He had to fight them, more than once, and had they united against him he might have been killed. But they never united. Their own personal animosities and angers kept them apart, as their misery held them together. And as time went on and his muscles hardened he was able to give a better account of himself. The time came when they let him alone, and when one day a big shocker fell off a stack and broke his leg and Dick set it, he gained their respect. They asked no questions, for their law was that the past was the past. They did not like him, but in the queer twisted ethics of the camp they judged the secret behind him by the height from which he had fallen, and began slowly to accept him as of the brotherhood of derelicts.

With his improvement in his physical condition there came, toward the end of the summer, a more rapid subsidence of the flood of the long past. He had slept out one night in the fields, where the uncut alfalfa was belled with purple flowers and yellow buttercups rose and nodded above him. With the first touch of dawn on the mountains he wakened to a clarity of mind like that of the morning. He felt almost an exaltation. He stood up and threw out his arms.

It was all his again, never to lose, the old house, and David and Lucy; the little laboratory; the church on Sunday mornings. Mike, whistling in the stable. A wave of love warmed him, a great surging tenderness. He would go back to them. They were his and he was theirs. It was at first only a great emotion; a tingling joyousness, a vast relief, as of one who sees, from a far distance, the lights in the windows of home. Save for the gap between the drunken revel at the ranch and his awakening to David's face bending over him in the cabin, everything was clear. Still by an effort, but successfully, he could unite now the two portions of his life with only a scar between them.

Not that he formulated it. It was rather a mood, an impulse of unreasoning happiness. The last cloud had gone, the last bit of mist from the valley. He saw Haverly, and the children who played in its shaded streets; Mike washing the old car, and the ice cream freezer on Sundays, wrapped in sacking on the kitchen porch. Jim Wheeler came back to him, the weight of his coffin dragging at his right hand as he helped to carry it; he was kneeling beside Elizabeth's bed, and putting his hand over her staring eyes so she would go to sleep.

The glow died away, and he began to suffer intensely. They were all lost to him, along with the life they represented. And already he began to look back on his period of forgetfulness with regret. At least then he had not known what he had lost.

He wondered again what they knew. What did they think? If they believed him dead, was that not kinder than the truth? Outside of David and Lucy, and of course Bassett, the sole foundation on which any search for him had rested had been the semi-hysterical recognition of Hattie Thorwald. But he wondered how far that search had gone.

Had it extended far enough to involve David? Had the hue and cry died away, or were the police still searching for him? Could he even write to David, without involving him in his own trouble? For David, fine, wonderful old David— David had deliberately obstructed the course of justice, and was an accessory after the fact.

Up to that time he had drifted, unable to set a course in the fog, but now he could see the way, and it led him back to Norada. He would not communicate with David. He would go out of the lives at the old house as he had gone in, under a lie. When he surrendered it would be as Judson Clark, with his lips shut tight on the years since his escape. Let them think, if they would, that the curtain that had closed down over his memory had not lifted, and that he had picked up life again where he had laid it down. The police would get nothing from him to incriminate David.

But he had a moment, too, when surrender seemed to him not strength but weakness; where its sheer supineness, its easy solution to his problem revolted him, where he clenched his fist and looked at it, and longed for the right to fight his way out.

When smoke began to issue from the cook-house chimney he stirred, rose and went back. He ate no breakfast, and the men, seeing his squared jaw and set face, let him alone. He worked with the strength of three men that day, but that night, when the foreman offered him a job as pacer, with double wages, he refused it.

"Give it to somebody else, Joe," he said. "I'm quitting."

"The hell you are! When?"

"I'd like to check out to-night."

His going was without comment. They had never fully accepted him, and comings and goings without notice in the camp were common. He rolled up his bedding, his change of under-garments inside it, and took the road that night.

The railroad was ten miles away, and he made the distance easily. He walked between wire fences, behind which horses moved restlessly as he passed and cattle slept around a water hole, and as he walked he faced a situation which all day he had labored like three men to evade.

He was going out of life. It did not much matter whether it was to be behind bars or to pay the ultimate price. The shadow that lay over him was that he was leaving forever David and all that he stood for, and a woman. And the woman was not Elizabeth.

He cursed himself in the dark for a fool and a madman; he cursed the infatuation which rose like a demoniac possession from his early life. When that failed he tried to kill it by remembering the passage of time, the loathing she must have nursed all these years. He summoned the image of Elizabeth to his aid, to find it eclipsed by something infinitely more real and vital. Beverly in her dressing-room, grotesque and yet lovely in her make-up; Beverly on the mountain-trail, in her boyish riding clothes. Beverly.

Probably at that stage of his recovery his mind had reacted more quickly than his emotions. And by that strange faculty by which an idea often becomes stronger in memory than in its original production he found himself in the grip of a passion infinitely more terrible than his earlier one for her. It wiped out the memory, even the thought, of Elizabeth, and left him a victim of its associated emotions. Bitter jealousy racked him, remorse and profound grief. The ten miles of road to the railroad became ten miles of torture, of increasing domination of the impulse to go to her, and of final surrender.

In Spokane he outfitted himself, for his clothes were ragged, and with the remainder of his money bought a ticket to Chicago. Beyond Chicago he had no thought save one. Some way, somehow, he must get to New York. Yet all the time he was fighting. He tried again and again to break away from the emotional associations from which his memory of her was erected; when that failed he struggled to face reality; the lapse of time, the certainty of his disappointment, at the best the inevitable parting when he went back to Norada. But always in the end found his face turned toward the East, and her.

He had no fear of starving. If he had learned the cost of a dollar in blood and muscle, he had the blood and the muscle. There was a time, in Chicago, when the necessity of thinking about money irritated him, for the memory of his old opulent days was very clear. Times when his temper was uncertain, and he turned surly. Times when his helplessness brought to his lips the old familiar blasphemies of his youth, which sounded strange and revolting to his ears.

He had no fear, then, but a great impatience, as though, having lost so much time, he must advance with every minute. And Chicago drove him frantic. There came a time there when he made a deliberate attempt to sink to the very depths, to seek forgetfulness by burying one wretchedness under another. He attempted to find work and failed, and he tried to let go and sink. The total result of the experiment was that he wakened one morning in his lodging-house ill and with his money gone, save for some small silver. He thought ironically, lying on his untidy bed, that even the resources of the depths were closed to him.

He never tried that experiment again. He hated himself for it.

For days he haunted the West Madison Street employment agencies. But the agencies and sidewalks were filled with men who wandered aimlessly with the objectless shuffle of the unemployed. Beds had gone up in the lodgings-houses to thirty-five cents a night, and the food in the cheap restaurants was almost uneatable. There came a day when the free morning coffee at a Bible Rescue Home, and its soup and potatoes and carrots at night was all he ate.

For the first time his courage began to fail him. He went to the lakeside that night and stood looking at the water. He meant to fight that impulse of cowardice at the source.

Up to that time he had given no thought whatever to his estate, beyond the fact that he had been undoubtedly ad-

judged legally dead and his property divided. But that day as
he turned away from the lake front, he began to wonder
about it. After all, since he meant to surrender himself before long, why not telegraph collect to the old offices of
the estate in New York and have them wire him money?
But even granting that they were still in existence, he knew
with what lengthy caution, following stunned surprise, they
would go about investigating the message. And there were
leaks in the telegraph. He would have a pack of newspaper
hounds at his heels within a few hours. The police, too. No,
it wouldn't do.

The next day he got a job as a taxicab driver, and that
night and every night thereafter he went back to West
Madison Street and picked up one or more of the derelicts
there and bought them food. He developed quite a system
about it. He waited until he saw a man stop outside an
eating-house, look in and then pass on. But one night he
got rather a shock. For the young fellow he accosted looked
at him first with suspicion, which was not unusual, and later
with amazement.

"Captain Livingstone!" he said, and checked his hand as
it was about to rise to the salute. His face broke into a
smile, and he whipped off his cap. "You've forgotten me,
sir," he said. "But I've got your visiting card on the top of
my head all right. Can you see it?"

He bent his head and waited, but on no immediate reply
being forthcoming, for Dick was hastily determining on a
course of action, he looked up. It was then that he saw
Dick's cheap and shabby clothes, and his grin faded.

"I say," he said. "You *are* Livingstone, aren't you? I'd
have known——"

"I think you've made a mistake, old man," Dick said,
feeling for his words carefully. "That's not my name, anyhow. I thought, when I saw you staring in at that window——
How about it?"

The boy looked at him again, and then glanced away.

"I was looking, all right," he said. "I've been having a
run of hard luck."

It had been Dick's custom to eat with his finds, and thus
remove from the meal the quality of detached charity. Men
who would not take money would join him in a meal. But
he could not face the lights with this keen-eyed youngster.
He offered him money instead.

"Just a lift," he said, awkwardly, when the boy hesitated. "I've been there myself, lately."

But when at last he had prevailed and turned away he was conscious that the doughboy was staring after him, puzzled and unconvinced.

He had a bad night after that. The encounter had brought back his hard-working, care-free days in the army. It had brought back, too, the things he had put behind him, his profession and his joy in it, the struggles and the aspirations that constitute a man's life. With them there came, too, a more real Elizabeth, and a wave of tenderness for her, and of regret. He turned on his sagging bed, and deliberately put her away from him. Even if this other ghost were laid, he had no right to her. . . . . . .

Then, one day, he met Mrs. Sayre, and saw that she knew him.

Chapter Thirty-seven

WALLIE STARED at his mother. His mind was at once protesting the fact and accepting it, with its consequences to himself. There was a perceptible pause before he spoke. He stood, if anything, somewhat straighter, but that was all.

"Are you sure it was Livingstone?"

"Positive. I talked to him. I wasn't sure myself, at first. He looked shabby and thin, as though he'd been ill, and he had the audacity to pretend at first he didn't know me. He closed the door on me and——"

"Wait a minute, mother. What door?"

"He was driving a taxicab."

He looked at her incredulously.

"I don't believe it," he said slowly. "I think you've made a mistake, that's all."

"Nonsense. I know him as well as I know you."

"Did he acknowledge his identity?"

"Not in so many words," she admitted. "He said I had made a mistake, and he stuck to it. Then he shut the door and drove me to the station. The only other chance I had was at the station, and there was a line of cabs behind us, so I had only a second. I saw he didn't intend to admit anything, so I said: 'I can see you don't mean to recognize me, Doctor Livingstone, but I must know whether I am to say at home that I've seen you.' He was making change for me at the time—I'd have known his hands, I think, if I hadn't seen anything else—and when he looked up his face was shocking. He said, 'Are they all right?' 'David is very ill,' I said. The cars behind were waiting and making a terrific din, and a traffic man ran up then and made him move on. He gave me the strangest look as he went. I stood and waited, thinking he would turn and come back again at the end of the line, but he didn't. I almost missed my train."

Wallie's first reaction to the news was one of burning anger and condemnation.

"The blackguard!" he said. "The insufferable cad! To have run away as he did, and then to let them believe him dead! For that's what they do believe. It is killing David Livingstone, and as for Elizabeth— She'll have to be told, mother. He's alive. He's well. And he has deliberately deserted them all. He ought to be shot."

"You didn't see him, Wallie. I did. He's been through something, I don't know what. I didn't sleep last night for thinking of his face. It had despair in it."

"All right," he said, angrily pausing before her. "What do you intend to do? Let them go on as they are, hoping and waiting; lauding him to the skies as a sort of superman? The thing to do is to tell the truth."

"But we don't know the truth, Wallie. There's something behind it all."

"Nothing very creditable, be sure of that," he pronounced. "Do you think it is fair to Elizabeth to let her waste her life on the memory of a man who's deserted her?"

"It would be cruel to tell her."

"You've got to be cruel to be kind, sometimes," he said oracularly. "Why, the man may be married. May be anything. A taxi driver! Doesn't that in itself show that he's hiding from something?"

She sat, a small obese figure made larger by her furs, and stared at him with troubled eyes.

"I don't know, Wallie," she said helplessly. "In a way, it might be better to tell her. She could put him out of her mind, then. But I hate to do it. It's like stabbing a baby."

He understood her, and nodded. When, after taking a turn or two about the room he again stopped in front of her his angry flush had subsided.

"It's the devil of a mess," he commented. "I suppose the square thing to do is to tell Doctor David, and let him decide. I've got too much at stake to be a judge of what to do."

He went upstairs soon after that, leaving her still in her chair, swathed in furs, her round anxious face bent forward in thought. He had rarely seen her so troubled, so uncertain of her next move, and he surmised, knowing her, that her emotions were a complex of anxiety for himself with Elizabeth, of pity for David, and of the memory of Dick Livingstone's haggard face.

She sat alone for some time and then went reluctantly up

the stairs to her bedroom. She felt, like Wallie, that she had too much at stake to decide easily what to do.

In the end she decided to ask Doctor Reynolds' advice, and in the morning she proceeded to do it. Reynolds was interested, even a little excited, she thought, but he thought it better not to tell David. He would himself go to Harrison Miller with it.

"You say he knew you?" he inquired, watching her. "I suppose there is no doubt of that?"

"Certainly not. He's known me for years. And he asked about David."

"I see." He fell into profound thought, while she sat in her chair a trifle annoyed with him. He was wondering how all this would affect him and his prospects, and through them his right to marry. He had walked into a good thing, and into a very considerable content.

"I see," he repeated, and got up. "I'll tell Miller, and we'll get to work. We are all very grateful to you, Mrs. Sayre——"

As a result of that visit Harrison Miller and Bassett went that night to Chicago. They left it to Doctor Reynolds' medical judgment whether David should be told or not, and Reynolds himself did not know. In the end he passed the shuttle the next evening to Clare Rossiter.

"Something's troubling you," she said. "You're not a bit like yourself, old dear."

He looked at her. To him she was all that was fine and good and sane of judgment.

"I've got something to settle," he said. "I was wondering while you were singing, dear, whether you could help me out."

"When I sing you're supposed to listen. Well? What is it?" She perched herself on the arm of his chair, and ran her fingers over his hair. She was very fond of him, and she meant to be a good wife. If she ever thought of Dick Livingstone now it was in connection with her own reckless confession to Elizabeth. She had hated Elizabeth ever since.

"I'll take a hypothetical case. If you guess, you needn't say. Of course it's a great secret."

She listened, nodding now and then. He used no names, and he said nothing of any crime. "The point is this," he finished. "Is it better to believe the man is dead, or to know that he is alive, but has cut himself off?"

"There's no mistake about the recognition?"

"Somebody from the village saw him in Chicago within a day or two, and talked to him."

She had the whole picture in a moment. She knew that Mrs. Sayre had been in Chicago, that she had seen Dick there and talked to him. She turned the matter over in her mind, shrewdly calculating, planning her small revenge on Elizabeth even as she talked.

"I'd wait," she advised him. "He may come back with them, and in that case David will know soon enough. Or he may refuse to, and that would kill him. He'd rather think him dead than that."

She slept quietly that night, and spent rather more time than usual in dressing that morning. Then she took her way to the Wheeler house. She saw in what she was doing no particularly culpable thing. She had no great revenge in mind; all that she intended was an evening of the score between them. "He preferred you to me, when you knew I cared. But he has deserted you." And perhaps, too, a small present jealousy, for she was to live in the old brick Livingstone house, or in one like it, while all the village expected ultimately to see Elizabeth installed in the house on the hill.

She kept her message to the end of her visit, and delivered her blow standing.

"I have something I ought to tell you, Elizabeth. But I don't know how you'll take it."

"Maybe it's something I won't want to hear."

"I'll tell you, if you won't say where you heard it."

But Elizabeth made a small, impatient gesture. "I don't like secrets, Clare. I can't keep them, for one thing. You'd better not tell me."

Clare was nearly balked of her revenge, but not entirely.

"All right," she said, and prepared to depart. "I won't. But you might just find out from your friend Mrs. Sayre who it was she saw in Chicago this week."

It was in this manner, bit by bit and each bit trivial, that the case against Dick was built up for Elizabeth. Mrs. Sayre, helpless before her quiet questioning, had to acknowledge one damning thing after another. He had known her; he had not asked for Elizabeth, but only for David; he looked tired and thin, but well. She stood at the window watching Elizabeth go down the hill, with a feeling that she had just seen something die before her.

Chapter Thirty-eight

ON THE NIGHT Bassett and Harrison Miller were to return from Chicago Lucy sat downstairs in her sitting-room waiting for news.

At ten o'clock, according to her custom, she went up to see that David was comfortable for the night, and to read him that prayer for the absent with which he always closed his day of waiting. But before she went she stopped before the old mirror in the hall, to see if she wore any visible sign of tension.

The door into Dick's office was opened, and on his once neat desk there lay a litter of papers and letters. She sighed and went up the stairs.

David lay propped up in his walnut bed. An incredibly wasted and old David; the hands on the log-cabin quilt which their mother had made were old hands, and tired. Sometimes Lucy, with a frightened gasp, would fear that David's waiting now was not all for Dick. That he was waiting for peace.

There had been something new in David lately. She thought it was fear. Always he had been so sure of himself; he had made his experiment in a man's soul, and whatever the result he had been ready to face his Creator with it. But he had lost courage. He had tampered with the things that were to be and not he, but Dick, was paying for that awful audacity.

Once, picking up his prayer-book to read evening prayer as was her custom now, it had opened at a verse marked with an uneven line:

"I will arise and go to my Father, and will say unto Him, Father, I have sinned again Heaven and before Thee, and am no more worthy to be called Thy son."

That had frightened her. . . . .

David's eyes followed her about the room.

"I've got an idea you're keeping something from me, Lucy."

"I? Why should I do that?"

"Then where's Harrison?" he demanded, querulously.

She told him one of the few white lies of her life when she said: "He hasn't been well. He'll be over to-morrow." She sat down and picked up the prayer-book, only to find him lifting himself in the bed and listening.

"Somebody closed the hall door, Lucy. If it's Reynolds, I want to see him."

She got up and went to the head of the stairs. The light was low in the hall beneath, and she saw a man standing there. But she still wore her reading glasses, and she saw at first hardly more than a figure.

"Is that you, Doctor Reynolds?" she asked, in her high old voice.

Then she put her hand to her throat and stood rigid, staring down. For the man had whipped off his cap and stood with his arms wide, looking up.

Holding to the stair-rail, her knees trembling under her, Lucy went down, and not until Dick's arms were around her was she sure that it was Dick, and not his shabby, weary ghost. She clung to him, tears streaming down her face, still in that cautious silence which governed them both; she held him off and looked at him, and then strained herself to him again, as though the sense of unreality were too strong, and only the contact of his rough clothing made him real to her.

It was not until they were in her sitting-room with the door closed that either of them dared to speak. Or perhaps, could speak. Even then she kept hold of him.

"Dick!" she said. "Dick!"

And that, over and over.

"How is he?" he was able to ask finally.

"He has been very ill. I began to think—Dick, I'm afraid to tell him. I'm afraid he'll die of joy."

He winced at that. There could not be much joy in the farewell that was coming. Winced, and almost staggered. He had walked all the way from the city, and he had had no food that day.

"We'll have to break it to him very gently," he said.

"And he mustn't see me like this. If you can find some of my clothes and Reynolds' razor, I'll——" He caught suddenly to the back of a chair and held on to it. "I haven't taken time to eat much to-day," he said, smiling at her. "I guess I need food, Aunt Lucy."

For the first time then she saw his clothes, his shabbiness and his pallor, and perhaps she guessed the truth. She got up, her face twitching, and pushed him into a chair.

"You sit here," she said, "and leave the door closed. The nurse is out for a walk, and she'll be in soon. I'll bring some milk and cookies now, and start the fire. I've got some chops in the house."

When she came back almost immediately, with the familiar tray and the familiar food, he was sitting where she had left him. He had spent the entire time, had she known it, in impressing on his mind the familiar details of the room, to carry away with him.

She stood beside him, a hand on his shoulder, to see that he drank the milk slowly.

"I've got the fire going," she said. "And I'll run up now and get your clothes. I—had put them away." Her voice broke a little. "You see, we— You can change in your laboratory, Richard, can't you? If you go upstairs he'll hear you."

He reached up and caught her hand. That touch, too, of the nearest to a mother's hand that he had known, he meant to carry away with him. He could not speak.

She bustled away, into her bright kitchen first, and then with happy stealth to the store-room. Her very heart was singing within her. She neither thought nor reasoned. Dick was back, and all would be well. If she had any subconscious anxieties they were quieted, also subconsciously, by confidence in the men who were fighting his battle for him, by Walter Wheeler and Bassett and Harrison Miller. That Dick himself would present any difficulty lay beyond her worst fears.

She had been out of the room only twenty minutes when she returned to David and prepared to break her great news. At first she thought he was asleep. He was lying back with his eyes closed and his hands crossed on the prayer-book. But he looked up at her, and was instantly roused to full attention by her face.

"You've had some news," he said.

"Yes, David. There's a little news. Don't count too much on it. Don't sit up. David, I have heard something that makes me think he is alive. Alive and well."

He made a desperate effort and controlled himself.

"Where is he?"

She sat down beside him and took his hand between hers.

"David," she said slowly, "God has been very good to us. I want to tell you something, and I want you to prepare yourself. We have heard from Dick. He is all right. He loves us, as he always did. And—he is downstairs, David."

He lay very still and without speaking. She was frightened at first, afraid to go on with her further news. But suddenly David sat up in bed and in a full, firm voice began the Te Deum Laudamus. "We praise thee, O God: we acknowledge thee to be the Lord. All the earth doth worship thee, the Father everlasting."

He repeated it in its entirety. At the end, however, his voice broke.

"O Lord, in thee have I trusted—I doubted Him, Lucy," he said.

Dick, waiting at the foot of the stairs, heard that triumphant pæan of thanksgiving and praise and closed his eyes.

It was a few minutes later that Lucy came down the stairs again.

"You heard him?" she asked. "Oh, Dick, he had frightened me. It was more than a question of himself and you. He was making it one of himself and God."

She let him go up alone and waited below, straining her ears, but she heard nothing beyond David's first hoarse cry, and after a little she went into her sitting-room and shut the door. . . . .

Whatever lay underneath, there was no surface drama in the meeting. The determination to ignore any tragedy in the situation was strong in them both, and if David's eyes were blurred and his hands trembling, if Dick's first words were rather choked, they hid their emotion carefully.

"Well, here I am, like a bad penny!" said Dick huskily from the doorway.

"And a long time you've been about it," grumbled David. "You young rascal!"

He held out his hand, and Dick crushed it between both of his. He was startled at the change in David. For a moment he could only stand there, holding his hand, and trying to keep his apprehension out of his face.

"Sit down," David said awkwardly, and blew his nose with a terrific blast. "I've been laid up for a while, but I'm all right now. I'll fool them all yet," he boasted, out of his happiness and content. "Business has been going to the dogs, Dick. Reynolds is a fool."

"Of course you'll fool them." There was still a band around Dick's throat. It hurt him to look at David, so thin and feeble, so sunken from his former portliness. And David saw his eyes, and knew.

"I've dropped a little flesh, eh, Dick?" he inquired. "Old bulge is gone, you see. The nurse makes up the bed when I'm in it, flat as when I'm out."

Suddenly his composure broke. He was a feeble and apprehensive old man, shaken with the tearless sobbing of weakness and age. Dick put an arm across his shoulders, and they sat without speech until David was quiet again.

"I'm a crying old woman, Dick," David said at last. "That's what comes of never feeling a pair of pants on your legs and being coddled like a baby." He sat up and stared around him ferociously. "They sprinkle violet water on my pillows, Dick! Can you beat that?"

Warned by Lucy, the nurse went to her room and did not disturb them. But she sat for a time in her rocking-chair, before she changed into the nightgown and kimono in which she slept on the couch in David's room. She knew the story, and her kindly heart ached within her. What good would it do after all, this home-coming? Dick could not stay. It was even dangerous. Reynolds had confided to her that he suspected a watch on the house by the police, and that the mail was being opened. What good was it?

Across the hall she could hear Lucy moving briskly about in Dick's room, changing the bedding, throwing up the windows, opening and closing bureau drawers. After a time Lucy tapped at her door and she opened it.

"I put a cake of scented soap among your handkerchiefs," she said, rather breathlessly. "Will you let me have it for Doctor Dick's room?"

She got the soap and gave it to her.

"He is going to stay, then?"

"Certainly he is going to stay," Lucy said, surprised. "This is his home. Where else should he go?"

But David knew. He lay, listening with avid interest to Dick's story, asking a question now and then, nodding over Dick's halting attempt to reconstruct the period of his confusion, but all the time one part of him, a keen and relentless inner voice, was saying: "Look at him well. Hold him close. Listen to his voice. Because this hour is yours, and perhaps only this hour."

"Then the Sayre woman doesn't know about your coming?" he asked, when Dick had finished.

"No."

"Still, she mustn't talk about having seen you. I'll send Reynolds up in the morning."

He was eager to hear of what had occurred in the long interval between them, and good, bad and indifferent Dick told him. But he limited himself to events, and did not touch on his mental battles, and David saw and noted it. The real story, he knew, lay there, but it was not time for it. After a while he raised himself in his bed.

"Call Lucy, Dick."

When she had come, a strangely younger Lucy, her withered cheeks flushed with exercise and excitement, he said:

"Bring me the copy of the statement I made to Harrison Miller, Lucy."

She brought it, patted Dick's shoulder, and went away. David held out the paper.

"Read it slowly, boy," he said. "It is my justification, and God willing, it may help you. The letter is from my brother, Henry. Read that, too." . . . .

Lucy, having got Dick's room in readiness, sat down in it to await his coming. Downstairs, in the warming oven, was his supper. His bed, with the best blankets, was turned down and ready. His dressing-gown and slippers were in their old accustomed place. She drew a long breath.

Below, Doctor Reynolds came in quietly and stood listening. The house was very still, and he decided that his news, which was after all no news, could wait. He went into the office and got out a sheet of note-paper, with his name at the top, and began his nightly letter to Clare Rossiter.

"My darling," it commenced.

Above, David lay in his bed and Dick read the papers in his hand. And as he read them David watched him. Not once, since Dick's entrance, had he mentioned Elizabeth. David lay still and pondered that. There was something wrong about it. This was Dick, their own Dick; no shadowy ghost of the past, but Dick himself. True, an older Dick, strangely haggard and with gray running in the brown of his hair, but still Dick; the Dick whose eyes had lighted at the sight of a girl, who had shamelessly persisted in holding her hand at that last dinner, who had almost idolatrously loved her.

And he had not mentioned her name.

When he had finished the reading Dick sat for a moment with the papers in his hand, thinking.

"I see," he said finally. "Of course, it's possible. Good God, if I could only think it."

"It's the answer," David said stubbornly. "He was prowling around, and fired through the window. Donaldson made the statement at the inquest that some one had been seen on the place, and that he notified you that night after dinner. He'd put guards around the place."

"It gives me a fighting chance, anyhow." Dick got up and threw back his shoulders. "That's all I want. A chance to fight. I know this. I hated Lucas—he was a poor thing and you know what he did to me. But I never thought of killing him. That wouldn't have helped matters. It was too late."

"What about—that?" David asked, not looking at him. When Dick did not immediately reply David glanced at him, to find his face set and pained.

"Perhaps we'd better not go into that now," David said hastily. "It's natural that the readjustments will take time."

"We'll have to go into it. It's the hardest thing I have to face."

"It's not dead, then?"

"No," Dick said slowly. "It's not dead, David. And I'd better bring it into the open. I've fought it to the limit by myself. It's the one thing that seems to have survived the shipwreck. I can't argue it down or think it down."

"Maybe, if you see Elizabeth——"

"I'd break her heart, that's all."

He tried to make David understand. He told in its sordid details his failure to kill it, his attempts to sink memory and conscience in Chicago and their failure, the continued re-moteness of Elizabeth and what seemed to him the flesh and blood reality of the other woman. That she was yesterday, and Elizabeth was long ago.

"I can't argue it down," he finished. "I've tried to, des-perately. It's a—I think it's a wicked thing, in a way. And God knows all she ever got out of it was suffering. She must loathe the thought of me."

David was compelled to let it rest there. He found that Dick was doggedly determined to see Beverly Carlysle. After that, he didn't know. No man wanted to surrender himself for trial, unless he was sure himself of whether he was innocent or guilty. If there was a reasonable doubt—but what did it matter one way or the other? His place was gone, as he'd made it, gone if he was cleared, gone if he was convicted.

"I can't come back, David. They wouldn't have me."

After a silence he asked:

"How much is known here? What does Elizabeth know?"

"The town knows nothing. She knows a part of it. She cares a great deal, Dick. It's a tragedy for her."

"Shall you tell her I have been here?"

"Not unless you intend to see her."

But Dick shook his head.

"Even if other things were the same I haven't a right to see her, until I've got a clean slate."

"That's sheer evasion," David said, almost with irritation.

"Yes," Dick acknowledged gravely. "It is sheer evasion."

"What about the police?" he inquired after a silence. "I was registered at Norada. I suppose they traced me?"

"Yes. The house was watched for a while; I understand they've given it up now."

In response to questions about his own condition David was almost querulous. He was all right. He would get well if they'd let him, and stop coddling him. He would get up now, in spite of them. He was good for one more fight before he died, and he intended to make it, in a court if necessary.

"They can't prove it, Dick," he said triumphantly. "I've been over it every day for months. There is no case. There never was a case, for that matter. They're a lot of pin-headed fools, and we'll show them up, boy. We'll show them up."

But for all his excitement fatigue was telling on him. Lucy tapped at the door and came in.

"You'd better have your supper before it spoils," she said. "And David needs a rest. Doctor Reynolds is in the office. I haven't told him yet."

The two men exchanged glances.

"Time for that later," David said. "I can't keep him out of my office, but I can out of my family affairs for an hour or so."

So it happened that Dick followed Lucy down the back stairs and ate his meal stealthily in the kitchen.

"I don't like you to eat here," she protested.

"I've eaten in worse places," he said, smiling at her. "And sometimes not at all." He was immediately sorry for that, for the tears came to her eyes.

He broke as gently as he could the news that he could not stay, but it was a great blow to her. Her sagging chin quivered piteously, and it took all the cheerfulness he could summon and all the promises of return he could make to soften the shock.

"You haven't even seen Elizabeth," she said at last.

"That will have to wait until things are cleared up, Aunt Lucy."

"Won't you write her something then, Richard? She looks like a ghost these days."

Her eyes were on him, puzzled and wistful. He met them gravely.

"I haven't the right to see her, or to write to her."

And the finality in his tone closed the discussion, that and something very close to despair in his face.

For all his earlier hunger he ate very little, and soon after he tiptoed up the stairs again to David's room. When he came down to the kitchen later on he found her still there, at the table where he had left her, her arms across it and her face buried in them. On a chair was the suitcase she had hastily packed for him, and a roll of bills lay on the table.

"You must take it," she insisted. "It breaks my heart to think—Dick, I have the feeling that I am seeing you for the last time." Then for fear she had hurt him she forced a determined smile. "Don't pay any attention to me. David will tell you that I have said, over and over, that I'd never see you again. And here you are!"

He was going. He had said good-bye to David and was going at once. She accepted it with a stoicism born of many years of hail and farewell, kissed him tenderly, let her hand linger for a moment on the rough sleeve of his coat, and then let him out by the kitchen door into the yard. But long after he had gone she stood in the doorway, staring out. . . . .

In the office Doctor Reynolds was finishing a long and carefully written letter.

"I am not good at putting myself on paper, as you know, dear heart. But this I do know. I do not believe that real love dies. We may bury it, so deep that it seems to be entirely dead, but some day it sends up a shoot, and it either lives, or the business of killing it has to be begun all over again. So when we quarrel, I always know——"

Chapter Thirty-nine

THE EVENING had shaken Dick profoundly. David's appearance and Lucy's grief and premonition, most of all the talk of Elizabeth, had depressed and unnerved him. Even the possibility of his own innocence was subordinated to an overwhelming yearning for the old house and the old life.

Through a side window as he went toward the street he could see Reynolds at his desk in the office, and he was possessed by a fierce jealousy and resentment at his presence there. The laboratory window was dark, and he stood outside and looked at it. He would have given his hope of immortality just then to have been inside it once more, working over his tubes and his cultures, his slides and microscope. Even the memory of certain dearly-bought extravagances in apparatus revived in him, and sent the blood to his head in a wave of unreasoning anger and bitterness.

He had a wild desire to go in at the front door, confront Reynolds in his smug complacency and drive him out; to demand his place in the world and take it. He could hardly tear himself away.

Under a street lamp he looked at his watch. It was eleven o'clock, and he had a half hour to spare before train-time. Following an impulse he did not analyze he turned toward the Wheeler house. Just so months ago had he turned in that direction, but with this difference, that then he went with a sort of hurried expectancy, and that now he loitered on the way. Yet that it somehow drew him he knew. Not with the yearning he had felt toward the old brick house, but with the poignancy of a long past happiness. He did not love, but he remembered.

Yet, for a man who did not love, he was oddly angry at the sight of two young figures on the doorstep. Their clear voices came to him across the quiet street, vibrant and full of youth. It was the Sayre boy and Elizabeth.

He half stopped, and looked across. They were quite oblivious of him, intent and self-absorbed. As he had viewed Reynolds' unconscious figure with jealous dislike, so he viewed Wallace Sayre. Here, everywhere, his place was filled. He was angry with an unreasoning, inexplicable anger, angry at Elizabeth, angry at the boy, and at himself.

He had but to cross the street and take his place there. He could drive that beardless youngster away with a word. The furious possessive jealousy of the male animal, which had nothing to do with love, made him stop and draw himself up as he stared across.

Then he smiled wryly and went on. He could do it, but he did not want to. He would never do it. Let them live their lives, and let him live his. But he knew that there, across the street, so near that he might have raised his voice and summoned her, he was leaving the best thing that had come into his life; the one fine and good thing, outside of David and Lucy. That against its loss he had nothing but an infatuation that had ruined three lives already, and was not yet finished.

He stopped and, turning, looked back. He saw the girl bend down and put a hand on Wallie Sayre's shoulder, and the boy's face upturned and looking into hers. He shook himself and went on. After all, that was best. He felt no anger now. She deserved better than to be used to help a man work out his salvation. She deserved youth, and joyousness, and the forgetfulness that comes with time. She was already forgetting.

He smiled again as he went on up the street, but his hands as he buttoned his overcoat were shaking.

It was shortly after that that he met the rector, Mr. Oglethorpe. He passed him quickly, but he was conscious that the clergyman had stopped and was staring after him. Half an hour later, sitting in the empty smoker of the train, he wondered if he had not missed something there. Perhaps the church could have helped him, a good man's simple belief in right and wrong. He was wandering in a gray no-man's land, without faith or compass.

David had given him the location of Bassett's apartment house, and he found it quickly. He was in a state of nervous irritability by that time, for the sense of being a fugitive was constantly stressed in the familiar streets by the danger of recognition. It was in vain that he argued with himself that only the police were interested in his movements, and the casual roundsman not at all. He found himself shying away from them like a nervous horse.

But if he expected any surprise from Bassett he was disappointed. He greeted him as if he had seen him yesterday, and explained his lack of amazement in his first words.

"Doctor Livingstone telephoned me. Sit down, man, and let me look at you. You've given me more trouble than any human being on earth."

"Sorry," Dick said awkwardly, "I seem to have a faculty of involving other people in my difficulties."

"Want a drink?"

"No, thanks. I'll smoke, if you have any tobacco. I've been afraid to risk a shop."

Bassett talked cheerfully as he found cigarettes and matches.

"The old boy had a different ring to his voice to-night. He was going down pretty fast, Livingstone; was giving up the fight. But I fancy you've given him a new grip on the earth."

When they were seated, however, a sort of awkwardness developed. To Dick, Bassett had been a more or less shadowy memory, clouded over with the details and miseries of the flight. And Bassett found Dick greatly altered. He was older than he remembered him. The sort of boyishness which had come with the resurrection of his early identity had gone, and the man who sat before him was grave, weary, and much older. But his gaze was clear and direct.

"Well, a good bit of water has gone over the dam since we met," Bassett said. "I nearly broke a leg going down that infernal mountain again. And I don't mind telling you that I came within an ace of landing in the Norada jail. They knew I'd helped you get away. But they couldn't prove it."

"I got out, because I didn't see any need of dragging you down with me. I was a good bit of a mess just then, but I could reason that out, anyhow. It wasn't entirely unselfish, either. I had a better chance without you. Or thought I did."

Bassett was watching him intently.

"Has it all come back?" he inquired.

"Practically all. Not much between the thing that happened at the ranch and David Livingstone's picking me up at the cabin."

"Did it ever occur to you to wonder just how I got in on your secret?"

"I suppose you read Maggie Donaldson's confession."

"I came to see you before that came out."

"Then I don't know, I'm afraid."

"I suppose you would stake your life on the fact that Beverly Carlysle knows nothing of what happened that night at the ranch?"

Dick's face twitched, but he returned Bassett's gaze steadily.

"She has no criminal knowledge, if that is what you mean."

"I am not so sure of it."

"I think you'd better explain that."

At the cold anger in Dick's voice Bassett stared at him. So that was how the wind lay. Poor devil! And out of the smug complacence of his bachelor peace Bassett thanked his stars for no women in his life.

"I'm afraid you misunderstand me, Livingstone," he said easily. "I don't think that she shot Lucas. But I don't think she has ever told all she knows. I've got the coroner's inquest here, and we'll go over it later. I'll tell you how I got onto your trail. Do you remember taking Elizabeth Wheeler to see 'The Valley?' "

"I had forgotten it. I remember now."

"Well, Gregory, the brother, saw you and recognized you. I was with him. He tried to deny you later, but I was on. Of course he told her, and I think she sent him to warn David Livingstone. They knew I was on the trail of a big story. Then I think Gregory stayed here to watch me when the company made its next jump. He knew I'd started, for he sent David Livingstone the letter you got. By the way, that letter nearly got me jailed in Norada."

"I'm not hiding behind her skirts," Dick said shortly. "And there's nothing incriminating in what you say. She saw me as a fugitive, and she sent me a warning. That's all."

"Easy, easy, old man. I'm not pinning anything on her. But I want, if you don't mind, to carry this through. I have every reason to believe that, some time before you got to Norada, the Thorwald woman was on my trail. I know that I was followed to the cabin the night I stayed there, and that she got a saddle horse from her son that night, her son by Thorwald, either for herself or some one else."

"All right. I accept that, tentatively."

"That means that she knew I was coming to Norada. Think a minute; I'd kept my movements quiet, but Beverly Carlysle knew, and her brother. When they warned David they warned her."

"I don't believe it."

"If you had killed Lucas," Bassett asserted positively, "the Thorwald woman would have let the Sheriff get you, and be damned to you. She had no reason to love you. You'd kept her son out of what she felt was his birthright."

He got up and opened a table drawer.

"I've got a copy of the coroner's inquest here. It will bear going over. And it may help you to remember, too. We needn't read it all. There's a lot that isn't pertinent."

He got out a long envelope, and took from it a number of typed pages, backed with a base of heavy paper.

" 'Inquest in the Coroner's office on the body of Howard Lucas,' " he read. " 'October 10th, 1911.' That was the second day after. 'Examination of witnesses by Coroner Samuel J. Burkhardt. Mrs. Lucas called and sworn.' " He glanced at Dick and hesitated. "I don't know about this to-night, Livingstone. You look pretty well shot to pieces."

"I didn't sleep last night. I'm all right. Go on."

During the reading that followed he sat back in his deep chair, his eyes closed. Except that once or twice he clenched his hands he made no movement whatever.

Q. "What is your name?"

A. "Anne Elizabeth Lucas. My stage name is Beverly Carlysle."

Q. "Where do you live, Mrs. Lucas?"

A. "At 26 East 56th Street, New York City."

Q. "I shall have to ask you some questions that are necessarily painful at this time. I shall be as brief as possible. Perhaps it will be easier for you to tell so much as you know of what happened the night before last at the Clark ranch."

A. "I cannot tell very much. I am confused, too. I was given a sleeping powder last night. I can only say that I heard a shot, and thought at first that it was fired from outside. I ran down the stairs, and back to the billiard room. As I entered the room Mr. Donaldson came in through a window. My husband was lying on the floor. That is all."

Q. "Where was Judson Clark?"

A. "He was leaning on the roulette table, staring at the—at my husband."

Q. "Did you see him leave the room?"

A. "No. I was on my knees beside Mr. Lucas. I think when I got up he was gone. I didn't notice."

Q. "Did you see a revolver?"

A. "No. I didn't look for one."

Q. "Now I shall ask you one more question, and that is all. Had there been any quarrel between Mr. Lucas and Mr. Clark that evening in your presence?"

A. "No. But I had quarreled with them both. They were drinking too much. I had gone to my room to pack and go home. I was packing when I heard the shot."

Witness excused and Mr. John Donaldson called.

Q. "What is your name?"

A. "John Donaldson."

Q. "Where do you live?"

A. "At the Clark ranch."

Q. "What is your business?"

A. "You know all about me. I'm foreman of the ranch."

Q. "I want you to tell what you know, Jack, about last night. Begin with where you were when you heard the shot."

A. "I was on the side porch. The billiard room opens on to it. I'd been told by the corral boss earlier in the evening that he'd seen a man skulking around the house. There'd been a report like that once or twice before, and I set a watch. I put Ben Haggerty at the kitchen wing with a gun, and I took up a stand on the porch. Before I did that I told Judson, but I don't think he took it in. He'd been lit up like a house afire all evening. I asked for his gun, but he said he didn't know where it was, and I went back to my house and got my own. Along about eight o'clock I thought I saw some one in the shrubbery, and I went out as quietly as I could. But it was a woman, Hattie Thorwald, who was working at the ranch.

"When I left the men were playing roulette. I looked in as I went back, and Judson had a gun in his hand. He said, 'I found it, Jack.' I saw he was very drunk, and I told him

to put it up, I'd got mine. It had occurred to me that I'd better warn Haggerty to be careful, and I started along the
verandah to tell him not to shoot except to scare. I had
only gone a few steps when I heard a shot, and ran back.
Mr. Lucas was on the floor dead, and Judson was as the
lady said. He must have gone out while I was bending over
the body."

Q. "Did you see the revolver in his hand?"

A. "No."

Q. "How long between your warning Mr. Clark and the
shot?"

A. "I suppose I'd gone a dozen yards."

Q. "Were you present when the revolver was found?"

A. "No, sir."

Q. "Did you see Judson Clark again?"

A. "No, sir. From what I gather he went straight to the
corral and got his horse."

Q. "You entered the room as Mrs. Lucas came in the
door?"

A. "Well, she's wrong about that. She was there a little
ahead of me. She'd reached the body before I got in. She
was stooping over it."

Bassett looked up from his reading.

"I want you to get this, Livingstone," he said. "How did
she reach the billiard room? Where was it in the house?"

"Off the end of the living-room."

"A large living-room?"

"Forty or forty-five feet, about."

"Will you draw it for me, roughly?"

He passed over a pad and pencil, and Dick made a
hasty outline. Bassett watched with growing satisfaction.

"Here's the point," he said, when Dick had finished. "She
was there before Donaldson, or at the same time," as Dick
made an impatient movement. "But he had only a dozen
yards to go. She was in her room, upstairs. To get down in
that time she had to leave her room, descend a staircase,
cross a hall and run the length of the living-room, forty-
five feet. If the case had ever gone to trial she'd have had
to do some explaining."

"She or Donaldson," Dick said obstinately.

Bassett read on:

Jean Melis called and sworn.

Q. "Your name?"

A. "Jean Melis."

Q. "Have you an American residence, Mr. Melis?"

A. "Only where I am employed. I am now living at the Clark ranch."

Q. "What is your business?"

A. "I am Mr. Clark's valet."

Q. "It was you who found Mr. Clark's revolver?"

A. "Yes."

Q. "Tell about how and where you found it."

A. "I made a search early in the evening. I will not hide from you that I meant to conceal it if I discovered it. A man who is drunk is not guilty of what he does. I did not find it. I went back that night, when the people had gone, and found it beneath the carved woodbox, by the fireplace. I did not know that the Sheriff had placed a man outside the window."

"Get that, too," Bassett said, putting down the paper. "The Frenchman was fond of you, and he was doing his blundering best. But the Sheriff expected you back and had had the place watched, so they caught him. But that's not the point. A billiard room is a hard place to hide things in. I take it yours was like the average."

Dick nodded.

"All right. This poor boob of a valet made a search and didn't find it. Later he found it. Why did he search? Wasn't it the likely thing that you'd carried it away with you? Do you suppose for a moment that with Donaldson and the woman in the room you hid it there, and then went back and stood behind the roulette table, leaning on it with both hands, and staring? Not at all. Listen to this:

Q. "You recognize this revolver as the one you found?"

A. "Yes."

Q. "You are familiar with it?"

A. "Yes. It is Mr. Clark's."

Q. "You made the second search because you had not examined the woodbox earlier?"

A. "No. I had examined the woodbox. I had a theory that——"

Q. "The Jury cannot listen to any theories. This is an inquiry into facts."

"I'm going to find Melis," the reporter said thoughtfully, as he folded up the papers. "The fact is, I mailed an advertisement to the New York papers to-day. I want to get that theory of his. It's the servants in the house who know what is going on. I've got an idea that he'd stumbled onto something. He'd searched for the revolver, and it wasn't there. He went back and it was. All that conflicting evidence, and against it, what? That you'd run away!"

But he saw that Dick was very tired, and even a little indifferent. He would be glad to know that his hands were clean, but against the intimation that Beverly Carlysle had known more than she had disclosed he presented a dogged front of opposition. After a time Bassett put the papers away and essayed more general conversation, and there he found himself met half way and more. He began to get Dick as a man, for the first time, and as a strong man. He watched his quiet, lined face, and surmised behind it depths of tenderness and gentleness. No wonder the little Wheeler girl had worshipped him.

It was settled that Dick was to spend the night there, and such plans as he had Bassett left until morning. But while he was unfolding the bed-lounge on which Dick was to sleep, Dick opened a line of discussion that cost the reporter an hour or two's sleep before he could suppress his irritation.

"I must have caused you considerable outlay, one way and another," he said. "I want to defray that, Bassett, as soon as I've figured out some way to get at my bank account."

Bassett jerked out a pillow and thumped it.

"Forget it." Then he grinned. "You can fix that when you get your estate, old man. Buy a newspaper and let me run it!"

He bent over the davenport and put the pillow in place. "All you'll have to do is to establish your identity. The institutions that got it had to give bond. I hope you're not too long for this bed."

But he looked up at Dick's silence, to see him looking at him with a faint air of amusement over his pipe.

"They're going to keep the money, Bassett."

Bassett straightened and stared at him.

"Don't be a damned fool," he protested. "It's your money. Don't tell me you're going to give it to suffering humanity. That sort of drivel makes me sick. Take it, give it away if you like, but for God's sake don't shirk your job."

Dick got up and took a turn or two around the room.

Then, after an old habit, he went to the window and stood looking out, but seeing nothing.

"It's not that, Bassett. I'm afraid of the accursed thing. I might talk a lot of rot about wanting to work with my hands. I wouldn't if I didn't have to, any more than the next fellow. I might fool myself, too, with thinking I could work better without any money worries. But I've got to remember this. It took work to make a man of me before, and it will take work to keep me going the way I intend to go, if I get my freedom."

Sometime during the night Bassett saw that the light was still burning by the davenport, and went in. Dick was asleep with a volume of Whitman open on his chest, and Bassett saw what he had been reading.

"You broken resolutions, you racking angers, you short-lived ennuis;
Ah, think not you shall finally triumph, my real self has yet to come forth.
It shall march forth over-mastering, till all lie beneath me,
It shall stand up, the soldier of unquestioned victory."

Bassett took the book away and stood rereading the paragraph. For the first time he sensed the struggle going on at that time behind Dick's quiet face, and he wondered. Unquestioned victory, eh? That was a pretty large order.

Chapter Forty

LESLIE WARD had found the autumn extremely tedious. His old passion for Nina now and then flamed up in him, but her occasional coquetries no longer deceived him. They had their source only in her vanity. She exacted his embraces only as tribute to her own charm, her youth, her fresh young body.

And Nina out of her setting of gaiety, of a thumping piano, of chattering, giggling crowds, of dancing and bridge and theater boxes, was a queen dethroned. She did not read or think. She spent the leisure of her mourning period in long hours before her mirror fussing with her hair, in trimming and retrimming hats, or in the fastidious care of her hands and body.

He was ashamed sometimes of his pitilessly clear analysis of her. She was not discontented, save at the enforced somberness of their lives. She had found in marriage what she wanted; a good house, daintily served; a man to respond to her attractions as a woman, and to provide for her needs as a wife; dignity and an established place in the world; liberty and privilege.

But she was restless. She chafed at the quiet evenings they spent at home, and resented the reading in which he took refuge from her uneasy fidgeting.

"For Heaven's sake, Nina, sit down and read or sew, or do something. You've been at that window a dozen times."

"I'm not bothering you. Go on and read."

When nobody dropped in she would go upstairs and spend the hour or so before bedtime in the rites of cold cream, massage, and in placing the little combs of what Leslie had learned was called a water-wave.

But her judgment was as clear as his, and even more pitiless; the difference between them lay in the fact that while he rebelled, she accepted the situation. She was cleverer than he was; her mind worked more quickly, and she had the adaptability he lacked. If there were times when she wearied him, there were others when he sickened her. Across from her at the table he ate slowly and enormously. He splashed her dainty bathroom with his loud, gasping cold baths. He flung his soiled clothing anywhere. He drank whisky at night and crawled into the lavender-scented sheets redolent of it, to drop into a heavy sleep and snore until she wanted to scream. But she played the game to the limit of her ability.

Then, seeing that they might go on the rocks, he made a valiant effort, and since she recognized it as an effort, she tried to meet him half way. They played two-handed card games. He read aloud to her, poetry which she loathed, and she to him, short stories he hated. He suggested country walks and she agreed, to limp back after a half mile or so in her high-heeled pumps.

He concealed his boredom from her, but there were nights when he lay awake long after she was asleep and looked ahead into a future of unnumbered blank evenings. He had formerly taken an occasional evening at his club, but on his suggesting it now Nina's eyes would fill with suspicion, and he knew that although she never mentioned Beverly Carlysle, she would neither forget nor entirely trust him again. And in his inner secret soul he knew that she was right.

He had thought that he had buried that brief madness, but there were times when he knew he lied to himself. One fiction, however, he persisted in; he had not been infatuated with Beverly. It was only that she gave him during those few days something he had not found at home, companionship and quiet intelligent talk. She had been restful. Nina was never restful.

He bought a New York paper daily, and read it in the train. "The Valley" had opened to success in New York, and had settled for a long run. The reviews of her work had been extraordinary, and when now and then she gave an interview he studied the photographs accompanying it. But he never carried the paper home.

He began, however, to play with the thought of going to New York. He would not go to see her at her house, but he would like to see her before a metropolitan audience, to add his mite to her triumph. There were times when he fully determined to go, when he sat at his desk with his hand on the telephone, prepared to lay the foundations of the excursion by some manipulation of business interests. For months, he never went further than the preliminary movement.

But by October he began to delude himself with a real excuse for going, and this was the knowledge that by a strange chain of circumstance this woman who so dominated his secret thoughts was connected with Elizabeth's life through Judson Clark. The discovery, communicated to him by Walter Wheeler, that Dick was Clark had roused in him a totally different feeling from Nina's. He saw no glamour of great wealth. On the contrary, he saw in Clark the author of a great unhappiness to a woman who had not deserved it. And Nina, judging him with deadly accuracy, surmised even that.

That he was jealous of Judson Clark, and of his part in the past, he denied to himself absolutely. But his resentment took the form of violent protest to the family, against even allowing Elizabeth to have anything to do with Dick if he turned up.

"He'll buy his freedom, if he isn't dead," he said to Nina, "and he'll come snivelling back here, with that lost memory bunk, and they're just fool enough to fall for it."

"I've fallen for it, and I'm at least as intelligent as you are."

Before her appraising eyes his own fell.

"Suppose I did something I shouldn't and turned up here with such a story, would you believe it?"

"No. When you want to do something you shouldn't you don't appear to need any excuse."

But, on the whole, they managed to live together comfortably enough. They each had their reservations, but especially after Jim's death they tacitly agreed to stop bickering and to make their mutual concessions. What Nina never suspected was that he corresponded with Beverly Carlysle. Not that the correspondence amounted to much. He had sent her flowers the night of the New York opening, with the name of his club on his card, and she wrote there in acknowledgment. Then, later, twice he sent her books, one a biography, which was a compromise with his conscience, and later a volume of exotic love verse, which was not. As he replied to her notes of thanks a desultory correspondence had sprung up, letters which the world might have read, and yet which had to him the savor and interest of the clandestine.

He did not know that that, and not infatuation, was behind his desire to see Beverly again; never reasoned that he was demonstrating to himself that his adventurous love life was not necessarily ended; never acknowledged that the instinct of the hunter was as alive in him as in the days before his marriage. Partly, then, a desire for adventure, partly a hope that romance was not over but might still be waiting around the next corner, was behind his desire to see her.

Probably Nina knew that, as she knew so many things; why he had taken to reading poetry, for instance. Certain it is that when he began, early in October, to throw out small tentative remarks about the necessity of a business trip before long to New York, she narrowed her eyes. She was determined to go with him, if he went at all, and he was equally determined that she should not.

It became, in a way, a sort of watchful waiting on both sides.

Then there came a time when some slight excuse offered, and Leslie took up the shuttle for forty-eighty hours, and wove his bit in the pattern. It happened to be on the same evening as Dick's return to the old house.

He was a little too confident, a trifle too easy to Nina.

"Has the handle of my suitcase been repaired yet?" he asked. He was lighting a cigarette at the time.

"Yes. Why?"

"I'll have to run over to New York to-morrow. I wanted Joe to go alone, but he thinks he needs me." Joe was his partner.

"Oh. So Joe's going?"

"That's what I said."

She was silent. Joe's going was clever of him. It gave authenticity to his business, and it kept her at home.

"How long shall you be gone?"

"Only a day or two." He could not entirely keep the relief out of his voice. It had been easy, incredibly easy. He might have done it a month ago. And he had told the truth; Joe was going.

"I'll pack to-night, and take my suitcase in with me in the morning."

"If you'll get your things out I'll pack them." She was still thinking, but her tone was indifferent. "You won't want your dress clothes, of course?"

"I'd better have a dinner suit."

She looked at him then, with a half contemptuous smile. "Yes," she said slowly. "I suppose you will. You'll be going to the theater."

He glanced away.

"Possibly. But we'll be rushing to get through. There's a lot to do. Amazing how business piles up when you find you're going anywhere. There won't be much time to play."

She sat before the mirror in her small dressing-room that night, ostensibly preparing for bed but actually taking stock of her situation. She had done all she could, had been faithful and loyal, had made his home attractive, had catered to his tastes and tried to like his friends, had met his needs and responded to them. And now, this. She was bewildered and frightened. How did women hold their husbands?

She found him in bed and unmistakably asleep when she went into the bedroom. Man-like, having got his way, he was not troubled by doubts or introspection. It was done.

He was lying on his back, with his mouth open. She felt a sudden and violent repugnance to getting into the bed beside him. Sometime in the night he would turn over and throwing his arm about her, hold her close in his sleep; and it would be purely automatic, the mechanical result of habit.

She lay on the edge of the bed and thought things over. He had his good qualities. He was kind and affectionate to her family. He had been wonderful when Jim died, and he loved Elizabeth dearly. He was generous and open-handed. He was handsome, too, in a big, heavy way.

She began to find excuses for him. Men were always a child-like prey to some women. They were vain, and especially they were sex-vain; good looking men were a target for every sort of advance. She transferred her loathing of him to the woman she suspected of luring him away from her, and lay for hours hating her.

She saw Leslie off in the morning with a perfunctory good-bye while cold anger and suspicion seethed in her. And later she put on her hat and went home to lay the situation before her mother. Mrs. Wheeler was out, however, and she found only Elizabeth sewing by her window.

Nina threw her hat on the bed and sat down dispiritedly. "I suppose there's no news?" she asked.

"No."

Nina watched her. She was out of patience with Elizabeth, exasperated with the world.

"Are you going to go on like this all your life?" she demanded. "Sitting by a window, waiting? For a man who ran away from you?"

"That's not true, and you know it."

"They're all alike," Nina declared recklessly. "They go along well enough, and they are all for virtue and for the home and fireside stuff, until some woman comes their way. I ought to know."

Elizabeth looked up quickly.

"Why, Nina!" she said. "You don't mean——"

"He went to New York this morning. He pretended to be going on business, but he's actually gone to see that actress. He's been mad about her for months."

"I don't believe it."

"Oh, wake up," Nina said impatiently. "The world isn't made up of good, kind, virtuous people. It's rotten. And men are all alike. Dick Livingstone and Les and all the rest—tarred with the same stick. As long as there are women like this Carlysle creature they'll fall for them. And you and I can sit at home and chew our nails and plan to keep them by us. And we can't do it."

In spite of herself a little question of doubt crept that day into Elizabeth's mind. She had always known that they had not told her all the truth; that the benevolent conspiracy to protect Dick extended even to her. But she had never thought that it might include a woman. Once there, the very humility of her love for Dick was an element in favor of the idea. She had never been good enough, or wise or clever enough, for him. She was too small and unimportant to be really vital.

Dismissing the thought did no good. It came back. But because she was a healthy-minded and practical person she took the one course she could think of, and put the question that night to her father, when he came back from seeing David.

David had sent for him early in the evening. All day he had thought over the situation between Dick and Elizabeth, with growing pain and uneasiness. He had not spoken of it to Lucy, or to Harrison Miller; he knew that they would not understand, and that Lucy would suffer. She was bewildered enough by Dick's departure.

At noon he had insisted on getting up and being helped into his trousers. So clad he felt more of a man and better able to cope with things, although his satisfaction in them was somewhat modified by the knowledge of two safety-pins at the sides, to take up their superfluous girth at the waistband.

But even the sense of being clothed as a man again did not make it easier to say to Walter Wheeler what must be said.

Walter took the news of Dick's return with a visible brightening. It was as though, out of the wreckage of his middle years, he saw that there was now some salvage, but he was grave and inarticulate over it, wrung David's hand and only said:

"Thank God for it, David." And after a pause: "Was he all right? He remembered everything?"

"Yes."

But something strange in the situation began to obtrude itself into his mind. Dick had come back twenty-four hours ago. Last night. And all this time——

"Where is he now?"

"He's not here, Walter."

"He has gone away again, without seeing Elizabeth?"

David cleared his throat.

"He is still a fugitive. He doesn't himself know he isn't guilty. I think he feels that he ought not to see her until——"

"Come, come," Walter Wheeler said impatiently. "Don't try to find excuses for him. Let's have the truth, David. I guess I can stand it."

Poor David, divided between his love for Dick and his native honesty, threw out his hands.

"I don't understand it, Wheeler," he said. "You and I wouldn't, I suppose. We are not the sort to lose the world for a woman. The plain truth is that there is not a trace of Judson Clark in him to-day, save one. That's the woman."

When Wheeler said nothing, but sat twisting his hat in his hands, David went on. It might be only a phase. As its impression on Dick's youth had been deeper than others, so its effect was more lasting. It might gradually disappear. He was confident, indeed, that it would. He had been reading on the subject all day.

Walter Wheeler hardly heard him. He was facing the incredible fact, and struggling with his own problem. After a time he got up, shook hands with David and went home, the dog at his heels.

During the evening that followed he made his resolution,

not to tell her, never to let her suspect the truth. But he began to wonder if she had heard something, for he found her eyes on him more than once, and when Margaret had gone up to bed she came over and sat on the arm of his chair. She said an odd thing then, and one that made it impossible to lie to her later.

"I come to you, a good bit as I would go to God, if he were a person," she said. "I have got to know something, and you can tell me."

He put his arm around her and held her close.

"Go ahead, honey."

"Daddy, do you realize that I am a woman now?"

"I try to. But it seems about six months since I was feeding you hot water for colic."

She sat still for a moment, stroking his hair and being very careful not to spoil his neat parting.

"You have never told me all about Dick, daddy. You have always kept something back. That's true, isn't it?"

"There were details," he said uncomfortably. "It wasn't necessary——"

"Here's what I want to know. If he has gone back to the time—you know, wouldn't he go back to caring for the people he loved then?" Then, suddenly, her childish appeal ceased, and she slid from the chair and stood before him. "I must know, father. I can bear it. The thing you have been keeping from me was another woman, wasn't it?"

"It was so long ago," he temporized. "Think of it, Elizabeth. A boy of twenty-one or so."

"Then there was?"

"I believe so, at one time. But I know positively that he hadn't seen or heard from her in ten years."

"What sort of woman?"

"I wouldn't think about it, honey. It's all so long ago."

"Did she live in Wyoming?"

"She was an actress," he said, hard driven by her persistence.

"Do you know her name?"

"Only Her stage name, honey."

"But you know she was an actress!"

He sighed.

"All right, dear," he said. "I'll tell you all I know. She was an actress, and she married another man. That's all there is to it. She's not young now. She must be thirty now—if she's living," he added, as an afterthought.

It was some time before she spoke again.

"I suppose she was beautiful," she said slowly.

"I don't know. Most of them aren't, off the stage. Anyhow, what does it matter now?"

"Only that I know he has gone back to her. And you know it too."

He heard her going quietly out of the room.

Long after, he closed the house and went cautiously upstairs. She was waiting for him in the doorway of her room, in her nightgown.

"I know it all now," she said steadily. "It was because of her he shot the other man, wasn't it?"

She saw her answer in his startled face, and closed her door quickly. He stood outside, and then he tapped lightly.

"Let me in, honey," he said. "I want to finish it. You've got a wrong idea about it."

When she did not answer he tried the door, but it was locked. He turned and went downstairs again. . . . .

When he came home the next afternoon Margaret met him in the hall.

"She knows it, Walter."

"Knows what?"

"Knows he was back here and didn't see her. Annie blurted it out; she'd got it from the Oglethorpe's laundress. Mr. Oglethorpe saw him on the street."

It took him some time to drag a coherent story from her. Annie had told Elizabeth in her room, and then had told Margaret. She had gone to Elizabeth at once, to see what she could do, but Elizabeth had been in her closet, digging among her clothes. She had got out her best frock and put it on, while her mother sat on the bed not even daring to broach the matter in her mind, and had gone out. There was a sort of cold determination in her that frightened Margaret. She had laughed a good bit, for one thing.

"She's terribly proud," she finished. "She'll do something reckless, I'm sure. It wouldn't surprise me to see her come back engaged to Wallie Sayre. I think that's where she went."

But apparently she had not, or if she had she said nothing about it. From that time on they saw a change in her; she was as loving as ever, but she affected a sort of painful brightness that was a little hard. As though she had clad herself in armor against further suffering.

Chapter Forty-one

FOR MONTHS Beverly Carlysle had remained a remote and semi-mysterious figure. She had been in some hearts and in many minds, but to most of them she was a name only. She had been the motive behind events she never heard of, the quiet center in a tornado of emotions that circled about without touching her.

On the whole she found her life, with the settling down of the piece to a successful run, one of prosperous monotony. She had re-opened and was living in the 56th Street house, keeping a simple establishment of cook, butler and maid, and in the early fall she added a town car and a driver. After that she drove out every afternoon except on matinee days, almost always alone, but sometimes with a young girl from the company.

She was very lonely. The kaleidoscope that is theatrical New York had altered since she left it. Only one or two of her former friends remained, and she found them uninteresting and narrow with the narrowness of their own absorbing world. She had forgotten that the theater was like an island, cut off from the rest of the world, having its own politics, its own society divided by caste, almost its own religion. Out of its insularity it made occasional excursions to dinners and weekends; even into marriage, now and then with an outlander. But almost always it went back, eager for its home of dressing-room and footlights, of stage entrances up dirty alleys, of door-keepers and managers and parts and costumes.

Occasionally she had callers, men she had met or who were brought to see her. She saw them over a tea-table, judged them remorselessly, and eliminated gradually all but one or two. She watched her dignity and her reputation with the care of an ambitious woman trying to live down the past, and she succeeded measurably well. Now and then a critic spoke of her as a second Maude Adams, and those notices she kept and treasured.

But she was always uneasy. Never since the night he had seen Judson Clark in the theater had they rung up without her brother having carefully combed the house with his eyes. She knew her limitations; they would have to ring down if she ever saw him over the footlights. And the season had brought its incidents, to connect her with the past. One night Gregory had come back and told her Jean Melis was in the balcony. The valet was older and heavier, but he had recognized him.

"Did he see you?" was her first question.

"Yes. What about it? He never saw me but once, and that was at night and out of doors."

"Sometimes I think I can't stand it, Fred. The eternal suspense, the waiting for something to happen."

"If anything was going to happen it would have happened months ago. Bassett has given it up. And Jud's dead. Even Wilkins knows that."

She turned on him angrily.

"You haven't a heart, have you? You're glad he's dead."

"Not at all. As long as he kept under cover he was all right. But if he is, I don't see why you should fool yourself into thinking you're sorry. It's the best solution to a number of things."

"What do you suppose brought Jean Melis here?"

"What? To see the best play in New York. Besides, why not allow the man a healthy curiosity? He was pretty closely connected with a hectic part of your life, my dear. Now buck up, and for the Lord's sake forget the Frenchman. He's got nothing."

"He saw me that night, on the stairs. He never took his eyes off me at the inquest."

She gave, however, an excellent performance that night, and nothing more was heard of the valet.

There were other alarms, all of them without foundation. She went on her way, rejected an offer or two of marriage, spent her mornings in bed and her afternoons driving or in the hands of her hair-dresser and manicure, cared for the flowers that came in long casket-like boxes, and began to feel a sense of security again. She did not intend to marry, or to become interested in any one man.

She had hardly given a thought to Leslie Ward. He had come and gone, one of that steady procession of men, mostly married, who battered their heads now and then like night beetles outside a window, against the hard glass of her ambition. Because her business was to charm, she had been charming to him. And could not always remember his name!

As the months went by she began to accept Fred's verdict that nothing was going to happen. Bassett was back and at work. Either dead or a fugitive somewhere was Judson Clark, but that thought she had to keep out of her mind. Sometimes, as the play went on, and she was able to make her solid investments out of it, she wondered if her ten years of retirement had been all the price she was to pay for his ruin; but she put that thought away too, although she never minimized her responsibility when she faced it.

But her price had been heavy at that. She was childless and alone, lavishing her aborted maternity on a brother who was living his prosperous, cheerful and not too moral life at her expense. Fred was, she knew, slightly drunk with success; he attended to his minimum of labor with the least possible effort, had an expensive apartment on the Drive, and neglected her except when he needed money. She began to see, as other women had seen before her, that her success had, by taking away the necessity for initiative, been extremely bad for him.

That was the situation when, one night late in October, the trap of Bassett's devising began to close in. It had been raining, but in spite of that they had sold standing room to the fire limit. Having got the treasurer's report on the night's business and sent it to Beverly's dressing-room, Gregory wandered into his small, low-ceiled office under the balcony staircase, and closing the door sat down. It was the interval after the second act, and above the hum of voices outside the sound of the orchestra penetrated faintly.

He was entirely serene. He had a supper engagement after the show, he had a neat car waiting outside to take him to it, and the night's business had been extraordinary. He consulted his watch and then picked up an evening paper. A few moments later he found himself reading over and over a small notice inserted among the personals.

"Personal: Jean Melis, who was in Norada, Wyoming, during the early fall of 1911, please communicate with L 22, this office."

The orchestra was still playing outside; the silly, giggling crowds were moving back to their seats, and somewhere Jean Melis, or the friends of Jean Melis, who would tell him of it, were reading that message.

He got his hat and went out, forgetful of the neat car at the curb, of the supper engagement, of the night's business, and wandered down the street through the rain. But his first uneasiness passed quickly. He saw Bassett in the affair, and probably Clark himself, still living and tardily determined to clear his name. But if the worst came to the worst, what could they do? They could go only so far, and then they would have to quit.

It would be better, however, if they did not see Melis. Much better; there was no use involving a simple situation. And Bev could be kept out of it altogether, until it was over. Ashamed of his panic he went back to the theater, got a railway schedule and looked up trains. He should have done it long before, he recognized, have gone to Bassett in the spring. But how could he have known then that Bassett was going to make a lifework of the case?

He had only one uncertainty. Suppose that Bassett had learned about Clifton Hines?

By the time the curtain rang down on the last act he was his dapper, debonair self again, made his supper engagement, danced half the night, and even dozed a little on the way home. But he slept badly and was up early, struggling with the necessity for keeping Jean Melis out of the way.

He wondered through what formalities L 22, for instance, would have to go in order to secure a letter addressed to him? Whether he had to present a card or whether he walked in, demanded his mail and went away. That thought brought another with it. Wasn't it probable that Bassett was in New York, and would call for his mail himself?

He determined finally to take the chance, claim to be L 22, and if Melis had seen the advertisement and replied, get the letter. It would be easy to square it with the valet, by saying that he had recognized him in the theater and that Miss Carlysle wished to send him a box.

He had small hope of a letter at his first call, unless the Frenchman had himself seen the notice, but his anxiety drove him early to the office. There was nothing there, but he learned one thing. He had to go through with no formalities. The clerk merely looked in a box, said "Nothing here," and went on about his business. At eleven o'clock he went back again, and after a careful scrutiny of the crowd presented himself once more.

"L 22? Here you are."

He had the letter in his hand. He had glanced at it and had thrust it deep in his pocket, when he felt a hand on his shoulder. He wheeled and faced Bassett.

"I thought I recognized that back," said the reporter, cheerfully. "Come over here, old man. I want to talk to you."

But he held to Gregory's shoulder. In a corner Bassett dropped the friendliness he had assumed for the clerk's benefit, and faced him with cold anger.

"I'll have that letter now, Gregory," he said. "And I've got a damned good notion to lodge an information against you."

"I don't know what you're talking about."

"Forget it. I was behind you when you asked for that letter. Give it here. I want to show you something."

Suddenly, with the letter in his hand, Bassett laughed and then tore it open. There was only a sheet of blank paper inside.

"I wasn't sure you'd see it, and I didn't think you'd fall for it if you did," he observed. "But I was pretty sure you didn't want me to see Melis. Now I know it."

"Well, I didn't," Gregory said sullenly.

"Just the same, I expect to see him. The day's early yet, and that's not a common name. But I'll take darned good care you don't get any more letters from here."

"What do you think Melis can tell you, that you don't know?"

"I'll explain that to you some day," Bassett said cheerfully. "Some day when you are in a more receptive mood than you are now. The point at this moment seems to me to be, what does Melis know that you don't want me to know? I suppose you don't intend to tell me?"

"Not here. You may believe it or not, Bassett, but I was going to your town to-night to see you."

"Well," Bassett said sceptically, "I've got your word for it. And I've got nothing to do all day but to listen to you."

To his proposition that they go to his hotel Gregory assented sullenly, and they moved out to find a taxicab. On the pavement, however, he held back.

"I've got a right to know something," he said, "considering what he's done to me and mine. Clark's alive, I suppose?"

"He's alive all right."

"Then I'll trade you, Bassett. I'll come over with what I know, if you'll tell me one thing. What sent him into hiding for ten years, and makes him turn up now, yelling for help?"

Bassett reflected. The offer of a statement from Gregory was valuable, but, on the other hand, he was anxious not to influence his narrative. And Gregory saw his uncertainty. He planted himself firmly on the pavement.

"How about it?" he demanded.

"I'll tell you this much, Gregory. He never meant to bring the thing up again. In a way, it's me you're up against. Not Clark. And you can be pretty sure I know what I'm doing. I've got Clark, and I've got the report of the coroner's inquest, and I'll get Melis. I'm going to get to the bottom of this if I have to dig a hole that buries me."

In a taxicab Gregory sat tense and erect, gnawing at his blond mustache. After a time he said:

"What are you after, in all this? The story, I suppose. And the money. I daresay you're not doing it for love."

Bassett surveyed him appraisingly.

"You wouldn't understand my motives if I told you. As a matter of fact, he doesn't want the money."

Gregory sneered.

"Don't kid yourself," he said. "However, as a matter of fact I don't think he'll take it. It might cost too much. Where is he? Shooting pills again?"

"You'll see him in about five minutes."

If the news was a surprise Gregory gave no evidence of it, except to comment:

"You're a capable person, aren't you? I'll bet you could tune a piano if you were put to it."

He carried the situation well, the reporter had to admit; the only evidence he gave of strain was that the hands with which he lighted a cigarette were unsteady. He surveyed the obscure hotel at which the cab stopped with a sneering smile, and settled his collar as he looked it over.

"Not advertising to the world that you're in town, I see."

"We'll do that, just as soon as we're ready. Don't worry."

The laugh he gave at that struck unpleasantly on Bassett's ears. But inside the building he lost some of his jauntiness. "Queer place to find Judson Clark," he said once.

And again:

"You'd better watch him when I go in. He may bite me." To which Bassett grimly returned: "He's probably rather particular what he bites."

He was uneasily conscious that Gregory, while nervous and tense, was carrying the situation with a certain assurance. If he was acting it was very good acting. And that opinion was strengthened when he threw open the door and Gregory advanced into the room.

"Well, Clark," he said, cooly. "I guess you didn't expect to see me, did you?"

He made no offer to shake hands as Dick turned from the window, nor did Dick make any overtures. But there was no enmity at first in either face; Gregory was easy and assured, Dick grave, and, Bassett thought, slightly impatient. From that night in his apartment the reporter had realized that he was constantly fighting a sort of passive resistance in Dick, a determination not at any cost to involve Beverly. Behind that, too, he felt that still another battle was going on, one at which he could only guess, but which made Dick somber at times and grimly quiet always.

"I meant to look you up," was his reply to Gregory's nonchalant greeting.

"Well, your friend here did that for you," Gregory said, and smiled across at Bassett. "He has his own methods, and I'll say they're effectual."

He took off his overcoat and flung it on the bed, and threw a swift, appraising glance at Dick. It was on Dick that he was banking, not on Bassett. He hated and feared Bassett. He hated Dick, but he was not afraid of him. He lighted a cigarette and faced Dick with a malicious smile.

"So here we are, again, Jud!" he said. "But with this change, that now it's you who are the respectable member of the community, and I'm the—well, we'll call it the butterfly."

There was unmistakable insult in his tone, and Dick caught it.

"Then I take it you're still living off your sister?"

The contempt in Dick's voice whipped the color to Gregory's face and clenched his fist. But he relaxed in a moment and laughed.

"Don't worry, Bassett," he said, his eyes on Dick. "We haven't any reason to like each other, but he's bigger than I am. I won't hit him." Then he hardened his voice. "But I'll remind you, Clark, that personally I don't give a God-damn whether you swing or not. Also that I can keep my mouth shut, walk out of here, and have you in quod in the next hour, if I decide to."

"But you won't," Bassett said smoothly. "You won't any more than you did it last spring, when you sent that little letter of yours to David Livingstone."

"No. You're right. I won't. But if I tell you what I came here to say, Bassett, get this straight. It's not because I'm afraid of you, or of *him*. Donaldson's dead. What value would Melis's testimony have after ten years, if you put him on the stand? It's not that. It's because you'll put your blundering foot into it and ruin Bev's career, unless I tell you the truth."

It was to Bassett then that he told his story, he and Bassett sitting, Dick standing with his elbow on the mantel-piece, tall and weary and almost detached.

"I've got to make my own position plain in this," he said. "I didn't like Clark, and I kept her from marrying him. There was one time, before she met Lucas, when she almost did it. I was away when she decided on that fool trip to the Clark ranch. We couldn't get a New York theater until November, and she had some time, so they went. I've got her story of what happened there. You can check it up with what you know."

He turned to Dick for a moment.

"You were drinking pretty hard that night, but you may remember this: She had quarreled with Lucas at dinner that night and with you. That's true, isn't it?"

"Yes."

"She went to her room and began to pack her things. Then she thought it over, and she decided to try to persuade Lucas to go too. Things had begun all right, but they were getting strained and unpleasant. She went down the stairs, and Melis saw her, the valet. The living-room was dark, but there was a light coming through the billiard room door, and against it she saw the figure of a man in the doorway. He had his back to her, and he had a revolver in his hand. She ran across the room when he heard her and when he turned she saw it was Lucas. Do you remember, Jud, having a revolver and Lucas taking it from you?"

"No. Donaldson testified I'd had a revolver."

"Well, that's how we figure he'd got the gun. She thought at once that Lucas and you had quarreled, and that he was going to shoot. She tried to take it from him, but he was drunk and stubborn. It went off and killed him."

Bassett leaned forward.

"That's straight, is it?"

"I'm telling you."

"Then why in God's name didn't she say that at the inquest?"

"She was afraid it wouldn't be believed. Look at the facts. She'd quarreled with Lucas. There had been a notorious situation with regard to Clark. And remember this. She *had* done it. I know her well enough, however, to say that she would have confessed, eventually, but Clark had beaten it. It was reasonably sure that he was lost in the blizzard. You've got to allow for that."

Bassett said nothing. After a silence Dick spoke:

"What about the revolver?"

"She had it in her hand. She dropped it and stood still, too stunned to scream. Lucas, she says, took a step or two forward, and fell through the doorway. Donaldson came running in, and you know the rest."

Bassett was the first to break the silence.

"She will be willing to testify to that now, of course?"

"And stand trial?"

"Not necessarily. Clark would be on trial. He's been indicted. He has to be tried."

"Why does he have to be tried? He's free now. He's been free for ten years. And I tell you as an honest opinion that the thing would kill her. Accident and all, she did it. And there would be some who'd never believe she hadn't tired of Lucas, and wanted the Clark money."

"That's a chance she'll have to take," Bassett said doggedly.

"The only living witness who could be called would be the valet. And remember this: for ten years he has believed that she did it. He'll have built up a story by this time, perhaps unconsciously, that might damn her."

Dick moved.

"There's only one thing to do. You're right, Gregory. I'll never expose her to that."

"You're crazy," Bassett said angrily.

"Not at all. I told you I wouldn't hide behind a woman. As a matter of fact, I've learned what I wanted. Lucas wasn't murdered. I didn't shoot him. That's what really matters. I'm no worse off than I was before; considerably better, in fact. And I don't see what's to be gained by going any further."

In spite of his protests, Bassett was compelled finally to agree. He was sulky and dispirited. He saw the profound anticlimax to all his effort of Dick wandering out again, legally dead and legally guilty, and he swore roundly under his breath.

"All right," he grunted at last. "I guess that's the last word, Gregory. But you tell her from me that if she doesn't reopen the matter of her own accord, she'll have a man's life on her conscience."

"I'll not tell her anything about it. I'm not only her brother; I'm her manager now. And I'm not kicking any hole in the boat that floats me."

He was self-confident and slightly insolent; the hands with which he lighted a fresh cigarette no longer trembled, and the glance he threw at Dick was triumphant and hostile.

"As a man sows, Clark!" he said. "You sowed hell for a number of people once."

Bassett had to restrain an impulse to kick him out of the door. When he had gone Bassett turned to Dick with assumed lightness.

"Well," he said, "here we are, all dressed up and nowhere to go!"

He wandered around the room, restless and disappointed. He knew, and Dick knew, that they had come to the end of the road, and that nothing lay beyond. In his own unpleasant way Fred Gregory had made a case for his sister that tied their hands, and the crux of the matter had lain in his final gibe: "As a man sows, Clark, so shall he reap." The moral issue was there.

"I suppose the Hines story goes by the board, eh?" he commented after a pause.

"Yes. Except that I wish I'd known about him when I could have done something. He's my half-brother, any way you look at it, and he had a rotten deal. Sometimes a man sows," he added, with a wry smile, "and the other fellow reaps."

Bassett went out after that, going to the office on the chance of a letter from Melis, but there was none. When he came back he found Dick standing over a partially packed suitcase, and knew that they had come to the end of the road indeed.

"What's the next step?" he asked bluntly.

"I'll have to leave here. It's too expensive."

"And after that, what?"

"I'll get a job. I suppose a man is as well hidden here as anywhere. I can grow a beard—that's the usual thing, isn't it?"

Bassett made an impatient gesture, and fell to pacing the floor. "It's incredible," he said. "It's monstrous. It's a joke. Here you are, without a thing against you, and hung like Mahomet's coffin between heaven and earth. It makes me sick."

He went home that night, leaving word to have any letters for L 22 forwarded, but without much hope. His last clutch of Dick's hand had a sort of desperate finality in it, and he carried with him most of the way home the tall, worn and rather shabby figure that saw him off with a smile. . . .

By the next afternoon's mail he received a note from New York, with a few words of comment penciled on it in Dick's writing. "This came this evening. I sent back the money. D." The note was from Gregory and had evidently enclosed a one-hundred dollar bill. It began without superscription: "Enclosed find a hundred dollars, as I imagine funds may be short. If I were you I'd get out of here. There has been considerable excitement, and you know too many people in this burg."

Bassett sat back in his chair and studied the note.

"Now why the devil did he do that?" he reflected. He sat for some time, thinking deeply, and he came to one important conclusion. The story Gregory had told was the one which was absolutely calculated to shut off all further inquiry. They had had ten years; ten years to plan, eliminate and construct; ten years to prepare their defense, in case Clark turned up. Wasn't that why Gregory had been so assured? But he had not been content to let well enough alone; he had perhaps overreached himself.

Then what was the answer? She had killed Lucas, but was it an accident? And there must have been a witness, or they would have had nothing to fear. He wrote out on a bit of paper three names, and sat looking at them:

Hattie Thorwald

Jean Melis

Clifton Hines.

Chapter Forty-two

ELIZABETH HAD quite definitely put Dick out of her heart. On the evening of the day she learned he had come back and had not seen her, she deliberately killed her love and decently interred it. She burned her notes and his one letter and put away her ring, performing the rites not as rites but as a shameful business to be done with quickly. She tore his photograph into bits and threw them into her waste basket, and having thus housecleaned her room set to work to houseclean her heart.

She found very little to do. She was numb and totally without feeling. The little painful constriction in her chest which had so often come lately with her thoughts of him was gone. She felt extraordinarily empty, but not light, and her feet dragged about the room.

She felt no sense of Dick's unworthiness, but simply that she was up against something she could not fight, and no longer wanted to fight. She was beaten, but the strange thing was that she did not care. Only, she would not be pitied. As the days went on she resented the pity that had kept her in ignorance for so long, and had let her wear her heart on her sleeve; and she even wondered sometimes whether the story of Dick's loss of memory had not been false, evolved out of that pity and the desire to save her pain.

David sent for her, but she wrote him a little note, formal and restrained. She would come in a day or two, but now she must get her bearings. He was to know that she was not angry, and felt it all for the best, and she was very lovingly his, Elizabeth.

She knew now that she would eventually marry Wallie Sayre if only to get away from pity. He would have to know the truth about her, that she did not love any one; not even her father and her mother. She pretended to care for fear of hurting them, but she was actually frozen quite hard. She did not believe in love. It was a terrible thing, to be avoided by any one who wanted to get along, and his avoiding was really quite simple. One simply stopped feeling.

On the Sunday after she had come to this comfortable knowledge she sat in the church as usual, in the choir stalls, and suddenly she hated the church. She hated the way the larnyx of Henry Wallace, the tenor, stuck out like a crabapple over his low collar. She hated the fat double chin of the bass. She hated the talk about love and the certain rewards of virtue, and the faces of the congregation, smug and sure of salvation.

She went to the choir master after the service to hand in her resignation. And did not, because it had occurred to her that it might look, to use Nina's word, as though she were crushed. Crushed! That was funny.

Wallie Sayre was waiting for her outside, and she went up with him to lunch, and afterwards they played golf. They had rather an amusing game, and once she had to sit down on a bunker and laugh until she was weak, while he fought his way out of a pit. Crushed, indeed!

So the weaving went on, almost completed now. With Wallie Sayre biding his time, but fairly sure of the result. With Jean Melis happening on a two-days' old paper, and reading over and over a notice addressed to him. With Leslie Ward, neither better nor worse than his kind, seeking adventure in a bypath, which was East 56th Street. And with Dick wandering the streets of New York after twilight, and standing once with his coat collar turned up against the rain outside of the Metropolitan Club, where the great painting of his father hung over a mantelpiece.

Now that he was near Beverly, Dick hesitated to see her. He felt no resentment at her long silence, nor at his exile which had resulted from it. He made excuses for her, recognized his own contribution to the catastrophe, knew, too, that nothing was to be gained by seeing her again. But he determined finally to see her once more, and then to go away, leaving her to peace and to success.

She would know now that she had nothing to fear from him. All he wanted was to satisfy the hunger that was in him by seeing her, and then to go away.

Curiously, that hunger to see her had been in abeyance while Bassett was with him. It was only when he was alone again that it came up; and although he knew that, he was unconscious of another fact, that every word, every picture of her on the great boardings which walled in every empty lot, everything, indeed, which brought her into the reality of the present, loosened by so much her hold on him out of the past.

When he finally went to the 56th Street house it was on impulse. He had meant to pass it, but he found himself stopping, and half angrily made his determination. He would follow the cursed thing through now and get it over. Perhaps he had discounted it too much in advance, waited too long, hoped too much. Perhaps it was simply that that last phase was already passing. But he felt no thrill, no expectancy, as he rang the bell and was admitted to the familiar hall.

It was peopled with ghosts, for him. Upstairs, in the drawing-room that extended across the front of the house, she had told him of her engagement to Howard Lucas. Later on, coming back from Europe, he had gone back there to find Lucas installed in the house, his cigars on the table, his photographs on the piano, his books scattered about. And Lucas himself, smiling, handsome and triumphant on the hearth rug, dressed for dinner except for a brocaded dressing-gown, putting his hand familiarly on Beverly's shoulder, and calling her "old girl."

He wandered into the small room to the right of the hall, where in other days he had waited to be taken upstairs, and stood looking out of the window. He heard some one, a caller, come down, get into his overcoat in the hall and go out, but he was not interested. He did not know that Leslie Ward had stood outside the door for a minute, had seen and recognized him, and had then slammed out.

He was quite steady as the butler preceded him up the stairs. He even noticed certain changes in the house, the door at the landing converted into an arch, leaded glass in the dining-room windows beyond it. But he caught a glimpse of himself in a mirror, and saw himself a shabby contrast to the former days.

He faced her, still with that unexpected composure, and he saw her very little changed. Even the movement with which she came toward him with both hands out was familiar.

"Jud!" she said. "Oh, my dear!"

He saw that she was profoundly moved, and suddenly he was sorry for her. Sorry for the years behind them both, for the burden she had carried, for the tears in her eyes.

"Dear old Bev!" he said.

She put her head against his shoulder, and cried unrestrainedly; and he held her there, saying small, gentle, soothing things, smoothing her hair. But all the time he knew that life had been playing him another trick; he felt a great tenderness for her and profound pity, but he did not love her, or want her. He saw that after all the suffering and waiting, the death and exile, he was left at the end with nothing. Nothing at all.

When she was restored to a sort of tense composure he found to his discomfort that woman-like she intended to abase herself thoroughly and completely. She implored his forgiveness for his long exile, gazing at him humbly, and when he said in a matter-of-fact tone that he had been happy, giving him a look which showed that she thought he was lying to save her unhappiness.

"You are trying to make it easier for me. But I know, Jud."

"I'm telling you the truth," he said, patiently. "There's one point I didn't think necessary to tell your brother. For a good while I didn't remember anything about it. If it hadn't been for that—well, I don't know. Anyhow, don't look at me as though I willfully saved you. I didn't."

She sat still, pondering that, and twisting a ring on her finger.

"What do you mean to do?" she asked, after a pause.

"I don't know. I'll find something."

"You won't go back to your work?"

"I don't see how I can. I'm in hiding, in a sort of casual fashion."

To his intense discomfiture she began to cry again. She couldn't go through with it. She would go back to Norada and tell the whole thing. She had let Fred influence her, but she saw now she couldn't do it. But for the first time he felt that in this one thing she was not sincere. Her grief and abasement had been real enough, but now he felt she was acting.

"Suppose we don't go into that now," he said gently. "You've had about all you can stand." He got up awkwardly. "I suppose you are playing to-night?"

She nodded, looking up at him dumbly.

"Better lie down, then, and—forget me." He smiled down at her.

"I've never forgotten you, Jud. And now, seeing you again—I——"

Her face worked. She continued to look up at him, piteously. The appalling truth came to him then, and that part of him which had remained detached and aloof, watching, almost smiled at the irony. She cared for him. Out of her memories she had built up something to care for, something no more himself than she was the woman of his dreams; but with this difference, that she was clinging, woman-fashion, to the thing she had built, and he had watched it crumble before his eyes.

"Will you promise to go and rest?"

"Yes. If you say so."

She was acquiescent and humble. Her eyes were soft, faithful, childlike.

"I've suffered so, Jud."

"I know."

"You don't hate me, do you?"

"Why should I? Just remember this: while you were carrying this burden, I was happier than I'd ever been. I'll tell you about it some time."

She got up, and he perceived that she expected him again to take her in his arms. He felt ridiculous and resentful, and rather as though he was expected to kiss the hand that had beaten him, but when she came close to him he put an arm around her shoulders.

"Poor Bev!" he said. "We've made pretty much a mess of it, haven't we?"

He patted her and let her go, and her eyes followed him as he left the room. The elder brotherliness of that embrace had told her the truth as he could never have hurt her in words. She went back to the chair where he had sat, and leaned her cheek against it.

After a time she went slowly upstairs and into her room. When her maid came in she found her before the mirror of her dressing-table, staring at her reflection with hard, appraising eyes. . . . .

Leslie's partner, wandering into the hotel at six o'clock,

found from the disordered condition of the room that
Leslie had been back, had apparently bathed, shaved and
made a careful toilet, and gone out again. Joe found himself unexpectedly at a loose end. Filled with suppressed
indignation he commenced to dress, getting out a shirt,
hunting his evening studs, and lining up what he meant to
say to Leslie over his defection.

Then, at a quarter to seven, Leslie came in, top-hatted
and morning-coated, with a yellowing gardenia in his
buttonhole and his shoes covered with dust.

"Hello, Les," Joe said, glancing up from a laborious
struggle with a stud. "Been to a wedding?"

"Why?"

"You look like it."

"I made a call, and since then I've been walking."

"Some walk, I'd say," Joe observed, looking at him
shrewdly. "What's wrong, Les? Fair one turn you down?"

"Go to hell," Leslie said irritably.

He flung off his coat and jerked at his tie. Then, with it
hanging loose, he turned to Joe.

"I'm going to tell you something. I know it's safe with
you, and I need some advice. I called on a woman this
afternoon. You know who she is. Beverly Carlysle."

Joe whistled softly.

"That's not the point," Leslie declaimed, in a truculent
voice. "I'm not defending myself. She's a friend; I've got
a right to call there if I want to."

"Sure you have," soothed Joe.

"Well, you know the situation at home, and who Livingstone actually is. The point is that, while that poor kid at
home is sitting around killing herself with grief, Clark's
gone back to her. To Beverly Carlysle."

"How do you know?"

"Know? I saw him this afternoon, at her house."

He sat still, moodily reviewing the situation. His
thoughts were a chaotic and unpleasant mixture of jealousy,
fear of Nina, anxiety over Elizabeth, and the sense of a
lost romantic adventure. After a while he got up.

"She's a nice kid," he said. "I'm fond of her. And I
don't know what to do."

Suddenly Joe grinned.

"I see," he said. "And you can't tell her, or the family,

where you saw him!"

"Not without raising the deuce of a row."

He began, automatically, to dress for dinner. Joe moved around the room, rang for a waiter, ordered orange juice and ice, and produced a bottle of gin from his bag. Leslie did not hear him, nor the later preparation of the cocktails. He was reflecting bitterly on the fact that a man who married built himself a wall against romance, a wall compounded of his own new sense of responsibility, of family ties, and fear.

Joe brought him a cocktail.

"Drink it, old dear," he said. "And when it's down I'll tell you a few little things about playing around with ladies who have a past. Here's to forgetting 'em."

Leslie took the glass.

"Right-o," he said.

He went home the following day, leaving Joe to finish the business in New York. His going rather resembled a flight. Tossing sleepless the night before, he had found what many a man had discovered before him, that his love of clandestine adventure was not as strong as his caution. He had had a shock. True, his affair with Beverly had been a formless thing, a matter of imagination and a desire to assure himself that romance, for him, was not yet dead. True, too, that he had nothing to fear from Dick Livingstone. But the encounter had brought home to him the danger of this old-new game he was playing. He was running like a frightened child.

He thought of various plans. One of them was to tell Nina the truth, take his medicine of tears and coldness, and then go to Mr. Wheeler. One was to go to Mr. Wheeler, without Nina, and make his humiliating admission. But Walter Wheeler had his own rigid ideas, was uncompromising in rectitude, and would understand as only a man could that while so far he had been only mentally unfaithful, he had been actuated by at least subconscious desire.

His own awareness of that fact made him more cautious than he need have been, perhaps more self-conscious. And he genuinely cared for Elizabeth. It was, on the whole, a generous and kindly impulse that lay behind his ultimate resolution to tell her that her desertion was both wilful and cruel.

Yet, when the time came, he found it hard to tell her. He took her for a drive one evening soon after his return, forcibly driving off Wallie Sayre to do so, and eying surreptitiously now and then her pale, rather set face. He found a quiet lane and stopped the car there, and then turned and faced her.

"How've you been, little sister, while I've been wandering the gay white way?" he asked.

"I've been all right, Leslie."

"Not quite all right, I think. Have you ever thought, Elizabeth, that no man on earth is worth what you've been going through?"

"I'm all right, I tell you," she said impatiently. "I'm not grieving any more. That's the truth, Les. I know now that he doesn't intend to come back, and I don't care. I never even think about him, now."

"I see," he said. "Well, that's that."

But he had not counted on her intuition, and was startled to hear her say:

"Well? Go on."

"What do you mean, go on?"

"You brought me out here to tell me something."

"Not at all. I simply——"

"Where is he? You've seen him."

He tried to meet her eyes, failed, cursed himself for a fool.

"He's alive and well, Elizabeth. I saw him in New York."

It was a full minute before she spoke again, and then her lips were stiff and her voice strained.

"Has he gone back to her? To the actress he used to care for?"

He hesitated, but he knew he would have to go on.

"I'm going to tell you something, Elizabeth. It's not very creditable to me, but I'll have to trust you. I don't want to see you wasting your life. You've got plenty of courage and a lot of spirit. And you've got to forget him."

He told her, and then he took her home. He was a little frightened, for there was something not like her in the way she had taken it, a sort of immobility that might, he thought, cover heartbreak. But she smiled when she thanked him, and went very calmly into the house.

That night she accepted Wallie Sayre.

Chapter Forty-three

BASSETT WAS having a visitor. He sat in his chair while that visitor ranged excitedly up and down the room, a short stout man, well dressed and with a mixture of servility and importance. The valet's first words, as he stood inside the door, had been significant.

"I should like to know, first, if I am talking to the police."

"No—and yes," Bassett said genially. "Come and sit down, man. What I mean is this. I am a friend of Judson Clark's, and this may or may not be a police matter. I don't know yet."

"You are a friend of Mr. Clark's? Then the report was correct. He is still alive, sir?"

"Yes."

The valet got out a handkerchief and wiped his face. He was clearly moved.

"I am glad of that. Very glad. I saw some months ago, in a newspaper—where is he?"

"In New York. Now Melis, I've an idea that you know something about the crime Judson Clark was accused of. You intimated that at the inquest."

"Mrs. Lucas killed him."

"So she says," Bassett said easily.

The valet jumped and stared.

"She admits it, as the result of an accident. She also admits hiding the revolver where you found it."

"Then you do not need me."

"I'm not so sure of that."

The valet was puzzled.

"I want you to think back, Melis. You saw her go down the stairs, sometime before the shot. Later you were confident she had hidden the revolver, and you made a second search for it. Why? You hadn't heard her testimony at the inquest then. Clark had run away. Why didn't you think Clark had done it?"

"Because I thought she was having an affair with another man. I have always thought she did it."

Bassett nodded.

"I thought so. What made you think that?"

"I'll tell you. She went West without a maid, and Mr. Clark got a Swedish woman from a ranch near to look after her, a woman named Thorwald. She lived at her own place and came over every day. One night, after Mrs. Thorwald had started home, I came across her down the road near the irrigator's house, and there was a man with her. They didn't hear me behind them, and he was giving her a note for some one in the house."

"Why not for one of the servants?"

"That's what I thought then, sir. It wasn't my business. But I saw the same man later on, hanging about the place at night, and once I saw her with him—Mrs. Lucas, I mean. That was in the early evening. The gentlemen were out riding, and I'd gone with one of the maids to a hill to watch the moon rise. They were on some rocks, below in the canyon."

"Did you see him?"

"I think it was the same man, if that's what you mean. I knew something queer was going on, after that, and I watched her. She went out at night more than once. Then I told Donaldson there was somebody hanging round the place, and he set a watch."

"Fine. Now we'll go to the night Lucas was shot. Was the Thorwald woman there?"

"She had started home."

"Leaving Mrs. Lucas packing alone?"

"Yes. I hadn't thought of that. The Thorwald woman heard the shot and came back. I remember that, because she fainted upstairs and I had to carry her to a bed."

"I see. Now about the revolver."

"I located it the first time I looked for it. Donaldson and the others had searched the billiard room. So I tried the big room. It was under a chair. I left it there, and concealed myself in the room. She, Mrs. Lucas, came down late that night and hunted for it. Then she hid it where I got it later."

"I wish I knew, Melis, why you didn't bring those facts out at the inquest."

"You must remember this, sir. I had been with Mr. Clark for a long time. I knew the situation. And I thought that he had gone away that night to throw suspicion from her to himself. I was not certain what to do. I would have told it all in court, but it never came to trial."

Bassett was satisfied and fairly content. After the Frenchman's departure he sat for some time, making careful notes and studying them. Supposing the man Melis had seen to be Clifton Hines, a good many things would be cleared up. Some new element he had to have, if Gregory's story were to be disproved, some new and different motive. Suppose, for instance . . . .

He got up and paced the floor back and forward, forward and back. There was just one possibility, and just one way of verifying it. He sat down and wrote out a long telegram and then got his hat and carried it to the telegraph office himself. He had made his last throw.

He received a reply the following day, and in a state of exhilaration bordering on madness packed his bag, and as he packed it addressed it, after the fashion of lonely men the world over.

"Just one more trip, friend cowhide," he said, "and then you and I are going to settle down again to work. But it's some trip, old arm-breaker."

He put in his pajamas and handkerchiefs, his clean socks and collars, and then he got his revolver from a drawer and added it. Just twenty-four hours later he knocked at Dick's door in a boarding-house on West Ninth Street, found it unlocked, and went in. Dick was asleep, and Bassett stood looking down at him with an odd sort of paternal affection. Finally he bent down and touched his shoulder.

"Wake up, old top," he said. "Wake up. I have some news for you."

Chapter Forty-four

TO DICK the last day or two had been nightmares of loneliness. He threw caution to the winds and walked hour after hour, only to find that the street crowds, people who had left a home or were going to one, depressed him and emphasized his isolation. He had deliberately put away from him the anchor that had been Elizabeth and had followed a treacherous memory, and now he was adrift. He told himself that he did not want much. Only peace, work and a place. But he had not one of them.

He was homesick for David, for Lucy, and, with a tightening of the heart he admitted it, for Elizabeth. And he had no home. He thought of Reynolds, bent over the desk in his office; he saw the quiet tree-shaded streets of the town, and Reynolds, passing from house to house in the little town, doing his work, usurping his place in the confidence and friendship of the people; he saw the very children named for him asking: "Who was I named for, mother?" He saw David and Lucy gone, and the old house abandoned, or perhaps echoing to the laughter of Reynolds' children.

He had moments when he wondered what would happen if he took Beverly at her word. Suppose she made her confession, re-opened the thing, to fill the papers with great headlines, "Judson Clark Not Guilty. A Strange Story."

He saw himself going back to the curious glances of the town, never to be to them the same as before. To face them and look them down, to hear whispers behind his back, to feel himself watched and judged, on that far past of his. Suppose even that it could be kept out of the papers; Wilkins amiable and acquiescent, Beverly's confession hidden in the ruck of legal documents; and he stealing back, to go on as best he could, covering his absence with lies, and taking up his work again. But even that uneasy road was closed to him. He saw David and Lucy stooping to new and strange hypocrisies, watching with anxious old eyes the faces of their neighbors, growing defiant and hard as time went on and suspicion still followed him.

And there was Elizabeth.

He tried not to think of her, save as of some fine and tender thing he had once brushed as he passed by. Even if she still cared for him, he could, even less than David and Lucy, ask her to walk the uneasy road with him. She was young. She would forget him and marry Wallace Sayre. She would have luxury and gaiety, and the things that belong to youth.

He was not particularly bitter about that. He knew now that he had given her real love, something very different from that early madness of his, but he knew it too late. . . . .

He looked up at Bassett and then sat up.

"What sort of news?" he asked, his voice still thick with sleep.

"Get up and put some cold water on your head. I want you to get this."

He obeyed, but without enthusiasm. Some new clue, some hope revived only to die again, what did it matter? But he stopped by Bassett and put a hand on his shoulder.

"Why do you do it?" he asked. "Why don't you let me go to the devil in my own way?"

"I started this, and by Heaven I've finished it," was Bassett's exultant reply.

He sat down and produced a bundle of papers. "I'm going to read you something," he said. "And when I'm through you're going to put your clothes on and we'll go to the Biltmore. The Biltmore. Do you get it?"

Then he began to read.

"I, the undersigned, being of sound mind, do hereby make the following statement. I make the statement of my own free will, and swear before Almighty God that it is the truth. I am an illegitimate son of Elihu Clark. My mother, Harriet Burgess, has since married and is now known as Hattie Thorwald. She will confirm the statements herein contained.

"I was adopted by a woman named Hines, of the city of Omaha, whose name I took. Some years later this woman married and had a daughter, of whom I shall speak later.

"I attended preparatory school in the East, and was sent during vacations to a tutoring school, owned by Mr. Henry Livingstone. When I went to college Mr. Livingstone bought a ranch at Dry River, Wyoming, and I spent some time there now and then.

"I learned that I was being supported and sent to college from funds furnished by a firm of New York lawyers, and that aroused my suspicion. I knew that Mrs. Hines was not my mother. I finally learned that I was the son of Elihu Clark and Harriet Burgess.

"I felt that I should have some part of the estate, and I developed a hatred for Judson Clark, whom I knew. I made one attempt to get money from him by mail, threatening to expose his father's story, but I did not succeed.

"I visited my mother, Hattie Thorwald, and threatened to kill Clark. I also threatened Henry Livingstone, and his death came during a dispute over the matter, but I did not kill him. He fell down and hit his head. He had a weak heart.

"My foster-sister had gone on the stage, and Clark was infatuated with her. I saw him a number of times, but he did not connect me with the letter I had sent. My foster-sister's stage name is Beverly Carlysle.

"She married Howard Lucas and they visited the Clark ranch at Norada, Wyoming, in the fall of 1911. I saw my sister there several times, and as she knew the way I felt she was frightened. My mother, Hattie Thorwald, was a sort of maid to her, and together they tried to get me to go away."

Bassett looked up.

"Up to that point," he said, "I wrote it myself before I saw him." There was a note of triumph in his voice. "The rest is his."

"On the night Lucas was killed I was to go away. Bev had agreed to give me some money, for the piece had quit in June and I was hard up. She was going to borrow it from Jud Clark, and that set me crazy. I felt it ought to be mine, or a part of it anyhow.

"I was to meet my mother in the grounds, but I missed her, and I went to the house. I wasn't responsible for what I did. I was crazy, I guess. I saw Donaldson on the side porch, and beyond him were Lucas and Clark, playing roulette. It made me wild. I couldn't have played roulette that night for pennies.

"I went around the house and in the front door. What I meant to do was to walk into that room and tell Clark who

I was. He knew me, and all I meant to do was to call Bev down, and mother, and make him sit up and take notice. I hadn't a gun on me.

"I swear I wasn't thinking of killing him then. I hated him like poison, but that was all. But I went into the living-room, and I heard Clark say he'd lost a thousand dollars. Maybe you don't get that. A thousand dollars thrown around like that, and me living on what Bev could borrow from him.

"That sent me wild. Lucas took a gun from him, just after that, and said he was going to put it in the other room. He did it, too. He put it on a table and started back. I got it and pointed it at Clark. I'd have shot him, too, but Bev came into the room.

"I want to exonerate Bev. She has been better than most sisters to me, and she has lied to try to save me. She came up behind me and grabbed my arm. Lucas had heard her, and he turned. I must have closed my hand on the trigger, for it went off and hit him.

"I was in the living-room when Donaldson ran in. I hid there until they were all gathered around Lucas and had quit running in, and then I got away. I saw my mother in the grounds later. I told her where the revolver was and that they'd better put it in the billiard room. I was afraid they'd suspect Bev.

I have read the above statement and it is correct. I was legally adopted by Mrs. Alice Ford Hines, of Omaha, and use that signature. I generally use the name of Frederick Gregory, which I took when I was on the stage for a short time.

(Signed) CLIFTON HINES.

Bassett folded up the papers and put them in the envelope. "I got that," he said, "at the point of a gun, my friend. And our friend Hines departed for the Mexican border on the evening train. I don't mind saying that I saw him off. He held out for a get-away, and I guess it's just as well."

He glanced at Dick, lying still and rigid on the bed.

"And now," he said. "I think a little drink won't do us any harm."

Dick refused to drink. He was endeavoring to comprehend the situation; to realize that Gregory, who had faced him with such sneering hate a day or so before, was his half-brother.

"Poor devil!" he said at last. "I wish to God I'd known. He was right, you know. No wonder——"

Sometime later he roused from deep study and looked at Bassett.

"How did you get the connection?"

"I saw Melis, and learned that Hines was in it somehow. He was the connecting link between Beverly Carlylse and the Thorwald woman. But I couldn't connect him with Beverly herself, except by a chance. I wired a man I knew in Omaha, and he turned up the second marriage, and a daughter known on the stage as Beverly Carlysle."

Bassett was in high spirits. He moved about the room immensely pleased with himself, slightly boastful.

"Some little stroke, Dick!" he said. "What price Mr. Judson Clark to-night, eh? It will be worth a million dollars to see Wilkins' face when he reads that thing."

"There's no mention of me as Livingstone in it, is there?"

"It wasn't necessary to go into that. I didn't know— Look here," he exploded, "you're not going to be a damned fool, are you?"

"I'm not going to revive Judson Clark, Bassett. I don't owe him anything. Let him die a decent death and stay dead."

"Oh, piffle!" Bassett groaned. "Don't start that all over again. Don't pull any Enoch Arden stuff on me, looking in at a lighted window and wandering off to drive a taxicab."

Suddenly Dick laughed. Bassett watched him, puzzled and angry, with a sort of savage tenderness.

"You're crazy," he said morosely. "Darned if I understand you. Here I've got everything fixed as slick as a whistle, and it took work, believe me. And now you say you're going to chuck the whole thing."

"Not at all," Dick replied, with a new ring in his voice. "You're right. I've been ten sorts of a fool, but I know now what I'm going to do. Take your paper, old friend, and for my sake go out and clear Jud Clark. Put up a headstone to him, if you like, a good one. I'll buy it."

"And what will you be doing in the meantime?"

Dick stretched and threw out his arms.

"Me?" he said. "What should I be doing, old man? I'm going home."

Chapter Forty-five

LUCY CROSBY was dead. One moment she was of the quick, moving about the house, glancing in at David, having Minnie in the kitchen pin and unpin her veil; and the next she was still and infinitely mysterious, on her white bed. She had fallen outside the door of David's room, and lay there, her arms still full of fresh bath towels, and a fixed and intense look in her eyes, as though, outside the door, she had come face to face with a messenger who bore surprising news. Doctor Reynolds, running up the stairs, found her there dead, and closed the door into David's room.

But David knew before they told him. He waited until they had placed her on her bed, had closed her eyes and drawn a white coverlet over her, and then he went in alone, and sat down beside her, and put a hand over her chilling one.

"If you are still here, Lucy," he said, "and have not yet gone on, I want you to carry this with you. We are all right, here. Everybody is all right. You are not to worry."

After a time he went back to his room and got his prayer-book. He could hear Harrison Miller's voice soothing Minnie in the lower hall, and Reynolds at the telephone. He went back into the quiet chamber, and opening the prayer-book, began to read aloud.

"Now is Christ risen from the dead, and become the first fruits of them that slept——"

His voice tightened. He put his head down on the side of the bed.

He was very docile that day. He moved obediently from his room for the awful aftermath of a death, for the sweeping and dusting and clean curtains, and sat in Dick's room, not reading, not even praying, a lonely yet indomitable old figure. When his friends came, elderly men who creaked in and tried to reduce their robust voices to a decorous whisper, he shook hands with them and made brief, courteous replies. Then he lapsed into silence. They felt shut off and uncomfortable, and creaked out again.

Only once did he seem shaken. That was when Elizabeth came swiftly in and put her arms around him as he sat. He held her close to him, saying nothing for a long time. Then he drew a deep breath.

"I was feeling mighty lonely, my dear," he said.

He was the better for her visit. He insisted on dressing that evening, and on being helped down the stairs. The town, which had seemed inimical for so long, appeared to him suddenly to be holding out friendly hands. More than friendly hands. Loving, tender hands, offering service and affection and old-time friendship. It moved about sedately, in dark clothes, and came down the stairs red-eyed and using pocket-handkerchiefs, and it surrounded him with love and loving kindness.

When they had all gone Harrison Miller helped him up the stairs to where his tidy bed stood ready, and the nurse had placed his hot milk on a stand. But Harrison did not go at once.

"What about word to Dick, David?" he inquired awkwardly, "I've called up Bassett, but he's away. And I don't know that Dick ought to come back anyhow. If the police are on the job at all they'll be on the lookout now. They'll know he may try to come."

David looked away. Just how much he wanted Dick, to tide him over these bad hours, only David knew. But he could not have him. He stared at the glass of hot milk.

"I guess I can fight this out alone, Harrison," he said. "And Lucy will understand."

He did not sleep much that night. Once or twice he got up and tip-toed across the hall into Lucy's room and looked at her. She was as white as her pillow, and quite serene. Her hands, always a little rough and twisted with service, were smooth and rested.

"You know why he can't come, Lucy," he said once. "It doesn't mean that he doesn't care. You have to remember that." His sublime faith that she heard and understood, not the Lucy on the bed but the Lucy who had not yet gone on to the blessed company of heaven, carried him back to his bed, comforted and reassured.

He was up and about his room early. The odor of baking muffins and frying ham came up the stair-well, and the sound of Mike vigorously polishing the floor in the hall.

Mixed with the odor of cooking and of floor wax was the scent of flowers from Lucy's room, and Mrs. Sayre's machine stopped at the door while the chauffeur delivered a great mass of roses.

David went carefully down the stairs and into his office, and there, at his long deserted desk, commenced a letter to Dick.

He was sitting there when Dick came up the street. . . . . .

The thought that he was going home had upheld Dick through the days that followed Bassett's departure for the West. He knew that it would be a fight, that not easily does a man step out of life and into it again, but after his days of inaction he stood ready to fight. For David, for Lucy, and, if it was not too late, for Elizabeth. When Bassett's wire came from Norada, "All clear," he set out for Haverly, more nearly happy than for months. The very rhythm of the train sang: "Going home; going home."

At the Haverly station the agent stopped, stared at him and then nodded gravely. There was something restrained in his greeting, like the voices in the old house the night before, and Dick felt a chill of apprehension. He never thought of Lucy, but David . . . . The flowers and ribbon at the door were his first intimation, and still it was David he thought of. He went cold and bitter, standing on the freshly washed pavement, staring at them. It was all too late. David! *David!*

He went into the house slowly, and the heavy scent of flowers greeted him. The hall was empty, and automatically he pushed open the door to David's office and went in. David was at the desk writing. David was alive. Thank God and thank God, David was alive.

"David!" he said brokenly. "Dear old David!" And was suddenly shaken with dry, terrible sobbing.

There was a great deal to do, and Dick was grateful for it. But first, like David, he went in and sat by Lucy's bed alone and talked to her. Not aloud, as David did, but still with that same queer conviction that she heard. He told her he was free, and that she need not worry about David, that he was there now to look after him; and he asked her, if she could, to help him with Elizabeth. Then he kissed her and went out.

He met Elizabeth that day. She had come to the house, and after her custom now went up, unwarned, to David's

room. She found David there and Harrison Miller, and—
it was a moment before she realized it—Dick by the
mantel. He was greatly changed. She saw that. But she had
no feeling of pity, nor even of undue surprise. She felt
nothing at all. It gave her a curious, almost hard little
sense of triumph to see that he had gone pale. She marched
up to him and held out her hand, mindful of the eyes on her.

"I'm so very sorry, Dick," she said. "You have a sad
home-coming."

Then she withdrew her hand, still calm, and turned to
David.

"Mother sent over some things. I'll give them to Minnie," she said, her voice clear and steady. She went out,
and they heard her descending the stairs.

She was puzzled to find out that her knees almost
gave way on the staircase, for she felt calm and without
any emotion whatever. And she finished her errand, so
collected and poised that the two or three women who had
come in to help stared after her as she departed.

"Do you suppose she's seen him?"

"She was in David's room. She must have."

Mindful of Mike, they withdrew into Lucy's sitting-room
and closed the door, there to surmise and to wonder. Did
he know she was engaged to Wallie Sayre? Would she
break her engagement now or not? Did Dick for a moment
think that he could do as he had done, go away and jilt a
girl, and come back to be received as though nothing had
happened? Because, if he did . . . . . .

To Dick Elizabeth's greeting had been a distinct shock.
He had not known just what he had expected; certainly he
had not hoped to pick things up where he had dropped
them. But there was a hard friendliness in it that was like
a slap in the face. He had meant at least to fight to win
back with her, but he saw now that there would not even
be a fight. She was not angry or hurt. The barrier was more
hopeless than that.

David, watching him, waited until Harrison had gone,
and went directly to the subject.

"Have you ever stopped to think what these last months
have meant to Elizabeth? Her own worries, and always
this infernal town, talking, talking. The child's pride's been
hurt, as well as her heart."

"I thought I'd better not go into that until after—until later," he explained. "The other thing was wrong. I knew it the moment I saw Beverly and I didn't go back again. What was the use? But—you saw her face, David. I think she doesn't even care enough to hate me."

"She's cared enough to engage herself to Wallace Sayre!"

After one astounded glance Dick laughed bitterly.

"That looks as though she cared!" he said. He had gone very white. After a time, as David sat silent and thoughtful, he said: "After all, what right had I to expect anything else? When you think that, a few days ago, I was actually shaken at the thought of seeing another woman, you can hardly blame her."

"She waited a long time."

Later Dick made what was a difficult confession under the circumstances.

"I know now—I think I knew all along, but the other thing was like that craving for liquor I told you about—I know now that she has always been the one woman. You'll understand that, perhaps, but she wouldn't. I would crawl on my knees to make her believe it, but it's too late. Everything's too late," he added.

Before the hour for the services he went in again and sat by Lucy's bed, but she who had given him wise counsel so many times before lay in her majestic peace, surrounded by flowers and infinitely removed. Yet she gave him something. Something of her own peace. Once more, as on the night she had stood at the kitchen door and watched him disappear in the darkness, there came the tug of the old familiar things, the home sense. Not only David now, but the house. The faded carpet on the stairs, the old self-rocker Lucy had loved, the creaking faucets in the bathroom, Mike and Minnie, the laboratory,—united in their shabby strength, they were home to him. They had come back, never to be lost again. Home.

Then, little by little, they carried their claim further. They were not only home. They were the setting of a dream, long forgotten but now vivid in his mind, and a refuge from the dreary present. That dream had seen Elizabeth enshrined among the old familiar things; the old house was to be a sanctuary for her and for him. From it and from her in the dream he was to go out in the morning; to it and to her he was to come home at night, after he had done a man's work.

The dream faded. Before him rose her face of the morning, impassive and cool; her eyes, not hostile but indifferent. She had taken herself out of his life, had turned her youth to youth, and forgotten him. He understood and accepted it. He saw himself as he must have looked to her, old and worn, scarred from the last months, infinitely changed. And she was young. Heavens, how young she was! . . . . .

Lucy was buried the next afternoon. It was raining, and the quiet procession followed Dick and the others who carried her light body under grotesquely bobbing umbrellas. Then he and David, and Minnie and Mike, went back to the house, quiet with that strange emptiness that follows a death, the unconscious listening for a voice that will not speak again, for a familiar footfall. David had not gone upstairs. He sat in Lucy's sitting-room, in his old frock coat and black tie, with a knitted afghan across his knees. His throat looked withered in his loose collar. And there for the first time they discussed the future.

"You're giving up a great deal, Dick," David said. "I'm proud of you, and like you I think the money's best where it is. But this is a prejudiced town, and they think you've treated Elizabeth badly. If you don't intend to tell the story——"

"Never," Dick announced, firmly. "Judson Clark is dead." He smiled at David with something of his old humor. "I told Bassett to put up a monument if he wanted to. But you're right about one thing. They're not ready to take me back. I've seen it a dozen times in the last two days."

"I never gave up a fight yet." David's voice was grim.

"On the other hand, I don't want to make it uncomfortable for her. We are bound to meet. I'm putting my own feeling aside. It doesn't matter—except of course to me. What I thought was—— We might go into the city. Reynolds would buy the house. He's going to be married."

But he found himself up against the stone wall of David's opposition. He was too old to be uprooted. He liked to be able to find his way around in the dark. He was almost childish about it, and perhaps a trifle terrified. But it was his final argument that won Dick over.

"I thought you'd found out there's nothing in running away from trouble."

Dick straightened.

"You're right," he said. "We'll stay here and fight it out together."

He helped David up the stairs to where the nurse stood waiting, and then went on into his own bedroom. He surveyed it for the first time since his return with a sense of permanency and intimacy. Here, from now on, was to center his life. From this bed he would rise in the morning, to go back to it at night. From this room he would go out to fight for a place again, and for the old faith in him, for confiding eyes and the clasp of friendly hands.

He sat down by the window and with the feeling of dismissing them forever retraced slowly and painfully the last few months; the night on the mountains, and Bassett asleep by the fire; the man from the cabin caught under the tree, with his face looking up, strangely twisted, from among the branches; dawn in the alfalfa field, and the long night tramp; the boy who had recognized him in Chicago; David in his old walnut bed, shrivelled and dauntless; and his own going out into the night, with Lucy in the kitchen doorway, Elizabeth and Wallace Sayre on the verandah, and himself across the street under the trees; Beverly, and the illumination of his freedom from the old bonds; Gregory, glib and debonair, telling his lying story, and later on, flying to safety. His half-brother!

All that, and now this quiet room, with David asleep beyond the wall and Minnie moving heavily in the kitchen below, setting her bread to rise. It was anti-climactic, ridiculous, wonderful.

Then he thought of Elizabeth, and it became terrible.

After Reynolds came up he put on a dressing-gown and went down the stairs. The office was changed and looked strange and unfamiliar. But when he opened the door and went into the laboratory nothing had been altered there. It was as though he had left it yesterday; the microscope screwed to its stand, the sterilizer gleaming and ready. It was as though it had waited for him.

He was content. He would fight and he would work. That was all a man needed, a good fight, and work for his hands and brain. A man could live without love if he had work.

He sat down on the stool and groaned.

Chapter Forty-six

ONE THING DICK knew must be done and got over with. He would have to see Elizabeth and tell her the story. He knew it would do no good, but she had a right to the fullest explanation he could give her. She did not love him, but it was intolerable that she should hate him.

He meant, however, to make no case for himself. He would have to stand on the facts. This thing had happened to him; the storm had come, wrought its havoc and passed; he was back, to start again as nearly as he could where he had left off. That was all.

He went to the Wheeler house the next night, passing the door twice before he turned in and rang the bell, in order that his voice might be calm and his demeanor unshaken. But the fact that Micky, waiting on the porch, knew him and broke into yelps of happiness and ecstatic wriggling almost lost him his self-control.

Walter Wheeler opened the door and admitted him.

"I thought you might come," he said. "Come in."

There was no particular warmth in his voice, but no unfriendliness. He stood by gravely while Dick took off his overcoat, and then led the way into the library.

"I'd better tell you at once," he said, "that I have advised Elizabeth to see you, but that she refuses. I'd much prefer——" He busied himself at the fire for a moment. "I'd much prefer to have her see you, Livingstone. But—I'll tell you frankly—I don't think it would do much good."

He sat down and stared at the fire. Dick remained standing.

"She doesn't intend to see me at all?" he asked, unsteadily.

"That's rather out of the question, if you intend to remain here. Do you?"

"Yes."

An unexpected feeling of sympathy for the tall young

man on the hearth rug stirred in Walter Wheeler's breast.

"I'm sorry, Dick. She apparently reached the breaking point a week or two ago. She knew you had been here and hadn't seen her, for one thing." He hesitated. "You've heard of her engagement?"

"Yes."

"I didn't want it," her father said drearily. "I suppose she knows her own business, but the thing's done. She sent you a message," he added after a pause. "She's glad it's cleared up and I believe you are not to allow her to drive you away. She thinks David needs you."

"Thank you. I'll have to stay, as she says."

There was another uncomfortable silence. Then Walter Wheeler burst out:

"Confound it, Dick, I'm sorry. I've fought your battles for months, not here, but everywhere. But here's a battle I can't fight. She isn't angry. You'll have to get her angle of it. I think it's something like this. She had built you up into a sort of superman. And she's—well, I suppose purity is the word. She's the essence of purity. Then, Leslie told me this to-night, she learned from him that you were back with the woman in the case, in New York."

And, as Dick made a gesture:

"There's no use going to him. He was off the beaten track, and he knows it. He took a chance, to tell her for her own good. He's fond of her. I suppose that was the last straw."

He sat still, a troubled figure, middle-aged and unhandsome, and very weary.

"It's a bad business, Dick," he said.

After a time Dick stirred.

"When I first began to remember," he said, "I wanted whisky. I would have stolen it, if I couldn't have got it any other way. Then, when I got it, I didn't want it. It sickened me. This other was the same sort of think. It's done with."

Wheeler nodded.

"I understand. But she wouldn't, Dick."

"No. I don't suppose she would."

He went away soon after that, back to the quiet house and to David. Automatically he turned in at his office, but Reynolds was writing there. He went slowly up the stairs. . . .

Ann Sayre was frankly puzzled during the next few days. She had had a week or so of serenity and anticipation, and although things were not quite as she would have had them, Elizabeth too impassive and even Wallie rather restrained in his happiness, she was satisfied. But Dick Livingstone's return had somehow changed everything.

It had changed Wallie, too. He was suddenly a man, and not, she suspected, a very happy man. He came back one day, for instance, to say that he had taken a partnership in a brokerage office, and gave as his reason that he was sick of "playing round." She rather thought it was to take his mind off something.

A few days after the funeral she sent for Doctor Reynolds.

"I caught cold at the cemetery," she said, when he had arrived and was seated opposite her in her boudoir. "I really did," she protested, as she caught his eye. "I suppose everybody is sending for you, to have a chance to talk."

"Just about."

"You can't blame us. Particularly, you can't blame me. I've got to know something, doctor. Is he going to stay?"

"I think so. Yes."

"Isn't he going to explain anything? He can't expect just to walk back into his practise after all these months, and the talk that's been going on, and do nothing about it."

"I don't see what his going away has to do with it. He's a good doctor, and a hard worker. When I'm gone——"

"You're going, are you?"

"Yes. I may live here, and have an office in the city. I don't care for general practise; there's no future in it. I may take a special course in nose and throat."

But she was not interested in his plans.

"I want to know something, and only you can tell me. I'm not curious like the rest; I think I have a right to know. Has he seen Elizabeth Wheeler yet? Talked to her, I mean?"

"I don't know. I'm inclined to think not," he added cautiously.

"You mean that he hasn't?"

"Look here, Mrs. Sayre. You've confided in me, and I know it's important to you. I don't know a thing. I'm to stay on until the end of the week, and then he intends to take hold. I'm in and out, see him at meals, and we've had a little desultory talk. There is no trouble between the two families. Mr. Wheeler comes and goes. If you ask me, I think Livingstone has simply accepted the situation as he found it."

"He isn't going to explain anything? He'll have to, I think, if he expects to practise here. There have been all sorts of stories."

"I don't know, Mrs. Sayre."

"How is Doctor David?" she asked, after a pause.

"Better. It wouldn't surprise me now to see him mend rapidly."

He met Elizabeth on his way down the hill, a strange, bright-eyed Elizabeth, carrying her head high and a bit too jauntily, and with a sort of hot defiance in her eyes. He drove on, thoughtfully. All this turmoil and trouble, anxiety and fear, and all that was left a crushed and tragic figure of a girl, and two men in an old house, preparing to fight that one of them might regain the place he had lost.

It would be a fight. Reynolds saw the village already divided into two camps, a small militant minority, aligned with Dick and David, and a waiting, not particularly hostile but intensely curious majority, who would demand certain things before Dick's reinstatement in their confidence.

Elizabeth Wheeler was an unconscious party to the division. It was, in a way, her battle they were fighting. And Elizabeth had gone over to the enemy.

Late that afternoon Ann Sayre had her first real talk with Wallie since Dick's return. She led him out onto the terrace, her shoulders militant and her head high, and faced him there.

"I can see you are not going to talk to me," she said. "So I'll talk to you. Has Dick Livingstone's return made any change between Elizabeth and you?"

"No."

"She's just the same to you? You must tell me, Wallace. I've been building so much."

She realized the change in him then more fully than ever, for he faced her squarely and without evasion.

"There's no change in her, mother, but I think you and I will both have to get used to this: she's not in love with me. She doesn't pretend to be."

"Don't tell me it's still that man!"

"I don't know." He took a turn or two about the terrace. "I don't think it is, mother. I don't think she cares for anybody, that way, certainly not for me. And that's the trouble." He faced her again. "If marrying me isn't going to make her happy, I won't hold her to it. You'll have to support me in that, mother. I'm a pretty weak sister sometimes."

That appeal touched her as nothing had done for a long time. "I'll help all I can, if the need comes," she said, and turned and went heavily into the house.

Chapter Forty-seven

DAVID WAS satisfied. The great love of his life had been given to Dick, and now Dick was his again. He grieved for Lucy, but he knew that the parting was not for long, and that from whatever high place she looked down she would know that. He was satisfied. He looked on his work and found it good. There was no trace of weakness nor of vacillation in the man who sat across from him at the table, or slammed in and out of the house after his old fashion.

But he was not content. At first it was enough to have Dick there, to stop in the doorway of his room and see him within, occupied with the prosaic business of getting into his clothes or out of them, now and then to put a hand on his shoulder, to hear him fussing in the laboratory again, and to be called to examine divers and sundry smears to which Dick attached impressive importance and more impressive names. But behind Dick's surface cheerfulness he knew that he was eating his heart out.

And there was nothing to be done. Nothing. Secretly David watched the papers for the announcement of Elizabeth's engagement, and each day drew a breath of relief when it did not come. And he had done another thing secretly, too; he did not tell Dick when her ring came back. Annie had brought the box, without a letter, and the incredible cruelty of the thing made David furious. He stamped into his office and locked it in a drawer, with the definite intention of saving Dick that one additional pang at a time when he already had enough to bear.

For things were going very badly. The fight was on.

It was a battle without action. Each side was dug in and entrenched, and waiting. It was an engagement where the principals met occasionally on the neutral ground of the streets, bowed to each other and passed on.

The town was sorry for David and still fond of him, but it resented his stiff-necked attitude. It said, in effect, that when he ceased to make Dick's enemies his it was willing to be friends. But it said also, to each other and behind its hands, that Dick's absence was discreditable or it would be explained, and that he had behaved abominably to Elizabeth. It would be hanged if it would be friends with him.

It looked away, but it watched. Dick knew that when he passed by on the streets it peered at him from behind its curtains, and whispered behind his back. Now and then he saw, on his evening walks, that line of cars drawn up before houses he had known and frequented which indicated a party, but he was never asked. He never told David.

It was only when the taboo touched David that Dick was resentful, and then he was inclined to question the wisdom of his return. It hurt him, for instance, to see David give up his church, and reading morning prayer alone at home on Sunday mornings, and to see his grim silence when some of his old friends were mentioned.

Yet on the surface things were much as they had been. David rose early, and as he improved in health, read his morning paper in his office while he waited for breakfast. Doctor Reynolds had gone, and the desk in Dick's office was back where it belonged. In the mornings Mike oiled the car in the stable and washed it, his old pipe clutched in his teeth, while from the kitchen came the sounds of pans and dishes, and the odor of frying sausages. And Dick splashed in the shower, and shaved by the mirror with the cracked glass in the bathroom. But he did not sing.

The house was very quiet. Now and then the front door opened, and a patient came in, but there was no longer the crowded waiting-room, the incessant jangle of the telephone, the odor of pungent drugs and antiseptics.

When, shortly before Christmas, Dick looked at the books containing the last quarter's accounts, he began to wonder how long they could fight their losing battle. He did not mind for himself, but it was unthinkable that David should do without, one by one, the small luxuries of his old age, his cigars, his long and now errandless rambles behind Nettie.

He began then to think of his property, his for the claiming, and to question whether he had not bought his peace at too great a cost to David. He knew by that time that it was not fear, but pride, which had sent him back empty-handed, the pride of making his own way. And now and then, too, he felt a perfectly human desire to let Bassett publish the story as his vindication and then snatch David

away from them all, to some luxurious haven where—
that was the point at which he always stopped—where
David could pine away in homesickness for them!

There was an irony in it that made him laugh hopelessly.

He occupied himself then with ways and means, and
sold the car. Reynolds, about to be married and busily
furnishing a city office, bought it, had it repainted a bright
blue, and signified to the world at large that he was at the
Rossiter house every night by leaving it at the curb. Sometimes, on long country tramps, Dick saw it outside a farm-
house, and knew that the boycott was not limited to the town.

By Christmas, however, he realized that the question of
meeting their expenses necessitated further economies, and
reluctantly at last they decided to let Mike go. Dick went
out to the stable with a distinct sinking of the heart, while
David sat in the house, unhappily waiting for the thing to
be done. But Mike refused to be discharged.

"And is it discharging me you are?" he asked, putting
down one of David's boots in his angry astonishment.
"Well, then, I'm telling you you're not."

"We can't pay you any longer, Mike. And now that the
car's gone——"

"I'm not thinking about pay. I'm not going, and that's
flat. Who'd be after doing his boots and all?"

David called him in that night and dismissed him again,
this time very firmly. Mike said nothing and went out, but
the next morning he was scrubbing the sidewalk as usual,
and after that they gave it up.

Now and then Dick and Elizabeth met on the street, and
she bowed to him and went on. At those times it seemed
incredible that once he had held her in his arms, and that
she had looked up at him with loving, faithful eyes. He suffered so from those occasional meetings that he took to
watching for her, so as to avoid her. Sometimes he wished
she would marry Wallace quickly, so he would be obliged
to accept what now he knew he had not accepted at all.

He had occasional spells of violent anger at her, and of
resentment, but they died when he checked up, one after
the other, the inevitable series of events that had led to the
catastrophe. But it was all nonsense to say that love never
died. She had loved him, and there was never anything so
dead as that love of hers.

He had been saved one thing, however; he had never seen her with Wallie Sayre. Then, one day in the country while he trudged afoot to make one of his rare professional visits, they went past together in Wallie's bright roadster. The sheer shock of it sent him against a fence, staring after them with an anger that shook him.

Late in November Elizabeth went away for a visit, and it gave him a breathing spell. But the strain was telling on him, and Bassett, stopping on his way to dinner at the Wheelers', told him so bluntly.

"You look pretty rotten," he said. "It's no time to go to pieces now, when you've put up your fight and won it."

"I'm all right. I haven't been sleeping. That's all."

"How about the business? People coming to their senses?"

"Not very fast," Dick admitted. "Of course it's a little soon."

After dinner at the Wheelers', when Walter Wheeler had gone to a vestry meeting, Bassett delivered himself to Margaret of a highly indignant harangue on the situation in general.

"That's how I see it," he finished. "He's done a fine thing. A finer thing by a damned sight than I'd do, or any of this town. He's given up money enough to pay the national debt—or nearly. If he'd come back with it, as Judson Clark, they wouldn't have cared a hang for the past. They'd have licked his boots. It makes me sick."

He turned on her.

"You too, I think, Mrs. Wheeler. I'm not attacking you on that score; it's human nature. But it's the truth."

"Perhaps. I don't know."

"They'll drive him to doing it yet. He came back to make a place for himself again, like a man. Not what he had, but what he was. But they'll drive him away, mark my words."

Later on, but more gently, he introduced the subject of Elizabeth.

"You can't get away from this, Mrs. Wheeler. So long as she stands off, and you behind her, the town is going to take her side. She doesn't know it, but that's how it stands. It all hangs on her. If he wasn't the man he is, I'd say his salvation hangs on her. I don't mean she ought to take him back; it's too late for that, if she's engaged. But a little friendliness and kindness wouldn't do any harm. You too.

Do you ever have him here?"

"How can I, as things are?"

"Well, be friendly, anyhow," he argued. "That's not asking much. I suppose he'd cut my throat if he knew, but I'm a straight-to-the-mark sort of person, and I know this: what this house does the town will do."

"I'll talk to Mr. Wheeler. I don't know. I'll say this, Mr. Bassett. I won't make her unhappy. She has borne a great deal, and sometimes I think her life is spoiled. She is very different."

"If she is suffering, isn't it possible she cares for him?"

But Margaret did not think so. She was so very calm. She was so calm that sometimes it was alarming.

"He gave her a ring, and the other day I found it, tossed into a drawer full of odds and ends. I haven't seen it lately; she may have sent it back." . . . .

Elizabeth came home shortly before Christmas, undeniably glad to be back and very gentle with them all. She set to work almost immediately on the gifts, wrapping them and tying them with methodical exactness, sticking a tiny sprig of holly through the ribbon bow, and writing cards with neatness and care. She hung up wreaths and decorated the house, and when she was through with her work she went to her room and sat with her hands folded, not thinking. She did not think any more.

Wallie had sent her a flexible diamond bracelet as a Christmas gift and it lay on her table in its box. She was very grateful, but she had not put it on.

On the morning before Christmas Nina came in, her arms full of packages, and her eyes shining and a little frightened. She had some news for them. She hadn't been so keen about it, at first, but Leslie was like a madman. He was so pleased that he was ordering her that sable cape she had wanted so. He was like a different man. And it would be July.

Elizabeth kissed her. It seemed very unreal, like everything else. She wondered why Leslie should be so excited, or her mother crying. She wondered if there was something strange about her, that it should seem so small and unimportant. But then, what was important? That one got up in the morning, and ate at intervals, and went to bed at night? That children came, and had to be fed and washed and tended, and cried a great deal, and were sick now and then?

She wished she could feel something, could think it vital

whether Nina should choose pink or blue for her layette, and how far she should walk each day, and if the *chauffeur* drove the car carefully enough. She wished she cared whether it was going to rain to-morrow or not, or whether some one was coming, or not coming. And she wished terribly that she could care for Wallie, or get over the feeling that she had saved her pride at a cost to him she would not contemplate.

After a time she went upstairs and put on the bracelet. And late in the afternoon she went out and bought some wool, to make an afghan. It eased her conscience toward Nina. She commenced it that evening while she waited for Wallie, and she wondered if some time she would be making an afghan for a coming child of her own. Hers and Wallace Sayre's.

Suddenly she knew she would never marry him. She faced the future, with all that it implied, and she knew she could not do it. It was horrible that she had even contemplated it. It would be terrible to tell Wallie, but not as terrible as the other thing. She saw herself then with the same clearness with which she had judged Dick. She too, leaving her havoc of wrecked lives behind her; she too going along her headstrong way, raising hopes not to be fulfilled, and passing on. She too.

That evening, Christmas eve, she told Wallie she would not marry him. Told him very gently, and just after an attempt of his to embrace her. She would not let him do it.

"I don't know what's come over you," he said morosely. "But I'll let you alone, if that's the way you feel."

"I'm sorry, Wallie. It—it makes me shiver."

In a way he was prepared for it but nevertheless he begged for time, for a less unequivocal rejection. But he found her, for the first time, impatient with his pleadings.

"I don't want to go over and over it, Wallie. I'll take the blame. I should have done it long ago."

She was gentle, almost tender with him, but when he said she had spoiled his life for him she smiled faintly.

"You think that now. And don't believe I'm not sorry. I am. I hate not playing the game, as you say. But I don't think for a moment that you'll go on caring when you know I don't. That doesn't happen. That's all."

"Do you know what I think?" he burst out. "I think

you're still mad about Livingstone. I think you are so mad about him that you don't know it yourself."

But she only smiled her cool smile and went on with her knitting. After that he got himself in hand, and—perhaps he still had some hope. It was certain that she had not flinched at Dick's name—told her very earnestly that he only wanted her happiness. He didn't want her unless she wanted him. He would always love her.

"Not always," she said, with tragically cold certainty. "Men are not like women; they forget."

She wondered, after he had gone, what had made her say that.

She did not tell the family that night. They were full of their own concerns, Nina's coming maternity, the wrapping of packages behind closed doors, the final trimming of the tree in the library. Leslie had started the phonograph, and it was playing *Stille Nacht, heilige Nacht.*

Still night, holy night, and only in her was there a stillness that was not holy.

They hung up their stockings valiantly as usual, making a little ceremony of it, and being careful not to think about Jim's missing one. Indeed, they made rather a function of it, and Leslie demanded one of Nina's baby socks and pinned it up.

"I'm starting a bank account for the little beggar," he said, and dropped a gold piece into the toe. "Next year, old girl" . . . . . .

He put his arm around Nina. It seemed to him that life was doing considerably better than he deserved by him, and he felt very humble and contrite. He felt in his pocket for the square jeweler's box that lay there.

After that they left Walter Wheeler there, to play his usual part at such times, and went upstairs. He filled the stockings bravely, an orange in each toe, a box of candy, a toy for old time's sake, and then the little knickknacks he had been gathering for days and hiding in his desk. After all, there were no fewer stockings this year than last. Instead of Jim's there was the tiny one for Nina's baby. That was the way things went. He took away, but also He gave.

He sat back in his deep chair, and looked up at the stockings, ludicrously bulging. After all, if he believed that He gave and took away, then he must believe that Jim was where he had tried to think him, filling a joyous, active place in some boyish heaven.

After a while he got up and went to his desk, and getting pen and paper wrote carefully.

"Dearest: You will find this in your stocking in the morning, when you get up for the early service. And I want you to think over it in the church. It is filled with tenderness and with anxiety. Life is not so very long, little daughter, and it has no time to waste in anger or in bitterness. A little work, a little sleep, a little love, and it is all over.

"Will you think of this to-day?"

He locked up the house, and went slowly up to bed. . . . .

Elizabeth found the letter the next morning. She stood in the bleak room, with the ashes of last night's fire still smoking, and the stockings overhead not festive in the gray light, but looking forlorn and abandoned. Suddenly her eyes, dry and fiercely burning for so long, were wet with tears. It was true. It was true. A little work, a little sleep, a little love. Not the great love, perhaps, not the only love of a man's life. Not the love of yesterday, but of to-day and to-morrow.

All the fierce repression of the last weeks was gone. She began to suffer. She saw Dick coming home, perhaps high with hope that whatever she knew she would understand and forgive. And she saw herself failing him, cold and shut away, not big enough nor woman enough to meet him half way. She saw him fighting his losing battle alone, protecting David but never himself; carrying Lucy to her quiet grave; sitting alone in his office, while the village walked by and stared at the windows; she saw him, gaining harbor after storm, and finding no anchorage there.

She turned and went, half blindly, into the empty street.

She thought he was at the early service. She did not see him, but she had once again the thing that had seemed lost forever, the warm sense of his thought of her.

He was there, in the shadowy back pew, with the grill behind it through which once insistent hands had reached to summon him. He was there, with Lucy's prayer-book in his hand, and none of the peace of the day in his heart. He knelt and rose with the others.

"Oh God, who makest us glad with the yearly remembrance of the birth of Thy Son——"

Chapter Forty-eight

DAVID WAS beaten; most tragic defeat of all, beaten by those he had loved and faithfully served.

He did not rise on Christmas morning, and Dick, visiting him after an almost untasted breakfast, found him still in his bed and questioned him anxiously.

"I'm all right," he asserted. "I'm tired, Dick, that's all. Tired of fighting. You're young. You can carry it on, and win. But I'll never see it. They're stronger than we are."

Later he elaborated on that. He had kept the faith. He had run with courage the race that was set before him. He had stayed up at night and fought for them. But he couldn't fight against them.

Dick went downstairs again and shutting himself in his office fell to pacing the floor. David was right, the thing was breaking him. Very seriously now he contemplated abandoning the town, taking David with him, and claiming his estate. They could travel then; he could get consultants in Europe; there were baths there, and treatments—

The doorbell rang. He heard Minnie's voice in the hall, not too friendly, and her tap at the door.

"Some one in the waiting-room," she called.

When he opened the connecting door he found Elizabeth beyond it, a pale and frightened Elizabeth, breathless and very still. It was a perceptible moment before he could control his voice to speak. Then:

"I suppose you want to see David. I'm sorry, but he isn't well to-day. He is still in bed."

"I didn't come to see David, Dick."

"I cannot think you want to see me, Elizabeth."

"I do, if you don't mind."

He stood aside then and let her pass him into the rear office. But he was not fooled at all. Not he. He had been fooled enough. He knew why she had come, in the kindness of her heart. (She was so little. Good heavens, a man could crush her to nothing!) She had come because she was sorry for him, and she had brought forgiveness. It was like her. It was fine. It was damnable.

His voice hardened, for fear it might be soft.

"Is this a professional visit, or a Christmas call, Elizabeth? Or perhaps I shouldn't call you that."

"A Christmas call?"

"You know what I mean. The day of peace. The day of—what do you think I'm made of, Elizabeth? To have you come here, gentle and good and kind——"

He got up and stood over her, tall and almost threatening.

"You've been to church, and you've been thinking things over, I know. I was there. I heard it all, peace on earth, good will to men. Bosh. Peace, when there is no peace. Good will! I don't want your peace and good will."

She looked up at him timidly.

"You don't want to be friends, then?"

"No. A thousand times, no," he said violently. Then, more gently: "I'm making a fool of myself. I want your peace and good will, Elizabeth. God knows I need them."

"You frighten me, Dick," she said, slowly. "I didn't come to bring forgiveness, if that is what you mean. I came——"

"Don't tell me you came to ask it. That would be more than I can bear."

"Will you listen to me for a moment, Dick? I am not good at explaining things, and I'm nervous. I suppose you can see that." She tried to smile at him. "A—a little work, a little sleep, a little love, that's life, isn't it?"

He was watching her intently.

"Work and trouble, and a long sleep at the end for which let us be duly thankful—that's life, too. Love? Not every one gets love."

Hopelessness and despair overwhelmed her. He was making it hard for her. Impossible. She could not go on.

"I did not come with peace," she said tremulously, "but if you don't want it——" She rose. "I must say this, though, before I go. I blame myself. I don't blame you. You are wrong if you think I came to forgive you."

She was stumbling toward the door.

"Elizabeth, what *did* bring you?"

She turned to him, with her hand on the door knob.

"I came because I wanted to see you again."

He strode after her and catching her by the arm, turned her until he faced her.

"And why did you want to see me again? You can't still care for me. You know the story. You know I was here and didn't see you. You've seen Leslie Ward. You know my past. What you don't know——"

He looked down into her eyes. "A little work, a little sleep, a little love," he repeated. "What did you mean by that?"

"Just that," she said simply. "Only not a little love, Dick. Maybe you don't want me now. I don't know. I have suffered so much that I'm not sure of anything."

"Want you!" he said. "More than anything on this earth."

Bassett was at his desk in the office. It was late, and the night editor, seeing him reading the early edition, his feet on his desk, carried over his coffee and doughnuts and joined him.

"Sometime," he said, "I'm going to get that Clark story out of you. If it wasn't you who turned up the confession, I'll eat it."

Bassett yawned.

"Have it your own way," he said indifferently.

"You were shielding somebody, weren't you? No? What's the answer?"

Bassett made no reply. He picked up the paper and pointed to an item with the end of his pencil.

"Seen this?"

The night editor read it with bewilderment. He glanced up.

"What's that got to do with the Clark case?"

"Nothing. Nice people, though. Know them both."

When the night editor walked away, rather affronted, Bassett took up the paper and reread the paragraph.

"Mr. and Mrs. Walter Wheeler, of Haverly, announce the engagement of their daughter, Elizabeth, to Doctor Richard Livingstone."

He sat for a long time staring at it.